Shattered Moon

BOOK ONE OF THE PORTALS OF AYDEN

Kim Stokely

Kim Stokely/Createspace
Bellevue, NE
www.kimstokely.com
Book cover design by The Scarlett Rugers Design Agency
www.scarlettrugers.com
Map by Michael Weir: www.patreon.com/levilagann

Book Layout © 2015 BookDesignTemplates.com

A Shattered Moon/ Kim Stokely. -- 1st ed.
ISBN 978-1539318156

For my TNT girls.
Because each of you face battles every day, and I know you are
strong enough to win the war

CONTENTS

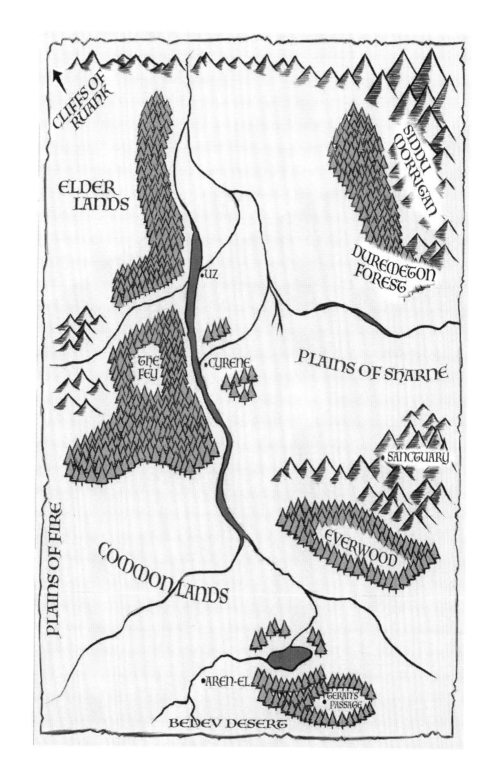

CHAPTER ONE

Waiting for an Asteroid

On a scale from one to ten—with one being a private limousine taking me and my boyfriend, Channing Tatum, into NYC to see the Broadway show of my choice; and ten being the apocalypse—this morning would normally have ranked at about a six. My mother only left me a half a cup of coffee in the carafe before she took off for work. Sour milk in the fridge meant I had to eat my generic Fruitios dry, leaving behind a coat of sugar that no amount of toothpaste could dislodge. When I attempted to spit out said toothpaste into the sink, it dribbled on my shirt, which meant I had to change clothes. That wouldn't have been so bad if, like any normal day, my best friends, Josh and Renee, had picked me up.

But no. On this one day, the most important of my teenage life, Josh shot me the text: *Sorry. U have to bus it today. C u @ school*

I had just enough time to change my shirt, grab my backpack, make the bus, and run to sociology before the bell rang. The fact that this all happened on my sixteenth birthday meant that so far, this day ranked out at a 9.5. I figured the only thing that could make it worse would be an asteroid the size of Kentucky screaming toward Earth. Instead, I got Ms. Farley's wrath.

I think I would have preferred the asteroid.

"Miss Foster?" The old woman sat hunched like a buzzard waiting to pick the meat off my sophomore bones. "May I see you at my desk, please?"

A small chorus of "oooooh's" followed me from the couple of kids paying attention.

"Would you mind explaining this?" Farley slapped a piece of paper on her desk.

I knew what the paper showed. My mother's name, Kennis Foster, written in bold letters with a horizontal line connected to a question mark. A perpendicular line joined her name to mine–Alystrine Foster. That was it. At least I had put my legal name, which I absolutely never used, on the project.

"Mrs. Farley—"

"Ms. Farley." I flinched at her interruption. Before I could apologize, she plowed on. "I am not now, nor have I ever been, married. And just because your mother hasn't married is no excuse for not completing this assignment."

I felt my cheeks warm with embarrassment. "I tried to explain to you before that—"

"She didn't just fall from the sky, did she?"

"No but she—"

"She must have a family, even if she chose to have a child by unconventional methods. You could have listed her mother and father. Her sisters—"

"I'm trying to explain—"

"What?" Farley's green eyes flashed behind her glasses like a hawk that spied its prey. "What are you trying to explain? That she's an alien? That she was born in a Petri dish? What could possibly explain her total lack of heritage except that you were too lazy to do the assignment?"

"Maybe the fact that she was dumped in an orphanage when she was a baby and raped by a gang of boys when she was a teenager!" A sudden silence fell over the classroom like a wall of concrete. My stomach did a somersault. *Why don't I think before I say things?* The fire in Farley's eyes dimmed as she processed what I'd said. "I tried to tell you that before, but you apparently didn't listen."

The spark lit up again. "Don't take that tone with me, young lady."

In the back of my head I heard my mother's voice urging me to be calm. To answer with respect. I ignored it. "You've just chewed me out and made me admit the most intimate details of my life in front of the entire class, and you're worried about my tone of voice?"

"Mr. Edecker's office." She opened her desk drawer, pulled out a stack of passes, scribbled her signature on the top paper, and then tore it off. "Now."

I snatched the pass from her hand. The stares of the other students made heat rise to cheeks again, probably turning them bright red. As I grabbed my backpack from the floor, Sophia Brennan whispered, "Are you okay?"

I snorted softly. "Just ducky."

Stalking down the hall, I recalculated the crap factor of this day to a record infinity. Ms. Farley had hated me from the moment I'd sat down in her class. I worked my buns off for her and never got anything above a B. Steffy Majors once told me she cheated off my paper during a test and she got an A minus while I got a C. Renee told me it was because Farley hated pretty girls. I wasn't gorgeous like my mother, but I knew I wasn't an ugly duckling either. I think it was my auburn hair that made Farley jealous. Her's was a mousy brown while mine, I had to admit, was long, thick, and this great deep brown with coppery highlights. A lot of people thought I got it from a bottle, but it was natural. It's the only part of my body I liked.

I arrived at the principal's office, handed my pass to the assistant behind the counter then took a seat in one of the teal plastic chairs along the wall. Our school colors were supposed to be green and silver, but the district must have gotten a discount on teal and white furniture because that's what was in the office and the classrooms. The clock on the wall ticked away the minutes to my doom.

I stared at the rabid rodent painted on the wall across from me. Our school mascot, a groundhog, was about as threatening as a baby bunny, but the painting made it seem positively evil.

The door to the principal's office swung open and out walked Edecker with his hand on the shoulder of a long-haired kid in a flannel shirt and torn jeans. "Let's see if we can go one week without another offense, okay, Jacobs?"

Jacobs shirked away from the principal and slunk past me.

Edecker's jowls shook as he ran his hand over his balding head. At least he had class enough to not do the comb-over thing. He glanced over in my direction. "You here to see me?"

I nodded as his assistant chimed, "Ms. Farley sent her down."

He pushed his wire frame glasses up onto the bridge of his nose then narrowed his eyes as he stared at me. "Foster, isn't it?"

I stood up. "Yes, sir." *See Mom, I can be polite when I'm not being chewed out.*

He scratched his double chin then pointed inside his office. "What's going on, Amy?"

"It's Ally, sir."

He shut the door behind us after I took a seat. "Ally. What are you here for?"

I launched in with my explanation as to what happened in Farley's class. Edecker folded his hands on his desk and listened intently. At least he seemed uncomfortable when I told him why I couldn't do Farley's family tree assignment. "You can call my mother. She'll tell you I'm telling the truth."

"You have to admit . . ." Edecker coughed nervously. "It does sound a bit far-fetched."

I leaned back in my chair and crossed my arms. "Call her."

He let out a long sigh as the passing bell rang. "I will. For now, go on to your next class."

From the side-long glances I got, I knew the kids in my Sociology class had begun spreading the news of my heritage. I did my best to ignore the stares as I booked my way up to my locker on the second floor. I had nothing to be ashamed of and neither did my mom. She'd been a victim, but didn't play that card. She had me when she was just a kid herself then went back to school to become a nurse. She'd made a good life for us and I wasn't going to let Ms. Farley or anyone else look down on her for having a tough start.

I turned the corner and saw my locker, covered in lime green streamers. Renee and Josh stood on either side, each holding a Mylar balloon.

"You're squashing the decorations, moron." Renee smacked her taller, thinner, twin brother. She squealed as she ran over to me. "Happy sixteenth, Ally!" Her spiked pink hair nearly took out my eye when she gave me a hug. Her balloon bounced against my head.

I pried myself loose from her enthusiastic embrace. "This is why you made me ride the bus?"

Josh shrugged. "Something had to be done to celebrate the momentous occasion of your birth." He leaned his skinny frame against a neighboring locker. "Here." He held out his balloon. It had a picture of a dog with a thermometer in its mouth. It read *Get Well Soon*. "Happy birthday. We still on for tonight?"

"Unless my mom grounds me after my run-in with Farley this morning." I squeezed between them and dialed the combination for my locker.

Renee clenched her fist as if she were going to start a protest. "Sophia texted me what happened. I can't believe Farley. She's a freaking fascist."

"Nice alliteration." Josh shook his head. "You don't even know what that means."

She jabbed Josh in the arm with her pointer finger. "Remember when Farley stabbed me?"

"She slipped with a pencil." He rubbed his bicep. "It was an accident."

"It still hurt."

The bell rang, signaling the end of the passing period. We had one minute to get to class. Another crush of adolescent humanity scurried by us. Maybe it was my imagination, but it sure seemed like most of them looked my way. Renee tied her Mylar balloon around my wrist before running to her Chem class. I put away my sociology book then grabbed my copy of *Julius Caesar* for English.

Josh propped himself against the neighboring locker. "Crappy way to start off your birthday. Sorry."

"Not your fault." I slammed the door. "Not entirely, anyway."

His eyebrows rose. "Hey, come on. The balloons and streamers have to make up for the bus." We walked toward our class, carried along by the tide of teenagers racing down the hall.

"I don't know. The bus smells weird. It's like Oscar Mayer and Axe got together to create a new cologne."

He pulled me out of the congested hallway toward the alcove by the stairs. "Don't worry about Farley."

"That report is worth forty percent of my grade."

Josh wrapped me in his arms. His chin rested on the top of my head. "Edecker will listen to your mom. They'll come up with something else for you to do."

No one gave better hugs. I took a deep breath and relaxed. "We better go. All I need is to be sent down to Edecker's office again today for being late."

We jogged down the hall, making it to our seats as the bell rang. Josh tied his balloon to the back of my chair while Renee's bobbed into my head as I sat down.

Tiffany Ross, the brunette who sat in front of me, turned around. "It's your birthday?"

I blinked in surprise. One of the popular crowd, the girl had never said a word to me before. "Uh, yeah."

Her nose wrinkled like she caught a whiff of the boys' bathroom. "I'm surprised your mother knew the date. Maybe she made it up. You can never trust a whore."

I jumped up and would have strangled her if Josh hadn't grabbed hold of my arm. "My mother has more class than a stuck-up bitch like you will ever have." I ripped myself away from Josh just as Mr. Andrews strolled in, carrying a cup of coffee.

"Open your books up to Act III scene two."

Tiffany spun back around in her seat. "Happy bastard . . . oops, I mean birthday."

"Ignore her," Josh whispered, pulling on the hem of my shirt so I had to sit down.

But I couldn't just ignore her. Instead, I drew stick figure doodles of an asteroid smooshing Tiffany Ross flat.

CHAPTER TWO

Got my Cake, Never Ate it

I'd just sat down in my Geometry class an hour later when a disembodied voice crackled over the intercom. "Mrs. Shields?"

"Yes?"

"Please send Ally Foster to the office."

"Will do." Mrs. Shields raised one eyebrow as she looked in my direction. "Got any idea what this is about?"

I stood up. "I had a run-in with Ms. Farley this morning."

Mrs. Shields let out a soft chuckle. Her blue eyes twinkled. "Say no more. If this is something to do with her, you'd better take your things with you."

I grabbed my book bag and headed to the principal's office. Again.

My heart jumped into my throat when I saw my mom through the office door window. I didn't think Edecker would get her down here so soon to talk about this morning's fiasco. *Where was an asteroid when you needed one?*

I kept my cool as I opened the door. The delinquent sitting where I'd waited earlier drooled as he stared at my mother. She'd pulled her long blonde hair up into a twist. Her white blouse fell open tastefully, giving the kid a good look at her creamy skin as she leaned over to sign a piece of paper on the counter. Her tight blue pencil skirt showed off her legs to their best advantage.

I took a deep breath. "Hey, Mom."

Instead of the glare of doom I'd been expecting, I got a huge smile. "Hello, birthday girl! You ready to party?"

"What?"

"I thought we could have an early birthday celebration since I have to work tonight." She dug her keys from her purse. "Get your things. I'll wait in the car."

I texted Renee to let her know that I wouldn't be at lunch. I skipped to my locker, grabbed my books and my balloons, then hurried to find out what my mom had planned.

It turned out she'd made an appointment at the DMV so I could take my driving test. Two hours, several forms and a myriad of lines later, I drove us to the Shore House for my birthday lunch. The small stone café overlooked Long Island Sound. We followed a waiter to a table for two by one of the picture windows toward the back of the restaurant. The afternoon sun sparkled on the white caps formed by the brisk spring wind. We ordered mozzarella sticks and Caesar salads with shrimp and diet colas. I stared at my license while we waited for our appetizer to arrive.

My mom held out her hand. "Let me see it again."

I passed it over to her. "Is it a law that all license pictures look like mug shots?"

"I think so." She inspected the card. "This isn't so bad. You look tired." She handed it back. "Didn't you sleep well last night?"

I slipped it into my wallet. "I think I was just worried about Farley."

"Did you work out that assignment?"

"No." I jabbed my straw into the soda. "I tried to talk to her before it was due and she wouldn't listen. Then she got all bent out of shape when I turned in what I had." I stirred the ice cubes around in a furious whirlpool. "I think the principal is going to be calling you soon."

"I'll get it straightened out. Try not to let it ruin your day." She peeled the wrapper from her straw and stuck it in her soda. "That's not all that kept you up, was it?" She always had a way of reading my mind.

"I had a nightmare."

She took a sip of her drink. "What about?"

"I was walking somewhere. You know how in a dream you know you're home, but it's not your real home?" Mom nodded. "It was like that. I was walking in a garden, and then there was a river. I could see the moon reflected in it. It was full and bright, but when I looked up in the sky, it shattered like glass." I struggled to remember what I'd seen. "There were faces in the shards. Yours, mine...people I didn't know, but somehow they were familiar. They called my name."

The creases between my mom's eyebrows deepened. "Have you had this dream before?"

"A couple times this week."

"The other faces? What did they look like?"

I struggled to remember, but the dream had faded.

The waiter came with our mozzarella sticks and marinara sauce.

"Your salads will be up in a few minutes, ladies. Can I get you a refill?"

My mother shook her head. "We're fine for now, thank you." She watched him leave then her focus returned to me. "I want you to keep a journal by your bed. If you have another dream like this one, I want you to write down everything you remember as soon as you wake up, okay?"

"It's not that big a deal."

"You never know what a dream can mean." She smiled, but it didn't reach her eyes. She pushed the plate toward me. "Birthday girl gets first choice."

I picked the one that had cracked open so cheese oozed out like lava. "How long do you have off today?"

"I'm doing the overnight shift for Becky, but I have to go in this afternoon to finish some reports." She watched me as she blew on her own steaming piece of mozzarella. "I want you to come to work with me today."

I tried to keep a string of melted cheese from sliding down my chin. "Josh and Renee are taking me out for pizza, remember?"

"You could help in the dining room during dinner."

I hope my groan signaled my lack of enthusiasm for the idea since I couldn't talk with my mouth full.

"I don't want to fight about this. You're coming."

"It's my birthday." I sucked in air to cool down the molten goo in my mouth. "I just want to relax."

Mom dropped her unfinished cheese stick onto her plate. "I don't want you to be alone tonight." She held up her hand to stop me from arguing. "Josh and Renee can pick you up from Meadow Hills."

She'd used *the tone.* I knew her mind was made up. "Can I at least take the car and meet them there?"

She seemed to look somewhere past me, as if someone else gave her the answer, then nodded.

We made small talk through our appetizer and salads. Mom insisted on getting me a piece of double chocolate cake.

"It's not an official birthday lunch without dessert." She gave the waiter our order and leaned over to me. "Besides, I haven't given you your present yet." She reached into her purse and brought out a small square package. She hesitated for a moment, as if undecided whether to give it to me or not, before handing it to me.

I undid the gold ribbon and tore the purple paper to reveal the jewelers box underneath. I lifted the lid and gasped.

Inside sat a ring made to look like tangled silver and gold branches. In the center was an oval amethyst. I pulled the ring out to look at it closer. A silver branch on the left and a gold one on the right, both so intricately carved they looked real, intertwined to cradle the purple stone. It was too big for my ring finger so I slipped over the knuckle of my middle finger. "It's beautiful."

My mother spoke so softly, I barely heard her. "It's time you have it."

"I don't know what to say." The amethyst looked to be an even deeper purple now that the ring was on my hand. "Thank you."

Her eyes glistened. She stared out the window.

"Mom? Are you okay?"

She nodded but didn't speak. Her already pale face turned an unearthly shade of white.

Goosebumps rose on my arms. "Mom?"

"I just need a moment." She walked swiftly to the back of the restaurant toward the restroom sign.

The waiter returned with my cake but I'd lost my appetite. "Can we get a box for this?" I asked. "We're a little fuller than we thought."

He returned a minute later with the box and our check just as my mother sat back down. She took a quick peek then threw three twenties down on the table. I knew our lunch hadn't been that much. She dabbed the corners of her eyes. "Let's go. You can drive."

We drove home in silence. I could tell my mom struggled to keep herself together and it scared me. She was the strongest person I knew. She rarely lost her temper, almost never cried. I didn't know what to do.

"Give me a minute," she said when I unlocked our condo. She ran upstairs then slammed the door to the bathroom. I stood outside, listening. It took me a moment before I heard her sobbing underneath the sound of the shower.

I backed away. Maybe she was upset because I was growing up. It wouldn't be long and we'd be thinking about colleges. Not that we could afford it, but I made good grades and was already prepping for the SATs.

I opened my closet to pick the outfit I'd wear to dinner with Josh and Renee. After pulling several out, I decided on a brown broomstick skirt. A little fancy for pizza, but I felt like dressing up for my birthday.

I combined it with a cream sweater and my new ankle boots with the two-inch stacked heels. I'd bought them off the clearance rack last week with Renee. This would probably be the last time I could wear them before sandal and flip-flop weather settled in. I folded everything up and put it in a gym bag so I could change after I'd helped serve dinner.

Mom came in about an hour later, ready to go to work. She'd redone her makeup. If you hadn't known she'd been crying, you'd think the puffiness around her eyes was from spring allergies. I sat up on my bed where I'd been reading *Julius Caesar*. She sat down next to me.

"I guess you're wondering what that was all about, huh?" She made a failed attempt to smile.

I nodded.

She stroked my cheek then pushed a piece of my reddish brown hair behind my ear. I'd always figured I must take after the boy who'd raped her because we didn't look anything alike. She was petite with ivory skin, blonde hair and deep brown eyes. I had blue-green eyes, more latte-colored skin and stood about four inches taller.

"I have to talk to you about something. Something very important."

"What?"

She glanced over at my alarm clock. Her eyes clouded as if she tried to recall some distant memory. "There's not enough time today. I don't want to upset your birthday."

"Just tell me!"

"Tomorrow." She took a deep breath. "Tell Josh and Renee you can't hang out with them. This may take a while." She stood up. "Take me to work and you can have the car tonight. Just be sure to pick me up in the morning."

Mom's mood seemed better by the time we got to Meadow Hills Nursing Home where she worked as head nurse. We walked past the nurse's station and several residents' rooms on the way to her office. Mrs. Finster sat in her wheelchair in the doorway to her room and waved. Mr. Morrison let out a loud groan as we went by.

My mother stopped. "Wait here." She walked over to the old man's bed. I'd never seen him out of it. She took his hand. She'd put her hair into a ponytail for work and it dropped over her shoulder as she leaned down to talk to him. I couldn't hear what she said so I took a step past the threshold.

Her head jerked up. "Get out!"

I stumbled back at the fear I saw in her eyes. She whispered something to Mr. Morrison then came out to the hallway.

"You know you're not supposed to go in there." My mother strode toward her office. "He's very weak. Any germs you carry might kill him."

"I know. But Becky had me go in last week to help her—"

She whirled around. "What?"

"It was just for a minute. I didn't touch him or anything."

She seemed panicked about something. "Did he see you?"

"What?"

"Were his eyes open? Did he see you?"

"No. I don't think so." I shook my head. "What would it matter if he did?"

She turned down the hall while fishing her keys from her purse. "I told you not to go into his room."

"I know, but Becky needed my help."

My mother unlocked her office door. "She's supposed to be a professional. She shouldn't be asking a child for help."

"I'm not a child." I slammed the door behind me before I realized how childish that made me seem. "I'm sixteen."

She rested her hand on her desk like she needed help standing. "That's what I've been afraid of."

"Why? What's going on?"

"Tomorrow." She shook her head "We'll talk tomorrow." She sank into the chair behind her desk.

"Why won't you tell me?"

She didn't look up from the file she'd opened. "Go see if they need help in the dining room."

"Don't order me around like I'm nobody." I swore under my breath. "It's my birthday. I shouldn't have to be here at all." I stopped whining when I saw the tears welling in her eyes again.

"I'm sorry." She bit her lower lip before going on. "I just . . . I need more time to explain everything."

I turned to go.

"Come find me before you leave, okay?"

"Sure." I spent the next hour pouring coffee and picking up napkins as the residents who were mobile came down to dinner. My cell phone buzzed.

Josh had texted, *We still on for pizza?*

I got my license and the car! Meet u there in 1 hr.

☺

I went to my mom's office to change but she wasn't there. After dressing, I went to the bathroom down the hall to fix my makeup. I played with my hair for a minute, trying to decide whether to pull it back or not. I opted for down then set off to find my mother before leaving.

"Ahhh . . . ."

Mr. Morrison groaned as I passed his room. Something drew me back to the doorway to take a look at the old man. He lay as he always had, arms strapped down by his sides to keep them from curling up onto his chest. He moaned again.

"Ahhhleee . . . ."

Had he just said my name? My heart raced. I glanced toward the nurses' station, but no one sat at the desk.

"Aaaly . . . ."

I stepped inside the room even though I knew my mom would be angry. I couldn't stop myself. "Mr. Morrison? Are you alright?"

His eyelids flew open and I jumped back. His eyes were young. A vibrant, iridescent blue sparkling with life.

"Aaaalysssstrine . . . ." His voice sounded like a breeze rushing through dead, fall leaves. It crackled. His breath sputtered in his chest. "Alystrine."

How does he know my name? No one but my mother calls me that. "What do you need, Mr. Morrison?"

"Ka . . . ."

I tried to focus on his mouth to figure out what he was saying. "What?"

His eyes stared into mine. These weren't the eyes of a man deep in a coma. I could see the intelligence behind them . . . inside him. The crystal blue drew me around to the side of the bed. He smiled.

"Kaaahm."

"What does that mean? What do you need?"

His eyes clouded with frustration. He moved his lips but nothing came out. His hand twitched. His voice creaked out of his chest again, "Haaand."

I stared at the gnarled hand bound to the bed. He wriggled his fingers.

"Hand?" I asked.

Mr. Morrison nodded.

I swallowed, grabbed his hand, and the world as I knew it disappeared.

CHAPTER THREE

The Passage

The old man's bony fingers dug into the fleshy part of my palm, anchoring my body to his, but some part of me was ripped away and thrown to the ceiling. I could see myself, still standing by the bed, a look of horror on my face. The walls of the room melted away. Then my soul, or whatever floated above the scene, got sucked back into the physical me. I lost hold of Mr. Morrison and found myself hurtling and spinning through a black tunnel. Wind roared around me. Someone called my name.

"Mom! Help!" I tried to yell, but the rushing wind merely caught my words and hurled them back to me.

Inside my head, it felt as if someone squeezed my brain in a huge vice. The pressure grew greater and greater as I picked up even more speed. I screamed, sure that my brain would explode at any moment.

Then my body slammed onto the ground and my head hit something hard.

Blackness still surrounded me but the wind and noise vanished. I tried to orientate myself. I couldn't straighten my arms. Four walls enclosed me. I felt around for a door knob or lock, but there was nothing to hold on to—the walls were smooth, like polished wood. I pushed against the first wall. It stood firm. The same with the second. The third wall seemed to give a little. I positioned my back against the opposite side then kicked out with both legs. The air filled with the sound of splintering wood. I kept kicking until I'd made a hole big enough to crawl through.

A cold breeze nipped at my face as I crawled out from my enclosure. I stood, my muscles protesting after the beating they'd taken through the . . . whatever. A pale silver half-moon provided little light. A dank, moldy smell hung on the wind. I recognized it from the fall camping trips Mom and I would go on—autumn leaves decaying on a wet forest floor. I tried without success to push back the panic rising in my chest.

Where am I?

My lungs sucked in the frigid air as if I were drowning. Maybe the atmosphere here, wherever here was, didn't have any oxygen. I gasped like a fish out of water, my chest aching with the effort.

Calm down. Focus. Take one deep breath.

I sucked in a lungful, held it then let the air out in a steady stream. I repeated the exercise until my heart rate slowed and my breathing returned to normal.

My eyes adjusted to the moonlight. I looked to see what I'd escaped from and made out a vertical box, about six feet tall. The wood had been polished smooth. The barest skeleton of a house stood around it. A few stacked stones and a couple of door frames were all that remained. Past the open walls, I could make out the shapes of trees. Lots of trees.

A strong gust of wind picked my hair up and blew it across my face. When it died down, I heard another sound—the soft thunder of hooves beating their way through the forest.

To me.

They're coming for me.

I don't know how I knew this, but the feeling was unmistakable. This army on horseback was coming for me and I somehow knew I didn't want them to find me. I stumbled across the uneven ground toward the woods. It would be impossible for me to outrun them. I didn't know where I was or what hid in the forest. I did the only thing that came to my mind and climbed the first tree that offered me a low branch to heave myself up.

I hadn't climbed a tree in a dress since I was seven and hadn't wanted to go to the holiday concert at school. Jimmy Muldoon told me he was going to bring his pet lizard to the concert and put it down my back. I'd been the only kid to fail music in the third grade but at least I'd been lizard-free.

Funny how I thought of that as the hard bark and branches tore my skirt and scratched my arms. I made it up about thirty feet before I stretched myself out along a decent sized limb, trying to blend in with the rest of the tree. I waited for whatever rode toward me to appear. It didn't take long.

Eight hooded men galloped into the clearing, all riding jet black horses barely visible against the ebony sky. They circled the ruins of the house. For almost a minute, the only movement came from the horses as they shifted their weight. The only sound came from their labored breathing. Half of the men carried torches. The firelight reflected off the horses' sweat like liquid gold and danced on the metal of the swords at the men's sides.

Two more men rode out of the trees. The first one held his hand out and an orb glowed in his palm. As he neared the remains of the house, the light in his hand shifted from a brilliant white to blue. He wore a long robe that looked like something out of *Harry Potter*. With his free hand he brushed the hood from his head. Because his clothes reminded me of a wizard's, I'd expected him to be old with a long white beard and hair. But even from this distance I could see he was clean shaven and had few wrinkles.

The second man's horse was white. He had broad shoulders and thick dark hair. The two jumped down from their mounts. The second man stood tall, a full head above the first. The wizard moved past the threshold of the house, as he did, the orb flashed red. He dropped it as if it burned his hand. The horses snorted, a few skittered back from their sentry.

"What is it, Quinn?" The tall man asked from where he stood by the doorframe.

"Someone's come through, My Lord."

The tall man walked to the wizard's side. "Is it the child?"

"I can't be sure."

The other man grabbed Quinn's shoulders and pulled him up so their faces were only inches apart. The orb's red glow cast both of them in crimson shadows.

"What can you tell me, Portal? Surely you can find something useful to say?" The sound of his voice chilled me more than the brisk wind that blew. It was as if the air froze with his breath. The insects of the forest grew silent. Even the horses stopped fidgeting.

Quinn's voice cracked as he spoke. "The Chrysaline . . . ."

"What?"

Quinn hesitated. "I can't get a reading with you so close. It doesn't . . . it doesn't like you."

The dark man let out a throaty chuckle. "No?"

The wizard shook his head.

The man let him go with a thrust of his hands. Quinn stumbled, nearly tripping over the orb which shifted back to white as the other man stepped outside the threshold of the house.

Quinn picked up the orb and carried it to the broken wall of the . . . closet or whatever it was... I'd escaped from. As he put the orb inside, the light turned to a lilac hue.

"What does it mean?" The dark man asked.

"It means . . . ." A breeze carried Quinn's whispered answer up to where I hid in the trees. "One of the royal family has returned."

Another gust of wind hid the grunt of disbelief I'd let out. *Royal family?* I may not know a lot about this place but I was sure the tall, scary guy would be mad if he found out it was just me.

I thought about revealing myself to them, hoping that once they realized I wasn't the person they were looking for they'd help me get back home. I couldn't bring myself to do it. Something about all those guards with their swords kept me quiet.

The tall man rested his hand on the wooden doorframe. "How long ago did they come through?"

Quinn shook his head. "It can't have been too long. We came as soon as the other Portals sensed this passage."

I pressed myself down onto the branch as the dark man turned to scan around him. He walked back to his horse then lifted himself up. "Search the woods. They can't have gotten far. They don't know the area."

"Lord Braedon, wait!"

"What is it?"

The orb turned white as the wizard moved away from the closet. "It isn't certain who came through." He hesitated for a moment. "It may be your wife."

"The Portal was instructed to call for the child."

Quinn wrapped the orb in a piece of cloth then placed it in a bag at his horse's side. "If she discovered that our Portals had connected with hers, she may have taken the passage herself."

"Pray that didn't happen." Lord Braedon's voice grew louder, piercing the darkness like sharp arrows. "Search the woods for the traveler. I want whoever came through that passage alive and I want them before the sun rises!"

They all galloped out of the clearing but Quinn. He pulled the orb out from his bag and led the horse to the edge of the woods opposite me. As he circled toward me the light shifted again to lilac. I held my breath, trying to keep as still as possible. He waited until the pounding of the horses' hooves grew distant, then he spoke.

"Follow the moon as it sets behind the hills. Find someone there to help you to the Sanctuary." He put the orb in the saddle bag and mounted his horse. "Etain's child, beware of the Black Guards. Do not try to out run them. If one approaches, climb as high as you can and remain still until it passes."

"Wait!" I called out, but the horse already carried Quinn into the forest behind me. I wanted to tell him I didn't know any Etain. I wanted to explain that I wasn't royalty, just some average sixteen-year-old. I wanted him to tell me how to get home.

An owl screech spooked me and I lost my balance. I spun round until I hung under the branch. The bark scraped the inside of my thighs through the thin gauze of my skirt. The cuts burned and I sucked in a breath through clenched teeth.

Wonderful.

I decided to drop to the branch below. My skirt tore as I released my legs. *Great.* Not that the material was doing a fantastic job of keeping me warm, but the gaping hole from my knee to my hip gave the wind even more access to my skin.

This branch was a little more solid than my last perch. I scooted along until my back rested against the trunk. I put one hand on the branch above me and one between my knees. Balanced again, I thought about what else I knew for sure. I had two options. Either I was dreaming, or this was real. The smell of decaying leaves from the forest floor wafted on the wind and I sneezed. My dreams may be vivid, but they'd never included odors before. I took a deep breath to calm my fraying nerves and tried to think clearly about my situation.

I wondered whether some form of my body still clutched onto Mr. Morrison's hand back at Meadow Hills or whether I'd totally disappeared through a weird break in the space time continuum. Josh was always reading sci-fi books and using terms like that. I didn't know which would be better. Either I'd soon be hooked up to some kind of life-support in an effort to keep my spiritless body alive, or my mom would be calling the cops trying to convince them I wasn't the type of teenager who'd run away. And let's be honest, even if they did believe her, no one would think to look for me here.

The night grew even colder. I figured it would be better to start moving and warm up than to let the sound of my chattering teeth be a signal for the . . . what had Quinn called them . . . Black Guards.

Climbing down a tree is always harder than climbing up one. Branches that once worked as great ladder rungs now appeared impossibly far away in the dark. By the time I reached the bottom, my skirt was in shreds and my body bled in more places. I tried to run across the clearing toward the house but stumbled, landing face down on the cold grass. I rolled over and stretched the kinks out of my muscles before walking again.

This time I made it to the house. Soot came off on my fingers when I rubbed the wooden door frame. I guess the stones around it protected it from the fire that consumed the rest of the house. Someone must have swept the debris from the floor. Nothing remained but dirt and grass. I made my way over and ran my hand along the wall of the chamber I'd come through. It wasn't a closet, as I'd originally thought, as there were no hangers or shelves. Although slightly charred, the wood was solid. Why hadn't it burned with the rest of the house? It stood alone, with nothing to protect it. I ducked through the hole I'd made. Maybe if I thought hard about home, this thing would transport me back. Repeating the words of Dorothy, I chanted, "There's no place like home, there's no place like home." Dumb, I know, but I was desperate.

Nothing.

I concentrated on Mr. Morrison and tried to send him some kind of psychic message to bring me home.

Still nothing.

I debated hiding in the box until daylight but thought the better of it. That Quinn guy had given me some idea of where to head for help, so I should probably follow it. I poked my head out and listened for hoof beats. Nothing but the rustling of leaves. I crawled out and checked the moon. It no longer stood directly over my head. I marked where it set and started off in that direction.

It had been over a year since my mom and I had been camping, but little things she'd taught me kept popping into my head. Stuff like the names of the different trees; the fact that moss grows on the north side of the trunks so I figured I was heading west. I had complained over the years that we never went anywhere fun like Disney World, but right now I was very thankful. Although not a big fan of walking around strange forests in the dark, at least I'd done it before.

I kept my pace slow. One, because I wanted to be able to hear the Black Guards if they approached and two, because the boots I wore were in no way made for hiking. They rubbed against my little toes and I knew I'd soon have blisters. I came to another clearing and searched for the moon to make sure I still traveled the right way. A layer of clouds moved in with the wind obscuring all but the faintest glow of light. I readjusted my path then headed back into the trees.

A low rumble of thunder vibrated across the sky, followed by another. Before long, heavy raindrops plopped through the leaves and pelted my face. An image of Eeyore the donkey came to my mind. I pictured a little black rain cloud hanging over my head and trailing me wherever I went.

Can this night get any worse?

As soon the thought went through my mind, I tried to take it back.

It was too late.

Between the next two rolls of thunder I made out the sound of horse's hooves. Lightning exploded above. I took a quick look at the trees around me. None had branches low enough that I could climb.

The pounding hooves came closer. Another flash illuminated the woods. I dove for a fallen pine off to my right. I pressed myself flat into the dirt, wriggling under the trunk as far as I could. A small gap between the ground and the tree allowed me to see.

A Black Guard galloped into view with the next blaze of lightning. He pulled up on the horse's reins as the thunder roared overhead. I held my breath. I hadn't appreciated how big these horses and riders were from safety of my other perch. From this perspective, the horse appeared to be the size of a Clydesdale, only leaner. The Black Guard rose up from the saddle like a tower. He circled for a moment, tilting his head from one side to another. *Was he trying to hear me? Smell me?* He came right up beside the trunk I hid under, then turned his mount to the tree next to me. The storm illuminated his gloved hand reaching out to touch the pine's trunk. He brought it back to his face and sniffed. With the next crash of thunder, he kicked the horse into a gallop and rode back toward the way I'd come.

I shivered on the ground, trying to get the courage to crawl out. A blinding light blazed and the air filled with the shriek of cracking wood as a tree behind me exploded. I jumped from my hiding place and ran. I couldn't see the moon, so I had no idea if I headed in the right direction. I couldn't hear a sound besides the pounding rain and thunder. I could only think about escaping. Getting out of this forest, out of the rain, out of this world, and back home.

CHAPTER FOUR

Not in Connecticut Anymore

"Well, now Seamus, what do we have here?"
I woke to find a white and black speckled goat nibbling at some hay by my head. I let out a yelp and backed up against the wooden slats of a barn. My brain struggled to clear out the foggy remains of sleep. *Did that goat just talk?*

I looked around and saw a woman with graying brown hair standing at the entrance to the pen. A few wrinkles lined the skin around her eyes and mouth. I could see she had once been beautiful. She rested her hands on her round hips then lifted an eyebrow in my direction.

She spoke with an accent. It reminded me of an Irish brogue. "I do not think you're from around here, are ye, girl?"

I shook my head, trying to remember how I'd gotten into this barn. Images of giant beasts on horseback and glowing orbs flashed through my mind. I'd hoped the nightmare of the storm and Black Guards had been just that, but as I pulled a strand of hay from my hair, I knew it'd all been true.

The woman's gaze shifted from my face to my torn clothing. The humor in her eyes faded. "Ye look like you've had a rough time of it." She tugged the goat away from my feet. "Would ye by chance be needin' some food, and maybe somethin' to drink?"

I slid myself up the wall. I couldn't find my voice, my throat parched and sore from the cold air I'd been panting throughout the night. Instead, I nodded.

"Come, follow me into the house. There might be somethin' the boys haven't eaten."

My knees buckled. I had to grab onto the wall to keep my balance.

The woman held out her hand. "Let me help ye." I took hold of her arm. "My name is Treasa."

"Thank you," I managed to croak before my throat closed up again.

My eyes protested when we left the dim inside of the barn for the harsh light outside. I lifted my free arm to block the sun.

"The house is just ahead a few more feet," Treasa crooned. "Not far now."

She led me across a muddy yard, the heels of my boots making sucking sounds as I stepped through the muck. Chickens squawked somewhere off to my right and cow bells rang in the distance. The smell of smoke drifted on the breeze. By the time we reached the house, my eyes had grown accustomed to the sun. I could make out brown mud and stone walls. Treasa pushed open a wooden door.

"Ye have a seat, and I'll see what the boys have left us to eat, shall I?" She led me over to a table in front of a stone fireplace. A pot of water hung over flames. I let my gaze roam around the room. There were no windows. The roof was made of thatched straw. Helplessness washed over me like a wave. I longed to get a message to my mom so she could come find me but doubted anyone in this place would understand the concept of cellphones or laptops. I put my head down on the table and sobbed.

I jumped when Treasa put her hand on my shoulder. "Shh, now. It's only me." She set down a wooden cup filled with water. I didn't stop to wipe my eyes or the snot running from my nose before I grabbed hold of it and drank down the cool liquid. It tasted sweet and pure, not like the stuff back home. The water peeled a layer of cotton from my throat.

Treasa took the cup and poured me another from a nearby pitcher. I tried to drink this one slower but my body desperately needed to rehydrate.

"Ye need more?"

"Please," I gasped.

She smiled and poured another cupful, leaving the jug on the table so I could help myself. She walked over to a shelf then unwrapped what looked to be the remains of a loaf of bread. I finished off the rest of the water while she gathered a few more things onto a plate. She put it down on the table then pulled a stool over to sit across from me.

I wanted to dive into the food but years of listening to my mother nag about manners forced me to stop.

The older woman's brown eyes watched me closely. "I've already eaten today. Ye help yourself."

I tore off a hunk of bread and shoved it into my mouth. Its grainy texture scratched my tongue. It tasted hearty, like the whole kernel had been used to make it. I took a piece of cheese to soften the bread. Its sharp tang woke my taste buds.

Treasa smiled. "Feelin' better?"

I nodded and kept eating.

"Good."

She didn't say anything else until I finished the bread, cheese and piece of jerky-like meat she'd given me. I wiped the last chunk of bread around the plate to pick up any leftover crumbs.

My throat sufficiently lubricated and my hunger satisfied, I finally found my voice. "Thank you."

"You're welcome." Her gaze drifted over my clothes again. I pulled at the torn shreds of my skirt, trying to cover my legs. She shook her head. "Don't fret. I'll find ye somethin' of mine ye can wear. Do ye want to tell me what happened?"

I let out a shuddering breath. What could I tell this woman that she would believe?

Her face filled with compassion. She leaned forward. "Was it a man? Against your will, was it?"

I sat up. "No ma'am. I wasn't raped."

The tension in her shoulders loosened. "That's good then." Whatever else has happened to ye, it will be easier to deal with." She leaned her elbows on the table. "You're not from around here." She reached out and fingered the sleeve of my sweater. "I've never felt wool like this before."

How do I explain cotton-polyester blend? "I live very far away."

"Aye?" She sat back on her stool. "How'd did ye get to our part of the land?"

My mind raced, trying to come up with some plausible answer since I knew she'd never believe the real one. "I . . . I got lost in the woods . . . trying to find . . . to find my family."

Treasa's brows furrowed together. "How did ye come to lose them? Were ye traveling together? Or was it the storm that drove ye apart?"

"No . . . we weren't together . . . I uh, lost them . . . before—"

"Oh." Her heavy sigh interrupted my rambling. "Ye mean to the sickness? Ye lost your parents to it, have ye?"

I grasped onto her explanation. "Yes."

"Tryin' to find some relatives ye can live with now?" She reached over to pat my arm as I nodded. "What town are ye seekin'?"

My brain came up with the place Quinn told me to find. "The Sanctuary."

Her brows rose in what I guessed was surprise. "Are ye related to one of the Brethren, then?" Her expression softened as she answered her own question. "Or have your family gone there seekin' medicine for the sickness?"

I nodded again.

The door to the hut flew open and a young boy with dirt on his face and disheveled brown hair ran inside. "Mum!"

Treasa rested her hand over her heart. "What are ye doin', ye little heathen? Scarin' yer mother like that?"

The boy's brown eyes twinkled as he laughed. "Sorry, Mum. But Teagan's caught us a feast!" He held up two rabbits, their necks at odd angles

Treasa stood and pulled the boy to her side. "Has he now? Well, praise to Ruahk then, for we have company today."

I tried to rearrange the shredded remains of my skirt to hide more of my legs as the boy's eyes widened at the sight of me.

"Galvyn, this is . . . . Oh, dearie me," Treasa chuckled. "I don't know yer name."

"Alystrine," I spit out my full name before I could self-edit. "But my family calls me Ally."

Treasa seemed to tense as she stared at me. "Alystrine?" Her voice whispered. She pulled Galvyn closer, as if protecting him from something. "That's a high name for a Commoner. Who do ye say your people are?"

I tried to swallow but my mouth was dry. Again, my brain answered on its own, the idea seeming to come from somewhere outside of me. "My parents are gone. I need to find the Sanctuary."

"I can take her! Can't I, Mum?" Galvyn fairly danced with excitement. "I'm old enough!"

She smiled weakly. "We'll see. Perhaps you and Teagan can go together."

"But he's gone into town to trade the other conies he caught today."

"Is that so?" Treasa's smile faded. "Then ye can ask him when he gets back. Go and muck out the barn fer me, will ye?"

His disappointment apparent, he still groaned, "Yes, ma'am," before heading toward the barn.

Sunshine spilled into the dark room, but I felt a foreboding darkness as Treasa continued to study me in silence. I shivered. Not from a chill, but from apprehension.

Treasa blinked, as if coming out from a trance. She shut the door then turned back to me. "We should see about gettin' ye somethin' decent to wear. Come here, lass."

I had to use the table to push myself up, my legs still stiff from last evening's trek through the forest. I forced myself not to think any more about my bizarre situation. If I did, I'd lose it entirely. Instead, I followed Treasa through the threshold into a smaller room.

Two mattresses lay on the floor, covered with what looked like dark woolen blankets. Straw poked out of the corners. My hostess opened a wooden chest shoved into the corner of the room. She rummaged through it for a moment before pulling out a cream linen slip with ruffles along the bottom.

"Here." She tossed the garment to me. "Put this on under your skirt."

I winced as I stood on one leg to step into it, the blisters on my feet flaring to life again. After a moment, I switched to balance on the other foot and then pulled the slip up to my waist. As Treasa was quite a few pounds heavier than me, I had to tie the drawstring tightly to keep it from slipping back down to the floor.

She watched me from the corner. "Who do ye seek? In the Sanctuary?"

No answer came to me this time. I could only stand mute in the center of the room like an idiot while my brain searched for something. Anything.

Treasa didn't blink. "Who are ye?"

"My name is Ally Foster. I. . . I got lost in the woods. I need to find the Sanctuary." If I kept repeating it to myself, maybe it would keep me from going crazy.

She stood. "But why the Sanctuary? Surely ye have people closer than that great journey."

I shook my head. "Is it very far away?"

"From here?" Treasa nodded. "Four days, at least."

The news hit me like a bucket of ice water. My knees buckled before I could get control of myself. I collapsed to the floor at the foot of the two beds. "Four days?" What would my mother think? That I'd run away? But I didn't take the car and my purse was probably still in Mr. Morrison's room. What about Josh and Renee? Another wave of tears washed over me.

Treasa clucked her tongue in a soothing way. "There now." She put her arm around my shoulder and scooted me toward one of the mattresses. "Rest for a bit."

I stretched myself. Each piece of straw poking into my skin reminded me of how far away I was from home.

Treasa placed the back of her hand across my forehead. "Thanks be, you've no fever. I don't think it's the sickness. You're tired is all."

I rolled away from her, my sobs making my breath come out in tiny hiccups. *I'm not tired, I'm lost. I'm stuck in a nightmare and I have no idea how to wake up.*

When I opened my eyes sometime later, the room was still light. I must not have slept for long. I lay on the uncomfortable mattress and listened to voices talking.

"No, don't wake her." Treasa's voice pierced through the fog of sleep still surrounding my brain.

"But why is she sleepin' in the middle of the day?" Galvyn whined.

"Because she spent the night wanderin' in the woods."

"Why?"

His mother's voice rose. "I'm not an Elder, am I? Do ye think I can read another's mind?"

I sat up. What was she talking about? Were there people here that could read minds?

"Look!" Galvyn cried. "She's up, Mum. See?"

Treasa swiped her hand across his ear. "It's your pesterin' that's woke her, ye heathen."

"Ow!" He ducked out of the way in case she wanted to punish him again. "I'm sorry, Miss. I didna mean to wake ye."

"It's all right." I stifled a yawn.

Treasa peered in at me. "Why don't ye let the boy show ye to the stream so ye can wash yourself?"

"That would be great." I started to put weight on my feet to stand, but my blisters screamed at me to stop. I took a moment to unzip my boots. It wasn't until I'd pulled them off that I caught sight of Treasa and Galvyn's stares. "What's wrong?"

Galvyn took a step. "Can I see it?"

"What? My boot?"

He nodded.

I held it out to him.

He took it like he thought it would explode. He didn't bring it close but studied it nonetheless. His fingers touched the laces and then the metal teeth of the zipper. "Is it magic?"

"It's a zipper."

"A what?" he whispered.

One look at Treasa's face and I knew that they'd never seen one before. "It's just a fancy way to fasten boots, instead of laces." I turned my attention to my socks. They'd gotten wet in the rain last night and then dried into a hard crust. I knew it was going to hurt to peel them off, but I had to do it. I steeled myself then yanked the first one off with a hiss of pain. Both onlookers echoed my sharp intake of breath.

Galvyn's expression was a mixture of horror and fascination. "What did ye do to deserve that torture?"

Several of my blisters oozed with bloody pus. Those that hadn't burst looked like massive white boils. I gestured toward my boots with my head. "They weren't made for the kind of running I did last night." I pulled my other sock off with a groan.

"Magic fasteners or not." Galvyn tossed my footwear on the ground. "I don't think ye should trade with this cobbler again."

I stood gingerly to my feet. "I think you're right."

"Show her to the stream." Treasa crossed the room to pick up a bucket. "Then you'd better get some milk. Tegan should be back soon and we'll have supper."

Galvyn took the wooden pail from his mother. "Aye. Follow me."

I tried not to wince as I walked, but wasn't always successful. I paused in the doorway. The day's sunshine had done nothing to dry the ground; the farmyard was thick with mud. I took a deep breath and stepped into it, relishing the cool on my feet but trying not to think of what kind of infection I might get from the dirt. I followed Galvyn about a quarter mile from the house to a fast moving creek, observing as I did that the farm consisted of the two-room house, a slightly larger barn, and a recently harvested field of crops.

My guide paused by the stream. "Here ye are, Miss."

He watched me closely as I waded into the water. The icy water cooled my blisters. I drew my skirt and Treasa's slip up around my legs so I could sit on a boulder and let my feet soak for a bit.

"I'll be in the barn if you need anything else."

"Thanks," I called as he scurried off to do his chores. Once my feet were numb, I popped the remaining blisters, hoping that if I had to run again, my boots might not hurt as much.

Afterwards, I let the water deaden the pain as I scanned the horizon. Clouds of bright pink and orange streaked across the sky. If the sun set in the West here, then the forest I'd run through last night started about a half mile to the South. Endless farmland seemed to cover the hills to the Northwest. Far in the distance, I thought I could make out the purple silhouette of mountains.

"Mom," I spoke quietly, my voice no louder than the running stream, "If you can hear me, please know I didn't run away because of our fight." I willed myself not to start crying again. "I'm trying to find my way back to you."

After a couple more minutes, I stepped out of the creek then stooped down to dry my feet off with the hem of my slip. I made my way over to the barn to find Galvyn. He sat cross-legged on the straw, one hand on a goat's neck, the other pulling on its . . . was it still called an udder on a goat? I'd eaten goat cheese before, but had never given thought to the fact that someone would actually milk the animal like a cow.

Galvyn laughed. "What's the matter, Miss? Ye look like ye never seen a goat before."

"I haven't seen anyone milk one before."

He looked surprised. "No? Do ye have a cow then?"

I shook my head.

"Where do ye get yer milk and cheese then?"

Somehow I didn't think he'd get the concept of a supermarket. "We traded for it."

"Aye? With what?"

I was saved from trying to explain the concept of credit cards by a shout from the yard. "Galvyn!" The new voice was deep and definitely male. "Come inside now! Hurry!"

The young boy jumped to his feet. "That'll be Tegan. He sounds mad." He herded the goat back into a stall and shut the gate behind it.

I picked up the half-filled bucket of milk and followed Galvyn back to the house. Treasa sat at the table, her hand over her mouth like she was holding back a scream. A young man stood in front of her. He appeared to be my age or a few years older, no more than twenty. His brown hair and dark eyes resembled his mother's. He turned as Galvyn and I entered the house.

"Shut the door," he ordered, his voice harsh. Galvyn hurried to obey as his older brother took a step toward me. "Are ye the one they're lookin' for?"

I clutched the pail to my chest as fear crept up from my stomach. "Who?"

"Tegan?" Galvyn came protectively to my side. "What's wrong?"

I could feel Tegan's anger. "The Black Guards."

Both Treasa and Galvyn gasped.

Tegan's hard gaze never left my face. "They're all over the village, lookin' for a traveler. Is it ye?"

I sensed Treasa's terror as she watched me. "I should have known."

Galvyn's eyes grew wide. "You're from the Other World?"

I hated feeling like I'd somehow betrayed this kind family who'd done nothing but try to help me. I couldn't find my voice. I didn't know if I was a traveler or not, but I did know I was the person the Black Guards were seeking. I took a step backward as Tegan came toward me.

"Is it ye they're lookin' for?"

"I think so."

Treasa moaned.

"I don't know why." I wanted to go to her, to try to explain what had happened, but Tegan moved to stop me. "Please, I don't know where I am. I don't know how I got here."

"Ye have to leave." Tegan stood only an inch or so taller than me, but he seemed much more solid than I was, like he could snap me in half in his anger.

"No!" Treasa jumped to her feet. "If she leaves now, they're sure to find her. She'll have no choice but to lead them here."

Tegan whirled to face his mother. "She cannot stay. If she's been here all day, as you've said, her scent will surely bring them by the morning."

Galvyn ran to Treasa's side. She wrapped her arms around him in a fierce hug. "We can cover it up. Burn some of the lavender and sage about."

"No." Tegan shook his head. "I'll take her to them. Maybe then they'll leave us alone."

The bucket slipped from my arms. Milk exploded at my feet when it hit the floor. "Please don't. I'm not who they think I am. The man . . . Quinn . . . he said I should get to the Sanctuary. I'd be safe there."

All three stared at me with fear in their eyes, but it was Treasa who asked, "Quinn? The Portal?"

"He had a long robe, he carried this orb thing."

Tegan grabbed my shoulders and shook me. "The Chrysaline? He had it with him?"

"I don't know what it was. It glowed different colors. He told me to follow the moon over the hill. That I would find help here."

"Did he now?" Tegan pushed me away. "He was wrong."

"But what did I do? I don't understand!"

The pity in Treasa's eyes frightened me as she let go of Galvyn and took a step toward me. "It's not what ye did, child. It's what Braedon will do if he finds we've helped ye."

At the mention of the tall man's name, the temperature in the room chilled a few degrees. I sensed she was right.

Treasa paced for a moment, muttering under her breath. I couldn't tell if she was praying or talking to herself. Finally she looked up. "I cannot, in good conscience, turn her over to the Black Guards. No one deserves that."

Tegan started to sputter a retort but she raised her hand and he stopped. She turned to me. "But neither can ye stay here." She glanced between the two of us. "Ye'll guide her to the Sanctuary. Start tonight by followin' the river back into the forest. Hopefully they'll not retrace their steps from today." She turned to Galvyn. "Run to the stream and fill the skin with water."

He grabbed what looked like a brown leather bag hanging from the wall then hurried outside.

Treasa took hold of my wrist and pulled me toward the little side room. "Ye'll need another shirt. Yours looks too different from what we wear. Tegan," she called over her shoulder. "Gather up some blankets and food. We've not much, but it should get ye to the Sanctuary."

Treasa knelt down by the wooden box again and searched through it before pulling out a blue buttoned shirt. "It's one of Tegan's, too big yet for Galvyn." She carried it over to me as Tegan yanked the woolen blankets off the mattress furthest from us.

I waited for Tegan to leave before putting on the shirt.

"Ye must do all Tegan tells ye." Treasa ordered as she sifted through her crate again. "If ye wish to get to the Sanctuary, ye must do everythin' he says, whether ye understand or no."

"I will." What choice did I have?

She held out a pair of knitted socks. "Maybe these will help your feet."

I doubted anything would help if I had to wear my boots again, but I took them anyway. I picked up my shoes and headed out to the other room to put them on.

Tegan knelt while rolling up the blankets. He paused when he caught sight of my boots. "She can't be wearin' those. Everyone will know she's a traveler."

His mother frowned. "You're right. Run along the creek tonight until the sunrise. She can go without them until ye reach the Everwood."

Tegan nodded then ripped the boots from my hands. "I'll stuff them in the blanket roll. It should hide her smell."

If I wasn't so petrified of my situation, I'd be paranoid about the way they all kept talking about my smell. I balled up Treasa's socks then reached over to give them to Tegan. His mother took hold of my hand to stop me. She stared at my ring. Her voice came out in a monotone. "Where did ye get this?"

"My mother gave it to me yesterday." I couldn't explain the dread oozing through me. "For my birthday."

Treasa's eyes remained glued to the ring. "And how old are ye now?"

"Sixteen."

She groaned.

Tegan squatted next to his mother. "What is it?"

His presence stirred her out of her trance, but she did not look at him. "It's a ring of succession."

Tegan and I spoke together. "What?"

She let go of my hand then stuffed potatoes into Tegan's makeshift pack. "There's a lot ye need to be told girl, but there's not enough time. Ye can ask the Brethren. They'll know the truth."

"Who are the Brethren?" I asked, but Galvyn ran back in before they could answer, the skin now sloshing with water.

"The clouds are out, so there'll be little light." He set the water down by Tegan. "Not that the Black Guards need light."

Tegan tied the blanket rolls together before slinging them over his shoulder so they rested next to his quiver and bow. I stood as he did. Treasa pulled him into an embrace.

"I'll be prayin' for ye." She leaned in closer and whispered something in his ear. His eyes darted toward me then he nodded. She pushed him away. "Now go before the Black Guards double back."

The young man opened the door and scanned the distant horizon. "Come on."

"Thank you," I said as I passed Treasa. "For everything."

She gave me a halting smile but said nothing.

I followed Tegan across the muddy yard to the side of the barn. When we were out of sight of the house, he backed me against the wall.

I pushed him away. "Back off."

He breathed hard through his nose. "I don't know who ye are or where yer from, and I don't think I want to know the truth. Tonight we'll have the cover of darkness, so we should be safe if we keep to the creek." He shook his finger at me like he was scolding a child. "Tomorrow we'll be out in the open with no cover until we get to the Everwood. If anyone stops us, don't say anythin', let me do the talkin'."

I smacked his hand away from my face. "What am I supposed to do, pretend to be mute?"

He glared at me. "The way ye talk. It's too different. Ye'll get us killed." He took a sweeping look all around us. Satisfied that the Black Guards were nowhere in sight, he shifted his pack and started toward the creek.

"Tegan?"

He let out a frustrated sigh. "What is it?"

"What did your mother say to you? She whispered something when you hugged."

He pursed his lips for a moment before he admitted, "She said if the Black Guards get close, I must save myself and not worry about savin' ye."

"What will they do to me?" I tried to swallow but my mouth was too dry. "If they catch me?"

"Pray they don't," he muttered as he walked away.

CHAPTER FIVE

Red Dew

We traveled throughout the night, our only conversation Tegan's whispered orders that I keep up. Just before dawn, we left the creek and started walking toward the east. As the first rays of sunlight cracked the gray horizon, we came to the edge of the woods. Dew sparkled on the grass like diamonds. Some drops even glistened red.

"It's beautiful," I whispered.

Tegan's gaze was focused up ahead, not on the ground. "What is?" He stopped to look back at me.

I smiled as I came to his side. "The grass. What makes the dew look so red?" My foot hovered over the ground.

"No!" Tegan tried to stop me but my toes had brushed the grass. My foot froze, like I'd stuck it in a vat of ice. Tegan yanked my arm, pulling me back into the trees. The freezing sensation traveled to my ankle.

"What's happening to me?" I reached down, hoping to rub some warmth back into my lifeless limb, but Tegan grabbed my hands.

"Don't touch it. It'll make it worse."

"How could it get worse?" I grunted at the painful sensation burning inside my leg.

"We have to get ye back to the creek and wash it off."

I tried to walk but couldn't. I stumbled to the ground. Tegan slipped his arms under mine to pull me up. The numbness had travelled to my knee and I couldn't put any weight on my leg. "What's happening to me?" My voice came out high pitched with terror. Would this numbness keep traveling? Would it freeze my entire leg? Then what? My lungs? My heart?

Tegan dragged me the quarter mile back to the creek. I tried not to cry, but panic consumed me. He grunted as he pushed me toward the water. "Lift up your skirt. You need to let the water wash the curse from you."

I staggered into the creek, pulling the skirts to my waist so I could kneel in the water without soaking the fabric, splashing some up onto my now numbed thigh. I swore under my breath. "What was that stuff?"

Tegan squatted by the creek bank. "It's Red Water, cursed by the Black Guards." He picked up a rock. "I've never seen it before. Only heard the stories." He rolled the pebble in his hand. "They say it freezes a man's soul, binding him to the Black Guard that gave it to him. Making him a slave forever to the demon."

"Is that going to happen to me? Or did we stop it in time?" I didn't like how shrill my voice sounded.

I couldn't read Tegan's expression. He seemed conflicted. He sat back on his heels as he watched me. "How far has the coldness spread?"

"It had been up to my hip, but seems to be shrinking."

"Are ye sure?"

I nodded. "I can feel my knee again."

"Wait a bit longer." He threw the pebble across the creek. "Make sure it's all gone before ye get out."

The birds in the trees began singing as sunlight filtered down through the trees. When I could wiggle my toes freely, I stood up, letting my skirts fall down as I did. "It's gone."

His brown eyes watched me intently. "Give me yer hand."

I reached toward him. He squeezed my fingers tightly while muttering some kind of chant. When he finished, he studied me again. "Did you feel anything then? When I said a prayer?"

"Not a thing."

Tegan sighed as he let go of me. "Then I believe you're free of it." His forehead wrinkled as if he was thinking hard about something. "I don't know if the curse was in ye long enough for the beast to have connected with ye, but we'll have to wait until the sun burns off the dew before we try and cross out of the forest again."

I stepped out of the creek. "Connected?"

"They have the power to join with people's minds. If it's seen through your eyes, it'll know where ye are."

"Is there any way to tell if it did?"

Tegan shook his head. "None that I know of. Except that it'll be upon us soon. Did ye sense anythin'? A presence inside of ye?"

"No." I shook the water from my feet. "Just the cold."

The same conflicted expression passed over his face. "Then I think you'll be fine." He pulled out half a loaf of bread and ripped off two pieces. "We may as well eat somethin' while we wait to leave the forest."

I munched on my breakfast, trying not to dwell on what had almost happened to me. I had to survive another three nights in this place before Treasa said we'd reach the Sanctuary. I hoped I'd make it, but every day brought strange new dangers. I pushed the thought out of mind and concentrated instead on chewing the hard bread until I could swallow it without choking. By the time we finished eating, the dew had burned off the grass. Tegan made me put my boots on for the first mile of our journey. Popping the blisters and Treasa's socks helped alleviate some of the pain, but not for long. Once the forest was out of sight behind us, I sat down to take them off again.

Tegan waited impatiently. "We must hurry today. We've lost a lot of time." He paced in front of me. "And don't forget, if we meet anyone on the road, stay quiet. I'll do the talkin'." I handed him my boots. He stuffed them into one of the blanket rolls. "How's yer leg feel?"

"Fine now." I even hopped on it to prove how good it felt now I wasn't wearing my boots.

"Then let's get going." With that, he turned his back to me and set off through the meadow.

The sun was well past the horizon and still the boy said nothing to me. As I was supposed to be mute, I hadn't said anything either. I had a lot to consider during that time, but my bleeding feet and aching muscles kept most rational thought from making it into my brain. I refused to complain to Tegan, no matter how much pain I was in. I didn't appreciate the way he'd looked at me back at the creek. Like I was to blame for all this. It would be my fault if anything happened to his family, even though I had no idea what was going on.

My stomach growled. Tegan turned around. "What was that?"

I glared at him, trying to make my eyes say, *I'm mute remember?*

"Was that you?"

I nodded.

He turned away. "Try not to be so loud."

I stuck my tongue out at his back. "I'm sorry if my starvation annoys you," I muttered.

"You're not starvin'."

Great. He had super hearing. I tried to get my mind off my hunger by examining my surroundings. The tall grassy meadow we'd been walking in had become rockier. A herd of sheep grazed on a hillside to our right. The shadow of mountains loomed in the distance. I wondered if that's where we were headed.

We climbed a gentle hill. From the crest, I could see a road about a mile away on which several carts traveled. Tegan stopped, shaded his eyes and peered to the left. I did the same, making out a walled town a few miles away.

"Are we stopping there?" I asked.

Tegan shook his head. "It would be best not to. The less people who see ye, the better."

I had thought the same thing, but the idea of a bed at the local inn and a nice hot meal had crossed my mind as well.

"We'll follow the road north for a bit, then turn off." He thrust his chin toward the horizon. "We need to get across the river at the foot of the mountains by nightfall tomorrow."

If I had to guess, I'd estimate our journey to be another thirty or forty miles. I closed my eyes and willed myself not to cry.

His feet crunched on the dry grass. "What are ye waitin' for? We don't have time to waste."

Every muscle in my body hurt. I didn't want to go any farther.

"Come on now!" Tegan called from somewhere below.

I took a deep breath and forced my legs to move. My joints, muscles, and head screamed in protest. I refused to look up at the mountains. If I kept my eyes down, I could concentrate on taking one step at a time.

I could hear Tegan mumbling when I reached the bottom of the hill. Something inside me snapped. "Do you have something you want to say to me?"

He kept walking and muttering.

"Look. Just say what it is. I'm not going anywhere until you do."

He spun around. The wind blew his shaggy brown hair into his eyes, but he didn't brush it away. "I said at this rate, I might as well give a shout to tell the Black Guards where ye are. Yer movin' so slow." His brogue thickened with his anger. I could barely understand him. "Do ye not realize the danger yer in? The danger ye've put my family in?"

"Do I realize?" I screamed at him. "Are you kidding? Two nights ago

I took an old man's hand, and the next thing I knew I was in the amusement park ride from hell. My insides were ripped out and shoved back inside me, I spun around in a black hole for what seemed like forever, and then I smacked down in some wooden box I had to beat my way out of." I took a step toward him. "I've had giant men with huge swords chasing me through a forest, while being pelted with icy rain and having trees explode around me. I haven't eaten anything but a couple of scraps of bread and some cheese, and I haven't slept more than a couple of hours in two nights." I thrust my finger at his chest. "Believe me, I appreciate all you and your mother have done for me, but I'm tired of you looking at me like this was my fault. I haven't done anything. I don't know where I am, and all I want to do is get the hell out of here. I'm sorry if I'm not moving fast enough for you, but I'm doing the best I can."

He stood still. I couldn't read what he was thinking behind his eyes. "Are ye through?"

I balled my hand into a fist at my side and forced myself not to slug him.

"Can we get goin'? I'd like to be away from the Traders' Road before mid-day. Too many people could see us."

I growled in reply and walked past him. I heard him grunt behind me, then jog up to take the lead. "Ye don't even know which way to go."

"I know where I'd like you to go," I mumbled. I'd never met a more infuriating person. If he wasn't my only hope to get back home, I'd push him down the next hill just to watch him roll.

My legs gave out at dusk, even though we'd seemed to come no closer to the mountains. I swear I'd walked on a treadmill all day, moving constantly, but getting nowhere. Tegan found us shelter in a small grove of apple trees on the edge of a field. I picked several while Tegan unrolled the blankets and set out another heel of bread.

I passed him two of the apples. "It's getting cold."

He eyed me as he bit into the fruit, then tilted his head toward a farmhouse about a mile away. "We can't risk a fire being seen."

I sighed heavily. At least he was letting me rest for the night.

Although I was starving, I could barely finish my meager meal before my body forced me to lay down. I watched the stars fight to be seen through the gray clouds racing across the sky. I hoped it wouldn't rain, although I didn't think even that would get me to move again before morning.

Tegan's soft brogue cut through the silence. "Are ye still awake?"

I yawned. "Barely."

He snorted a laugh. "I was just wonderin'. Is it like this? Where ye live?"

I thought about the White Mountains in New Hampshire, where my mom and I would camp. "In some places."

"But not everywhere?"

I shook my head but realized he wouldn't be able to see the gesture in the dark. "No. There are a lot more people where I come from. And different kinds of houses and buildings." I had to stop for a moment, an overwhelming sense of homesickness threatening to overtake me. "Do you get many . . . what did you call them . . .travelers here? Many people like me?"

His voice floated through the darkness. "Not anymore. Many years ago, before I was born, there are lots of tales of people comin' through the passages. It's how we survived, actually."

"What do you mean?"

"The people had grown sickly. Too much in-breedin'. It was one of the early kings, Gedeon, who first passed through to your world. He brought people back with him. They married those that were here."

"Really?" I would have to look up strange disappearances when I got home. Maybe instead of UFO's, people were getting sucked into this place.

"You've not heard of us then, where ye live?"

"No." I yawned again. My brain sinking into the welcome fog of unconsciousness. Tegan spoke again. "What?"

"I asked what your name is."

"I'm Ally . . . Ally Foster."

He grunted. "I'm sorry I was so hard on ye this afternoon, Ally Foster. It's only . . . I was afraid . . . being so close to the town . . . to the roads . . . that we'd be seen."

"It's okay." I rolled over to my side, surprised to see his silhouette laying a few feet from me. The moon broke through the clouds at that moment and I could see his eyes open, watching me. "I'm sorry I freaked out on you. I just don't understand how I even got here, never mind all the stuff about Black Guards and curses."

"Is there no evil in the Other World?"

I chuckled softly. "Plenty. But not this magical kind. Just people hurting people."

"Aye." He sighed. "We have that kind of evil here, too."

A woman screamed in the distance. I sat up, my heart beating fast.

"Don't worry," Tegan rose so he rested on one arm. "It's only a fox."

"Are you sure?" I could barely catch my breath.

"Certain. It's an awful sound, but you'll see, it'll come fairly regular."

As if on cue, the animal shrieked again. I waited for another cry before I lowered myself to my blanket. Shivering, I pulled one side over me. *Like a human burrito.* I thought, regretting the food analogy as my stomach groaned loudly.

Tegan laughed. "It's a good thing we're so far from the farmhouse. Any closer and they'd be out lookin' for the bear."

"Sorry." I hugged my tummy, hoping to quiet it down.

"When we get to the Everwood, I'll go huntin' for some meat."

Exhaustion tugged at my brain. "Will that be tomorrow?" He may have answered me, but I didn't hear it before sleep claimed me for its own.

CHAPTER SIX

Not Rock

After a pre-dawn breakfast consisting of a strip of jerky and a couple more apples, Tegan and I set off on another day of walking. By mid-day, I broke under the monotony. The mountains were still in the distance but we hadn't seen anyone since yesterday afternoon, so I figured it was okay to talk.

"Tegan?"

I picked up my pace to catch up with him. He seemed startled when I came to his side, as if I'd woken him. "Can I ask you something?"

He nodded.

"I've been trying to figure things out. Back at your house, when I told you about the guy . . . Quinn . . . you asked if he was the portal. What's a portal?"

"A Portal is not a what, it's a who. Portals . . . they're special people."

"What makes them special?"

He shifted the blanket rolls across his back. "Some can talk to the spirits of the unseen realm. Some can see the Other World."

"You mean where I come from?"

"Aye." He lifted his head, his eyes seeming to focus on the mountains looming ahead of us. "All Portals can travel in the passages."

I shook my head. "What are the passages?"

"I'm not really sure. But Portals can use them to travel great distances in an instant. Some can even go between our worlds. Some can bring people with them."

"Do they do that a lot?"

"No. There are few Portals left now. Only a handful. And the way is hard, so I've been told." A corner of his mouth lifted in a smile. "Although you say it was amusing."

I let out a choked laugh. "I never said that."

He turned to me, his face a mask of surprise. "Aye, yesterday, when ye were havin' your rant. You said it was an amusing ride . . . ."

My brain struggled to remember. "I said it was like an amusement park ride from hell! Not an amusing ride!"

He shrugged. "A park where you are amused is not a good thing?"

"Not if it's from hell!"

"What's hell?"

"It's a place you don't want to go. Filled with demons and fire."

He made a general sound of understanding. "Like the Outside?" He continued when I didn't give him a response. "The Outside is a place of darkness and weepin'. Of separation from Ruahk."

I swatted the air as we walked through a swarm of gnats. "Who's Rock?"

Tegan grunted. "Not rock . . . Ruahk." He pronounced the word slowly. "Roo-ahk. He's the one who made our world."

"God, you mean?" A gnat tried to fly into my eye. I blinked rapidly to keep it out.

"Aye. He's God. Do ye not know of him in your world?"

"Not by that name." I had to stop. The stupid bug had gotten stuck in my lash.

"Here." Tegan turned and cupped my chin. He lifted my face so he could get a good look at my eye. A moment later, his finger brushed across my eyelash. He continued to stare down at me even after he'd flicked the bug away. A strange electricity seemed to course through my body.

"You got it." My voice came out in a husky whisper. I tried to clear my throat. "Thank you."

He stepped backward. "Aye." His demeanor turned brusque. "We must hurry now. I want to cross the river before nightfall."

I stood a moment longer, trying to shake the odd feelings that had come over me when we'd touched.

"Hurry now!" Tegan called over his shoulder.

I ran to catch up with him, but couldn't keep up with his longer strides unless I wanted to jog, which wasn't an option since I wasn't wearing shoes. Instead, he left me behind again, lost in my own thoughts.

Behind the mountains, the sun painted the sky in iridescent oranges, purples, and reds. The bright colors glowed against the coming grey of twilight. If I hadn't been exhausted, the beauty would have taken my breath away. As it was, I tried to lock the vision somewhere in the back of my memory for a time when I wasn't so tired.

Ahead flowed a river, about sixty feet wide. It looked shallow, but the current was fast. Several ducks paddled near the reeds along the shore. They lowered their heads under the water to pick out some morsel for dinner.

Dinner . . . food.

My stomach growled.

Tegan stopped by the river bank to pull off his leather boots and roll up his pants. He looked over his shoulder as I trudged up behind him. "It would be best if ye took off the skirt my mother gave ye, and carried it to keep it dry. The water is cold this time of year. You'll want somethin' warm to wear when night falls."

I undid the ties that held the slip up. It fell to my ankles. I wrapped it around my neck. The shredded fabric of my broomstick skirt did little to keep me warm, but at least it kept my legs covered. I held up Treasa's slip. "Do I need to hold it over my head, or will it be okay if I keep it around my shoulders?"

"Shoulders should be fine." He stood up and scrutinized me before speaking again. "It's not too deep, but frigid, and the current is swift."

My body stiffened, but I nodded. "I'm ready."

I followed him down the bank. He paused to fill up his flask before stepping out into the water. It came up past his knees. Several long strides brought him out to the middle of the river. "It'll be worse if ye wait. Come on now."

He reached a hand out toward me and I walked in, determined not to think about the cold. That worked great until the first numbing steps wore off and the icy water stabbed at my legs. My brain ceased to function. I stood frozen, unable to move or breathe.

Tegan grabbed my hand and yanked me through the current. "Come on!" We'd taken a couple more steps when he must have missed his footing on one of the slippery rocks beneath our feet. He stumbled, but righted himself without falling in past his thighs.

I was not so fortunate.

He'd wrenched me forward before letting go of my hand. The mossy rocks gave me no traction. I plunged into the water, the current dragging me downstream. The shocking cold numbed the rest of my body instantly.

For a moment, I thought about letting myself float face down until I drowned. At least then, the aching pain and fear would be gone. But I knew my mother would never forgive me for giving up. She'd pounded that mantra into my head since I could remember: "You have to be strong, Alystrine. You never know what life is going to throw at you."

My knee grazed the bottom of the river bed. I reached out and took hold of a slimy boulder. Sputtering, I lifted my head out of the water. Tegan sloshed toward me, a look of panic on his face.

"Get to the other side," I shouted over the rushing river. "I can make it from here."

He looked as if he didn't believe me. He took another step.

"Go!" I found my footing and stood. He waited until I'd moved a few more paces in the direction of the shore before he crossed over himself. He ran down the bank then held out his hand to help me up.

"We have to get ye out of those clothes," he said as I pulled my feet from the mucky bank.

I raised an eyebrow. "And what do you propose I wear?" His mother's skirt lay around my shoulders like a drowned cat.

"You'll have to wrap yourself in a blanket. We'll hang the clothes from a tree and pray we don't get rain tonight." He towed me up the hill.

My teeth chattered. "Could we have a fire?"

"It's a risk, with the Guards looking for you. The heat will draw them. Maybe in the morning."

My body trembled. Tegan actually gave me a look of pity. At the top of the hill, he stopped and took the blanket rolls from his pack. "Take off your shirt at least. You'll catch your death if you don't."

He unrolled one of the blankets and threw me my boots. "Best to put these on, too." He held the blanket out to me. I motioned for him to turn around then slipped off his shirt and my bra. I wrapped the blanket around me, enjoying its warmth but not the itchy texture of the wool. I sat down to put on my boots. "You can turn around now."

He cocked his head toward the nearby mountains. "It would be best to get to the Everwood before dark. Can ye make it?"

I couldn't stop my teeth from chattering, so I just nodded. He sat down to put his own boots back on then unrolled his pants. They were damp but not soaked through. When he was done, he set off for the mountains.

By now, the glorious sunset had faded and the murky light of twilight settled in around us. From the forest came the sound of a variety of insects and birds settling down for the night. I slogged along behind Tegan as quickly as I could, but my body still hadn't warmed up and the agony in my feet had escalated because of my boots.

The leaves crunched under us as we made our way into the Everwood. We didn't travel far before Tegan stopped inside a small break in the trees. "Go ahead and sit down. We cannot go farther in the dark."

My knees gave out. I collapsed onto the ground, landing on a dead branch and letting out a woof of pain.

Tegan walked over. "Give me your wet clothes. I'll hang them up."

I thrust the wadded mess up to him. He shook out the shirt and slip and hung them from a limb. He held up my bra. "What is this?"

"It's a bra." I was grateful I had chosen a generic cream one instead of hot pink.

"A what?"

"Women don't wear them here?"

"For what purpose?" He stared at me then back at my underwear.

For the first time since this whole ordeal began, I chuckled. "You're a smart boy. Figure it out."

His face scrunched up as he looked again at my bra. Understanding flashed in his eyes. He threw it away, relieved to get it out of his hands. It landed on a higher branch than the rest of my clothes. He muttered something under his breath while I giggled again.

He sat down about ten feet away from me in the clearing. "I'll make us a fire in the mornin'." He unrolled the other blanket and wrapped it around himself. "We can use it to dry out your clothes a bit as well."

"Can we have something to eat then, too?"

"Aye. I'll go huntin' in the mornin' and get us some meat."

I closed my eyes and tried to think of something besides how cold and hungry I was. Nothing helped. The remains of my gauze skirt clung around my legs and kept me from drying more. I shimmied out of it and my underwear, careful to keep the blanket over me to hide what I was doing. I walked over to hang them next to my other clothes. I felt Tegan's eyes on me and I wondered if he was thinking the same thing I was–that except for my boots, I was now naked under the blanket.

I couldn't face him. I wasn't attracted to him or anything, but I think that made it worse. I'd imagined what it might be like to be alone with a guy, but I'd never seen this scenario in my head—naked and alone in the woods with a total stranger. I kept my eyes down and found a sturdy tree to rest my back against. I tried to generate more body heat by curling my legs up into my chest.

Neither of us spoke as the night's black fingers closed in. The songbirds quit their frantic evening tunes only to be replaced by the screech of an owl. I was glad the trees hid the moonlight. It meant I couldn't see Tegan and he couldn't see me. I shifted against the tree, trying to find a more comfortable position. Maybe if I could get him talking again, I could forget about how cold I was. "Tegan?"

"Aye?" He answered with a yawn.

"What's so special about the Sanctuary? Why did that Quinn guy tell me to go there?"

I could hear leaves crunch as he shifted on the ground. "It's where the Brethren live."

"Who are the Brethren?"

"They're Elders who want to live more in our society. They study. They pray. They know the most about the healin' arts and science."

"And who are the Elders?" I wrapped my arms around my legs. Nothing seemed to warm the clamminess of my skin.

He let out a noise—part sigh, part groan. "The Elders are those that originally came to live here. Their land's protected. Ye cannot cross their borders unless you're with one of them."

I blew some breath into my hands to try and thaw my fingers. "And what are the Brethren going to do for me?"

"If anyone knows how to get ye back to your home, it'll be them." He grew quiet and I thought maybe he'd gone to sleep. I shifted my body so I lay flat on the ground but my muscles practically convulsed with shivers.

Tegan spoke softly from the black. "Are ye still cold?"

"I can't seem to get any warmer."

The owl screeched again. It took a moment for Tegan to speak. "I could come near to ye. I did not get as wet. Ye could share my warmth." His voice caught in his throat. "I fear you'll fall ill if ye can't get warm is all."

"You promise you won't try anything?"

"By Ruahk, I swear I'll not lay a hand on ye." The leaves rustled under his feet as he shuffled over to me. "Ye have to get warm and we cannot risk a fire. I swear to ye, I'll not take advantage of . . . of . . . the situation."

Maybe I was being naïve, but I was freezing and he was dry. At least, dryer. "All right." He must not have been able to see me on the ground because he kicked me in the back. "Hey!" I called. "I'm down here."

"Sorry." He spread his blanket out on the ground beside me. "Now you come towards me."

I scooted back until I felt his body. I knew he couldn't see anything in the dark but still I hesitated to unwrap myself from my own covers. He rolled to his side so that he rested against me. Spooning, my mother called it. It was weird being so close to a stranger. I should have been scared, but I wasn't. I guess I was too tired.

I finally began to get warm, but felt him shiver. I maneuvered the blanket so that he could have some, confident the darkness would keep me hidden.

His breathing, which had sped up for a few minutes, now slowed and deepened. He shifted a little closer, his breath caressing my neck. He mumbled something.

"What?" I yawned.

"Goodnight, Ally Foster. Sleep well."

And I did. Until I dreamed.

CHAPTER SEVEN

Keeping Silent

I dreamed of Mr. Morrison. But not the Mr. Morrison I'd seen the night I went through the passage. He was different, but the same, the way people often are in dreams. I stood by the bed in his room, but he wasn't in it.

"Alystrine?"

I looked up, and there he stood. He didn't have wrinkles anymore. His thin white hair was now thick and sandy brown. The eyes were the same though. Crystal blue. "Alystrine..."

I backed away. "Don't touch me! I don't want to go back!"

His face clouded with sadness. "I'm sorry."

"Sorry? Do you know what I've been through?" I skirted around him and tried to run to the door that wavered in and out of focus behind him.

He grabbed my arm. My skin went cold where he touched me. "You have to listen . . . ."

I tried to pull away. "No, I don't. I don't have to do anything you say." With my other hand I reached for the door. My mom appeared.

"Alystrine!" she called. "Listen."

I stretched toward her, but as I did, she floated farther away. "Let me go!" I turned back to Mr. Morrison, my free hand beating against his chest. Only it wasn't him.

It was Lord Braedon.

My fist did little damage against his thick leather breastplate. He seized my wrist, holding it in a vice-like grip before twisting my arm around my back and pulling me to his chest. His cold black eyes were a startling contrast to Mr. Morrison's. They stared down at me.

"Come to me, Etain's child." He smiled then, but it did nothing to soften the hardness of his face. "Come to me."

Mr. Morrison appeared back in his bed. An old man again. He groaned.

"Be quiet, Portal," growled Lord Braedon as he continued to hold me captive. "The child concerns you no more."

Wake up! My mother's voice called from somewhere in the back of my mind. *Break the binding before he finds you!*

The dark man dug his fingers even deeper into my arm, causing it to go numb.

Wake!

I wrenched myself away from him with strength I didn't know I possessed, and my body hurtled downward. Before I struck the bottom of whatever pit I dropped through, I woke up.

I sat up in the clearing, panting tiny clouds of fog into the air. Sunlight danced on the branches above me. Goose pimples sprang over my naked chest. I grabbed the blanket and looked for Tegan. He wasn't there.

I backed myself against the tree trunk behind me and scoped out the clearing. A fire crackled nearby with my clothes hanging stiffly over it. Tegan's pack lay where he'd left it the night before but he, his quiver and bow were nowhere to be seen. I'd hoped he'd only gone hunting and not left me alone for good.

I scanned the clearing again and gasped. A blond-haired boy crouched among the trees opposite me. He appeared to be my age or maybe a few years older. His cheeks reddened, contrasting the light peach fuzz on his chin. I pulled my knees up to my chest then glanced over to where my clothes hung. I looked back at the boy.

Neither of us spoke.

Do I have to keep up the mute act if Tegan isn't here?

The blond boy coughed and ducked his head. He spoke in the same lilting tones as Tegan and his mother. "I'm sorry if I frightened ye. I saw the fire and thought I might get somethin' to eat."

I shook my head.

He stared at me, his cheeks still rosy from blushing. It angered me to know this strange boy had seen more of me than anyone else had besides my mom. I know I hadn't exactly been sleeping in a locked house but still, I thought Tegan would have protected me. My hand snaked out from the blanket until I found a rock. I hurled it at him. It struck the tree beside him with enough force to knock off a piece of bark. The bark landed in his hair.

"Now what did ye do that for? I'm not after harmin' ye!" He stood and walked into the clearing. He was shorter than Tegan, but broader through the shoulders. Back home, he would have been on the football team, I'm sure.

I sat with my arms clutching my knees, staring longingly at my clothes. If I wasn't naked I'd make a run for it, but doubted I'd get far wrapped in a blanket and the air was too cold to escape without it. Still, I pushed myself up as he approached, ready to escape if he came much closer.

The boy stopped about ten feet from me, his arms spread out to his side. "I promise, I'll not hurt ye."

"No, you'll not, I'll see to that." Tegan stood behind the newcomer with his bow drawn and an arrow pointed at the other boy's back.

Blondie turned his head and then, to my surprise, smiled.

Tegan lowered the arrow. "Brice? What are ye doing sneakin' around the woods this early in the day?"

"I should ask ye the same thing." His gaze flickered to me. He turned red again. "That is . . . um . . . well I didn't know."

Tegan shoved his friend's shoulder. "Don't be daft. It's nothin' like that."

Brice raised an eyebrow. "No?"

A rabbit hung limply from Tegan's belt. He untied it and set to skinning it as he spoke. "She's a relative. A bit simple in the head. Her family sent her to get help from The Brethren for the pox. It's spread to her village. Mum's makin' me take her."

Brice nodded. "We're on the same mission then. The pox has hit my family. There's no medicine left in town." He took a step toward me. "What's your name?"

Tegan stood up before I could answer. "I told ya, she's simple. She doesn't speak."

The blond boy's head tilted to one side. He looked between me and Tegan for a moment. "A mute, is she?"

"Aye." Tegan finished preparing the rabbit then stuck the carcass on a stick and held it over the fire. "She slipped crossin' the river last night. We needed to try and dry her clothes, before she caught a chill."

Brice reached out to touch my shirt. "It's still damp. Ye didn't do a very good job with the fire last night."

Tegan glared up at him. "I didn't want them to burn, did I? Make yourself useful man and bring it closer, so she can make herself presentable. Think how she must feel with you here now. A stranger and all, and she's no clothes on."

The newcomer took down my shirt and held it out over the fire, turning it from time to time while I watched from my spot under the tree. Tegan glanced over at me and gave me a small shrug which I took to mean, "What else could I do?" I suppose he was right. If he knew this kid then it would be suspicious if he tried to make him leave. The boys talked about their families and people they knew in the village. Tegan managed to stake the rabbit in the dirt so that he could fetch the potatoes from his pack. He cut two of them up then threw them in the pot he'd brought along. He placed that in the flames.

Brice stood up. "I think this is dry now." He held it out to me. I maneuvered the blanket so that I could get my arm out without flashing him. He stared like he'd never seen a bare arm before, his cheeks glowing pink yet again before he stepped away.

I pulled the shirt under the blanket, trying to hide my smirk as Tegan snuck my bra and underwear off the branch. He stuffed them inside his shirt before his friend turned around. Brice took Treasa's slip and held it out over the flames to dry while Tegan circled behind him to toss me my underwear. They landed at my feet. I dragged them under the blanket with the toe of my boot. They were still damp, but not soaking wet. I got them on then put on the warm shirt. Once at least my top half was decent, I dropped the blanket so it wrapped around my waist like a skirt. I waddled over and took the slip from Brice. He couldn't look me in the eye. Tegan turned the rabbit.

"If ye want," Brice offered, "I could take her to The Sanctuary, as I'm going that way."

My heart skipped a beat, waiting for Tegan's answer.

"She'll be needin' someone to bring her back as well."

Would he really leave me with this stranger? I know I'd only known Tegan for a day, but he'd proven I could trust him.

Brice shrugged. "I could get her back to your farm. Ye could take her from there."

Tegan cocked his head as if considering the suggestion then frowned. "Me mother would kill me. Leavin' a simple girl with the likes of you."

I found I'd been holding my breath. I let it out in relief.

Brice smacked the darker boy's head. "And what are ye implyin'? That I'm not an honorable man?"

"I'm not implyin' anythin'," Tegan laughed as he punched his friend's arm. "I know yer not to be trusted!"

"And what proof do ye have?"

"There's talk all over the village of yer wicked ways!"

The grease from the rabbit sizzled in the flames as the two

continued to joke. My stomach growled as the smell of the cooking meat caused my mouth to water. Both boys stopped fighting.

"Was that you?" Brice asked, his eyes wide.

Tegan grinned. "Aye, she's got an appetite. Sounds like a bear, her stomach does."

I stuck my tongue out at them both, and turned the slip to warm the other side. By the time breakfast was ready, the slip had dried off enough that I could put it on. I peeled what remained of my broomstick skirt off the branch.

Tegan shook his head. "It's not worth tryin' to save that." He put it in the fire. His eyes held mine as he did it. *We can't leave any signs*. The damp cloth let off a thick gray smoke as it burned. Now all I had from home were the crummy boots I had to wear, and the ring my mother had given me.

Tegan cut off a piece of the rabbit. "Here ye go." He held it out to me. "Quiet that beast in your belly."

Two days ago my stomach would have turned at the thought of eating a helpless bunny rabbit, but as I hadn't had anything substantial since the salad I'd eaten with my mom, I had no problem biting into Bugs. The meat was a little tough and greasy, with a smoky flavor to it, but it wasn't bad.

Tegan speared a potato, held it away from the fire to cool, then tossed it to me. I missed smothering the spud with butter and sour cream. We made short work of the food, rinsing it down with river water from the flasks the boys carried. I poked at the remains of my skirt in the fire as Tegan picked up the blankets and cooking pot and stuffed them into his pack.

"Ready?" Brice asked.

I scraped some dirt up with my boot then kicked it over the smoldering flames. I noticed Brice studying my feet. His gaze lifted to mine. His mouth opened as if he was going to say something but then snapped it shut.

He looked over at Tegan. "Did ye know the Black Guards are about?"

"Here? In the Everwood?"

"I didn't see them in the wood. But two were in the village yesterday."

"Aye?" Tegan shifted his pack. "What are they after?"

Brice glanced at me. "Strangers. Some say a traveler's come

through."

"A traveler?" Tegan asked. "There hasn't been a traveler in years." He started walking toward the denser forest. Brice jogged up next to him while I brought up the rear.

"I know. I thought all the passages were destroyed after the massacre, but I heard Old Eli sayin' there was one left. Geran placed a special protection on his that kept it alive."

"I don't believe it," Tegan said. "Braedon would not have left a passage he couldn't control."

Brice waved his hands at his sides. "Geran tricked him somehow, don't ye see?"

"No one can best Braedon."

"But what if it's true? What if a traveler has come?" His eyes flickered over to me. "What do ye think it means?"

Tegan put a hand on his friend's shoulder. "I think it means we best be careful. We don't want to meet up with the Black Guard here. They're none too friendly when they ask their questions, and worse when they don't like the answers ye give them."

CHAPTER EIGHT

Under the Stars

Sunbeams poked though the dense branches overhead, lighting our path with golden hues but doing little to warm the air. I wondered if I'd ever be warm again. We spent most of the morning climbing uphill. I said a silent thank-you to my mother for forcing me to hike with her in the summer, and work out at the gym during the long Connecticut winters. I would have done better if I'd been wearing hiking boots, and had some trail mix to munch on, but all in all, I had little difficulty keeping up with the boys. My feet were past the point of blistering; calluses had begun to form in their place.

Tegan, for the most part, kept silent as we climbed up the steep slope, but he'd look back every once in a while to make sure I followed. His eyes held a sparkle to them, and I began to hope he'd look my way more often. They were the only thing that could take my mind off of my situation.

Brice chattered on about all sorts of news—the pox in the village, his fight with another boy, the weather of late and of course, the traveler. After several hours I tuned him out and thought about the dream I'd had that morning. What had my mother meant when she told me to "break the binding?" Was it possible Lord Braedon could connect with me somehow in my dreams? I wished I'd had the opportunity to talk to Tegan about it. In the world I came from, I didn't think that kind of thing was possible, but who knew about this place? And what did it mean that Mr. Morrison was a portal? How did he end up in Meadow Hills? Had he known my mother? Did she know him?

The thought punched me in my gut. Somehow I knew it was true. My mother knew what Mr. Morrison was, that's why she never wanted me in his room. She knew about this place. She knew, and had never told me about it.

Tegan stopped walking. "What's the matter?" He'd caught sight of my face. "Ally? What's wrong?"

I couldn't look at them. If I did, I might cry. I lowered my head and pushed myself uphill. I passed Brice, but Tegan took hold of my arm. I let out a gasp as pain stabbed my muscles. I pulled away, rubbing the spot he'd held.

"What happened?" Tegan asked. "I barely touched ya."

I shook my head, wondering at the ache that still throbbed up to my shoulder. Tegan took my other arm. "She's scared of somethin'," he called over his shoulder to Brice. "Give me a moment to try and understand what she fears."

We passed the wide trunk of a tree and Tegan yanked me around so we were hidden. He pulled up the left sleeve of my shirt. Five round bruises could be seen on the flesh above my elbow. "Where did ye get these?"

My voice was soft, but urgent. "I don't know."

He put his hand around my arm to prove to himself, or me, that his grip was smaller than whoever had made the marks. He laid a finger on one of the bruises. "It's cold." He eyes bore into mine. "Who did this?"

"I had a dream," I whispered.

"When?"

"This morning, when you were gone."

He rested his hands on the tree behind me so that his arms made an arch over our heads. "What was it?"

I told him about Mr. Morrison being a portal. How Lord Braedon grabbed my arm and told me to come to him.

The color drained from his face. "Why did ye not tell me this before?"

"I'm mute, remember? And we had company." I shook my head. "How can a dream leave bruises?"

"He's using some dark spirits to reach out to ya. Do ye know why he wants ye so?"

"No."

He pulled my sleeve down. "They've left a mark on ya. They may be able to tell where ye are."

"From a dream? What kind of place is this?"

Tegan frowned. "For you? A dangerous one." He leaned around the tree. "Come on! She'll be all right now."

Brice hiked up the steep incline. "What's the matter with her?"

"All the talk about Black Guards earlier, I think." He put an arm around my shoulder. "Her father was killed by Guards when she was young. She got to rememberin' it."

I could tell Brice didn't believe a word of the story, but he nodded his head in sympathy. "Aye? That's a shame, isn't it?"

Tegan pushed me up the mountain. "We need to get out of here fast. I'm afraid of what she'll do if the Black Guards come this way."

"This far into the Everwood? It's never happened before."

Tegan glanced behind him. "There's always a first time."

I dreamed again that night of Mr. Morrison–the different Mr. Morrison, the one with the younger face and sandy blond hair. My body hurt too much to move. I looked up at him.

"Why?" I asked. "Why did you send me here?"

He didn't answer, but the lines in his face seemed to deepen with sorrow.

"Please . . ." My voice caught in my throat. "Please bring me home."

He mouthed the words, "I'm sorry."

In my dream, I wept. Sobbed. Gut wrenching cries. Mr. Morrison knelt down by my side and stroked my head. Then he touched my cheek. Only it was different. Real. I jerked awake.

Someone shuffled away.

"Mr. Morrison?" I half hiccupped, half whispered.

"No." Tegan moved back closer. "I heard ye cry out." I could just make out his silhouette in the dim light of the cave where we'd taken shelter for the night. "I came to see if I could help."

I wiped my face on the sleeves of my shirt and looked around for Brice. He lay in the corner by the glowing embers of the fire. His chest rose in the rhythmic pattern of sleep. "I had a dream. About home."

Tegan watched me for a moment. "Come outside."

I groaned. "I don't think I can move a muscle."

"I promise you'll be pleased. Bring your blanket."

I wrapped the blanket around my shoulders and hobbled with him to the mouth of the cave. The night air chilled my feet. It actually felt good, but I was glad I had an extra layer to keep my body warm. We walked until we came to a clearing.

We stood facing each other. Tegan put his hands on my shoulders. "Look up."

I lifted my eyes and my heart skipped a beat. Stars filled the sky. I'd never seen so many at one time. Behind them ran a swirling ribbon of white. A soft chuckle escaped my throat. "The Milky Way."

"What?"

"In school they'd tell us about the galaxy and how we were part of the Milky Way. That it was full of stars and planets." I lowered my eyes and looked at Tegan. "'I've never seen it like this."

"I know ye miss your home. I know everythin' is strange here to ye." He brushed the hair from my eyes. "But there's beauty here, too." His fingers lingered for a moment on my cheek.

His skin shone pale, almost silver, in the moonlight. I became aware of how close we stood to each other. A current of energy flowed between us. I tried to swallow, to step away, but I couldn't even take a breath.

"Look!" He turned me around and pointed up. I caught the last moments of a shooting star as it sailed across the sky. He wrapped his arms around my waist. "Tell me about your home. Do ye not see the stars where ye are?"

I leaned back against his chest, enjoying the warmth of his body. "We have too many lights. Not fire light. Brighter."

"Brighter, how?" His breath tickled my neck. I shivered.

"There's this stuff called electricity. It's what makes lightning flash in the sky. Someone figured out how to harness that energy and use it to light our houses."

"Tell me more."

"We have tall buildings." My head rose as he took a breath. "They call them skyscrapers because they touch the clouds."

He snorted softly in what sounded like disbelief.

"It's true! And we have machines we can fly in."

"Now I know yer tellin' a fib."

"No, I'm not. They're called airplanes and they can take you from one end of the world to the other in less than a day."

His arms tightened around my waist. I tried to remember how to breathe as I stared up at the stars.

"What are ye thinkin'?" he whispered.

I wasn't thinking about anything, except how weird it was to feel so safe, and yet scared, at the same time.

"Ally?"

I focused on the moon. "Men have been there."

"Where? The stars?"

"Not quite to the stars, but a few have gone to the moon."

"Yer making up stories."

I turned around to face him again. "I wouldn't lie to you. I swear it—"

Tegan stopped my words with a kiss. It was clumsy, and hard, and wonderful. My first real kiss. Josh and I had tried once when we were eleven or twelve, just as an experiment, but I don't think that counted. Not like this.

Tegan cupped my face with his hands. "I'm sorry." He sounded out of breath. "I shouldn't have done that."

Part of me agreed with him. I mean, we barely knew each other. I ignored that part. "Do it again," I whispered.

His fingers wrapped behind my neck so they entwined with my hair. For a moment our lips barely touched, but then he pressed his onto mine. A strange fluttering surged in my stomach. I brought my hands to his chest. I could feel his heart beating through the thin fabric of his shirt.

And then my stomach growled.

Loudly.

I couldn't help laughing, and neither could Tegan. He ran his hands through my hair. "I saved you a bit of pheasant I caught since ye fell asleep before supper." He kissed my forehead. "We'd best get back."

I limped to the cave where Tegan warmed the meat in the fire before giving it to me. We didn't talk. Brice still snored in the corner near us.

Tegan laid down while I ate. "Ye best try and get some rest. We should be there tomorrow night."

The last morsel went down hard. I started back to my corner of the cave but stopped. I didn't want to dream again. I didn't want to be alone. "Tegan?"

"Hmmm?"

I took a deep breath. "Would you hold me? Like last night?"

He rolled over and looked up at me. "Aye. If ye want me too."

I repeated the promise he'd made to me. "You'll not take advantage of the situation?"

He let out a soft snort of air. "No. I shall not."

I knelt down, unwrapped my blanket and spread it over us. He raised his arm so I could rest my head on his chest. My heart beat so hard I thought it would burst. I could hear Tegan's heart drumming almost as fast as mine. For a minute, I was too scared to move. I think Tegan felt the same way because he lay perfectly still, too. A rock dug uncomfortably into my back until I finally shifted to my side so my body curved against his. Our pulses slowed together as the embers of the fire dampened. The light in the cave faded. I drifted to sleep on the gentle tide of his breathing.

CHAPTER NINE

Ginessa's Pool

Brice shook me awake in the morning. "It's time to go."

I growled but sat up. Tegan was nowhere to be seen.

Brice grinned. "Ye sleep like the dead."

I thought about my dreams and my walk with Tegan but didn't disagree. I couldn't anyway since I was still pretending to be mute. I crept to the back of the cave. Finding my boots, I steeled myself for the of pain of putting them back on while Brice rolled up the blankets.

He handed me half a potato he pulled from the cooking pot. "It's not much of a breakfast, but tis somethin'."

I closed my eyes and pretended it was a Pop-Tart. We left the shelter and found Tegan waiting for us in the clearing. He smiled when he saw me but then glanced at the ground. "Did ye sleep well then, Cousin?"

Heat rushed to my cheeks. I nodded.

Brice looked between us. "What's wrong with the both of ye?"

Tegan grabbed his pack from Brice. "Nothin'." He reached over and took my hand. "We best get movin' if we're goin' to make the Sanctuary before they shut the gates."

By early afternoon, we'd stopped climbing and instead worked our way through a pass in the mountains. Sheer rock bordered either side of us. I missed the calls of the birds and the wind in the leaves. Even Brice grew quiet. Tension crackled through my body. At any moment I expected to hear the hoof beats of the Black Guards and there was nowhere in this pass to hide.

An avalanche had filled the gorge with innumerable rocks of varying size. Tegan picked up his pace, jumping from boulder to grass to boulder like a mountain goat as he selected a path. Brice and I scrambled behind him. This kind of hiking had never been a strong suit of mine and doing it in a long skirt and heels made it even more difficult. Brice fell back to help me over a couple of the trickier places.

He held out his hand to pull me up a particularly large stone that blocked our way. "Here ye go."

I started to say "Thank you," then tried to mask it as an unintelligible grunt. I felt stupid and Brice gave me a look like I was insane. We stood on top of the boulder and spied Tegan about a half mile ahead.

"Aye!" Brice called. "Wait up!" He turned to me with an impish grin. "He's as fast as a fox, that one. I've never been good at these rocks."

I smiled and tried to make my expression say, "You're doing just fine," but I don't know that he got it.

He jumped down from the boulder. I eyed the four to five foot drop with some trepidation. It wouldn't normally worry me, but more rocks lay on the ground below, which meant there wasn't much room for error. If I landed wrong, I'd wind up on one of those stones. If I had good luck, I'd just be bruised. As I hadn't been lucky lately, I figured I'd probably break my ankle.

Brice reached his arms up. "I'll catch ye."

I raised an eyebrow.

He laughed. "Yer taller than most girls I know, but you're not huge! Besides, I'm stronger than I look. Come on now."

I gave him an exaggerated sigh, then jumped. He caught me under my arms, but stumbled as my weight shifted. He clutched me to his chest in order to regain his balance. We stood for a moment, locked in a kind of embrace, before I pushed away.

He smiled. "There now. I told ye I'd catch ye."

I nodded, unnerved by the way his green eyes looked into mine. I could smell him as well, a musky scent of sweat and leaves.

He grabbed my right hand. "Tegan will be wonderin' where we are if I let ye distract me any longer."

I tried to pull my hand from his, but he wouldn't let go. Instead he chuckled. "I'm only teasin' ya. Ally, isn't it? That's what Tegan called ye?"

I nodded as he helped me up the next rock.

"It's not a name I've heard before. Is it short for somethin' else?"

I indicated it was.

He guessed the usual names, Alice and Allison, but I shook my head in response. He grew frustrated with the game. "You're a strange one, Miss Ally. I know there's more to ye than what he's told me."

Tegan jumped down from the boulder ahead of us. He eyed us with suspicion. "And what have ye two been doin'? Pickin' flowers?"

I frowned at him and lifted my slip up. *You try doing this in a skirt buddy, then we'll talk.* He held out his hand and I let him help me over the next boulder. He stayed with me as we made our way through the remainder of the pass. We stopped to rest on one of the last rocks. Tegan passed me his flask. I took a long drink, relishing the water even though it had warmed up some during the day. I gave it back to Tegan, as Brice had a flask of his own.

Tegan drained his before slinging it over his shoulder. "Come on. We want to make the Sanctuary before nightfall."

Brice and Tegan both took the lead as we headed downhill. The rocky terrain gave way again to forest and from the distance came the sound of rushing water. When we reached flat ground, the boys made a bee-line to the left. The ground sloped again, but this time toward a stream. We side-stepped down a mossy embankment. They both knelt to refill their flasks. The water bubbled lazily in its bed. I jumped out onto a rock in the middle of the creek, hop-scotching from dry stone to dry stone until I located the source of the rushing water I'd heard.

I caught my breath as I rounded a bend in the stream. Water fell from a cliff fifty feet above me, in a cascade about ten feet wide. The pool below churned with white foam. Tegan came up and nearly knocked me off my rock. He placed his hands on my waist to steady me.

"It's beautiful, is it not?"

I nodded.

He leaned in close, his warm breath tickling my ear. "It's called Ginessa's Pool."

"Ginessa?"

"It means 'the white one.'"

I could see why. As the water frothed onto the rocks, the breeze picked up clouds of white spray and carried it to the river bank. The whole place seemed magical.

"She was one of the Elders."

I glanced over my shoulder. "Where's Brice?"

I could feel Tegan chuckle against my back. "He's stuffin' his belly with blackberries he found. Do ye want some?"

I turned back to the waterfall. "In a minute."

I stood transfixed by the sight, letting the sound of crashing water wash over me. It soothed my nerves. I closed my eyes and leaned my head against Tegan's shoulder. I took a deep breath. The scent of moss and water drifted into my soul. For a moment, I let myself relax, let myself forget everything that had happened.

And then I heard the horses.

Truth be Told

Tegan's arm tightened around my waist. "Black Guards."

Brice splashed up the stream. "Do ye hear them?"

Tegan pulled me off the rock. We splashed in the water toward the opposite river bank. "Can ye climb a tree?" he yelled as we clawed our way up the embankment.

"Yes," I shouted, remembering too late I was supposed to be mute.

"Then do it!"

The three of us sprinted into the forest as the pounding hoof beats came closer. I lost Tegan as I searched the surrounding trees for one to climb. Brice came up behind me and grabbed my arm. A spear of pain jolted up to my shoulder and I stumbled. In the distance I heard a horse whinny.

Brice kept hold of my arm so I wouldn't fall. He pulled me toward a tree and boosted me up to a branch I wouldn't normally have been able to reach. When I'd gotten to the next limb, he hoisted himself up. I'd never moved faster in my life. I didn't see how we'd be hidden in broad daylight, but if the boys thought it was safer up in the trees, who was I to doubt?

I climbed as high as I could. Brice pulled himself up alongside me. We stood on a limb about thirty feet in the air holding the branch above us for balance. I turned my head in time to see two Black Guards cross the stream, their horses kicking water up around them. They raced up the embankment before the one in the lead raised his hand. They came to a stop below us. The horses made a restless circle as the Black Guards grunted to each other. I couldn't make out words. They steered the horses over to several trees, touching them and lifting their hands to their . . . *snouts?* From where we'd climbed, I couldn't make out details, but their noses definitely looked like a pig's.

Brice swore under his breath, "By Ruahk."

I turned, expecting to see him watching the Guards. Instead his eyes were focused behind us. I followed his gaze and saw Tegan with an arrow aimed at my chest. It wavered a moment when he knew I'd caught sight of him, but then he steadied himself.

I didn't know where to look; afraid if I took my eyes from Tegan he'd loose the arrow, but wanting to know what the Black Guards were doing. A strange trilling noise echoed through the forest. The horses reared. Below us, the wind picked up dead leaves, swirling them around in a giant eddy. The Black Guards turned and headed back the way they came. I looked at Tegan. He lowered the arrow as the horses crossed over the river.

We stared at each other for several moments. None of us moved until Tegan put the arrow into his quiver and slung the bow across his back.

"I'll go first," Brice said. He lowered himself down a couple of branches then waited for me. Tegan continued to watch us, his face pale. Finally, he started down his tree. I did the same. The boys had no difficulty dropping from limb to limb but they weren't doing it in a long skirt.

Tegan and Brice reached the ground at about the same time. Brice ran to his friend and pushed him in the chest. "No more lies. Ye tell me what's goin' on."

Tegan brushed Brice's hands away. "You'll not be tellin' me what to do."

I kept climbing down the tree as the two boys parried and hit each other. I couldn't make out everything they were saying but I knew enough to know they weren't playing around this time. I jumped from the last branch and raced over to them.

"Stop it!" I tried to insert myself between them. "Stop! The two of you!"

They kept swinging at each other. One of them hit me in the jaw, I couldn't tell who. I fell onto my back with a grunt. They stopped fighting and stood over me, both holding their hands down to help me up.

I rubbed my jaw, ignoring them. "Idiots."

"Who's an idiot?" Brice yelled. "He was goin' to kill ye, and ye don't seem at all upset about it."

"Keep quiet," Tegan said. "Ye don't know anythin'."

Brice squared his shoulders. "Ye had your arrow aimed at her heart. What more do I need to know?"

I stayed on the ground. "His mother told him to."

Both boys turned to stare at me.

"She did, right?" I asked Tegan. "When you hugged? She didn't just say to leave me if the Black Guards came. She said to kill me."

Tegan nodded, his eyes filled with shame. "I do not know why, but she made me promise. I had no choice."

Brice looked between the two of us. "One of ye better tell me what's goin' on."

I pushed myself up. "Come off it, you already know. All your talk about the traveler. You know it's me."

"I had a guess." He shrugged. "I knew ye could talk. I heard ye when I came upon ye dreamin' in the woods."

I smacked his arm. "Why didn't you say anything?"

"I figured you and Tegan had some reason to lie." He glared at his friend. "But I don't understand why you'd kill her. What's the meanin' in that?"

Tegan's brown hair fell across his eyes. "She dinna say. All I know is my ma was scared. I could feel it deep within her." He stared at the ground. "I'm sorry, Ally. I don't know that I could have done it. But she was adamant the Black Guards not get hold of ya."

Brice pulled a twig from my hair. "So, who are ye really and what are ye doin' here?"

"My name is Ally Foster. I traveled through a passage three nights ago. I have no idea why I'm here. All I'm sure about is that this Lord Braedon thinks I'm someone else. In my dream he called me 'Etain's child.'"

Both boys stood up straighter. They stared at me.

Frustration boiled up inside me. "What are you looking at? Who is Etain?"

Tegan stepped forward. "Etain was the heir to the throne after King Aldred died."

"What happened to him?"

Brice shook his head. "Etain was a woman. She was murdered."

"Let me guess," I said. "By Lord Braedon?"

Tegan took up the story. "It couldn't be proved, but it's certain he did. He had Etain murdered, but it's rumored she had a child before she died."

"What happened to it?" I asked.

Tegan brushed his hair from his eyes. "No one knows. Etain was murdered as well as her entire household. Burned, they were. Nothing left but rock and rubble."

"But Braedon swore he had nothing to do with the massacre," Brice said. "As they could not prove it, he's allowed to rule as regent over the land."

"But as he's not from the royal line," Tegan continued, "He cannot be king. He must answer to the Assembly in all things."

I rubbed my arm where the dream Braedon had left his mark. "I still don't know what this has to do with me."

Tegan's face mirrored my own worry. "I don't know either, but whatever spooked the Guards will not keep them away since you've been marked."

"What are they?" I asked. "The Black Guards?"

Brice frowned. "They're the offspring of the Fallen and the Mystics."

"The what and the who?"

Tegan took my hand and pulled me toward the river. "Have ye not heard of them before?"

"Not even in my nightmares."

"The Fallen are the Messengers who rebelled against Ruahk back in the time before the world began. Turned into demons, they were. Beasts of spirit."

I had always loved Mythology in school, but this was weird. We sloshed across the river. "I hate to ask this, but what are 'Messengers'?"

We scrambled up the opposite bank. "Like Ruahk, the Messengers are immortal. But they're not God. They were created to serve Him."

"So . . . the Fallen and the Messengers they're . . . supernatural or something?"

Tegan shrugged. "I don't know what that means. They're powerful, unseen beings, capable of great magic. The Messengers use theirs for good."

"And the Fallen are evil. Got it." I thought about this for a moment as Brice came along side me. "And the Mystics?"

"Ancestors of those King Gedeon led from your world to ours. They worship the Fallen."

I shivered as Tegan picked up the pace. "These Mystics are human right?"

Brice ran next to me. "Yes."

"Then how did they . . . you know . . . mate with the Fallen?"

"'Tis not known for certain." Brice said. "But the guards are not natural creatures. They should never have been born." We separated to go around a tree. He continued his explanation when we met on the other side. "They don't belong in the unseen world or ours."

"They're stronger than any natural beast, but they don't have eyes," Tegan called over his shoulder. "They make up for it with their keen sense of smell."

"But if you climb high enough above them," Brice added, "they lose your scent."

I didn't know why Treasa had demanded Tegan kill me rather than let the Black Guards take me prisoner. Was it to save me from whatever they might do to me? Or was it to save this world from Etain's child?

For their part, the boys kept quiet. Even Brice seemed preoccupied with his own questions about my identity and purpose here. Tegan kept us running over the flat ground for most of the afternoon, until the sun sank in the sky, too low to be seen over the trees. The wind that blew around us carried another sound.

I grabbed hold of Tegan's hand. "Are those voices?"

He squeezed mine back. "Aye, don't fear. We're nearing the Sanctuary. Others will be comin' to seek help from the Brethren."

A man and a woman called from up ahead, "Hullo!"

"Right," Tegan whispered to me. "Time for you to be mute again." He lifted his arm and returned their greeting. "Do you travel to the Sanctuary?"

The couple approached. The man stood a few inches taller than me, while his companion's head barely reached my shoulder. Dressed in the simple clothing of peasants, they appeared to be in their twenties.

The man shook hands with the boys. "Aye. And you?"

"Yes sir," Tegan answered. "The pox has reached our village. We've come seekin' medicine."

The stranger frowned slightly. "I see." He tilted his head toward me. "Carys saw your woman here, and hoped she might find a kindred spirit."

"My cousin does not speak," Tegan explained.

The man raised an eyebrow. "Perhaps the Brethren can heal her as well, no? They're mighty powerful."

The five of us walked together toward a sheer rock wall. Several others joined us as we made our way around the steep stone base. One man held a sick child in his arms. An elderly woman lay on a stretcher carried between two middle-aged men. Carys took my hand and pulled me aside from the group. Her blonde hair fell past her shoulders. Her blue eyes had a haunted look to them.

"Me and Hugh, we've been married five years." She held up her hand to indicate the number five. I guess she thought I might be deaf as well as mute. "Are you married to the other boy with you?"

I shook my head. At sixteen? No, thank you.

"Oh." She lowered her gaze. "I thought you might be married at least. Might understand a little of . . . ."

I tried to show empathy by patting her hand.

"It's just . . . we have not had a child yet. We're hoping the Brethren might have medicine of some kind."

I wondered again at these Brethren. How much power did they really have and how much was just the desperate wishes of an ignorant population?

The men let out a cheer as we came to a ramp carved into the stone. I dropped Carys's hand and let my gaze follow the incline of the slope up the side of the mountain. It rose so high and steep I couldn't see where the path ended.

"Are you all right?" Carys asked.

I gave her a weary nod. I could only hope these Brethren would be able to send me home because I didn't think I could travel another mile after I scaled this monstrosity. Tegan and Brice walked back to my side.

"Tis a hard climb," Tegan said, "but at the end there'll be food and rest, I promise."

They each took an arm. Brice whispered, "If ye need me to carry ye, I can."

Tegan glared at him. "She won't be needin' to be carried. She's strong enough to do it on her own." I glanced at him, relishing the approval I saw in his eyes. "Ready?"

I strode forward, pulling the boys along with me. We fell in behind more pilgrims and started up the path. At its base, the stone road was wide enough for the three of us to walk side-by-side. As we climbed higher, the path grew narrower. No guardrails protected the far edge. I made the mistake of looking over and my stomach lurched. One misstep and there would be no way to survive the fall.

Tegan squeezed my hand. "Best not to look."

I had to take another deep breath before I could force my legs to move again. About a mile up, the path curved round the mountain and as it did, it tapered, now able to fit only two of us side-by-side. Brice seemed reluctant to let go of my hand but it was evident from Tegan's face that he planned on staying next to me.

The path grew steeper still. The men carrying the litter had to stop and rest. Everyone behind them had to stop as well. I leaned against the stone face. The forest wove below like a deep brown river through the mountains that surrounded us. The sun touched the horizon. It wouldn't be long before it sank out of sight. I motioned to it with my head.

Tegan frowned. "Aye, we have to keep movin'. We cannot climb the cliff road in the dark."

The two men must have heard him because they picked up their cargo and, with many groans, headed up the mountain. The path curved again and we were forced to walk single file. Tegan went ahead while Brice followed behind me. My knees argued with every new step. I put a hand on the wall to steady myself. The sun descended behind the mountains, causing the world around us to fade into the monotone color of the gray rock we scaled.

"They'll be closing the gate soon," called someone from behind us. "We must hurry!"

The men carrying the litter put it down again. "Ye'll have to pass us," groaned the one nearest to us. "We canna go any faster."

Tegan nodded before glancing my way. "Mind ye step careful."

The men flattened themselves against the sheer rock. Tegan faced the first one. It looked like he was going to hug him. He placed his hands on the wall on either side of the man as he slid his feet along the few remaining inches of the path. When he got to the litter, he tip-toed around the body of the woman. He performed the hugging maneuver around the second man.

"Come on," he called back to me. "Don't be afraid."

Too late. The muscles in my legs already quivered like jelly from the extended climb. I didn't know how I would keep my balance on the sliver of road that remained. Brice placed his hand on my back.

"Ye'll not fall. I'll see to that."

I smiled weakly at him. The line of people behind us grumbled as the sky grew darker. I repeated what I'd seen Tegan do, placing my hands on either side of the first man. Our bodies brushed together as I slid by him. I could smell the rank sweat that permeated his clothes. He gave me an almost toothless grin as I passed. I tried not to gag at his foul breath. I stepped carefully around the woman on the stretcher, then slipped past the next man. I took another step up the hill but had to lean against the wall as my knees buckled.

Tegan pulled me into an embrace. "You're doing fine. Not much more to go." He rested his hands on my shoulders. "We must be quick though."

Brice came up behind us. "Ye sure ye don't want me to carry ye?"

Although I dreaded the idea of walking anymore uphill, I hated the thought of plummeting over the side of the cliff with Brice even more. I patted his arm and shook my head. Setting my face in what I hoped was a look of determination, I indicated we should get moving again. We picked up our pace and pushed upward toward the sky.

The haze of twilight settled around us as we took another bend. The people ahead let out a cry and dashed forward.

"They're closin' the gate! Hurry!"

Tegan grabbed my hand, dragging me up the remainder of the path. The pilgrims streamed across the flat summit toward a man-made stone wall about fifty yards away. Two men in black hooded robes walked the wooden doors closed.

Cries of "Wait!" and "Hold the gate!" wailed as we ran toward the Sanctuary. I stumbled, sprawling face first on the dirt. Feet pounded around me, barely missing my head. Brice and Tegan pulled me up and helped me sprint the last few yards. Tegan let me go. He placed his body between the doors so the hooded men couldn't shut them.

"Do not bar the work of the Brethren," boomed a voice from inside the Sanctuary.

"Forgive me," Tegan stammered. "She must get in tonight."

Brice pushed me forward and I lurched into Tegan. We fell together inside the gate. Brice slid in behind us. The doors shut with a thud. People begged from the other side, but the men lowered bars across the entry to lock the gate.

I lay panting on my back beside Tegan, unable to move another inch. A man approached, his dark-skinned sandaled feet stopping by my head. His voice resonated within his chest, booming through the air like a bass drum. "Who are you to force your way into the home of the Brethren?"

"Please forgive us," Brice pleaded. He paused for a moment, breathing hard, as the few stragglers who'd entered before us moved away. "Please sir, she's a traveler. The Black Guards search for her."

For a moment, everything stood still, as if time stopped. I lay on the ground and prayed silently that someone here might help me as night draped its black cloak around us.

The deep-voiced man knelt down by my head. He brushed the hair out of my eyes then motioned to someone. Another robed man lowered a torch beside me.

The first man studied my face. His head was the size of a watermelon, but it wasn't out of proportion with his massive body. "Is it true?"

I swallowed hard, but couldn't answer.

"Is it true?" His rich voice carried easily in the dark, even though he whispered. He didn't have Tegan's lilting brogue.

I nodded.

He stood then lowered his hand. "Come, Child."

I placed my hand on his palm. It was swallowed by his huge, dark fist. He pulled me to a sitting position. My head swam. I don't know whether it was the lack of food, my exhaustion, or perhaps the altitude, but everything around me waffled in and out of focus. Gold lights sparkled on the periphery of my vision.

The bear of a man lifted me to my feet, pausing as his fingers touched the ring my mother had given me. He opened his fist and stared. He waved the torch bearer closer again, turning my hand so he could see the ring. He let out a sigh that sounded like air being released from a tomb.

Dropping my hand, he took a step back and bowed. "Your Majesty. Welcome home."

CHAPTER ELEVEN

The Sanctuary

"**M**y name is Sheridan." The hulking man gestured for us to follow him across the courtyard. "We've been praying for your safety."

"You don't understand." I struggled to catch up to him. "There's been a mistake."

He lifted an eyebrow. "The Messengers told us of your passage to our world."

"How did they know I was here?"

His wide eyes and huge, open mouth gave him a Jack-O-Lantern quality. "Ruahk knows everything." He paused as two black-robed men opened the doors to a stone building. "Come inside and take your rest."

The doors closed behind us with an ominous thud. My heart sped up in fear as my boot heels clacked against the flagstone floor. Torches lit the limestone hallways, casting odd shadows as we passed. At the end of the corridor, I could see a hundred or so people crowded into a room with long tables. The savory smell of garlic and beef hung in the air. My stomach growled.

Sheridan stopped next to a metal gate blocking off the entrance to another, narrower hallway. "Your servants may continue to the Common Hall if they wish to have dinner."

Brice started toward the crowd. "Thank you, Sir." He turned back when Tegan didn't follow. "Ye comin'?"

Tegan must have sensed my fear because he hesitated.

My voice cracked. "Can he stay?" I indicated to Tegan with a nod of my head.

Sheridan paused from examining the ring of skeleton keys in his hand. "I suppose, until one of the Brethren has been assigned, you may keep a servant with you."

I started to explain that Tegan wasn't a servant, but I caught the quick shake of his head. Maybe it would be best to play along until we knew what was going to happen.

Shivers raced down my spine as the metal gate opened with a horrendous squeal. Sheridan held it aside so Tegan and I could pass through. We had to press ourselves against the wall to let the huge man take the lead after the gate shrieked shut.

"This way, Your Majesty."

"Please," I murmured. "Don't call me that."

Sheridan glanced over his shoulder. "You have a ring of succession."

Frustration bubbled inside me. "It's a mistake. I don't know how my mother got this, but—"

"The Messengers foretold your coming. The Order will confirm you are Etain's heir."

We turned down another corridor. The hallways were getting darker. I reached out and found Tegan's hand. I grasped onto it as if I were drowning. "What's the Order?" I envisioned a kind of inquisition with instruments of torture.

Sheridan's deep voice echoed down the hall. "They are the heads of each of the divisions within the Brethren."

"What kind of divisions?"

"The heart, soul, and mind. Each of these is divided into more groups."

"Like what?"

He had to crane his neck to look down at me. "Take the mind; those are the sciences that we study— medicine, weather, the sky and alchemy. Heart is that which is good for our bodies— the kitchen, the grounds keeping, and agriculture."

He led us down another corridor. "The soul is the study of Ruahk and the unseen world around us." Sheridan's eyes fell on Tegan's hand clasped in mine. His gaze flickered to my face. I thought I caught a frown before he turned to lead us up a steep flight of stairs.

I froze—my body exhausted from the hike up the stone road that brought us here. I closed my eyes, let out a heavy sigh and reached out to gain support from the walls to push myself forward.

Before I took my first step, Tegan swept me up in his arms. I cried out in surprise as he shifted my body closer to his, then turned so he could walk sideways up the narrow flight. He called up when Sheridan glared down at us.

"Her Majesty is most weary from her journey. She could use the medicines of a healer to ease her pain."

Sheridan nodded and continued up the stairs.

"Sorry," I whispered up to Tegan, relieved that he wasn't grunting with exertion.

"For what?"

"That I'm such a wimp." Every muscle in my body hurt and my feet killed from three days of hiking in my stupid boots.

We were almost to the top. "I don't know what a wimp is, but it's been a hard journey for all of us, and Brice and I have done it before."

"I could have done it, you know." I rested my head on his shoulder. "With better shoes." I liked the way his chuckle resonated within his chest. Tegan carried me out of the stairwell into another hall. "You can put me down now."

He lowered his head and said softly, "But I don't want to."

My mom had always taught me to be independent. I'd never daydreamed about a knight in shining armor to rescue me from my problems. But after three days of running for my life, I figured it was okay to accept Tegan's chivalry. I leaned my head back against his shoulder, enjoying the feeling of safety his arms gave me.

Sheridan unlocked another door. "Here you are, Your Majesty." He pulled a torch down from the opposite wall to light the dark room. Tegan carried me inside then gently sat me down on the king-sized bed. A canopy of deep blue velvet hung overhead. He made his way to the corner of the room while Sheridan lit several sconces. Something in the stone blocks of the wall sparkled as the flames danced over them.

The huge man approached the side of the bed. "I will inform the Order of your presence. One of the other Brethren will be here shortly to wait on you, Your Majesty."

I groaned but figured it wasn't worth arguing with him again.

Sheridan bowed then left the room without closing the door.

I flopped back onto the bed. "This will beat sleeping in a cave." Running my fingers across the velvet blanket, I sighed with contentment. I heard Tegan's footsteps and raised my head to see what he was doing. He took my right foot in his hands and tried to pull off my boot.

"Ouch!"

He dropped my foot. "What'd I do?"

I sat back up. "You have to unzip it first."

His brow furrowed as he watched me take it off. "Let me try the other." He lifted my left foot, stared a moment, then fiddled with the zipper before pulling off the other boot.

I wiggled my toes and stretched my legs. I cried out when my right leg cramped up.

"What's wrong?" Tegan backed away as I jumped off the bed and tried to work out the Charlie Horse.

"It's a cramp." I waved him away when he tried to come near me. "It'll work itself out." I swore under my breath, stomping around like an idiot until the muscle relaxed.

"Better now?" Tegan asked.

I sighed with relief. "Much." I hopped back up onto the bed.

Tegan and I stared at each other.

I patted to the space next to me. "You want to sit down?"

"As I'm your servant, I think I had better stand."

"You're not my servant."

He stepped back. "If ye are who they think ye are, then yes, I am. Everyone is servant to the queen."

"But I'm not a queen. There's been some kind of mistake."

His eyes grew sad. "I don't think so."

I let out a breathy laugh. "If you knew me better, you'd know how stupid this all is." I slipped off the bed, grimacing when my sore feet hit the cold stone floor. "I'll admit, I think my mother had something to do with this place. But queen? I think she would have told me if it was anything that important."

We stood facing each other. That same weird current of electricity sparked between us like last night under the stars. Only the sound of our breathing broke the silence in the room. I wanted him to kiss me again. I tried to will him closer, but he remained frozen to the ground, his hands clenched into fists. I stepped closer.

A shrill voice broke the tension between us. "Your Majesty?" A hunchbacked man in a blue robe stood in the doorway.

"Who are you?"

"Malvin." He bowed. "I will be your personal assistant while you are with us. Your servant is free to go eat." He directed his next comments to Tegan. "Tali is in the hallway. He can show you the way to the dining hall."

Tegan started to leave.

My heart raced like I was clicking up the incline of a rollercoaster, waiting for the drop on the other side. I grabbed his arm. "You'll come back, won't you?"

He wouldn't look me in the eyes.

I turned to the hunchback. "I'll see him again, won't I?"

The little man smiled. "He's only going to eat, my lady. The Brethren won't send him away in the night."

I sighed with relief and let go of Tegan's arm. He stopped in the doorway to look back at me before disappearing into the hall. I hobbled to the bed, rubbing my temples as I walked.

"Healer Andrew will be here shortly. I am sure he will have something for your pains." He took a step toward me. "Until then, do you wish for something to eat?"

"I would love something to eat." I croaked. "And water, if you have it. Lots of water."

He scurried out into the hall and spoke to a person I couldn't see. A moment later he returned with a tray of food. He set it on a table near the bed. "I have sent for water to drink." He passed me a silver goblet. "You can start with this, My Lady."

I took a gulp without looking. The cool liquid burned my throat as I swallowed. I let out a sputtering cough. "What is this?"

"Is the wine not pleasing?" He seemed afraid. "I could fetch another, but this is considered our finest."

I shook my head. "I just wasn't expecting it." I stared into the cup, trying to decide whether to drink it or not. My thirst won out. I drained it. "Thank you."

He picked up a substantial looking bowl. "Would you like some stew, my lady?"

My stomach growled in answer as the rich, meaty aroma reached me.

The hunched man looked surprised, but didn't comment. I took the bowl and he handed me a wooden spoon. "You don't have to call me 'my lady' all the time. My name is Ally." The utensil he'd given me was the same size as one I'd use to stir cookie mix with back home. I held it rather awkwardly before dipping it into the stew. "What's your name again?"

"Malvin, my...I am Malvin."

"Malvin," I lifted the spoon up in a kind of toast. "Thanks."

"You're welcome."

The stew was warm and spicy, infused with a variety of flavors like curry and ginger. I made out lentils, onions and some kind of root vegetable in it along with red meat. I tried to eat slowly but it tasted so good, I found myself shoveling it in.

Malvin sat in a chair against the wall, watching me with interest.

I scraped the bowl with the spoon. "I'm sorry. I usually have better manners than this but I was starving."

He bounced up then handed me a hunk of dark bread.

"Thank you."

He sat back down.

I wiped the bowl with the bread, not wanting to waste a morsel of the wonderful stew. I had just finished eating when two other Brethren entered the room. One wore a blue robe and carried a pitcher. The other wore brown. Malvin stood, took the pitcher and filled my goblet. He passed it to me. I checked to make sure it held water. It did. I drained it then held the cup out to Malvin.

"More?" he asked.

"Yes, please."

We played the game several more times, me gulping down the water and him re-filling the cup as the brown-robed man set down a large wooden box, unlocked the clasps and pulled out several trays of bottles, instruments and envelopes. The other servant left with the empty food tray. I had finished all the water in the pitcher by the time the brown-robed man seemed satisfied. He lowered his hood, revealing a handsome face framed by thin, shoulder-length brown hair. He reminded me of Mr. El-Afandi, my geometry teacher, whose family was from Egypt. I couldn't judge his age. He appeared young, but I noticed deeply etched lines around his mouth and forehead.

His brown eyes shone with kindness as he turned to me. "I am Healer Andrew, my lady. Sheridan said you might be in need of me."

It hit me that the Brethren spoke with a strange accent. As if they'd learned English as a second language. Kind of like how my mother talked.

The healer approached the bed. "Do you think you could sit closer? So that I might examine you better?"

I swung my legs over the side. It stood at least three feet off the ground so I couldn't touch the floor. Andrew placed his fingers against my temple. I clenched my teeth as a jolt of pain stabbed through my brain.

He didn't release me but his touch softened. "You head hurts a great deal?"

"Yes, sir."

One of his eyebrows lifted, as if he were surprised I called him "sir." My feet caught his attention. He lifted each one, examining my scabby blisters and calluses. He muttered under his breath then turned to the wooden box on the table. From the deep center of it he pulled a mortar and pestle. He proceeded to open several paper envelopes and pour brightly colored powders and leaves into the mortar. He crushed them together with the pestle. The room filled with the scent of menthol and peppermint. He pulled out another bowl, poured a clear syrup into it, then mixed it with the powder he'd ground.

"Malvin, please bring me water so I may clean Her Majesty's feet."

I let out a growl as the hunched man left the room. "You don't have to call me Majesty. I'm not who you think I am."

Andrew glanced at me as he continued to stir the ointment. "The Order will obtain the truth. I would rather err on the side of formality. If you are Etain's daughter then you are the queen. If not, no harm will be done in treating you as one." The side of his mouth lifted in a grin. I couldn't help but chuckle. Of all the doctors I'd seen in my life, Healer Andrew had the best bedside manner.

I leaned over to get a closer look at what he was doing. "Do you have something for headaches in that box of tricks of yours?'

"Of course, but I want to wait until after the Order has talked to you. What I have will make you very tired."

I snorted under my breath. "I'm already very tired."

Malvin returned with a jug and towel.

Andrew scrubbed my feet with a white substance from his box. I winced as the gritty cream scraped not only the dirt from my feet but the scabs as well. Malvin rinsed them off, then Andrew massaged them with the ointment he'd made. The medicine brought me instant relief, easing the pain and cooling my feet.

Sheridan came to the doorway. "The Order is gathering in the Gold Hall. Is she well enough to join them?"

Andrew nodded. "For a short while." He held out his hand. "My Lady."

I let him help me off the bed, but shivered when my feet hit the floor.

He gripped my hand. "Stand for a moment."

"I'm alright," I lied. "Just stiff." The truth was I had a raging headache, my legs hurt and my arm throbbed where I'd been bruised by the dream Lord Braedon.

I tried not to shuffle my feet as I walked toward the bear-man, but my knees hurt so much I couldn't bend them. We walked down the marble hall and passed an open doorway. It appeared to be a dormitory of sorts. I nodded toward it. "What's that?"

"That's where the women sleep."

"Are there women in the Brethren?"

Sheridan chuckled. "No, my lady. It is for the pilgrims who come seeking our help. The men stay in the hall on the floor below."

"For people who want to help others, you sure make it hard to get here."

The huge man tilted his head, as if considering my question. "We do not bar anyone but the Fallen entrance to The Sanctuary, but we also want to be sure that only those with true need invade our studies." He sighed. "I will admit that The Keeper's demand that the gates close at sundown is a little harsh, but it is his right to make such rules."

Before I could ask more questions, we arrived at a spiral stone staircase. A blue robed man sat at a desk at the base of the stairs. He nodded at Sheridan and we climbed up. I had always thought I was in pretty good shape, but the exercise I'd gotten over the past two days proved differently. My knees hurt so much, I had to climb the steps one at a time while I used the walls to bear some of my weight.

"My lady? Are you unwell?"

"The road up here is a little steeper than my legs are used to. I've discovered muscles I didn't know I had."

I grunted, pulling myself up to the top of the stairs. Torches lit another long hall that Sheridan and I walked down. We turned a corner and I found myself standing in an atrium. To my right stood two Brethren dressed in black robes flanking double doors of dark wood. The atrium was about thirty feet in width and a stone staircase to my left led back to the lower floors.

One of the black robed men knocked on the door with a wooden staff and it swung open. Sheridan placed a hand on my shoulder. "The Order waits."

CHAPTER TWELVE

The Order

Butterflies flew evasive maneuvers in my stomach as I passed through the giant doorway. *What if The Order can't help me? How will I ever get home?*

Five gold columns lined each side of a room half the size of a football field. There were no windows and the white marble walls glowed yellow in the torchlight. I made my way down the aisle toward the far end where two tiered platforms stood. Wooden benches lined each platform and thirty or so of the Brethren sat on them. Like Sheridan and Andrew, most of these men had darker skin, ranging in hue from caramel to dark brown, although some were lighter skinned, like me.

As I drew nearer, I saw Tegan and Brice standing in front of the men. I almost called out to them, but then I heard Tegan speaking.

"No sir, she has no idea of the ring's significance, or knowledge of who Etain was."

A bald headed man in a black robe rubbed his chin before turning to Brice, "And you concur? The girl is unaware of the import of her presence here?"

Brice nodded. "Yes, sir."

The bald man stood as he saw me. The others on the platforms followed suit, causing a sound like a crashing wave to echo throughout the marble room. Tegan and Brice separated so I could stand between them. All the ease and friendship we shared on our journey had disappeared. Their pale faces barely acknowledged me as I stood before the Order.

A gray-haired man in a red robe stepped forward on the first tier. "Girl, what is your name?"

"Ally . . . Alystrine Foster."

At the mention of my name, a murmur swelled among the Order.

"You are a traveler?" The gray-haired man frowned. "You have come from the other world?"

I took a moment to swallow. "Yes, sir."

His dark eyes watched me intently. "These boys tell us that you had no idea of our world before you came through the passage."

"That's true."

A younger member of the Order, also wearing a red robe, stepped up. "That is impossible. One has to know of a passage or a portal in order to come through."

The men above me muttered to each other.

"I'd never heard of passages until I got here. If I'd known Mr. Morrison was a portal, I would never have taken his hand."

The younger man shook his head. "There have been no portals by that name." He looked around at the others. "She's either mistaken," He paused. "Or she's lying."

I moved toward the platform. "I know what happened to me. I may not understand it, but I know!"

A booming knock came from the wooden doors behind me. The Brethren stirred as the doors opened. A white-robed man ran down the aisle. "Is she here?"

"Devnet," called the bald-headed man, his tone one of annoyance.

"I am sorry to come unannounced, Faolan." The new arrival spoke as he rushed toward us. "But the Messengers told me she had come." He continued running until he stood about ten feet from me. He stopped then and stared. "You are here."

He looked familiar. I struggled to remember where I'd seen him before. His dark blond hair was cut short and his face was clean shaven. He had the same light tan skin as me. He came a step closer. I could see his blue-green eyes searching mine, as if he were trying to recall where he'd seen me before as well. They sparkled in the torch light, causing the butterflies in my stomach to take flight again.

I gasped. "You have eyes like his."

One of the men behind me asked, "Like whose?"

"Like Mr. Morrison."

"Morrison?" Devnet asked. "Who is he?"

"The man who sent me here. He has eyes like yours, only bluer."

His face clouded for a moment before brightening with a smile. "Not Morrison. Maris's son."

I shook my head. "What?"

The bald man spoke. "Explain yourself, Devnet."

Devnet looked up at the others. "Geran must have used that name to hide in the other world. He would keep his identity by honoring our mother."

"Your mother?" I asked. "Then he's . . . ?"

The man smiled at me. "My brother, yes."

My heart leapt. "Then you can send me back!"

"Oh no, Your Majesty. I am not a portal."

My shoulders sagged. "But . . . can't you talk to him somehow? Reach him? Tell him to bring me back?"

The man's smile faded. "I have been talking to him, Your Majesty. He told me he'd been compromised. A dark spirit had found a way into his dreams and used him to call to you. He told me you had come through."

"Who is she, Devnet?" asked the bald-headed man. "Is she Etain's daughter?"

"Can you not see it, Faolan?" He gestured toward me. "The hair is Etain's copper brown. And the lips are the Queen's. She has my brother's height." He took another step toward me. "And she has my eyes."

I backed away from him. My body shivered, although I didn't feel cold. "What are you saying?"

"I'm saying that you are my niece. Etain and Geran's daughter. Heir to the throne of Ayden."

"No, my mother's name is Kennis. Kennis Foster. She works at Meadow Hills Nursing Home." I willed myself not to collapse as the air in the room grew hotter. "I never heard of Etain or Geran until I came to this place."

My gaze flickered between Tegan and Brice, desperate for some kind of reassurance. I didn't get it. Tegan's brown eyes were wide with surprise. Brice kept his focus on the Brethren. I looked at Devnet, the man who claimed to be my uncle. "I just want to go home. Please." I turned to the Order who sat like members of a jury, judging me. "Please." My breath caught in my throat as I tried not to cry. "Can't one of you send me home?"

Faolan's face softened with sympathy. "There are no more portals among the Brethren, Your Majesty. Your father, Geran, was the only one to escape Lord Braedon's wrath."

"My father?" An image of Mr. Morrison flashed into my mind. That old, decrepit man was my father? And who was Kennis Foster; the woman I'd believed was my mother for sixteen years? I stepped away from the men on the platforms, my arm brushing Tegan's. He tried to steady me as I stumbled backward. I caught my balance and stared at

Devnet.

"You're wrong. My mother wouldn't lie to me. I'm not who you think I am." My mind grasped at this new hope. Devnet reached a hand toward me but I smacked it away. "You're wrong! All of you!" I bolted down the aisle toward the double doors.

Pandemonium broke out behind me, but I didn't care. I didn't care about the stinging pain in my legs as I pounded down the marble floor. I didn't care about this world and its murdered queen and its passages and portals. The only things I cared about were back home in Connecticut. I flung myself at the door, searching for handles that weren't there. My fists beat against the heavy wood but they wouldn't open.

I turned. Tegan raced down the aisle toward me, followed by Brice, Devnet and the rest of the Order. The solid door blocked my way. I furtively scanned the room for a window or another door but found none. The men formed a half circle around me. "You have no right to keep me here!"

"Ally, think." Tegan moved toward me. "There's nowhere to go." He took hold of my hand, his grip firm, but comforting.

I tried to steady myself in his gaze. "I want to go home."

He clasped his other hand over mine as he shook his head. "The Black Guards will hunt ye down if ye leave the Sanctuary."

I knew he was right, but it did nothing to calm my fears about the men who held me captive in this place. I glanced over their faces, trying to find one that I could trust. Only Devnet and the bald-headed man gave me any kind of sympathy. The rest looked either angry or scandalized.

"Please," I whispered to the bald man. "I'm so tired. Can I have some time to think about everything you've told me?"

Faolan smiled. "Of course, Your Majesty. We were so curious to find out the truth we did not stop to consider all it might entail for you." He touched the doors behind me and they swung opened. "Sheridan!"

The bear-man waited on a marble bench in the corner of the atrium.

"Please, take Lady Alystrine back to her room. See to it that a Healer is provided to help her with anything she needs."

Devnet, Tegan and Brice followed me out of the doors.

"Wait!" called the younger man with the red robe who had doubted me earlier. He pointed to Tegan and Brice. "The servants must stay with the other men in the dormitory downstairs."

"They're not servants, they're my friends."

He glared at me with barely hidden malice. "Nevertheless, they are not allowed on the women's floor."

Tegan took my hand. "Don't worry about us. Ye get some rest."

Brice nodded. "We'll see ye in the morning."

I looked to Faolan. He smiled. "You have nothing to fear, Your Majesty."

I shuddered and gave Tegan's hand a squeeze. He squeezed mine back before leaning forward and whispering in my ear, "You're safe here. I promise."

Sheridan and Devnet accompanied me back to the opulent room I'd been in earlier. Healer Andrew took one look at me as I came through the door and jumped up from the chair he'd been sitting in.

"You look terrible." Andrew put an arm around my shoulder and led me to the bed. "Is it your head? Does it still bother you?"

I nodded but couldn't say anything. Too many questions danced around my brain. My body hurt in too many places. My heart ached from all the lies my mother had told me.

The healer helped me jump up onto the mattress. He poured a powder from one of his small envelopes and mixed it with some water in a gold cup on the table. "Drink this. It will ease your pain and give you a dreamless sleep."

I gulped down the medicine, gagging at the bitter taste. I folded myself down on the bed. Someone pulled the covers over me as I shut my eyes.

Several clicks and scrapes signaled Healer Andrew closed up his box of medicines. "What did the Order say? Is she Etain's child?"

"Yes," Devnet's voice answered. "Geran described her to me and I can see them both in her."

"What was Kennis thinking? To keep it hidden from her all this time?"

"I cannot fathom." Devnet's fingers brushed the hair from my face. "But there is no doubt. She is the queen."

CHAPTER THIRTEEN

Goodbye

The Healer had been true to his word. I slept without dreaming. It was only when someone pushed aside the curtains from the room's window that I cracked my eyelids open. The hunchback, Malvin, scurried about the room, directing one man to bring in a tray and instructing yet another to pour water into a bowl on the table. I closed my eyes and rolled away from the light.

"Alystrine?"

I opened one eye. Devnet smiled down at me. I shut it again.

He chuckled under his breath. "I know you're awake. You've been stirring for a while." His fingers stroked my hair. "I'm afraid you can't run away from this reality, even in your dreams. You may as well wake up and deal with it."

I groaned. "You sound like my mother." I fought back the anger that surged through me. "I mean the woman I *thought* was my mother." I pushed myself up and plumped a pillow against the headboard.

Devnet frowned. "Kennis may not have given you birth, but she sacrificed everything to give you life. You must not think ill of her."

"Sorry if I don't jump on your bandwagon, but it's a little tough for me to forgive her right now."

"When you know the truth, you will understand."

I didn't like sounding like such a snarky teenager but my attitude was driven by the overwhelming sense of betrayal I felt. "Yeah well, it will be nice to finally have someone tell me the truth. I guess I'm some kind of royalty here but what does that mean? Why did Lord Braedon call me here? What am I supposed to do?"

My uncle sat back into his chair. "Why don't you have something to eat? It may put you in a better mood. Then perhaps we'll talk."

I turned my attention to Malvin when he coughed lightly. The little man stood waiting with a tray of food by the side of my bed. I straightened my legs and he passed me my breakfast. I ate my porridge and thick brown toast in moody silence. When I reached for the silver goblet of water on the table, Malvin jumped up to give it to me.

I looked over at Devnet. "Aren't you going to eat anything?"

"I've been up for several hours and have already broken my fast."

"What time is it?"

"Almost mid-morning."

Another robed man stepped into the doorway. He carried something in his arms. Malvin ran over to take it.

"Your Majesty, we were able to find a dress suitable for you to wear." The hunched man laid the garment over the back of a chair. "Would you like to change after your meal?"

I drained the water from my goblet. "Is there someplace I could shower first?" From the look on Malvin's face, I guessed he'd never heard of a shower. I glanced at Devnet and saw the same lack of comprehension. I tried again. "Someplace I could bathe?"

Malvin's head bobbed up and down. "I understand, Your Majesty. I'll ask." The little man dashed out the door.

I turned back to Devnet. "I feel bad that he seems to have to do anything I say. I don't like ordering people around."

"Malvin's gift is service. He finds contentment in helping others." Devnet stood. "Your two companions will need to leave the Sanctuary after the mid-day meal."

"What?" My heart gave a weird flutter in my chest. "Why can't they stay?"

"It is the rule of the Sanctuary. Once you have received what you have come for, you must leave. Your friends are in with the Healers this morning, waiting for the medicine they seek for their village."

"But Tegan wasn't here for medicine. He came because of me."

Devnet nodded. "He came to show you the way. And now that you are here, he must leave."

I didn't understand the near panic rising up inside me. "But why can't he stay? I need him here."

"The Brethren will see to your every need and protection until you decide on a plan. You will lack for nothing."

Except a friend. I pushed the tray off my lap and flopped back on the bed. Devnet sighed. I heard him moving around, but I'd pulled the covers over my head so I couldn't see what he was doing. Several minutes later, footsteps pattered into the room.

"Your Majesty?"

I yanked the velvet blanket from my face.

Malvin's eyes widened. "Faolan has given his permission for you to use the Sanctified Pool. Shall I show you the way?"

I threw off the covers and jumped out of the bed without looking at Devnet. Malvin took the dress from the chair and led me down the hall. The medicine Healer Andrew had given me must have been some kind of muscle relaxant as I had none of the excruciating pain or stiffness I'd had the night before. I followed Malvin down a staircase, through a stone archway and outside to a courtyard. Many Brethren walked around but I didn't see any of the regular people that had traveled up the stone road.

I quickened my step so I could catch up with the hunched man. "Where are all the pilgrims?"

"Faolan thinks it best to keep you out of sight as much as possible, Your Majesty. We've been going through the private wings of the sanctuary that few but the Brethren are allowed to see."

The crisp air helped clear the remaining cobwebs of sleep from my brain. A line of trees ran down the center of the courtyard, their bright red leaves standing out against the drab stone used to make the buildings. Brown vines ran snake-like up and down the walls. Perhaps in the spring the courtyard bloomed with green ivy and flowers, but now its barren appearance made me even more depressed.

Malvin ducked into a narrow corridor. We twisted and turned through several more before he led me out to another courtyard, then finally stopped at a wooden door. He dropped his voice to a whisper.

"This is the Sanctified Pool, Your Majesty. It is where the Brethren go to cleanse themselves before they are called to a time of prayer, fasting or a special task. Faolan has decreed that you may use it as you have a great many decisions to make."

He opened the door and hung the dress up on a hook. I still hadn't gotten a good look at it but it appeared to be made of cream velvet with green brocade trim. I stepped inside the room. The humidity of the place slapped my face like a wet towel.

Malvin pointed to the pool. "There are steps down into the water and benches to sit on. Faolan suggests you take some time to pray while you are in the pool that Ruahk would give you discernment regarding your future." He lifted his arm in the direction of a shelf, cut into the stone wall. "You'll find soap and lotions to cleanse with over there." He bowed as he backed out of the door. "I'll wait for you in the courtyard, Your Majesty."

I relished the freedom of stripping off my filthy clothes. The heavy air of the room kept me from feeling any chill. I walked over to the edge of the pool. Candles lined the stone walls, casting just enough light to see. Wisps of steam rose from the surface, while a spring bubbled up in the center. I stuck my big toe in the water and sucked in a breath at the near scalding temperature. I guess the pool was meant to purify the Brethren by burning sin and dirt from their bodies.

I stepped onto the first stair, waiting to adjust to the heat before going down to the bottom. The water came up level to my chin. I walked out to the middle and let the spring's bubbles dance over my skin. I imagined this was how an ice cube felt in a glass of carbonated soda, only much warmer. I knelt so that my head sunk below the surface and scrubbed my scalp with my fingertips, trying to dislodge three days' worth of oil and dirt. When I couldn't hold my breath any longer, I rose back up.

I glided through the pool to the shelf Malvin had pointed out then picked up a bar of soap the size of a soup can. As I ran it over my arms, a strong smell of cleaner reached my nose. I sneezed. I worried the harsh chemicals might hurt my skin, but used it anyway, desperate to get the grime of the woods off my body.

I found a jar on the shelf whose aroma didn't remind me of the disinfectant the janitors used at school. I poured some of the creamy liquid into my palm and scrubbed it into my hair, pleased with the light floral and lemon scent that now hung in the air. I rinsed the lather off in the pool then washed my hair one more time so I could smell it again.

Once I was done, I sat on the bench along the side. Faolan had suggested I use my time here to pray. I'd never really prayed before, except in times of extreme duress, like before math tests, so I felt a little awkward. "God," I whispered. "If you really are up there, I'm asking for your help. Whoever you are, please, help me to do the right thing in this world. Help me make the right choices. And if there's any way you could get me home so I wouldn't have to rule at all, that would be great." I paused for a moment, unsure of what to do next. "Thanks."

I waited for some kind of sign that God or Ruahk existed and that he'd heard me, but nothing happened. Bathing had helped my mood though. I thought I could handle whatever my Uncle Devnet wanted to talk to me about. I lifted myself to the upper edge of the pool and allowed my skin to air dry as I French braided my hair, then knotted it to keep it in place at the base of my neck.

Standing, I used my hands to brush off the moisture that remained on my skin. I took the dress down from the hook and realized it was actually two garments. The first was a light cream linen dress with voluminous sleeves that narrowed to cuffs at the wrist. I slipped that over my head, glad to find it didn't fit too snug. The second dress was sleeveless, with a full skirt made of cream velvet. The bodice of green brocade was made to look like a fitted corset over the top of the cream material. I stepped into it and discovered whoever originally owned the dress had been a little shorter and heavier than me. I reached behind to zip it up, but found the entire back needed to be laced. Making my way outside I found Devnet standing in the courtyard instead of Malvin.

He smiled when he caught sight of me. "I know you probably don't want to hear this, but you look very much like your mother."

I shrugged. "I always figured I must look like my father because I didn't look anything like my . . . like Kennis."

"Here, let me help you with that." He stepped around behind me and laced my dress. "Your companions are almost done with their meal. Faolan has arranged for you to say goodbye in one of the study rooms."

The peace I'd felt in the pool faded, but I figured it wouldn't look good if I begged for Brice and Tegan to remain. Devnet tied off the laces. I ducked back into the pool room to retrieve my clothes.

"I can take them for you if you'd like," Devnet said.

"That's okay. I need to give them back to Tegan. They're his mother's."

"I almost forgot." He ran over and picked something up off a stone bench. "Here you go."

He passed me a pair of embroidered slippers. The soles were leather while the tops were decorated with a floral design in bright green, blue and red thread. I stepped into them. "Thanks."

Devnet took my arm and led me through a maze of hallways until we arrived at the place he desired. He knocked on the door before opening it to allow me to enter first.

Tegan and Brice stood together at the far end of the room, studying a bookshelf that stretched from the floor to the high ceiling. Three wooden tables sat in the middle of the room each flanked by four chairs on each side. An odor of dust and leather permeated the air. The boys turned as I entered, their eyes widening with surprise. As I didn't have a mirror, I could only guess what I looked like. I assumed by their faces, I made an impressive sight.

They both bowed at the waist. "Your Majesty."

I walked between two of the tables and held his mother's clothes out to Tegan. "Here. I wish I could have washed them before I gave them back but there wasn't a laundromat nearby."

His puzzled look made me laugh.

"I don't think I could explain it to you." I thrust the clothes into his arms. "Just tell your mom thank you for me. Okay?"

He nodded but didn't say anything. I didn't know how to respond to his awkwardness so I chose to ignore it and turned my attention to Brice. "Did the Healers give you the medicine you need?"

Brice coughed before speaking. "Yes, Your Majesty. Thank you, Your Majesty."

I blew out a loud raspberry sound, causing the boys' mouths to drop open. "Will you two stop it? You're acting like we don't know each other. No matter what happens in the future, you'll always be my friends."

Their shoulders relaxed. Brice dipped his head toward me. "Ye don't look like the same girl in that fancy dress."

"They're only clothes. It's still me underneath."

A crimson blush rose up from his neck to enflame his face and I realized he was remembering the sight he'd caught of me in the woods. I slapped his arm. "Now, that, I order you to forget! Understand?"

He ducked his chin. "I'll try."

I turned to Tegan and my own cheeks warmed at his frank stare. I had only known the boy for three days and yet I knew I would never forget him. I tried to swallow the lump in my throat before I spoke.

"I can't thank you enough. For everything." I looked down at the floor and studied my shoes, willing myself to stay in control.

"It was my pleasure."

I lifted my head and stared into his eyes. "The one thing I'll be grateful for, if I become queen, will be the chance to properly reward you and your family for all you did for me."

The corner of his mouth turned up in a soft smile. "There will be no need for that, my lady, if you will promise to serve wisely."

"I promise."

Sheridan's massive form appeared in the doorway behind them. "I'm sorry, Your Majesty. Your companions must leave now."

My heart raced in my chest. I tried to think of something else to say. "Do you have everything you need for the trip?"

Sheridan held up two leather packs. "I have supplies here. Food for them and medicine for their village."

I took a deep breath. "Good."

Brice stepped backward. "Goodbye, Your Majesty. I wish ye well."

My eyes welled up. Tegan bowed, then spun on his heels. He crossed to the door in two long strides.

"Wait!" I ran over and gave Brice a quick hug. The blond boy's cheeks flushed pink again. I let him go then took a step to Tegan. "Please, Tegan. Look at me."

He glanced over his shoulder. I saw the tears glistening in his eyes. I turned him around so I could embrace him. I didn't care about the shocked look on Sheridan's face. I kissed Tegan's cheek. "I'll never forget you," I whispered. "Never." I pushed him away, but he put his hands on my shoulders so that we stood face to face. He mouthed the words he spoke with no voice, not wanting anyone but me to know what he said.

"I'll remember ye, Ally Foster. Always."

CHAPTER FOURTEEN

Learning My Past

I reached out and grabbed the corner of one of the tables for support as Sheridan escorted my friends away. My mind had to tell my heart to keep beating. The reality of my situation pressed so heavy on my chest, I could hardly breathe. I had no friends. No clue as to what my life here would be like. No way to get back home. I wanted nothing more than to collapse to the floor in a puddle of tears and cry for hours.

Devnet whispered behind me, "They will be fine, Alystrine."

I let out a shuddering breath. "It's not them I'm worried about."

"You will be fine as well."

I let out another long sigh, then looked at my uncle. "Now what?"

He took my arm in his. "Let's go for a walk." He wasn't any bigger than me so when I groaned and kept my feet planted, he had to stop. Confusion shadowed his blue-green eyes. "What's wrong?"

"When you say 'walk,' what are you talking about?" I fixed him with what I hoped was a regal stare. "I am not walking up steep spiral staircases, scaling cliff roads, or traipsing through the woods today."

My uncle's chuckle brought a smile to my own lips. "Only one small staircase. I thought you might like to sit in the roof gardens. It's a beautiful day."

My eyes narrowed as I let him lead me out of the study. "You'd better be sure it's a *small* staircase, or else."

We walked down another hallway before ascending a narrow spiral flight of steps, up to the Sanctuary's roof. The earlier fog had burned away and the sun blazed against a radiant blue sky. We followed a meandering stone path through various beds, now lying dormant in anticipation of winter. Devnet guided me over to a stone bench at the farthest corner of the roof.

He sat down and patted the space next to him. "The walls will block the wind."

I didn't sit down right away but leaned over the wall behind him so that I could look out over the Sanctuary grounds. Devnet came to stand by my side.

I studied the Sanctuary, realizing why I hadn't gotten a sense of how it was laid out. There were three large buildings, including the one where I stood, that sat parallel to each other on the mountain's summit. A courtyard ran between each of the buildings. A series of random sized structures wound their way about the perimeter. Some were towers, some looked like bricked-in hallways, some rectangles and some squares.

I snorted as I surveyed the jumbled layout. "You guys needed to hire an architect."

Devnet arched an eyebrow. "A what?"

"Someone to help you design this place. It makes no sense."

Creases etched his forehead as he concentrated on the view. "I never thought about it before. It's all familiar to me now."

We stared out over the Sanctuary in silence before I finally asked the question that was bothering me the most. "What did my mom . . . Kennis, have to do with all of this?"

"She was Etain's sister."

I took a breath of the crisp fall air as I tried to make sense of everything I'd learned. "So she's really my aunt?"

"Yes." Devnet's hands gripped the edge of the stone wall, his knuckles turned white. "It's a long story, one that you'll eventually have to know, but I think it best to be told by someone other than me. Suffice to say that once Lord Braedon's ambitions became known, your entire family worked together to save your life and bring you to safety."

I folded my arms on the wall and rested my head in the crook of my elbow. "Tell me about my parents. What were they like?"

Devnet looked out over the Sanctuary but his eyes seemed to be focused on some distant memory. "I know more about Geran, of course, since he is my brother."

"How much older is he than you?"

"Only a few years." He must have sensed my confusion because he continued, "The amount of power he used to transport you and Kennis through the passage took a toll on him physically. That, and the fact time moves faster in your world. I'm not sure why or how."

"What was he like?"

Devnet smiled. "He always took responsibility for me and our other brother. Geran never stepped out of line and he tried to make sure Asher and I didn't either. He was taller than most men and very brave."

I tried to combine this description of my father with the skeletal man back at Meadow Hills. It didn't work. Geran should only be in his forties if Devnet told the truth, not on his death bed. I pushed myself from the wall then sat down on the stone bench. "And my mother? What was she like?"

He turned away from me, his gaze looking distant again. "She was the most beautiful woman I've ever known. Skin like alabaster marble and hair your color, that deep reddish brown." He came over to sit by my side. "Her eyes were green like the grass in springtime and her laugh was infectious."

I scratched out a pattern in the dirt with the toes of my embroidered slippers. "How did they meet?"

Devnet stretched his legs out straight. "At their betrothal ceremony. Her brother, King Aldred, had arranged the marriage. Etain was fifteen and Geran twenty."

"What happened after that?"

Devnet shrugged. "Geran returned to the Sanctuary while Etain stayed in the king's court."

An ant crawled across the top of my slipper. I thought about squishing him, but decided to be merciful and let it live. "Then what happened?"

"A year later, they were married at King Aldred's palace."

I sat up. "What do you mean?"

My uncle shook his head. "I don't understand. What do you want to know?"

"Did they see each other during that year?"

"Of course not."

"They met that one time and that was it?"

Devnet bent his knees and placed his hands in his lap. "They exchanged a letter or two before the wedding, but they only come face to face at the betrothal."

"Wow." I pondered this for a moment. "Did they even like each other?"

My uncle grinned. "Yes, they liked each other. In time, they grew to love each other."

I shook my head. "I can't imagine marrying someone I didn't love. Someone I didn't even know."

Devnet went quiet.

I waited, but he didn't speak. "What's wrong?"

His lips pursed together in a worried fashion. "Things are different here, Alystrine. I don't know how things were done in your world, but . . . ."

A seed of dread dropped into my stomach. I could feel its slender roots growing through my body. "But what?"

"You must know, you have to understand, that you may be called to do the same thing. Marry someone not because of love, but because it is the best for the country. Royal marriages are often arranged to bring peace and security first. If you are lucky then friendship and even love may grow."

I folded my arms across my waist. "But I'll be queen. Won't I get to choose who I'll marry?"

Lines creased my uncle's forehead. "Yes. No one can force your decision, but you may be asked to sacrifice the desires of your heart, for the safety of your people."

I stood up. Another ant ran across the stone in front of me. I squashed it. "Can we talk about something else?"

Devnet's eyes watched me for a moment, a quiet sadness spilling out from them. "Of course, Your Majesty."

I bristled. I resented his subtle hint that I might try and avoid the subject of my new position, but it wouldn't disappear. I walked across the rooftop to the opposite side. Below, Brethren in dark green robes carried buckets and baskets to and from several barns. A small herd of sheep grazed in a fenced pasture while several cows mooed nearby. Beyond the barns, fields were tiered into the hillside. I'd assumed the Sanctuary would stand alone like a fortress on top of the mountain, but it was actually a vibrant, self-sustaining community.

My uncle came up behind me. I pointed to the men below. "The men who work with the animals, they wear green robes?"

Devnet nodded.

"And the blue robes? Are they the men who work inside the Sanctuary?"

"They are the cooks and housekeepers, yes."

"The healer wore a brown robe."

My uncle walked over to the wall and leaned against it. "The Brethren who study the things of science; they all wear the brown."

I thought about the men I had seen in the Golden Hall last night. In particular, the young guy who accused me of lying. "What about red?"

Devnet's head tilted to the side in an awkward kind of nod as if he knew who I was thinking about. "Zaccur and those in red study the laws. They are involved with the Council that governs Ayden."

I pointed to his white robe. "What do you do here?"

He brushed his hand down his sleeves, cleaning off unseen dirt. "Those of us in white are dedicated to the spiritual realm. We study the old texts, we pray. Some can communicate with the unseen world and some are called to be Portals to the other world."

My legs grew stiff from standing so I wandered along one of the stone paths. "What's your gift?"

"I am able to see the unseen world. The Messengers give me insight into this world and sometimes tell me the future."

"Sounds creepy."

He shrugged. "Most of the time, it is a blessing. They offer peace. They help give discernment in times of turmoil. And for me, they've served as a connection with my brother."

"Could you speak with him?"

"Not as you and I are speaking. More in pictures than in words."

I paused. "Did he know who I was?"

"Of course."

I kicked a pebble launching it into one of the garden beds. "I wasn't supposed to go in his room. Mom said he was too fragile and might pick up an infection."

"Kennis always feared Braedon might be able to open a connection through your father." He let out a sigh. "And she was right. She would often sit with Geran however, and tell him about you."

I kicked another rock. "He could hear her?"

Devnet seemed surprised at my question. "Of course. He could speak as well."

"But he spent all the time in bed!" The thought that he'd actually been fully functioning all those years, but unable or unwilling to move freely, tore at my heart. "I don't understand."

Devnet put his hands in the pockets of his robe and paced down the path. "It's difficult to explain. I told you the effort it took to transport you and Kennis to the other world exacted a tremendous toll on him. At first, his body went into stasis as a way to survive." The wind picked up as we walked in the middle of the roof. "Kennis was able to keep him alive until she could find healers who could give him nourishment and medicine."

I thought about the IV tubes he'd had stuck in his arms and guessed the healers had been doctors.

"Later, as he came out of the stasis state, he and Kennis agreed it would be better for him to pretend to stay that way. It would preserve his life longer and it would protect you."

"How did they figure that?"

"Geran knew if he made the passage back to Ayden he would be killed. Braedon had decreed all the Portals destroyed unless they bowed to him, something Geran would never do. Your father also knew there was no way he could live in the other world, your world, without being with you. He was a strong man, but not that strong. If you and he had formed an emotional bond, even one of friendship, Braedon would have found you sooner."

My uncle stopped as we approached the exit from the gardens. "Kennis and your father gave up everything they had in order to keep you safe." He pulled his hood up as the wind blew even stronger. "Many people have sacrificed their homes, their families, even their lives so you could survive. So you might, one day, return to Ayden and rule again as the rightful heir to the throne."

My stomach did a somersault. "I didn't ask any of them to. I never wanted this kind of responsibility."

Devnet fixed me with his gaze. "Nevertheless, it has been given to you. There is no going back to your former life, Alystrine. You are here now, in Ayden, and you must accept that. You may either take up the task ahead of you, or you can choose to hide in obscurity. There is no other choice."

CHAPTER FIFTEEN

The Keeper of the Keys

The door to the stairwell swung open.

"There you are," Malvin panted. "Faolan has requested a meeting with you, Your Majesty."

"Is anything wrong?" Devnet asked.

Malvin put a hand on the door frame. "I've been searching through the Sanctuary for you. No one knew where you'd gone."

"Too bad you don't have cellphones here," I quipped under my breath.

The little man frowned. "What?"

"A little other world humor. Sorry."

"Where is Faolan?" my uncle asked. "I can bring Alystrine while you take a few minutes to rest."

"Thank you," gasped the hunchback. "He's in his private chambers."

We made our way down the stairs and through the back hallways of the Sanctuary. As we passed other Brethren, their conversations stopped. They turned to stare. Some bowed.

"What's going on?" I whispered to Devnet. "They weren't doing this before."

"My guess is, Faolan made some kind of announcement at the service before mid-meal regarding your presence here."

We turned a corner and ran into several young men wearing red robes and carrying books. We careened into each other. Leather bound volumes littered the floor.

"Why don't you watch where you're going?" one of the men groaned as he and his friends knelt to pick up the books.

"I'm sorry." I stooped to help them. "We didn't see you."

Devnet grabbed my elbow and pulled me back up. The mark Braedon had given me came to life. I gasped. Devnet must have thought I was annoyed at him because he whispered, "You lower yourself to no one but Ruahk. No matter what the reason."

Two of the boys glanced up, their scowls turning to looks of embarrassment. "We're sorry, your . . . your . . . ." They kicked their companion who still scrambled on his knees.

"What?" He picked up a volume by my foot and his gaze traveled slowly up to my face. I tried to suppress a smile. His cheeks turned redder than his robe.

"I'm so sorry, your royal Highness...Majesty...Queen."

"I'm not queen yet," I chuckled. "Please don't look so worried." I ignored my uncle's command and bent down to pick up the last book which had skidded behind me. I passed it to the boy on the floor. "Here you go."

"Thank you, your . . . Uh . . . ."

"Your Majesty," Devnet offered. He reached for my arm again but I stepped away. He knit his brows, but said nothing until we were out of earshot of the others. "I told you not to bow to them."

I rubbed my arm trying to ease the throbbing pain. "I wasn't bowing, I was picking up a book."

His eyes clouded. "What is wrong with your arm?"

"I forgot to ask the healer about it last night. I've been marked."

Devnet stopped walking. "What?"

The cuffs of my sleeves had no buttons so I couldn't show him the bruises. "I had a dream about Lord Braedon. In it, he grabbed my arm. Tegan said I'd been marked."

His face paled. "You should have spoken of this before now."

I fought back the anxiety that crept up my spine. "I had a few other things on my mind. Besides, it hadn't hurt today until you touched it."

Devnet started walking again. "We'll ask Faolan about it. Perhaps the healers have something that can break the binding."

"Can he find me here? Lord Braedon?"

"Can he find you? Yes. But he and his army cannot attack the Sanctuary in order to take you."

"Why not?"

We turned down another hallway. "The Messengers protect us here. Their power provides a shield to keep us safe."

I sighed with relief. "Devnet?"

"Hmmm?"

"Who is Faolan? Is he, like, the head of the Brethren or something?"

Devnet nodded. "He is the Keeper of the Keys. His is the last word in any dispute within the Sanctuary." We stopped in front of a dark wooden door flanked by a black robed man. "We're here to see Faolan."

The guard knocked on the door.

"Enter," a voice called.

I passed through the doorway but the guard put a hand out to stop my uncle.

The Keeper of the Keys had his arms folded on his desk. "Devnet? I thought Malvin was escorting the queen here."

"He'd searched the Sanctuary for us and was out of breath. I offered to bring Alystrine."

The bald man's eyes twinkled when he smiled. "Why don't you take your own rest? I didn't see you at mid-meal." His face darkened so that the words he said were more of a command than an offer. "Tell Abner in the kitchen and he'll give you some bread and cheese."

Devnet opened his mouth but then shut it again when he took note of Faolan's expression. He nodded to me. "I'll wait outside for you."

Faolan waved a hand. "Don't worry yourself. I'll see she's brought back to her rooms. You should check in with Goram as well. The head of your division would like to hear what you have learned today."

The black robed guard shut the door on my uncle. I was left alone with the head of the Brethren.

A slat in the stone wall to my right offered the room's primary source of light. A candle flickered on Faolan's desk from the breeze that blew. A round table with chairs sat in the far corner. Faolan motioned to it.

"Sit down, Your Majesty."

I sat in one of the wooden chairs as the bald man stood and walked over to a set of bookcases behind him. My palms sweated. I tried to wipe them inconspicuously on my dress.

Faolan pulled a book from the shelf. "I trust you had a good night's sleep?"

"Uh-huh," I mumbled, then cleared my throat. "Yes, sir."

"No need for formalities. You far outrank me."

"Isn't there a ceremony or something I have to go through first in order to be queen?"

"Officially, yes. But as a member of the Brethren, I accept your authority as coming from Ruahk." He slid the book onto his desk. "I serve you, My Lady."

Although an imposing figure with his height, bald head and dark coloring, his soothing voice and reassuring words put me at ease. I sat back in the chair. "What did you want to see me about?"

"I know you've probably been asking a lot of questions about your parents and I'm sure you have a lot more, but I'd like to know about you." He put the book down on his desk then came to sit in the chair opposite me. "Tell me about yourself. How old are you now?"

My left hand played with the ring my mother had given me. "I'm sixteen."

Something flashed behind his eyes, but I couldn't decipher it. He folded his hands in front of his face with his index fingers pointing up. It reminded me of the old children's rhyme. *This is the church, this is the steeple.*

Faolan pressed his lips against the tip of his "steeple." "I have a limited knowledge of the other world. Where did you and Kennis live?"

"We had a condo . . . a small house. In Guilford."

"Did you have a farm?"

I laughed. I had a tough enough time keeping houseplants alive. "No, sir. In my world, only a few people still farm. Others work in all kinds of different jobs. My mom worked as a nurse in a home where sick and elderly people stay when their families can't take care of them."

"A nurse? For the elders, not the children?"

"More like a healer."

"I see." Faolan nodded. "And what did you do? What was your work?"

I traced the grain of the wood on the table with my fingertip. "I didn't work, I went to school."

The bald man's eyes narrowed. "What is that?"

"It's a place where kids go to learn."

He leaned forward. "Children of royalty?"

"No." I shook my head. "All children can go to school. We learn reading, science, math. Like the men here do."

Faolan lowered his hands. "You can read?"

"Yes, sir. And write. I'm pretty good at math too, although geometry was kicking my a—" I stopped myself from swearing in front of the head of the Brethren.

"A woman who can read." He cocked his head. "It is a different world."

I couldn't tell if the knowledge of my abilities pleased him or not. He just sat there staring at me. I had to break his gaze. I twisted the ring on my finger. "Renee was a whiz at math," I finally said. "She and

Josh tutored me enough so I passed, but it never really clicked for me."

His brown eyes fairly glowed with intensity. "And who are Renee and Josh?"

"They're my best friends." I paused and swallowed the lump that crept up into my throat. "Or, they were."

"Of course you grieve their loss." He placed a hand over mine. "What were they like?"

"Renee was funny and smart. And tough. She was always sticking up for me in school."

"And . . . Josh was it?"

I shrugged. Losing Josh hurt the most. He'd been a great listener. "He had a quiet strength. A tender heart. He was always there when I needed someone to talk to."

Faolan watched me for a moment. "And have you been betrothed yet?"

"What?"

"Has a marriage been arranged for you?"

I laughed nervously. "I'm too young to be married."

The Keeper continued to stare. "I thought perhaps, this Josh you spoke of."

I gave my head an emphatic shake. "We're just friends. Nothing else."

He sat back in his chair. "Has Devnet said when he'll take you to the Elders?"

"I didn't know I had to go anywhere else."

The bald man's eyes widened in surprise. "He didn't tell you? Perhaps he was waiting until you felt stronger."

"Aren't you guys Elders?"

"Yes." Faolan nodded, but his eyes shifted to the floor. "But they keep to the strict laws of our past, unlike we of the Brethren, who are trying to build a bridge between all the people of Ayden."

"Where do they live?"

"Outside of the Elder Wood. On the plains of Uz."

"Uz?" I giggled. It sounded too much like "Oz."

Faolan smiled. "What amuses you?"

I stifled another chuckle. "It reminds me of someplace else. A place I saw in a movie. A story," I explained when he scowled in confusion. "A children's story."

The bald man stood and walked back to his desk. "I won't bore you anymore today, talking to an old man." He picked up a bell and rang it. "I'll have someone bring you back to your room."

"There's something my uncle wanted me to ask you about. If you don't mind."

"Of course not. What is it?"

"Tegan, the boy who brought me here, told me I'd been marked by Lord Braedon."

Again Faolan's eyes glowed with interest. "Where?"

I touched my left arm. "Above my elbow. He did it in a dream."

The door opened and a blue robed man stepped into the room. "How may I serve you?"

Faolan sat down behind his desk. "Please take the queen back to her room. Make sure dinner is brought to her and see that a Healer is sent also." He nodded toward me. "Do not be afraid, my lady. I'll see to it the mark is removed before you leave the Sanctuary."

CHAPTER SIXTEEN

Demons and Messengers

I ate dinner alone, sitting at a desk that had been brought into my room sometime during the day. Soon after I finished, and put on linen nightgown for the evening, Healer Andrew came to my door.

"I'm glad it's you again," I said when I saw him. "Whatever you gave me last night was wonderful and I wanted to thank you."

He bowed his head. "I'm glad it helped, Your Majesty."

"My uncle wanted me to show you the mark I had on my arm. I think it's some kind of sign for Lord Braedon."

Andrew scowled. "Where?" He directed me to sit down and then examined the bruise. His brown eyes grew darker as he turned my arm to get a better look. He shook his head. "I am not sure if what I have will draw out this ill spirit. This is not a physical poison but a spiritual one."

I frowned. "But Faolan said you could get rid of it."

"I will try, My Lady. But it may take one of the white Brethren to free you of this mark." He picked up his wooden case and set it on the desk. He went through the ritual of sorting through the various shelves, envelopes and bottles before making the medicine.

He called to Malvin who sat outside the door. "Fetch me some hot water, please."

Malvin nodded and hurried off.

He turned to me. "Once again, this brew will make you tired, but unlike last night's, I'm afraid you will dream."

Malvin entered a minute later with a steaming mug to which Andrew added the powder he'd mixed together. Once it had steeped a few minutes, he brought it to me. "Drink it all."

I took a sip and gagged at the burning liquid. It tasted like ash and dirt. "It's awful!"

Andrew held the cup to my lips. "It is meant to draw out the evil. You have to drink it all to have any chance of its power healing you."

I held my nose and drank down the medicine. My stomach threatened to spew it up but I kept my mouth shut until the feeling passed. Andrew helped me lie back onto the pillows. "I've sent for your uncle. We will stand watch through the night."

"You don't have to do that. I'll be alright."

The healer shook his head. "This is a powerful potion to counteract dark spirits. One can never be sure what will happen."

I shivered. "I wish you had told me that before I drank it. Maybe I should have just left the mark."

"Oh no, Your Majesty. Having that mark means that once you left The Sanctuary you would not be under its protection anymore. Lord Braedon's Black Guards could find you, no matter where you hid in this land."

I lay on the bed, wondering what the potion would do. After a while I thought maybe I'd been spared any ill effects but then the room grew hot. I pushed off the top cover of the bed. Sweat beaded along my hairline. I rolled over and tried to look at Andrew, but he swam in and out of focus. "I don't think I like this." My heart raced. The walls of the room turned to liquid and melted onto the floor. "I don't like this at all."

He took my hand. "Try and relax. Do not fight the potion."

I couldn't catch my breath. I squeezed Andrew's hand. "Make it stop!" His distorted face did nothing to calm my fears. His voice sounded like he was trying to speak under water. I couldn't make out the words. I pulled away from him. "Make it stop!"

The bed rocked as if I floated out on an angry ocean. My stomach lurched with every roll. I thought for certain someone had lit me on fire. My skin burned and sweat streamed from every pore. I tore off the sheets and tried to rip off the linen dress I wore. I cried out to Andrew, to anyone who would listen, but my words came out in unintelligible groans.

Wisps of black smoke swirled and eddied above my bed, their gaseous tendrils reaching down toward me like skeleton fingers. I watched, transfixed as the dark clouds solidified into bizarre creatures. One had huge multi-lensed eyes, like a fly's. Its furry body resembled a rat's, but it had two pairs of wings on its back that beat furiously as it dodged and wove above my head. Another creature dropped from the canopy and landed on my stomach. A huge serpent, its scales iridescent green and black, slithered up my chest. I tried to beat it off but something held my arms at my side.

"Get it off!" I writhed on the bed, trying to force the snake away by wrenching my body from side to side. "Get it off!"

Andrew's muted voice tried to calm me but I couldn't understand the words. The serpent lifted itself up, then turned toward me. It looked like a man's face had been morphed into the snake's head. Terror gripped me. I screamed.

The snake grinned. "You cannot escape your destiny, Etain's child. Lord Braedon has made his bargain with us and we will see his plan fulfilled."

A long, forked tongue slid from its mouth and flicked my cheek. Where was Andrew? Why couldn't he get the thing off me? The sandpaper tongue licked my forehead.

"I taste your fear." It leered at me. "Give yourself to the Dark One and he will set you free. You will have power and wealth beyond your imagination."

"No!"

Another voice chanted from somewhere in the room, its indistinguishable words transformed into beads of light that floated up into the air.

The rat-fly buzzed down so it hovered above my head. "Etain's child, come to us. We can set you free."

"There are other things too." The serpent lowered his head so its tongue now darted around my ear. "Worlds of pleasure we can open up to you." The snake's breath brushed against my neck.

"Yes! Yes," The rat-fly laughed. "Feel it! Enjoy it!"

A bead of light the size of a penny flew down from the canopy and hit the rat. It squealed and gnashed its teeth. The serpent slid under my neck, wrapping itself around me like a scarf.

"She is our master's," it hissed as another ball of light pelted the rat-fly. "You cannot keep her from us."

The chanting in the room grew louder as more spheres of light flew around the bed. Spinning balls of white, blue, and yellow rained down like hail on the monsters. Each hit caused the demons to scream as their skin sizzled. Sharp pain stabbed my own body when the beads missed the snake and hit me instead. One of the lights attached itself to my arm. I screamed at the fire that engulfed the left side of my body. The snake roared, coiling around the orb, even as a tearing sensation consumed me. I shrieked as the light pulsated. With each throb, I sensed something being sucked out of my body. The white light of the orb on my arm turned gray, then black. The rat-creature and serpent dissolved back into smoke. The sphere on my arm swelled to the size of a grapefruit before tearing itself from the bruise. I cried out, sure that the orb ripped off skin and muscle. The bloated black light rose. Smaller balls danced around it as it hovered near the canopy, pulling threads of black from it and absorbing them into their own spheres. This odd ballet continued until no darkness remained. All the balls were white again and the size of ping pong balls. They circled above me for several minutes before returning, one by one, to the corner of the room.

I lay on the bed, drenched in sweat and panting hard. I blinked my eyes and stared at the canopy above me. Something cold touched my forehead. I screamed.

"It is only me."

I sat up and saw Healer Andrew with a cloth.

"Relax now. It is done." He lowered me to the bed then pressed the cloth to my face. I struggled to turn my head so I could see who still chanted in the corner. My uncle Devnet and another man in white knelt facing each other and holding hands. As my panting slowed, so did their prayers.

Devnet's eyes found mine. He let out a long breath. "It is over."

The other man let go of his hands and watched me. "She must have some of the Elder power in her to allow the spirits to attach so strong."

My uncle nodded as he leaned back against the wall. "She is Geran's daughter."

"Indeed. And your niece. You are both gifted." The white robed man stood. "I will leave you now." He approached the bed. His deeply lined face looked down on me. "I am sorry to have met you in this way, Your Majesty. But I am pleased that I could be of service to you."

Andrew put a hand on the older man's shoulder. "Thank you for your help, Goram."

The older man bowed then left the room.

Andrew patted my forehead with the cloth. "How do you feel now?"

"Not good."

"Have some water." He handed me a silver goblet, but my hands shook so hard I couldn't hold it. "Let me help you." Andrew lifted the cup to my lips and I took a sip.

Devnet sat at the foot of the bed. "Can you give her something to help her sleep?"

"No more drugs," I croaked. "Please." My head throbbed and my stomach ached.

"It's probably best if she doesn't have anything. I'm not sure how they would react together."

The linen slip I'd worn to bed was torn. I must have ripped off the sleeves in an effort to cool myself down. My left arm now had one massive black and blue mark instead of five small bruises. I looked up at my uncle. "What were those things?"

He glanced over at the healer. "What did you see?"

I shivered. "There were two of them. A serpent and some big rat with wings. Why didn't you get them off me?"

Devnet watched me with interest. "We did not see them."

"Didn't see them? But they were huge!" I turned to Andrew. "Were they hallucinations? Something the drug made me see?" The healer shrugged but his eyes stayed focused on my uncle.

Devnet leaned forward. "Did you see anything else?"

I nodded. "There were little balls of light that flew from the corner you and the other man were in. They attacked the ugly things." I shivered. "They made them disappear."

I could tell by the glances they exchanged that I'd said something significant. I fought the exhaustion that crept through my body. "The demon things? They spoke to me. They told me Lord Braedon had made a bargain with them. I belonged to their master. But I don't, do I?" I reached out and grabbed my uncle's robe. "Now that the mark is gone I don't belong to them, right?"

Devnet took my hand. "You are free of them now." His words were comforting but I could see in his eyes that something worried him. He patted my hand and put it down on the bed. "I had wanted to wait to bring you to the Elders, but now . . . ."

"What will they do?"

He helped me lay back down. "They are the wisest of our people. They will want to test your abilities."

I yawned as my uncle stroked my hair. "Are your parents still there?"

"My mother, yes. My father died many years ago." He kissed my forehead. "Go to sleep, Alystrine. You must get some rest."

I sat up after he left the room. Healer Andrew busied himself, putting away all of his medicines and straightening up the bed. The remains of my sleeves hung around my wrists. He pulled them off.

I ran my hand over the bruise. It hurt, but not like Braedon's had.

"Why does he want me, Andrew? Is it to kill me?"

The healer wouldn't look at me. Instead he tied the remnants of linen into a ball and put them in his pocket.

"I don't think he wants to kill me." I watched Andrew as I spoke, trying to judge his reaction. "He needs something from me, but I don't know what."

The healer's brown eyes glanced toward me then he closed his wooden box and locked all the buckles up.

"Why won't you tell me what you know?"

His hands gripped the sides of the box. "Because I don't know anything for sure. All we have are guesses."

"Then what's your guess?"

"I won't tell you."

"Why not?"

"Because it is only a theory, not fact." He turned to me. "I will not have you worrying about conjecture and fantasy. You have enough to concern yourself." His face softened as he watched me. "You need to rest."

I let him tuck me back under the covers. He bent down to blow out the candle by my bedside.

"Don't!"

He stopped. "What is wrong?"

"Can you leave it?" It had been years since I'd slept with a nightlight but I wanted one tonight.

"Of course." He stood up. "I will take the torch, however."

"Okay."

He took the torch from the wall and carried it toward the door. "Good night, My Lady. Malvin sleeps outside the door should you need anything."

"Goodnight, Andrew."

I lay awake for some time thinking about the creatures and what they'd said. I thought through the various plans Braedon might have for me. I came up with all kinds of torture he might put me through so I'd officially abdicate the throne.

I rolled over to my side and tried to think about something else. Josh and Renee came to my mind. I wondered what they were doing now. Devnet said time passed more quickly back home, so I wondered how long I'd actually been missing. *Was my mom trying to find me? Could Geran . . . my father . . . transport her back or had he used up all his power?*

I turned over onto my back again and stared at the canopy. I couldn't shake the image of the rat-fly buzzing around my head. I sat up and swung my legs over the side of the bed. It didn't matter that I was exhausted. Sleep would be a long time coming tonight.

I padded over to the tapestry that hung in front of the window. A thick cord hung nearby. I looped it around the heavy wool curtain and tied a loose knot to keep it pulled aside. Wooden shutters still blocked the window. I fiddled with the latch until it came loose, then swung the shutters open.

The cool night air blew in, lifting some of the staleness out of my room. The candle's flame flickered like a strobe light. Goose pimples popped up on my skin. I rested my hands on the stone window sill and peered out over the Sanctuary.

Nothing moved except the wind. Candles burned in a few other windows. *What time is it? How long did I battle with the rat-fly and the serpent?* I shivered and looked up to the sky, amazed again by the amount of stars I could see.

I thought of Tegan's kiss and my lips tingled. I pressed my fingers to my mouth in a stupid attempt to feel it again. *How far did he and Brice make it on their journey today?* I traced our steps back and thought they'd probably made it to the cave where we'd spent the night.

Growling under my breath, I pushed myself away from the window. I didn't want to think about this boy I'd never see again. I didn't want to hear his soft brogue whispering in my ear. I didn't want to feel his arms around my waist.

The solitary candle cast an amber pool of light near my bed, but left the rest of the large room hidden in gray shadows. I shuddered. Did any other creatures lurk in the dark corners? I hadn't been afraid of the Boogeyman for years, but now I wondered whether kids in my world could really see monsters hiding in the closets. Maybe they were attuned to an unseen world, just like the Portals of Ayden.

I crossed to the nightstand. Picking up the candle, I walked around to every corner and even checked under the bed to make sure nothing waited to put its mark on me again while I dreamed.

Nothing.

Yet.

But I wasn't asleep either. I returned the candle to the nightstand. I wanted to climb back into the bed and drift into a peaceful dream. As demons or Lord Braedon would more than likely make an appearance, I opted for staying awake. I pulled the top cover off the bed. Wrapping myself up in the velvet blanket I waddled over to the window. The sill was about two feet wide and a little more than waist high. I freed my arms and pulled myself up onto the ledge. I wedged myself in the corner so I wouldn't fall out.

The moon rose huge and silver over the mountains. I studied it. It looked like the same moon I'd seen all my life. *Where exactly was Ayden?* I remembered the dream I'd had the night before my birthday, about the moon shattering into pieces. I thought about the faces I'd seen in the shards. *Had Tegan's and Braedon's been in the moon as well? Or am I picturing them there now because of all that's happened?* I shifted on the sill. The tapestry curtain came loose, falling across the window and hiding the room from my view.

The tension in my shoulders faded. If I didn't have to look at the room with the huge canopy bed and stone walls, I didn't have to be reminded that I wasn't home. If I stared at the moon with its gray eyes and mouth grinning back at me, I could pretend for a little while that I was back in Connecticut.

I pictured myself sitting out on the playground in the elementary school with Josh and Renee. We spent summer evenings out on the swings talking about all the things that seemed so important at the time. Parents and school and future plans. Funny how my dreams never included being a queen.

I pulled the blanket up to my neck and rested my head against the wall. "Please." I whispered my prayer to the moon. "Let me go home." I sat in the window sill, willing myself not to cry.

CHAPTER SEVENTEEN

Welcome to Ayden

"**A**re you ready?" My uncle asked the following morning as he studied my face. We stood outside yet another wooden door guarded by men in black robes. "You must meet with the Council of the Order so you can begin to understand the country you are to rule."

I toyed with the silky gauze bell sleeves of my new dress. The deep blue velvet bodice fit snug against my ribs, but the full skirt of the empire waist still gave me room to breathe. "Will you stay?"

He shook his head. "The Order will want to meet with you alone."

"But if I want you there?" My palms grew sweaty.

He took my hands. "It would be best if you went alone." His face was grave. "If the Order perceives that you rely on me, it could give them cause for concern."

"I've read history books. Queens are allowed counselors." I found myself squeezing his fingers in my worry. "Can't I choose you as a counselor?"

He returned my firm grip. "When you are truly queen, then yes, I can openly serve as one of your counselors. Until then, you must appear to be agreeable to all advice the Order wants to give you." He let go of one of my hands and cupped my chin. "Ayden stands at a crossroads, Alystrine. Your coming here has upset the delicate balance that Braedon achieved when your mother was killed and Kennis disappeared. There are many forces at work, both seen and unseen. Some, like me, rejoice at your return. But others . . ." His eyes darkened and he dropped his hand. "Others have been corrupted by the power Braedon has granted them in the absence of a true monarch. You must step carefully until you are crowned queen. You can do this Alystrine. I believe in you."

No. You believe in your brother's child. But I don't know who that is.

Devnet gave me a look of concern. "Are you ready?"

"No. I'd like to know my enemies before I go in there."

"Pray for discernment." He leaned closer to my ear. "You glimpsed the Messengers of Ruahk last night. Pray they guard you today. Ask

Ruahk to clear your mind and give you understanding." He stood back from me. "I will be praying the same."

I turned to face the black robed guards. They opened the doors and stood aside. One called out, "Alystrine, daughter of Her Majesty Etain, Queen of Ayden."

The Order sat around a massive round table about thirty feet in diameter that dominated the room. The Brethren reminded me of carousel horses as they stood in their various colored robes. I fought back a nervous giggle. The pairs of colored robes around the room suggested that two men represented each division in the Council. There were no windows to the room, the only light coming from torches placed along the gray stone walls.

Faolan indicated the large wooden chair next to him. "Your Majesty, this, is your seat."

Two men in red robes stood on the other side of the chair whispering to each other. Zaccur was the dark-haired man but I didn't know the older one's name. I fought back the anger Zaccur's expression pulled from me. His hatred was palpable. I refused to let him intimidate me, choosing to ignore him instead. I took Devnet's advice and sent up a silent plea for help discerning who I could trust and who I couldn't.

The Order waited for me to take my seat before all but Faolan sat down. "My Lady, let me take this opportunity to officially welcome you to the Sanctuary of the Elders and the Council of the Order."

I sensed from the awkward silence that I was supposed to say something. "Thank you."

Faolan sat down beside me. "Now gentlemen, let each division head introduce himself and the nature of his work in the Sanctuary."

"Excuse me, Faolan." Years of public school had entrenched a love of note taking in me. Weird, I know, but I liked having something to do while people lectured. "Could I have some paper and a pen?"

The bald man looked confused. "My Lady?"

"I have a lot to learn. I want to make sure I remember everything from today." My quick gaze around the room proved my request was unusual. "I'd like to write things down."

A low murmur travelled around the table as Faolan stared at me as if I'd I grown another head. "Of course, Your Majesty." He ordered one of the guards at the door to locate writing material. "Should we wait until they arrive before we begin the introductions?"

I already felt like a monkey on display at the zoo by the way the Order watched me. "No. Go ahead and start."

The blue robed man to Faolan's left stood and introduced himself as Jorash, the Keeper of the Sanctuary. With his thick gray hair and beard, he reminded me of Gandalf from *The Lord of the Rings*. He talked for some time about the running of the Sanctuary, primarily how many Brethren were housed permanently, how many temporarily, the average number of pilgrims per night and so on.

A knock on the door interrupted him. Jorash paused while another blue robed man ran in with a large sheet of thick, yellow paper, a quill and a jar of ink. I stared at the tools for a moment and let out a long sigh. The Brethren watched me with fascination as I tried to figure out how to use the quill.

"Is anything wrong?" Faolan asked.

"I forgot you wouldn't have pens I'm used to." I picked up the quill and dipped the tip in the ink. "Give me a minute to practice."

He lifted his eyebrow in an amused fashion as I proceeded to make a huge blot on the paper. After a couple of more tries, I got the hang of how much ink it would take to write. My notes would have to be sparse.

I looked toward Jorash. "Can I ask how many men work for you?"

He seemed pleased at my interest and gave me a breakdown of the men in each service; the kitchen, the serving staff, the cleaners. I wrote the numbers down, relieved at how well I was doing.

I took down more notes as Nathan, dressed in a brown robe, stood to explain about his division. I remembered Devnet told me that those in brown dealt with the sciences, including the healing arts. The head of the agricultural division gave me an accounting of all the animals and produce under the Sanctuary's management. I forced myself to concentrate on what he said and resisted the urge to doodle on the paper.

I recognized the white-robed man who spoke next as the man who'd prayed with Devnet to remove the mark from my arm. I almost thanked him for his help but something stopped me. A thought of instant clarity told me to keep everything about the night before a secret.

"I am Goram, Your Majesty." His round, lined face looked at me. In his eyes, I read his approval of my action, or inaction. I swear I could hear his voice in my head, even as he spoke about what kinds of

services the Brethren under him performed. *Good, Your Majesty.*
Devnet has spoken to me of what you saw. The others need not know of
your abilities yet.

I tried to keep my face neutral as I nodded toward him. *I don't*
know if you can hear me, but I understand.

His eyes twinkled. I think he must have heard me. Out loud, he
brought up the subject of the Messengers.

"I've heard people mention them before," I interrupted. "They're
servants of your god, right?"

"My god?" Goram raised his hands to his side in a kind of shrug. "Is
he not your god as well?"

I pretended to study an ink blot on the parchment.

"Did Kennis not instruct you?"

I shook my head.

"I see."

A rumble of disapproval, like a wave, traveled through the men
around the table. I tried to take the focus away from my mother. "So,
when people say a Messenger has spoken to them, it's like they've
spoken to your god?"

The white haired man's head tilted to one side. "In a manner, yes.
The Messengers do his will."

"How do they speak to you?"

"Primarily in dreams or visions. Sometimes, in our prayers." He
nodded to the older man in red who sat next to me. "Perhaps it would
be best if Javan could explain our history to you. Then you would
better understand our faith."

The gray-haired Javan exchanged glances with Zaccur before
standing. With his imposing stature he loomed over me. "You are
certain Kennis told you nothing about this world?"

"Yeah." His animosity flowed toward me in unseen waves. I
wondered if anyone else in the room could feel it. "I'm sure."

Javan sneered. "Then I will go slowly so as not to confuse you."

I wanted to slap him but instead gave him what I hoped was a
winning smile. "I'll stop you if I have any questions."

He took a deep breath. "Before the world, there was Ruahk. He
existed before time, before space, before anything. Out of himself he
created others to serve him. We call them the Messengers. They exist
with him, in the unseen world. A place beyond time. A place beyond
our reality. Like Ruahk, the Messengers are immortal. But they are not

God. They were created by God to serve Him."

Javan closed his eyes. "Ruahk created the earth and the sky. He created the land and the seas and all the plants that grow. He created the animals that live in the water and those that breathe the air. The last animal he created was man. And into man, he placed his breath, so that man would be able to think and speak with him.

"Now discord arose among the Messengers." Javan opened his eyes and stared at me. "Some were jealous of men and the love that Ruahk showed them. Others wanted the love and worship that men gave God. So they rebelled. But they could not defeat Ruahk and He cast them out of the unseen realm. In darkness they wandered, until they found their way to earth, and into the lives of men."

A chill ran down my spine from the expression on Javan's face; a combination of fear and something else. Desire?

"We call these Messengers 'The Fallen,' for they fell from the grace of Ruahk. They tempted men, telling them to betray their creator and seek power of their own. When Ruahk discovered mans' betrayal, he grieved. He had made a place of flawless beauty and now evil corrupted it. In his anger, he cast men out into the wilderness of the earth. He placed faithful Messengers at the portals to guard his perfect land so that men, and the Fallen, could never re-enter."

"I've heard this story," I whispered. It sounded like one Renee had read me once from her children's Bible when we were six or seven. I remembered the picture of a woman reaching out to pick an apple. We'd giggled because we could tell she was naked even though she stood behind a fern.

Javan ignored me and continued. "Now, with their rebellion, men had discovered all kinds of sin and they gave themselves over to every desire of their heart. Nothing was beyond their imagination. And it came to pass that another group of Messengers left the unseen realm. These servants did not desire the power of Ruahk, but the pleasures of the flesh. They sought out the daughters of men and they lay with them. In the eyes of Ruahk, the children of these unions were abominations; creatures that were not men and not his servants. These became known as the Nephilim. Soon they populated the earth and Ruahk grew angry. He sought to destroy the world and all the evil that corrupted his creation."

I'd stopped taking notes long ago, engrossed in Javan's story and the intensity with which he told it.

"But, there was one among the Messengers who remained faithful to Ruahk, even though many of his brothers had chosen sin. His name was Jehoel. When he learned of Ruahk's plan he sought to warn his brothers. Many scoffed at his predictions, but a few believed and shook in fear. Jehoel devised a strategy to save those of his brothers who were repentant. He approached the guardians of Ayden, the place of perfection, and told them of Ruahk's plan. He offered to guard the gates so they could help God take his revenge upon the earth. But instead of keeping them out, he allowed his brothers and the Nephilim–their children into the protected world so that they might survive Ruahk's wrath."

Many of the men around me lowered their heads as Javan continued. A few offered up prayers in low voices. Some even shed tears.

Javan's voice echoed off the stone walls. "And God sent a great flood to wipe out the children of men and the Nephilim. The Messengers who had lain with the daughters of men He called "The Lost," and He sent them into another realm. A realm of darkness and torture.

But those in Ayden cried out to God. 'Please,' they pleaded. 'Have mercy on us.' And Ruahk saw that their hearts were sore with their sin and he forgave them. 'But you will no longer be my servants.' He took away their immortality and made them as men, prone to sickness, despair and death. But some retained a spark of their former selves in that they could see their brothers in the unseen realm and move between the portals to the other world. They called themselves 'The Elders' and sought to make a life for themselves and their families in Ayden."

I couldn't get the picture from the children's Bible out of my head. "Eve," I said under my breath as I finally remembered the naked woman's name.

Javan glared at me. "What?"

I tried to remember the story I'd read. "In my world, we tell the story a little bit different." I snapped my fingers as more of it came back to me. "Adam and Eve. They lived in a beautiful garden that God created. The Garden of Eden." I shivered as I said the name. Eden. Ayden. It had to be the same.

Faolan put a hand on my arm. "You are pale, Your Majesty. Are you unwell?"

I tried to answer him but couldn't seem to catch my breath. I knew Josh and Renee believed the story, but I never had. Landing in Eden was like waking up and finding myself in Oz. My mind struggled to make sense of this new reality.

"What is wrong?" Faolan asked.

"Nothing," It would take me some time to accept this but it wasn't something I could work out with a roomful of men staring at me. "I'm all right." I looked up at Javan. "You've told me your history, but what is your position in the Order?"

"I am the Keeper of the Law. I and the Brethren in my division study, advise, and serve as judges throughout Ayden in order to keep the peace and protect the people."

I wanted to ask him more, but the same niggling feeling I'd had before warned me not to. I glanced at Goram, but he sat with his hands folded on the table and his head lowered.

"May I ask you a question?" Javan's voice barely hid the contempt I could tell he had for me.

"Sure."

His eyes narrowed. "What do these scribblings tell you?"

"What?"

He thrust a finger at the parchment in front of me. "You had the Keeper of the Keys fetch you valuable paper and then you wrote nonsense on it. What was your purpose?"

I had to unclench my jaw before I could answer him. "It's not nonsense. It's English."

"And what is that?" He scoffed.

"That's the language we're speaking. I write in English."

A few men gasped. Even Goram lifted his head in surprise.

Javan picked up the paper. "You tell me you write in the language we speak?"

Now I was really confused. "Don't you?"

Javan seemed absorbed in trying to make sense of my notes. I turned to Faolan, who shook his head in answer to my question. Before he could explain further, the red robed man threw the paper down.

"Read it."

I lifted my eyebrows. "Excuse me?"

Faolan stood. "Javan, you are speaking to Etain's heir."

The gray-haired man bristled. He pressed his lips into a hard line then took a deep breath through his nose. "I apologize. Would you please read what you wrote? I am interested to hear how this new writing works."

I picked up the parchment. "Jorash, the Keeper of the Sanctuary. Forty-seven men work in the kitchen. Eight cooks, three in storeroom, sixteen cleaners and twenty servers." I looked up at Javan. "Do you want me to continue?"

The color of his face almost matched his robe. "No." He sat down.

Faolan held his hand out. "May I see this?"

I passed my notes to the bald man. His eyes scanned the page and he laughed. "How wonderful! You will have to teach us this new writing!"

A knock on the doors interrupted me before I could ask what language they wrote in. A blue robed man stepped forward as the doors opened.

"Your Majesty; Faolan; it is time for the mid-day meal."

The Keeper of the Keys gave back my notes. "It would be best if you returned to your room to eat, Your Majesty. The Brethren dine in the same hall as the pilgrims and they have not been told of your presence."

"That's fine." The Brethren stood as I rose from the table. Faolan escorted me to the door and passed me off to the blue robed man.

"Take her to her rooms." He made a small bow. "We would be honored if you would come back this afternoon."

I shrugged. "Sure."

I followed my guide away from the Council, down the private halls of the Sanctuary. I did a double take as we passed an open door and took a step back to look inside. Rows of bookshelves filled the room.

My guide stopped. "My Lady? Is something wrong?"

I'd been wondering what language the Brethren wrote in and thought this room might hold the answer. I handed my notes to the blue-robed man. "Take these to my room, please."

A look of panic crossed his face.

"I want to explore the library for a moment."

"But . . . but . . . I'm supposed escort you."

I'd had it with being ordered around. "And I'm telling you I want to stay here. Take my notes to my room. I know the way."

I spun on my heels and stepped into the library before he could argue with me anymore. Being heir to the throne of Ayden had to have some advantages, after all.

I wandered along the end of the aisles created by the rows of bookcases before picking one to explore. I ran my finger along the shelves as I walked down the row—no dust. The air was thick with the odor of the oil used to keep the wood polished. I caressed the leather bindings. They definitely weren't written in English. I stopped halfway down and pulled out a book. The thick parchment crinkled as the pages fell open. I stared at the words written down, enthralled by the beautiful artwork that adorned some of the letters.

Latin!

My mom had insisted I study Latin even though my friends all took Spanish. She wouldn't relent even when I'd pitched a huge fit and wouldn't speak to her for two days. Now I knew why. I guess it made sense . . . Somehow, the people of Ayden must have been in contact with people from Rome. I chuckled as I pictured a gladiator like Russel Crowe coming through a passage and preaching to the Elders.

My finger traced the words. I could only make out a few of them but at least I had a basic idea of what the book said. And if I had the beginnings of the language, maybe one of the Brethren could continue teaching it to me. I put the book back on the shelf and looked for a simpler one to start with.

I pulled another one down as several men entered the library, speaking in hushed tones.

"Hurry up, you two," a gravelly voice ordered. "Faolan will be angry if we're late for service."

"Be calm, Simon," a younger man replied. "We won't take long."

"Do you think she'll be there?" another younger sounding voice asked.

"Who?" Simon asked.

"Who do you think? The queen, of course."

I froze in my aisle, feeling guilty about eavesdropping on their conversation, but curious to know what they would say about me.

"I doubt it very much," the older voice answered. "Faolan wants to keep her presence hidden from the people."

"You've seen her though, haven't you?"

"Yes, Sebastian, I've seen her."

"What is she like? Is she pretty?"

Simon groaned. "Is that all you can think of? The girl will be queen of this land. Her mind and countenance matter more than her beauty."

I heard the soft brush of books being slipped back onto shelves.

"That means she's not pretty," Sebastian mumbled. "Or he would have said."

A sharp crack, followed by a yelp, echoed through the shelves. Simon's irritation was evident in his tone. "She will be your queen. Show some respect."

"Sorry."

No one spoke as they replaced several more books. Then Simon sighed. "She is young yet. Younger than Etain when she took the throne."

"How old is she?" the other boy asked.

"Just sixteen."

The two boys gasped.

"Yes," Simon said. "Still young, but old enough to rule without a regent. Without the Council."

"Will Braedon allow it?" Sebastian asked.

"He will have no choice if the Elders and the Council crown her."

The other boy spoke. "Why do you think he brought her here?"

I stepped closer to the voices so I could be sure to hear Simon's answer.

"He didn't know of Geran's passage. That much is sure. I think he believed he could force her to come through a passage he controlled."

Sebastian interrupted the older man. "Then he could have killed her and no one would have been the wiser."

"Not true," Simon disagreed. "The Messengers would have told one of the Elders. Besides, I don't agree that he wants her dead." Simon let out a slow breath. "I'm not sure of Ruahk's purpose. I fear for her."

"But if you don't think the Lord Regent wants to kill her, what else is there to be afraid of?" Sebastian asked.

"Try and use your brain for a moment. Think of her position. From all accounts, she was told nothing of this world or her role in it. She is alone here, without a friend, and Braedon is not the only man who needs her to secure his power."

Simon's voice dropped and I tried to still my breath so I could hear what he had to say.

"There are those, even within these walls, who would use her for their own gain. Members of the Order, of the Council, even her own uncle. You should be praying that Ruahk protects her from evil and gives her wisdom to discern whom she can trust."

Footsteps approached and the three stopped talking.

"My Lady?" A rasping voice called from the doorway.

Simon greeted the newcomer. "Good day, Malvin. Who are you looking for?"

"The queen. Seth was supposed to bring her back to her quarters for the mid-day meal but he said she stopped here. Have you seen her?"

"No. There has been no one here but us."

Malvin groaned. I feared he'd start running through the hallways looking for me again.

"I'm here." I stepped out from the aisle where I'd been hiding. "I'm sorry to make you worry. I was looking for a book."

Malvin stood in the doorway to my left while the three other men stood to my right. Their eyes grew round when they saw me. The older man, who I assumed was Simon, bowed at his waist. The two younger men followed his example.

"My Lady," Malvin said. "Your mid-day meal is ready. Faolan desires you to meet with the Council again as soon as you are satisfied."

I nodded toward him, but turned to Simon. Although he wore red robes like Zaccur and Javan, he didn't glare at me with malice.

"Your Majesty." He smiled as he stood from his bow–a warm grin that gave him the appearance of a kindly grandfather. "I trust you were not offended by our conversation. My students were only curious about you."

I took a step toward him. "You didn't offend me. In fact, I wanted to thank you for your prayers. You're right. I can use all the help I can get."

Malvin cleared his throat and I started to leave but hesitated at the doorway. "Simon?"

"Yes, My Lady?"

"Would you help me learn to read?" The look of shock that crossed his face made me laugh. I lifted the book I held in my hands. "I know a little Latin, but I'd like to understand more."

Again he gave me a kind smile. "It would be my honor."

"Could we meet here? After dinner?"

He bowed again. "I will be here."

I returned his smile and gave a small wave to the young men who stood dumbfounded behind him. "See you then."

CHAPTER EIGHTEEN

Assassination

I spent the evening hunched over one of the tables in the library. It had taken me almost an hour to read through the *Historia de Ayden*, a primer of sorts for the young men sent to study at the Sanctuary. Simon had been impressed that I could pronounce all the words in the book, but I'm sure he grew as frustrated as I did as I tried to translate them.

He patted my arm. "Do not worry so. You're doing very well." A shocked expression crossed his face and he drew his hand away. "I'm sorry, My Lady."

"For what?"

"For touching you." He shook his head. "I'm used to encouraging the boys. For most, it's their first time away from home. They miss their parents. I try and reassure them."

A pit in my stomach reminded me of how much I missed my own mother . . . or aunt . . . whatever Kennis was. "I know how they feel."

He nodded. "Perhaps we've read enough for one night. Why don't you try to summarize what you've learned so far about our history."

I flipped back through the colorful pages. "In Ayden, there are three races of people. The Elders, who are the descendants of the Nephilim; the Mystics, who came from my world; and the Commoners, whose ancestors come from both Mystics and Elders, or who accidently traveled through passages on their own. Commoners follow the laws of the Elders and it is their loyalty that keeps the Mystics from taking over Ayden."

"Very good." Simon clasped his hands together and rested them on the table. "Now. Why is there such animosity between the Mystics and the Elders?"

I turned ahead a few pages and re-read the Latin words. "King Gedeon found a way to create a passage between Ayden and my world. He thought it was an answer to prayer but he'd been deceived by one of the Fallen." I tried not to let my own prejudice show as I summarized the book. It was going to take longer than a day to accept that Ayden was Eden and that Gedeon was somehow tricked by an evil angel. And besides, what made the Mystics bad? Did Simon think everyone from my world was evil? I hurried on. "Gedeon believed the Mystics would accept the rule of the Elders, but they didn't. They practiced their own religion, including human sacrifices and the worship of the Fallen."

Simon nodded. "Very good. And where do you fit in?"

I shut the leather bound book. "I'm not really sure. Geran was one of the Elders, but what was my mother?"

"She was one of the noble class, as are you. A direct descendant of King Gedeon, but also of Common blood."

I let out a soft snort of laughter. "I still can't believe it."

A warm glow flooded Simon's eyes. "I can. There is much about you that speaks of your ancestors, even if you do not recognize it." He fought against a yawn. "You read very well. Who instructed you in our written language? Was it Kennis?"

I shook my head. "In the other world, all kids go to school. They don't all learn Latin, but that's what Kennis wanted me to take." I ran my fingers over the top of the book. "I guess I understand why now."

Simon's eyes twinkled. "I would love to see all children in Ayden educated." A slight frown formed on his lips. "But most would not see the reason for it. Why teach a child to read when they have no access to books, or When there are fields that need to be plowed?"

"But knowing how to read . . . that shouldn't be a luxury. There's power in books."

"Exactly why those in authority have never advocated teaching Commoners to read."

Now it was my turn to frown. "What do you mean?"

"Because it gives them power. When the laws of man and Ruahk are left in the hands of a chosen few, those laws can be warped to suit those who interpret them for the masses."

"Maybe I can change that." I stared at the book in my hand. "Could we meet here tomorrow for another lesson?"

He grinned mischievously, making him look like a gnome. "It's a bit radical, teaching a woman, but it is not expressly forbidden." He cupped his hand over his mouth and whispered, "Of course I won't tell Javan what I'm doing. No need stirring up trouble."

"I don't think he likes me."

Simon folded his hands. "He likes few people." The portly man seemed to shake off any misgivings as he stood up. "Shall I walk you back to your room?"

"I don't need a chaperone. I know the way."

"I'm sure you do. But Faolan has said you must be escorted at all times."

"Why?"

I waited as Simon pondered what to tell me. He studied me for a moment. "You should know the truth. He fears for you, as do we all. Ayden's government is too unsettled without a monarch on the throne. Too many factions war for power. You would be a valuable ally or a great enemy to many."

I nodded. "Devnet told me the same thing."

"Your uncle is a wise man, Your Majesty."

I stopped him before we left the library. "I heard you this afternoon. You said that even he might have his own reasons for wanting me here." Simon made his face neutral so I couldn't read his thoughts. "What do you think they are?"

The old man took my elbow and pulled me away from the entry. "He is a good man, your uncle. Although I do not have the privilege of knowing him well myself, I have heard that he is a man of courage and honor."

"But?"

"But he is a man who has lost much to Lord Braedon and the Mystics. I worry about his objectivity when it comes time for you to rule. He may desire revenge more than peace."

"What do you mean?"

"Not all the Mystics desire power. Not all follow the ancient religion. But your uncle may want to see them all punished for what the Lord Regent and his family have plotted."

I swallowed hard. "Thank you for being honest."

He bowed. "I find it too hard to lie. Come, let us get you to your room so you can rest."

I kept a candle burning on the nightstand again as I went to bed, but had too many thoughts churning in my head to go to sleep. My mind went over all the different things I'd learned during the day. I rolled over and started thinking about the night before and the balls of light that had helped get rid of the rat-fly and the serpent. Devnet had said I'd glimpsed the unseen world. I guessed the rat-fly and serpent were demons, but I'd always thought angels looked like men, not balls of light. Maybe they only looked like that to me.

I tossed over to my other side. This time I thought about Tegan. He said he'd always remember me. My heart felt weightless in my chest as I thought about the way he'd looked at me when he said it. I hadn't seen that look in anyone's eyes before. Was it love?

How could he love me after just a couple of days? I didn't know, but I knew I felt the same about him. Maybe it was the fact that we'd been thrown together. Maybe it was inevitable that we'd develop feelings for each other. My muscles relaxed and I drifted to sleep with thoughts of Tegan and the white pool of Ginessa.

I dreamed we waded together in the gentle stream, the noise of the waterfall drowning the sound of our breathing. Tegan cupped my face with his hands.

"I'll love you, Ally Foster. Always."

I reached my hands around his waist. "I love you, too."

He kissed my forehead then let me go. We walked toward the cascade. The spray clung to our clothes and sunlight sparkled on the water drops like crystals dancing in the air. Tegan grabbed my hand and pulled me to his chest. I laughed as he spun me around. He wrapped his arms around me, squeezing me tight. I couldn't breathe. He pulled me under the waterfall. The pounding water filled my mouth and nose when I tried to catch my breath. I tried to push him but he stood firm. I wrenched my hands away and scratched at his face. I tried to scream but the water stopped me.

Tegan placed a hand on my head, pushing me down until I knelt in the pool. He grabbed my neck and forced me under the water. Just like my dream of Lord Braedon, I knew that somehow, the things happening now were real. I reached out toward this dream Tegan, grabbed a handful of something and twisted.

A high-pitched scream echoed through my mind as I woke up. The candle I'd left burning had gone out, leaving the room in total blackness. I tried to sit, but something lay across my legs. I cried out and kicked at it, thinking the creatures from the other night had come back. Before I could yell again, someone grabbed my hair, forced my head back then covered my face with a pillow. I sucked in fabric when I tried to breathe. I reached up with my hand, raking my fingernails along my assailant's face. He grunted but kept the pillow in place.

I tried to scratch him again. He moved away so I couldn't reach him. I hit whatever I could, but my strength grew weaker the longer I went without breath. My heart hammered so hard within my chest, it sounded like someone pounding on a door. I sucked in one more breath but my mouth only filled with down, not air. I tried to lift my hand to strike again but couldn't. The last thing I remember thinking was that I never knew my heart could beat so loud.

"Breathe!" Rough hands shook me. "Almighty Ruahk, let her live!"

I sucked in a lungful of air. It burned my throat. A shaft of light cut through the darkness in my mind.

Someone shook me again. "Your Majesty! Breathe!"

I grabbed hold of the arms that held me, struggling to take another breath. This led to a fit of coughing. More people entered the room, a myriad of voices all talking at once.

"Look at me!" the person who held me ordered. "Open your eyes."

I had to blink a couple of times as the room now blazed with light. Faolan looked down at me.

"Thank Ruahk! She's alive." From over his shoulder, I could make out several Brethren holding the arms of two men in red robes. One of them was Zaccur. Malice radiated from his stare.

"Why?" My voice came out raspy and hoarse.

Zaccur's black eyes glared at me. Blood ran down his cheeks where I'd scratched him. "You know nothing of our world. To think you should rule over the Assembly!" He struggled against the men who held him.

Faolan let go of me as he turned his head toward the prisoners. "You have let the power of the Assembly corrupt you. You know she is the rightful heir to Ayden's throne."

The red robed man spat. "She is a foolish child. Only the Assembly can keep Lord Braedon from taking complete control."

The Keeper of the Keys let out a derisive laugh. "Lord Braedon holds Ayden in his iron grip. The Assembly has done nothing to curb his power." He looked back at me. "Only the true Queen can change the course of our world."

Devnet flew through the doorway. "Is she alive?"

"Yes." Faolan stood. "Come see for yourself."

My uncle ran to my side. "Were you hurt? Should we call for a healer?"

I shook my head. Tears pooled in my eyes.

"What can I do?"

I fell into his arms, crying. He held me close and rubbed my back. That's what I wanted; someone to make me feel safe. I realized now what a sheltered life Kennis had let me live. Never before had I feared for my life. Now every hour seemed to bring a new threat. No wonder she hadn't told me about this place. It would have haunted my dreams and made me paranoid to step outside of the house.

I heard the scuffling of feet as my would-be assassins were led away. Several other people came and went and still I sobbed on my uncle's shoulder until all my tears were spent.

"I think it best you take her from here soon," said Faolan.

I felt Devnet nod. "I had come to that conclusion earlier."

"Were you able to remove the mark?"

"Yes."

The two men remained silent for a moment before Faolan spoke again. "Did you see anything?"

My uncle didn't answer. Instead, he helped me sit back against the headboard. He tucked the covers around my legs. "How did those men get in?" He reached out touched my neck with his fingertips. "Wasn't there a guard posted?"

"We hadn't thought a guard was necessary in her own chambers. Malvin was sleeping in the doorway. Zaccur and his conspirator overpowered him and snuck in while she slept." His eyes filled with admiration. "She fought hard to free herself. She'd incapacitated the younger Brethren and managed to wound Zaccur, too."

Devnet's mouth curled up in a soft smile. "You carry the strength of your parents within you."

My throat hurt when I tried to talk. "Is Malvin all right?"

Faolan nodded. "He is being tended to in the infirmary, but he will heal."

Devnet took my hand and squeezed it. "I will stay here tonight. We will journey to the Elders tomorrow."

"Very well. I will break my fast with you in the morning." The Keeper of the Keys left the room, leaving my uncle and me alone.

"Why didn't . . . ." I coughed and tried to talk again.

Devnet held out his hand to stop me. "Why didn't I tell Faolan about what you saw?"

I nodded.

"The fact that you can see the unseen world is something I want to tell the Elders first. Especially now. After this." He straightened the bed clothes around me. "The less others know about your powers, the better."

I furrowed my eyebrows and scowled.

"Yes, powers. Your mother was not of pure Elder race like Geran. No one was sure if you would inherit any Elder gifts." He stroked my cheek. "But it's obvious that you have. Now we need to determine just what your skills are."

I tilted my head.

"You can see the unseen world, but is there more? Some of the Elders have more than one gift. Not many, but some. You may be one of them."

"Maybe a Portal?" I croaked.

His eyes held a mixture of optimism and sadness. "Maybe a portal. But they are rare, Alystrine. Do not get your hopes up." He rubbed his hands together. "Now, it's time for you to rest. We start a long journey tomorrow."

I groaned as I slid down into the bed.

"There won't be as many mountains this time. And I promise to find you some better shoes to wear." He pulled a chair over beside the bed. I took my hand out from under the blankets so I could hold his. "Don't worry, Alystrine. I will do everything in my power to keep you safe. I will never leave your side again."

I took a deep breath, letting it out slowly. "You promise?"

"I promise."

I wouldn't let him put out the torches that illuminated the room. Too much had happened in the dark tonight. I wanted to make sure that when I woke again, there would be light.

CHAPTER NINETEEN

Swallowed by Earth

A gentle wind caused dust to dance in the sunbeam that shone through the half-shuttered window. The Keeper's sitting room smelled of toast and butter. I sat next to my uncle, across a table from Faolan.

The Keeper of the Keys leaned on his elbows, waving a piece of bread as he spoke. "When do you leave?"

Devnet finished his mouthful of porridge. "I think after the mid-meal. I want to give Alystrine more time to rest before we go."

"Have you alerted the Elders?"

"Goram has made contact with them. They are expecting us."

I took a spoonful of the thick, oatmeal-like substance. The pasty texture stuck in my throat. I grabbed for a drink of water to try and push it down.

Faolan's face darkened. "Are you well?"

My eyes watered. I rubbed my neck. "It hurts." My voice sounded strange to my ears, like I spoke on a radio station that wasn't coming in well.

The bald man frowned. "Perhaps some broth would be better?" He picked up a bell, but I held out my hand to stop him.

"I'll be okay." I poured some water into the porridge to thin it out while Devnet and Faolan watched. I took another spoonful. This one went down easier. I gave the men a smile. "See?"

My uncle and his superior talked about the journey ahead, discussing various routes and places where we could rest along the way. I ate slowly, taking my time between each bite to make sure the food didn't get stuck again.

"How long do you think it will take?" Faolan asked.

"Maybe four days, if we take the easier path."

"You've decided on that way?"

Devnet glanced at me as I finished the last spoonful in my bowl. "I think it would be best. She's been through so much."

"Perhaps you're right, although it would be good to get her to the Elders sooner. She would be safer with them than . . ." he waved his hand in the air, "than anywhere else."

I tried unsuccessfully to stifle a yawn.

My uncle stood up, indicating that I should do the same. "I'll take her back to rest a few more hours while I get provisions ready."

Faolan rose and walked around the table to me. He bowed, took my hands and brought them up to his lips. "Your Majesty, I pray your journey be safe. I pray the Elders give you the knowledge you need. I pray you soon be allowed to assume the role you are destined to take in Ayden." He kissed my hands again before letting them go.

"Thank you for everything," I croaked.

He smiled. "You are welcome. Go in peace."

Devnet took my arm and led me from the Keeper's quarters. Once the door shut behind us, he pulled me quickly down the hall. The look on his face told me now was not a good time to ask questions. I knew from my past visit to Faolan that my uncle wasn't leading me back to my room. We crossed a courtyard and entered another building, taking a narrow staircase to a dark and musty basement.

Casks sat stacked along the far wall while shelves filled with baskets, jars and bags lined the other three. The stones on the walls glistened with moisture in the dim torchlight. My mom and I had stumbled on some caves once when we were hiking. This room had the same feel and smell.

"Where are we going?"

Devnet pulled a torch from the wall. "I hope you are not afraid of small places." He crossed the room to one of the columns of barrels. He felt along the rim of several until he found one that seemed to satisfy him. He stepped back and pulled on it. The cask swung open, revealing a small doorway. Beyond it, I could see nothing but darkness.

A damp breeze blew out from the tunnel like a sigh. I shivered. "What are we doing?'

"We're leaving now before anyone expects. There are too many eyes in the Sanctuary and not all are friendly."

"But . . ." I didn't want to tell my uncle I was scared. The tunnel looked like the throat of some giant beast that wanted to eat us. I grasped any excuse I could think of not to follow him. "But you promised me better shoes." I stared down at the beautiful embroidered slippers he'd given me the day before. "I can't travel in these."

I could read the impatience on my uncle's face. "You have to trust me, Alystrine."

Footsteps echoed in the stairwell behind us. Devnet pushed me into the secret hallway. He yanked the door shut and the flame on the torch bent low in the resulting draft. I bit my lip and prayed it wouldn't go out. It flickered, but then grew strong again. I followed my uncle, fighting back the terror gnawing at my gut.

I'd never thought I was claustrophobic, but then, I'd never been swallowed by the earth before. We moved hunch-backed through the tunnel. The smell of the dirt walls made me think of a freshly dug grave.

It seemed as if we traveled through the dank earth for hours. I didn't have a watch or cellphone so I couldn't judge the time. I was just about to ask him how much longer when we came to a wall of solid rock.

"Now what?" I asked.

The torch illuminated a narrow opening to our left. Devnet passed me the flame then squeezed through the hole.

He reached his hand back through. "Give me the light."

I did and was plunged into darkness. My throat tightened, making it difficult to breathe, until my uncle put the torch up to the hole. "Come."

I didn't think I could fit through the slender opening. Devnet was my height, but thinner than me. I put one leg through then wedged my body between the rocks. The rough surface scratched my cheek and snagged the fabric on my bodice. I felt like toothpaste being squeezed through a tube, grateful when I finally broke free and could take a full breath.

The cave we entered was larger than the secret passage, but no lighter. We twisted and turned through the caverns. I flinched when a drop of water dripped on my head and trickled down my arms. Devnet moaned at one point and made us double back through a corridor until he came to the fork we'd passed a few minutes earlier. We took a different path and soon I heard the sound of running water.

Devnet turned back to me. "This is the way. We are almost there."

We followed the river through the cave for what seemed like an eternity. Finally, I saw light about twenty feet ahead. My uncle dowsed the torch in the river before we slipped out of the cave's mouth.

"My lady," a voice called. "This way."

I squinted in the bright autumn sunshine, trying to see who had spoken. My uncle pointed up the hill ahead of us. I could make out the shape of a man waving to us from a clearing among the forest of birch trees surrounding us.

Devnet pulled me up the embankment. "Andrew, you made good time."

Now that my eyes had adjusted to the sun, I noticed the healer no longer wore his brown robe. Instead, he had on pants that tucked into leather boots at his knees. A blue woolen vest covered an ivory, long sleeved shirt. He reminded me of an adventurer from an Indiana Jones movie. He reached down at his feet and picked up a knapsack. "Here."

Devnet opened the pack and pulled out two pairs of pants and two dark brown tunics. He gave a set of clothes to me. "We need to put you in a disguise."

"I brought bandages as well," Andrew said.

My eyebrows furrowed. "What for?"

"It would be best, My Lady . . . ." He ran a hand through his shoulder length hair, clearly uncomfortable. "If you bound your . . . your chest. It will make you look more like a boy."

I looked at my uncle. "Is this really necessary?"

"You were nearly killed last night. I know there are others within the Brethren who wish you had never come, or worse, who want to bring you to Lord Braedon." He dug out a pair of boots and tossed them toward me. "I am thinking of any way I can to keep you safe."

I slipped on the pants then had Devnet help me untie the laces of my dress. The men turned their backs while I wrapped my chest. I wasn't exactly well-endowed, but by the time I finished, you'd never guess I ever had boobs. I put the brown tunic on and tied it with a piece of rope from the bag. "You can turn around now." I slipped on the boots, wriggling my toes inside the soft leather.

Andrew frowned as he studied me. "Take off the belt."

I looked up at him. "Why?"

"It gives you too much shape. You need to look like a young man."

I groaned and fumbled with the knot I'd made. The purple stone in my ring glowed bright against the shadows of the forest. "I should probably hide this somewhere, right?" I pulled on the band.

Devnet shook his head. "It will not come off."

I yanked on it, but the more I tugged, the smaller the ring seemed to become. "What the heck?"

"A ring of succession cannot be removed once the previous ruler has died. It will remain on your finger always."

"This is nuts." A kind of claustrophobic panic came over me. The ring seemed to be a chain shackling me to a prison cell.

Devnet rested his hand on my arm. "It is no use."

As soon as I stopped trying to pry it off, the ring loosened. I let out a slow breath and tried to relax. At least the band wouldn't cut off the circulation in my finger. I twisted the purple stone toward my palm. Hopefully, that would be enough to hide it from view.

Devnet gathered his new clothes up in his arms. "Did you bring a knife?"

Andrew swung a pack off his back and pulled a long blade out of the side pocket.

I eyed it suspiciously. "What's that for?"

My uncle's blue-green eyes stared into mine. "I think it best if we cut your hair."

My heart sank. My hair was the one thing I liked about my body. My thighs were too fat, my chin too pointed and my feet were big. But I never had a bad hair day. My thick brown and copper hair hung past my shoulders. I stepped away from Andrew. "Really?"

"It will be impossible to hide under a hat. No boy would keep it that long."

I swallowed hard. Andrew came up behind me and twisted my hair into a ponytail at the base of my neck. He raised the knife. "I am sorry."

I closed my eyes. "Just do it."

He sawed through my hair until it finally came free. My head felt ten pounds lighter. I turned and looked at the locks Andrew held in his hand. He ran back to the cave and threw the ponytail into the stream.

My uncle surveyed my new look with approval. He tilted his head toward the embankment. "I'll go down there to change."

Andrew returned and frowned at me. "Let me trim it a bit more."

"Do you want to make me bald?" I touched the nape of my naked neck as I took note of his shaggy dark hair. "Why do you get to keep yours so long?"

"Because I am older. And yours is uneven in the back. Give me a moment." He pulled a few strands of hair, sawing a bit more off before he was satisfied.

I peered over the embankment and spied my uncle next to the river. Devnet had put on the trousers and now pulled his white robe over his head. My breath caught in my throat. Vicious red scars crisscrossed his back like a road map. Barely an inch of skin was unmarked. A small cry escaped my throat.

Andrew drew me back. "Do not say anything to him, My Lady."

My body trembled. I couldn't form a complete thought. It was beyond my comprehension that anyone could do something so horrible to demand a punishment that severe. "What . . . who?"

Andrew leaned down to me, his voice barely above a whisper. "Your uncle was flayed for his part in your escape."

I looked up into his brown eyes. "My escape?"

The lines in his face seemed to deepen at the memory, making him appear older than his thirty or so years. "When you were a baby. Lord Braedon thought he'd killed your mother before she gave birth. Then the Portals told him you survived. He tortured Devnet, trying to discover where you hid."

I put my hand on his arm, trying to stop my body from shaking. "Braedon did that because of me?"

The healer's gaze softened. "Your uncle is devoted to you. From the day Etain announced she carried a child, Devnet promised his life to you."

I couldn't swallow past the lump in my throat. My uncle had said that many people had sacrificed for me, but I hadn't realized how much until this moment.

Andrew stiffened when Devnet climbed back up the embankment. "I was just examining the bruises from Zaccur's attack." His eyes flicked to mine. I gave him a nod to show I would keep quiet about what he'd revealed.

"I'm surprised he did not break her neck. The bruises seem deep."

The healer smiled. "Ruahk must have protected her, but her throat will be sore for several days, I'm sure."

Devnet stuffed our old clothes into his pack and slung it over his shoulder. "I think we should take the Fey path."

A cloud shifted in front of the sun. I shivered at the sudden drop in temperature.

The healer's face darkened. "The Fey? Are you certain? We are not heavily armed."

"I know." My uncle nodded. "But there are three of us. Hopefully that will be a good enough number to keep the brigands away."

"Brigands?" I asked.

Andrew slid his knife into a leather sheath and stuck it in his boots. "Thieves and ruffians, My Lady. They hide in the Fey because of the dense wood and spirits."

I groaned. "Thieves and spirits. Sounds like a great place."

Determination lined my uncle's face. "Those that seek us from the Sanctuary will take the western roads. I suspect the Black Guards patrol that path as well." He strode from the clearing. Andrew and I followed close, but I lost sight of him for a moment at he walked around a tree. From under his breath I heard him say, "And if the brigands and thieves can hide in the Fey, so can we."

CHAPTER TWENTY

Hiding in Plain Sight

After walking several hours though the birch forest, we came to an open plain. It had been days since I'd been away from the shelter of trees, or the walls of the Sanctuary, so the lack of enclosure unnerved me. There was no place to hide out here except for the areas of tall grass we came across. The autumn air was dry, but still cold. It carried the scent of dust and dirt.

The men of Ayden weren't talkers. Andrew, Devnet, and I spent the day walking in near silence, my throat too raw from my near strangulation to initiate conversation, and my escorts too consumed with their own thoughts to chat. The sun played hide-and-seek with thin gray clouds throughout the morning until I longed for my beloved jean jacket to warm my arms.

Our shadows barely fell past our feet when we came across a community of large tents. Not camping tents from L.L. Bean, more like something you'd see out in the desert with camels beside them. Their maroon and blue stripes stood out in stark contrast to the yellow grass and brown dirt around us. Several barefoot children in ragged tunics ran out to meet us. Their white teeth flashed against their deeply tanned skin. They grabbed our hands, tugged on our shirts and dragged us into a circle of about ten tents.

"Come! Come!" they jabbered in clipped, nasal tones. A few ran off into the largest tent calling, "Papa! Papa! Look!"

A tall man with a short, cropped, graying beard flung aside the flap of his tent. "What is it, Elam, that you disturb my afternoon slumber?"

One of the boys pointed to us. "Strangers, Papa. Look!"

The old man shaded his eyes and scrutinized us. I moved to stand behind my uncle, hoping my disguise wasn't as transparent as I thought it was.

He lowered his hand. "Welcome." He spoke with authority but I could hear the wariness in his greeting. "What brings you to the Plains of Sharne?"

Devnet took a step forward, his arms lifted to his side with the palms facing upward. He stopped, touched his thumb to his forehead, then his chest and then his lips. "May peace be with you, my lord." He bowed slightly at his waist. "Your servants are only passing through the plain."

The old man smiled and repeated the gesture my uncle had performed. "It is good to see one so young who knows the traditional greeting; so many have forgotten the ways of the Elders." He pulled one of the children to his side. "Run and tell your mothers we have guests."

The boy hurried on his errand while our host stepped aside and gestured to his tent. "Come out of the sun and have some refreshment."

We filed past him into the dim interior. Large pillows lay scattered across thick woolen rugs. My uncle positioned himself between Andrew and myself so I sat near the doorway with our host facing us. I wanted to sit with my legs stretched out in front of me but noted that the men all sat cross-legged, so I did the same.

The old man placed his hands on his knees facing upward. "My name is Eben. I am the lord of this small tribe."

"I am Olen," said my uncle then he gestured to Andrew. "And this is my brother-in-marriage, Elric." He put a hand on my knee. "And this is my son, Raanan."

Eben nodded toward Andrew. His eyes narrowed when he looked at me. I fought the urge to lower my gaze and instead, held his stare. The old man's head tilted to the side, like he wanted to ask me a question, but he was interrupted by the arrival of three veiled women. One carried a leather flask, one a basket of raisins, and the other a pitcher and a bowl.

"Ah, my beautiful wives, Ripath, Adah and Idra." His arm swept in an arc toward us. "Please make our guests welcome."

The women bowed then scurried toward Andrew. He took the flask and drank deeply before passing it to Devnet. The woman with the bowl helped the healer take off his boots and then washed his feet. My uncle passed me the flask after he took a swallow. I lifted the leather pouch to my lips and filled my mouth before I realized it held wine, not water. I sputtered as the alcohol burned my throat, relieved that I didn't spit it out. Devnet glared at me then nodded his head toward our host. I leaned forward to pass the flask to him.

As he took the wine, Eben stared at my hand. I pulled it away, hiding it in my lap. I twisted my ring again to make sure only the band could be seen. The old man drank, handing the pouch back to his first wife after he'd swallowed. The second woman moved on to wash my uncle's feet while Andrew took a handful of raisins from the bowl the third woman placed in front of us.

Eben scratched his beard. "Where are you from that you know the ways of the Elders?"

"We live in the Western lands," answered Andrew. "Many there still hold to the traditions of our ancestors."

"What brings you through Sharne?"

"We travel back to our home after seeking help from the Brethren."

Doubt drifted across the old man's face. "You have come too far south if you seek the Commonland. To turn east now will bring you into The Fey."

Andrew hesitated before answering. "Perhaps we will turn back then."

Eben's wife sat down in front of me while Devnet put his boots back on. I felt weird letting this woman take off my shoes and wash my feet. I'm sure they didn't smell good after sweating in leather all morning. She dried them with a towel hanging from her waist.

My uncle took a handful of raisins. "Thank you for your warning, Eben. We will indeed go north a way before turning toward home."

The old man reclined against a pillow at his side. He studied me as I grabbed some raisins. The lines in his forehead deepened. "Who desires to harm you?"

My uncle frowned. "What do you mean?"

"His neck." Eben thrust his chin toward me. "Has he offended someone, or have you?"

I sensed Devnet stiffen beside me. "We have done no harm, my lord."

Our host lifted his arms to his side in a gesture of surrender. "I have opened my tent to you, offered you my food and wine. You need not fear. Your enemy is now my enemy. I would lay down my life for yours." He raised his hand. "Ripath, offer our guests more wine."

The flask made its way between us again, only this time I took a smaller mouthful, enjoying the numbing sensation the alcohol had on my throat. I lifted the pouch toward Eben. He took it in one hand, but grabbed my wrist with the other. He sat up and pulled me toward him in one swift movement. I grunted in surprise. My uncle and Andrew came to their knees as I fell on the ground in front of the old man.

Devnet spoke softly. "Let my son go."

I pulled my legs up underneath me so that I no longer lay sprawled on the floor. I tried to wrench my hand away.

Eben held me fast. "The Black Guards have been riding across the plain. They came to my camp just yesterday, seeking a child."

I waited for Devnet to speak, but he didn't. Out of the corner of my eye, I saw Andrew's hand snake toward his boot and the knife sheathed there.

Eben's gaze flickered to the healer. "Do not attempt it." He kept his focus on Andrew as he called, "Sidon! Vaschel!"

Two young men strode into the tent carrying swords. Thick beards covered their faces, but did nothing to hide the fury in their eyes. They pointed their weapons at Devnet and Andrew.

I still knelt in front of the old man. I figured now would be a good time to beg. "Please don't hurt them."

"You swore your life for ours," My uncle's eyes speared Eben's. "You would break your oath?"

The old man's face hardened. "You have lied. I cannot be bound when you have first spoken false."

Devnet started to shake his head but stopped when the sword pressed into his neck. "What makes you think they search for my son?"

"They said the child would be wearing a ring, a ring of silver and gold strands woven together around a purple stone." He yanked my arm and turned my hand over. "This ring."

"Who do they say the child is?" Andrew asked.

Eben stared long at my face. "The Black Guards reveal nothing more. Only that the one who finds the child will be rewarded."

My stomach dropped.

"Torture and death await any who try and hide it."

The image of my uncle's back flashed across my mind. I wouldn't let anyone face that kind of agony for me again. I took a deep breath. "Turn me in, but let them go."

Devnet tried to duck away from the sword but Eben's son was too quick. He pulled my uncle back by his hair and laid the sword across his throat.

"No!" I cried. "Don't hurt them. They haven't done anything. I don't want anyone else to get hurt because of me."

Eben pulled me closer. I could smell the wine on his breath. His eyes raked over me as if trying to draw information from my soul. "Who are you?"

I tried to look toward my uncle to gauge what he wanted me to say. The old man grabbed my face and held it in front of his. "No! Not the words they want you to speak." I hissed in pain as his fingers dug into my cheeks. "The truth. Who are you?"

I took hold of his wrist and wrenched his hand away from me. His nails scratched my skin. Blood ran down my chin. Before he could grab me again, I stood up. Devnet and Andrew grunted as Eben's sons made sure they couldn't come to my rescue.

I glared down at the old man, pulling every ounce of courage I could find up from my soul. "My name is Alystrine, daughter of Etain and Geran. I am heir to the throne of Ayden."

CHAPTER TWENTY-ONE

Spirit Travel

Devnet groaned and sank down on his knees. Eben waved his hand. The two young men lowered their swords. The old man stood. I refused to step away from him. The blood from the scratches on my chin dripped down my neck.

Eben stared at me. "Etain's daughter?"

I nodded.

His eyes glistened. "Truly?"

"Yes."

He dropped to the floor, prostrating himself at my feet. His wives and the guards did the same. I looked over to my uncle and mouthed, *what do I do now?*

Tell them to rise, he mouthed back.

"Rise, Eben."

The old man remained on the ground. "Your Majesty, forgive me. I have wounded you in my ignorance. Do not release your anger on my family. I am to blame."

"I'm not going to hurt you. Please get up."

Eben raised his head. His face paled when I wiped away the blood that ran from the scratches on my chin.

"Idra! Fetch water and a cloth for the Queen's wound."

The small woman picked up the bowl she'd washed our feet with then emptied it outside the tent. Refilling it with fresh water from a clay pitcher, she dipped a new cloth in it and held it out to me. I pressed it against my cuts.

The old man continued to stare at me. Tears ran down his cheeks. "I can see it now. I can see your mother in you." He nodded, as if confirming something to himself. "Geran also." He looked to my uncle. "Can you not see Geran in her frame? The set of her shoulders?"

"You knew my parents?"

"I knew them well." His shoulders sank as if he carried a burden. "I served as one of the household guards for many years. I should have been there when they were killed, but they had allowed me to go home, to see my child born." He raised his head to look at me. "How did you survive?"

I shrugged. "I don't know."

Eben turned to my uncle. "How? I have seen the ruins of Etain and Geran's palace. I sifted through the rubble gathering the remains so something could be buried." A sob caught in his throat. "I found her majesty in her bed. Her husband by her side . . . his arms . . . his arms across her stomach, to protect the child."

The blood drained from Devnet's face. He moaned and seemed to fold in on himself. "I didn't know..."

Andrew placed his arm around my uncle. "You have held it in too long, my friend. Now is the time to share the tale."

"I cannot." Devnet gasped. "I cannot relive the pain."

The healer leaned over him. "You must. Alystrine needs to understand the sacrifices made for her life."

I knelt by Devnet's side. "Please. Tell me what happened."

He raised his head. My heart ached to see the agony etched in the lines of his face. Eben passed him the flask of wine and my uncle took a long drink. He wiped his mouth with the back of his hand. "Some twenty years ago, Aldred became king of Ayden. He was a wise and benevolent ruler who sought a way to bring peace to the land. He decided the best way to do this was through the marriages of himself and the two princesses, his sisters. He chose for himself one of the Common people so that they would continue to love and fight for him and their queen."

The wind moaned outside the tent. Its mournful sound emphasized the heartache I could read in Devnet's eyes. "For his sister Etain, because she was gentle and kind in spirit, he looked among the Elders for a husband. The Elders have no permanent leaders, so it was decided Etain's husband should come from one of the most gifted families. Several men were chosen as possible candidates. As Geran was the oldest from our family, he was sent to Uz to be questioned by Aldred. The king wasn't told that Geran was actually one of a set of twins. Our brother, Asher, was born just seconds after Geran, identical in every way but one. Asher had no tongue, so although he was as gifted and talented as Geran, he lived a life of quiet solitude among the Elders."

Devnet took another sip from the flask. "Geran impressed King Aldred with his talent and wisdom. It was decided he would marry the princess Etain. I've told you of their betrothal and marriage. Truly, they came to love each other and hoped for a child that would unite the Elders to the nobility. After two years, Etain became pregnant. They had a son."

I let out a choked gasp. "I have a brother?"

Devnet shook his head. "An illness struck the prince when he was three. When he died, Etain's grief was so heavy, many thought she would never recover. Over time she gave herself again to hope, and sought the love of my brother to heal her sorrow."

Devnet stopped a moment. He seemed to be gathering his thoughts before he continued on. "It was during this time that Princess Kennis turned fifteen, the age of betrothal. Kennis had a warrior's heart and a toughness of spirit, so Aldred knew she could marry one of the Mystics and not be overpowered by him. He sought out the son of the ruling Lord and arranged a marriage. A year later, Kennis wed Lord Braedon."

My heart skipped a beat. "Wait a minute . . . so Braedon is my uncle?"

"By marriage." Devnet nodded. "Aldred hoped that by uniting all the factions in marriage to the nobility, he might stop the civil strife that had been plaguing Ayden for a century."

Andrew and I jumped when the tent flap blew in from the howling wind. I shivered, more from nervousness than cold. Idra ran over to tie the flap down. Devnet continued, "Two years after Braedon and Kennis wed, Etain announced she again carried a child. Then, King Aldred and his queen died of an unexplained illness. Etain and Geran took the throne just months before their child was due. It was decided they would forgo the official coronation until after the child had been born, so as to avoid the risks the journey to Uz would have on the pregnancy."

"Kennis visited her sister and told her she suspected Braedon of poisoning their brother and his wife. She feared for the safety of Etain and her baby. If Etain died childless, Kennis and her offspring, Braedon's children, would inherit the throne. Geran had also been warned of Braedon's deceit, so he had prepared a passage to help Etain and his child to escape to the other world."

"The time came for Etain's 'laying in.' It is the period of weeks before a baby is born in which the mother rests and waits. It was at this time Kennis overheard the truth of her husband's treachery. He planned to murder Etain, Geran and their unborn child, then burn the house so no evidence remained. Kennis warned her sister, but Etain would not travel through the passage so close to the birth of her child. Geran and I pleaded with her but she refused. The stress was so great; the baby was born several weeks early. Too weak from the travails of childbirth, Geran would not risk transporting you or your mother through the passage. But Kennis knew Braedon planned to move within days to murder her sister. She came to the Elders and pleaded with them to take the baby into the other world. They refused until Geran granted his permission."

It was strange to listen to the story, knowing the baby Devnet spoke of was me. I had been born in this world. I turned my attention back to my uncle.

"Desperate, Asher and I accompanied Kennis back to Etain's bedside. Certain you would die if you remained in Ayden, your mother insisted Geran take you through the passage. She convinced Kennis to go with him to help raise you. To hide Geran's disappearance, my brother Asher remained by Etain's side. Since no one but the Elders knew of his existence it was assumed that Geran held vigil by his wife's bed until the birth of their child."

"What happened then?" I asked. "After I was sent away?"

"No one knows for sure how many men descended on their home. Some in the village said ten, others fifty or more." Devnet's eyes stared past me, as if he could see the throng coming to murder his family "They came the night after you escaped. The guards were pierced by a barrage of arrows. Servants were hunted down within the walls or slaughtered as they ran away. My brother and Etain were slain in their chambers and the entire house set alight to hide the evidence."

"So it was Asher they found with my mother?"

Tears again fell down my uncle's cheeks. "I hadn't known that he had stayed by Etain's side the whole time. That he played the part of protective father until the end." A groan escaped his throat and he bent forward. His shoulders heaved with sobs.

Heaviness settled within me as I watched my uncle grieve. I studied the faces of the others around me and the weight grew more intense. I didn't want to show the panic rising inside me so I stood and walked out of the tent.

"Your Majesty," Eben called.

I pretended not to hear him.

The children swarmed around me but I ignored them. They straggled off as I walked away from the encampment. A numbness spread throughout my body and mind, as if I'd detached myself from any emotion, any pain. The land stretched out before me. The sheer flatness of it was oppressive. The gray sky melted into the pale yellow plain with only the barest change in hues. I walked until I couldn't hear the sounds of the children in the camp, until only the wind spoke to me out on the barren earth.

My knees buckled and I dropped to the ground. I couldn't even cry—my soul too desolate from all I'd experienced over the last week. I don't know how long I knelt there staring into oblivion before soft footsteps crunched behind me. I didn't turn around, but waited to see who'd come.

Andrew knelt beside me. "Devnet will be well. It was good for him to finally release his grief."

I remained silent.

"What are you thinking of?"

I let out a breathy chuckle. "Everything. Nothing."

He rearranged himself so that he sat cross legged on the sand. He didn't speak. I didn't either for several more minutes. Instead we stared together at the monotony of the horizon.

Finally I whispered, "A week ago, I didn't even know this place existed. My biggest worry was whether my History teacher was going to flunk me and I might have to go to summer school. My life was simple. Good."

I couldn't bring myself to look at Andrew. Instead, I watched a large bird circle overhead. "I knew there was suffering and pain in my world, but it didn't affect me. It was someplace else. It happened to someone else. I collected cans for the food pantry and donated money to earthquake victims, but it wasn't real. It wasn't part of my life.

"And now . . . now I'm here and everything means something. People have been beaten . . . killed because of me and I don't know what I'm supposed to do." I rocked forward. "It's too much. Can't you all see that? I'm not the person you hoped I would be. I'm just Ally Foster. I shouldn't be here, running from people who want to kill me and trying to save the world."

Andrew's finger scratched random circles in the sand. "No one expects you to be more than you are." His finger stilled. He looked up at me. "The question you must answer is, who do you want to become?" He pushed himself up from the ground. "Decide that, Ally Foster, and the rest will be simple."

The healer returned to the camp, but I remained out on the plain. He'd made it sound so easy, but it wasn't. The choice had already been made for me, whether I wanted to admit it or not. Even if I could go back to my world now, things would never be the same. Six days ago, I just wanted to take my driver's test. Today, I wanted to make it through the night without someone trying to kill me. I snorted softly, *my priorities sure have shifted.* I knew my responsibilities lay here in Ayden. Even if I could return to my home, I'd be plagued with guilt for abandoning the land to Braedon and the Black Guards.

The sun shone white through the clouds. I ran my hands through my butchered hair and bowed my head. I wanted the chance to say goodbye to my old life. I knelt on the hard ground and thought about Josh and Renee. I took a deep breath and released the tension that gripped my neck and shoulders. I took another deep breath and let it out slowly as I tried to think about what my friends might be doing.

I pictured myself floating above my school. I could see the kids swarming out of the doors as the last bell rang. I followed Renee and Josh as they drove home. They didn't talk, even as they parked the car and entered their house. In my thoughts, I approached Renee. Her pink hair cast a sickly hue on her pale cheeks. I wondered if her lack of makeup and solemn mood had to do with me disappearing. I put my arms around her as she opened the refrigerator door and stared at the shelves. I tried to hold her tight but my arms slipped through her. "I'll miss you."

I turned to Josh. He sat at their kitchen table, staring into space. The dark circles under his eyes evidence of his lack of sleep. I leaned over his shoulder and whispered, "I hope you know how much I loved you. Even though I never said it." He put his head in his hands and let out a shuddering sigh.

I floated up through the roof of their house, down the street to our condo. My mom paced in the living room while she talked on the phone. I couldn't hear what she was saying, but she looked upset. I came to rest in front of her. She walked through me. Even though this scene played only in my mind, I shivered at the strange sensation of having someone pass through my spirit. Kennis froze. The phone dropped from her hand.

She turned around, her eyes searching the space where I stood. Her lips moved but no sound came out. "Alystrine?"

My heart started racing. Could she hear me? "Mom?"

She reached her hand out toward me and I tried to touch her. Our limbs were as insubstantial as smoke. I tried again, desperate to reach her, to prove to myself this wasn't a dream.

Her body relaxed. She stopped trying to find me. Instead, she lowered her head. Her voice echoed in my mind. *Can you hear me, Alystrine?*

Yes! Yes I can hear you!

Be strong. Take courage. You can walk the path that has been given you.

Doubt crept into my thoughts and the vision of my mother wavered. I focused my energy back on her. *I'm afraid.*

I believe in you! My mother shimmered like a mirage. She lifted her head. "Forgive me," she mouthed before she disappeared.

"I do," I whispered to the wind. The breeze swirled around me, as if it wrapped me in an embrace. I didn't know if I'd had some kind of paranormal dream, but I knew there was no turning back now. I'd have to see this through. Whether I lived through it or died trying, at least I'd know I'd attempted to do the right thing.

CHAPTER TWENTY-TWO

I'm Getting Married in the Morning

All eyes turned in my direction when I entered Eben's tent. The old man opened his arms and waved me to the center of the blankets.

"Come! Come and sit. My wives are making you a fine meal to celebrate your return."

I looked to my uncle. "Do we have time to eat, or should we be making our way to the Fey?"

"The Fey?" Eben frowned. "You cannot be thinking of going through there to get to the Elders?"

Devnet's voice sounded as tired as he looked. "We cannot risk the main roads, they'll be too heavily guarded and you can see our attempt to disguise her is futile."

The older man leaned forward with his elbows on his knees. "To take her to the Fey is dangerous."

Andrew folded his hands together. "I have argued the same but Devnet is adamant."

Eben focused his deep brown eyes on me as I sat down beside him. "There must be another way."

Andrew caught my attention and the corner of his mouth rose in a smile. "You seem more at peace."

"I realized there's no use wishing to go back to the way things were before. I have to accept what's happening now and move on from there. I let myself say goodbye." I glanced at my uncle. "Something weird happened."

"Weird?" His eyes narrowed.

"Strange." I paused and thought about my experience. "Is it possible that one part of your body . . . maybe like your soul or something . . . can that travel to the other world while your physical body stays here?"

Devnet sat down next to me. "Tell me everything."

"I wanted to see my home one more time. I thought about it really hard and I swear I was back there. I could see everything so clearly. And when I found my mother . . . ." Now that I spoke the words out loud, it seemed foolish. The men all waited expectantly for me to say something. "Never mind. I must have been dreaming."

My uncle frowned. "What did you see?"

I shrugged. "It wasn't what I saw, it's that we spoke to each other." My gaze flickered between Andrew, Devnet and Eben, hoping their expressions wouldn't say I was crazy.

Devnet sat up like a jolt of electricity had shocked him. "What did she say?"

"She told me she believed in me. That I should be strong and have courage."

"And how did she speak to you?"

"It was more like she thought the words and I could hear them."

Devnet's face brightened with excitement. "You are amazing, Alystrine. I cannot wait until the Elders have a chance to test you."

"You don't think I was dreaming?"

Devnet shook his head. "No. It is just another of your abilities." His forehead creased. "Are you sure you never experienced anything like this before you came here?"

"Never."

"Amazing."

The guard who'd held his sword to my uncle's throat entered the tent.

"What is it, Vaschel?" Eben asked.

The young man leaned down and whispered something to his father. Eben nodded. "My son tells me he has killed a goat in your honor. My wives are preparing it for your dinner." He clapped his hands together. "A feast to celebrate your return to Ayden, Your Majesty."

Goat? Add that to another of the foods I never thought I'd eat in my lifetime. "Thank you very much."

Eben took his son's wrist. "Get your brother Sidon and come back to the tent. But keep the little ones out tonight. We have much to discuss." Vaschel turned to leave, but his father didn't let go of him. "I have an idea." He pulled his son down to sit by his side. "What if we disguise the Queen as Vaschel's bride?"

Devnet, Andrew and I all looked at Eben in confusion.

"She would be fully veiled, as is our law for a betrothed woman in public. We can make certain the sleeves of her gown cover her hands to hide the ring."

Vaschel paled, but he didn't outright refuse his father's idea. His eyes couldn't seem to meet mine as his father and the Brethren hashed out the details of the plan.

"Wait a minute." I glanced between the men. "Don't I get a say in all this?"

Devnet ignored my interruption. "It might work."

"It is safer than trying to pass her off as a boy," Eben continued. "Few would violate our laws and demand she remove her covering,"

"But I don't want to get married yet." I turned to Vaschel. "No offense, but I'm not ready to marry anyone! Least of all a total stranger!"

Devnet sat next to Eben. "But what would be the reason for our journey?"

The old man grinned. "If you were stopped, you could explain that you go to the Elders to have the marriage blessed, as is tradition."

"Hey!" I jumped up and crossed my arms. At my shout, the men all went quiet. "I'm not doing this."

My uncle's forehead creased in thought, but it was Andrew who spoke. "It is a better plan than taking you through the Fey."

"I am not marrying him and that's final!"

A tense pause hung in the air before Eben, then Devnet, and soon all the men started to chuckle.

Frustration bubbled inside me. "This isn't funny. I'd rather go through your haunted forest than get married to a stranger."

Devnet had to catch his breath before he answered, "There would be no ceremony, Alystrine. You would not be actually be a bride, only disguised as one."

"Oh." I didn't appreciate being the source of their amusement, but I was relieved to understand their plan. I paced to the back of the tent to get rid of some of my nerves.

Later, over a scrumptious dinner of spiced goat meat, lentils and bread, the rest of Eben's family added their own creativity to the proposal. His wives seemed as giddy as if the wedding were actually going to take place. They could barely contain themselves through the meal until they could take me back to their tent to get me ready to play the part of blushing bride.

I yawned as I finished the last bite of goat on my plate. It had a slight bitter taste to it, but I'd learned I could stomach just about anything when food came so sporadically.

Devnet walked over to me and held out his hands to help me stand. "Try and get some rest. But send someone for me if you have any more visions like you had today. Or if you dream." He held me at arm's length. "We are outside of the protection of the Sanctuary and too far from the influence of the Elders."

I shuddered. "Will Braedon try and reach me through my dreams again?"

"I don't know." Devnet kissed my cheek. "I will pray to the Messengers tonight that they protect you."

I followed Eben's wives back to their tent. "I'm sorry," I said as they showed me the palette where I was to sleep. "I've forgotten your names."

The shortest one spoke up first. Her long black hair fell straight down to her shoulders. "I'm Ripath." She pointed to the tallest of the three wives. "This is Adah." The other woman bowed. Her green eyes and graceful way of moving made her seem like a cat.

"And I'm Idra," the third woman straightened up. She had beautiful light-brown hair, full of curls. "Make yourself comfortable, My Lady. Let us show you the gowns we can offer you."

I sat down on a pile of woolen blankets and propped my back with an overstuffed pillow. Eben's wives ran to a wooden chest. Each pulled out an armload of clothes. They placed them before me then picked them up one at a time to model them. I couldn't get over the striking hues of the gowns; crimson, hunter green, turquoise and saffron. Iridescent beads had been sewn on many of them to make them sparkle in the torchlight of the tent.

A jade green dress caught my eye. "That one looks beautiful."

Adah grabbed it and stood. "This was my wedding dress. It went well with my eyes." She peered at my face. "Yours have green in them too. This would be perfect for you."

"I don't want to take your wedding dress."

"Nonsense, My Lady. It would be an honor, and I have other gowns. Besides, you and I are almost the same height. You should have one of my dresses so the fit is right."

"But then I insist you have my veil!" cried Ripath. "And my headdress."

I laughed at their enthusiasm. I'd never go to my high school prom, but I imagine Renee and I might have sounded something like this if I had. I tried to suppress a yawn.

Idra, the oldest looking of the three wives, clapped her hands together. "The Queen needs to rest now. We will wake early in the morning and prepare her for the journey." The others put the clothes away while I took off my boots and lay down.

Ripath covered me with a blanket of soft wool. "Call us if you need anything. We are at your service."

"Thank you."

I pulled the blanket under my chin and rolled over. The wives put out the torches. I almost asked them to keep one burning. I wasn't over the assassination attempt the night before, although I didn't believe any of Eben's wives had it in for me. I rolled to my side and saw several gold spheres floating toward me. I started to cry out, but a sense a peace flooded my body. Stress flowed out of my muscles like rain down a gutter. The orbs hovered above me, one on either side of my bed. They elongated until they no longer floated but stood by me. I couldn't make out faces but the silhouettes were human. They reached out toward each other so that I lay under a canopy of golden light. I closed my eyes and drifted into sleep.

Idra woke me the next morning and insisted on taking me out to a creek nearby to bathe. A pink ribbon of sunlight ran across the horizon as we left the tent. "You must be washed and perfumed before we place the gown on you."

"You do realize I'm not really getting married, don't you?" I was beginning to have my doubts.

Her manner was like a drill sergeant or some strict boarding school matron as she stripped off my boy's clothing. "It must appear like the real thing." She pulled me toward the water. "Come now."

I looked at the river with some trepidation. "How cold is it?"

"Warmer than after the winter thaw." She eyed me with something close to contempt. "Come. There is no time to waste."

Ripath came up beside me, carrying a mean looking scrub brush and a bar of orange soap. The two of them dragged me into the water and I discovered my idea of freezing was very different than Idra's. I refused to let the women actually scrub my body but took the soap from them and did it myself. Idra insisted she be the one to wash my hair. She forced my head under the water then grabbed the soap from me so she could use it.

I came up for air. "Is it tradition that the bride turns blue on her wedding day?"

Idra tsked under her breath. "The little children behave better than you on bath day."

Any whining I did about wanting warm water would only make me sound more childish so I let the brusque woman finish her job before I ran back to the tent, naked, and dove under the blankets of my pallet.

Adah laughed. "Get out of there, Your Majesty. We must get you ready. There isn't much time."

The wives rubbed me down with scented oils of sandalwood and lavender. They fussed over what was left of my hair, shaking their heads in frustration that Andrew had cut it all off. Ripath put a salve on the cuts Eben's nails had left on my cheeks. Once I was polished, primped and dressed, they led me out to the courtyard where the men waited. Although all the men had a similar Middle Eastern appearance, Sidon and Vaschel's broad shoulders and long, black curls marked them as being the younger two of the group.

Sidon whispered something to his brother when they saw me. Vaschel turned beet red. Eben grinned while Devnet and Andrew nodded their heads in approval. They had borrowed clothes from Eben and his sons. Their long sleeved tunics fell almost to their ankles. Devnet's boasted broad blue and yellow stripes while Andrew's had brown and green stripes. The tops of their heads were wrapped in linen.

"Turn around, please." Eben made a twirling gesture with his arm. "Let us see what work my wives have done."

I spun around in the early glow of morning. Sunlight sparkled off the iridescent beads sewn along the gown's neck and chest. The filmy green fabric caught the breeze and billowed around me. It lifted the shimmering golden veil from my face. Ripath's jeweled headdress kept the light fabric from flying off my head.

Devnet took a step toward me. "You certainly look like a bride. Now Eben, you must tell her the rules."

I frowned under my veil. "Rules?"

"There are certain protocols you must follow, Your Majesty. You must never be out of Vaschel's sight. To do so means death in our traditions and there are those along the way that might insist we carry out the law immediately if they feel you are treating your husband falsely. Do you understand?"

I swallowed hard. "Don't leave Vaschel's sight. Got it."

"You may not talk to another man unless Vaschel is by your side. Even if he is in the same room with you, you cannot speak unless he stands next to you. And you may never remove the veil unless asked by Vaschel. As your husband, he alone decides who sees you and to whom you may speak."

I groaned inwardly at the repressive nature of these demands. I hoped all the people of Ayden didn't treat women as harshly.

"Do you understand the laws?" My uncle asked.

"Yeah. Basically I can't do anything unless Vaschel tells me I can."

"I'm afraid that's the gist of it. Will you be able to remember?"

"If it will save my life, I'll do just about anything."

Eben gestured to his sons. "Very well. Vaschel, take your bride's hand." Vaschel had donned a handsome outfit for our journey. Deep purple and gold stripes decorated a shorter tunic than my uncle's. The tunic stopped about mid-thigh and he wore cream linen pants underneath. An ivory and gold sash sat at his waist with a jeweled scabbard hanging from it. Instead of the plain linen head wrap, he wore a deep purple hat with jewels and beads set in an intricate geometric design. His brother Sidon chuckled as Vaschel took my hand.

His father glared at him. "You behave. If you weren't already betrothed, I would have asked you to perform this sacred duty."

Sidon straightened his face. "I'm sorry, Father. I will play my part as well and help to keep the queen safe."

"That's better." Eben hugged his sons then bowed to me. "You have the might of my two eldest sons to help you on your quest. May Ruahk bless you and keep you safe."

CHAPTER TWENTY-THREE

A Dark Stranger

I longed for the good old days when my mom would drive me anywhere I wanted to go or, now that they were over seventeen, Josh and Renee could take me in their car when we went anywhere. I was sick of walking. At least if I did become queen, I'd know exactly what every part of Ayden looked like.

Vaschel and I walked behind Sidon, and in front of Devnet and Andrew, throughout the morning. We headed north, following the winding bank of the river I'd bathed in. To the east, across the water, I made out another forest.

"Is that the Fey?" I asked Vaschel.

He nodded.

"Is it really as bad as everyone here seems to think it is?"

"I've never been in it." His dark brown eyes looked black through my veil. "I had a friend who ventured in and never returned, another who came back missing a hand. It is not safe."

I'd wondered if I should suggest we go through the Fey anyway, just to shorten our journey, but after Vaschel's comments, perhaps I didn't mind the longer walk.

By mid-afternoon, the river widened enough so that crude boats and rafts floated along it. Men called to each other as they hauled in nets of wriggling fish. We approached a walled city.

Sidon turned around. "This is Cyrene. We can find transport on one of the rafts to bring us past Uz to the juncture of this river and the Uphetes."

"Be sure to stay with Vaschel," My uncle called to me. "These port cities are full of disreputable men."

Ragtag groups of people mingled outside the city gates. Some bartered with various peddlers, others argued amongst themselves the way old people will just to pass the time. The posted guards didn't give us a second glance as we passed through.

Tented stalls and wagons lined the streets. Vendors tried to entice us over to see their merchandise. I clutched Vaschel's hand as we wove our way through the crowded market down to the wharf. I hadn't been around so many people in a while and I didn't want to lose him.

The crowds and the smells grew dirtier the closer we came to the port area of the city. Drunk men sprawled in doorways, women with heavily painted eyelids called down to us from windows. The air carried the odor of rotting fish, sweat and urine. Sidon and Devnet stopped short.

I looked up at Vaschel. "What's wrong?" We'd come up to the edge of the river. The wind played along the surface and caused lazy waves to lap up against the empty wooden docks.

"Where are the boats?" I asked my pretend fiancé.

"I do not know."

Sidon, Andrew, and Devnet approached a leathered-skinned man who sat working on a net by one of the piers. They talked for a moment or two, arms gesturing up and down the river. I tried not to worry when my uncle turned toward me, his face a mask of concern. The three men hurried back to us.

"What's wrong?" I asked.

Devnet put his hand on the small of my back then led Vaschel and I up the street. "We have a problem."

"I can see that," I muttered. "Where are we going?"

Andrew walked alongside us while Sidon jogged ahead a few paces. Andrew kept his head down and his voice low as he spoke. "Braedon has ordered all boats stopped and searched once they reach Uz. It means the captains are only able to make one trip a day up the river."

"So . . . what does that mean for us?"

"It means we have to spend the night at one of the taverns. We'll try and hire one of the captains to take us tomorrow."

I turned to my uncle. "But what about the blockade? I assume he's searching for me. Do you think this disguise will fool the Black Guards?"

Devnet's face paled. "No. They'll be able to recognize your scent, even with the perfumes Eben's wives gave you." His hand pressed against my back. "We'll have to disembark before the blockade and try and make our way around Uz by a different path."

Vaschel's hand squeezed mine. "Do not even consider the Fey, Your Majesty. It is far too dangerous."

"I think those Black Guards are more dangerous than those . . . ." I waved my free arm, trying to remember the word Devnet had used.

"Brigands and thieves. How bad can they be?"

Sidon glared at his brother then barked something in another language. Vaschel's brown eyes widened as he whispered something in return. He pulled me to a stop then railed at me in the same strange language.

I tried to yank my hand from his but he held me tight. "Let go of me!"

Andrew came up behind us, his voice soft, but firm. "We are being watched. Vaschel must be seen as disciplining you because you raised your voice to him."

"You've got to be kidding me?"

"Bow to him," Andrew ordered.

I swore under my breath.

"Do it now!" the healer growled. "Or you may be in danger of being whipped."

I continued my litany of whispered curses as I bowed toward Vaschel. There were some things that were definitely going to change if I became queen. Once I had seemed to apologize to my fiancé, we continued up the road.

Sidon entered a building ahead of us. He came out a few moments later, shaking his head. "There's a lot of us in the same position, having to wait for ferries out tomorrow morning."

He tried another tavern with no luck. He thrust his chin to his right. "The owner here said there might be room up this way."

We followed Sidon up a narrow alley. The gray stone buildings leaned in toward each other like children playing *London Bridge*. A group of unwashed men inspected us as we approached. Their stench of alcohol and sweat lingered after we'd passed them and I could feel the eyes of more than one of them on my back. I tried not to shiver in revulsion.

A wooden sign hung askew, having lost one of its hooks. The faded picture of a pig carrying a goblet on its back creaked on its hinges as the wind blew. Sidon ducked into the doorway underneath, coming out a moment later with a resigned grin.

"It's not the finest of establishments, but they have a room. We should be able to hire a captain here as well."

My eyes had trouble adjusting to the dark interior of the tavern. It had no windows and a thin haze of smoke from the fireplace hung like fog. Wooden beams lined the ceiling about eight feet above our heads.

The main room we'd stepped into had two rows of five wooden tables. Over one of them lay three men sprawled in various stages of inebriation. An open doorway led back to a kitchen area where two women, a mother and daughter perhaps, scurried about stirring various pots. A grizzled old man with few teeth stood behind a scarred oak bar. He waved us into the room.

"Come in." His high-pitched voice fit his gnome-like appearance. "Can I get ye a pint o' somethin'? Perhaps a skin o' wine?"

Andrew pulled several coins from the pouch at his side. "We'll have wine. When the meat is ready, we'll take a slab of that, and some bread and cheese if you have it."

The old man's eye's glowed as he pocketed the silver. "Of course, Sir."

We squeezed around a table in the far corner, away from the door. Vaschel and I sat with our backs toward the wall while Devnet, Sidon and Andrew sat opposite us, but turned so they could watch the entryway.

Our host came around the bar with a sack that sloshed as he walked. He eyed me as he passed the wine to Andrew. "You folks are a finer lot than usually come this way. What brings ye here?"

The healer nodded toward Vaschel and me. "We seek the Elders' blessing on their union."

The gnome-man lifted an eyebrow. "Aye? It's a dangerous time to be stickin' to the old ways. Ye may want to let the young ones forgo that ritual."

Devnet's voice sounded hard and dismissive when he spoke. "Nevertheless, my family will keep it."

Our host shrugged. "It's not for me to say. I'm only warning ye." He stared at my uncle. "A girl like her won't be safe in these parts for long."

I knew the old guy told the truth. The whole town gave me the creeps. Devnet held the man's gaze. "You have a room where she can sleep? With a door we can guard?"

The old man lifted his head toward the ceiling. It was then I noticed the ladder leading up to the second "floor," if you could call it that. A balcony about three feet wide ran above the bar. Behind the landing I made out four doors. I couldn't imagine the rooms being any more than eight feet wide. Sleeping quarters were going to be tight tonight.

Our host left us, but not before promising the arrival of dinner within the hour. Devnet rested his elbows on the table and leaned in. We all crowded together so we could hear his hushed tones.

"I think she'll be fine until dinner. After that, I want her to go upstairs. We'll take turns keeping watch down here. Sidon and I will take the first watch and hopefully find a captain willing to ferry us in the morning."

The others nodded but I felt useless. "Wouldn't it be safer to camp somewhere outside the city tonight? I'm not getting a good feeling about this place."

My uncle frowned. "The Black Guards will be patrolling the area. We'd have to travel days west to go around them. To go east now means entering the deepest part of the Fey."

My voice rose. "But we'll have to do one or the other when we abandon the boat before the city anyway."

Devnet's eyes flashed as he tried to reason with me. "We can walk around the edges of the Fey and meet up with our raft once the captain passes through the blockade."

"And what makes you think Braedon won't have his monsters patrolling the Fey?" My fist hit the table.

The four men looked at me, but didn't speak.

I watched them through the film of my veil. "Well?"

Andrew took a drink from the wine sack. "The Fey surrounds the Elder Lands. The Black Guards have never dared enter it before." He passed the drink to my uncle.

"Yeah, well, a lot of things have been changing since I've been here." I crouched closer toward them. "Tegan told me the Black Guards never went into the Everwood either, but they came."

Devnet sputtered as he swallowed. "What?"

I told the group about our encounter with the Black Guards at Ginessa's Pool, leaving out the part where Tegan had his arrow pointed at me. Not that I thought I'd see the boy again, but I didn't want to cast him in a negative light, just in case.

The blood drained from the Brethrens' face. Both men looked like they were going to be ill. Devnet took my hand. "Describe the sound you heard that sent them away."

"It was almost a bird call. A shrill, trilling noise."

Devnet tightened his grip. "You're sure?"

"Yes." I pulled my hand from his and rubbed my fingers. "Why?"

My uncle took another swig of wine. "One of the Brethren must have been keeping track of your progress through the woods. They had to have seen you through an Elderstone or some other magic."

"Why look so worried? Isn't that a good thing?"

Devnet passed the sack to Sidon. "Not if they kept it secret. I told the Council of your passage through. Someone wanted you away from Braedon, but not necessarily safely to the Sanctuary."

The wine finally made its way to me. "Zaccur and Javan, probably."

Andrew shivered. "But neither can communicate with the unseen world. They would have had to enlist the help of one in white."

I lifted my veil so I could take a drink from the sack before passing it to Vaschel. "Maybe they lied to the guy. He may have thought he was just helping me escape the Black Guards."

Andrew nodded. "It's possible." He rested a hand on Devnet's shoulder. "It is possible."

I bent forward. "Let's not get side-tracked from my initial question. If the Black Guards came that far into the Everwood, which they've never done before, what makes you think they won't go into the Fey?"

The fatigue in my uncle's eyes scared me. Through all of this he had seemed confident. Now, he just looked tired. "I don't know that they won't." He looked around at the other men at the table. "Anyone have any other ideas?"

The four men crowded together at one end of the table leaving me out of the conversation. My pride stung a little. I mean, I was the queen, wasn't I? Shouldn't I have the final say in what we were going to do? But my rational self understood that I had no idea of the physical or political landscape of Ayden. I needed to leave this decision to them and trust they knew what they were doing.

Two burly men came into the tavern. The smaller of the two called out, "Yaren! Bring us a pint!"

They sat at a nearby table, deep in discussion. Another man joined them and the grizzled owner brought them each a mug of ale. The room filled with various customers, all looking for a pint and a bite to eat.

A younger man entered. He caught my eye because of his age and coloring. While most of the men in the tavern appeared to be in their forties or fifties, the newcomer looked to be in his late twenties. His skin reminded me of creamy hot chocolate and he even radiated heat. His darker color surprised me because the people in the town had the lighter skin of the Commoners. The newcomer strode into the tavern with a cocky attitude, like he owned the place.

He flashed a bright smile to the tavern keeper. "Yaren! How are you?"

The older man grinned, but his eyes narrowed. "I be well, Kyran. And yourself?" He passed him a mug of ale. "We have'na seen ye around in a while."

A loud crash came from the kitchen and everyone lifted their heads toward the noise. One of the women I'd seen earlier ran out and threw her arms around the newcomer.

"Kyran! You're back!"

She stood no higher than the middle of his chest. Kyran picked her up with no apparent effort, spinning her around. The other men in the tavern called out rude comments and noises that didn't seem to please the tavern owner much.

Yaren slammed his hands down on the bar. "Julia! Get back to the kitchen!"

Kyran set her down. "You'd best obey your father, now."

The girl's full lips pouted until he swept her up again and kissed her. The cat calls of the other men rose in volume. He let her go with a pat on the behind. "Come sit with me when your work is done." He picked up the mug of ale from the bar and tipped it toward Yaren. "I promise to behave myself. Do not worry."

The young girl flitted away toward the kitchen, but not without casting a longing glance toward Kyran as he made his way to the empty table by the door. He sat down with his back to the wall, scanning the room. His gaze rested on my table. I turned my head away, glad my veil hid the fact that I still looked at him. It didn't matter. Kyran's eyes burned into mine.

My breath caught in my throat. Kyran held me in the same contempt as Zaccur and Javan. I shuddered and pulled my attention away from him. I didn't know whether he knew who I really was, or whether he didn't like my disguise, but he despised something about me. I had difficulty paying attention to what the others at my table were discussing. I'd never had so many people hate me before.

A couple more men wandered into the tavern, along with a woman I figured was a prostitute. Her threadbare blouse did nothing to hide her ample breasts. I guess the people of Ayden hadn't developed bras or corsets yet. It didn't matter much for a person like me, but this lady's boobs swung like full sacks of water. My companions stared at the woman as she meandered her way around the tables, until she found someone willing to buy her a pint of ale for her company.

I snapped my fingers. "Focus here, people. We have work to do." I glared at my uncle. "Besides, don't you take a vow of abstinence or something?"

My uncle looked confused. "What?"

"Don't the Brethren abstain from sex?"

"Whatever gave you that idea?"

"You dress like monks. There are no women at the Sanctuary. You keep the pilgrims separated."

Devnet's bemusement still registered on his features. "I don't know what a monk is, but it's true, while at the Sanctuary, we try and keep ourselves from. . . ." His cheeks turned pink.

"Sex," I whispered.

He swallowed. "But it is only to focus our thoughts on our work. Many of the Brethren are married and make regular trips home to be with their families."

I hadn't considered that possibility. "Are you married?"

His countenance fell. "No. But Andrew is."

I smiled. "Really?"

Andrew nodded.

"Do you have kids?"

"I have two boys and a baby girl." He let out a sigh. "She is probably walking by now. I have not seen her in over a year."

Yaren interrupted our conversation with a platter of meat and cheese and a basket of bread. Unlike the Sanctuary, there were no plates or utensils to eat with. I started to reach for a piece of bread, but stopped when the others bowed their heads.

They all spoke under their breath. "To you, Ruahk, we give thanks for this provision and this day."

The others lifted their heads and looked at me expectantly.

"Can we eat now?" I asked.

"You're the queen," whispered Devnet. "You must choose first."

I placed a piece of meat on a slice of bread and set it on the table with hesitation. I'm sure Yaren and his daughter didn't scrub with bleach. Who knew what kind of bacteria lurked in the grains of wood? I just had to hope my body would be resistant to the germs. I decided to start with a clean piece of cheese.

The awkwardness of trying to pass food under my veil so I could eat was outweighed by the anonymity it gave me. The thin gauze did little to distort my view of others, but I knew they couldn't see me. I stole another glance toward the corner where Kyran sat. He stared at me as before. I wondered why he loathed me so much. He didn't even know me.

Yes, I do.

His expression hadn't changed so I couldn't be sure the thought I'd heard was his. When Goram had spoken to my mind, he'd given me some kind of physical clue. Kyran took a sip from his ale then turned his focus to Julia.

The girl, maybe a few years older than me, served the other guests their food. Her mother made the rounds with a jug and refilled cups with ale if enough coins crossed her palm. Julia's mother wasn't much taller than her daughter but many pounds heavier. The woman probably could have rolled faster than she waddled. Her pink cheeks and warm demeanor brought laughter with measured respect from the men around the tables.

Julia returned to the kitchen then brought back a tray with bread and meat for Kyran. She curtsied as she placed it on his table. He took her hand, pulling her down onto his lap. She giggled as he kissed her palm.

"Aye, Kyran!" called Julia's mother. "Ye behave yourself now. I'll be watchin' ye"

"And what will you do, Rhoda?" Kyran kissed Julia's neck. "If your daughter leads me astray?

Rhoda wagged a finger in his direction. "I'll sit on ye, that's what, ye cur."

The crowd roared with laughter. Kyran made a face of exaggerated fear. "You'd kill me!"

The fat woman's eyebrows furrowed. "Aye. A slow and painful death."

The patrons howled again, but the dark man steadied his gaze. "Never fear, my lady. I am a man of honor. Your daughter is safe with me."

The prostitute pulled herself up from the table. "Play all ye like with the girl. When you're ready for a real woman, ye come see me!"

The drunk man who'd paid for her ale yanked her back down. "Yer mine first tonight, Dearie."

"But there'll be plenty of time for more when yer done."

I looked away as she kissed his cheek and he reached up to fondle her breast. I hoped I'd never be so desperate that I would sell my body for a pint of ale.

I finished the meat and cheese then nibbled on the bread as my companions continued to think of a plan to get me to the Elders. My eyes were drawn back to Kyran and Julia in the corner. He fed her a piece of meat. She sucked on his fingers.

Gross. I'd always hated when girls acted like that in the cafeteria, fawning over a guy like they couldn't live without him.

Kyran's hand ran up and down Julia's back. She squirmed closer to him. He drew her in and kissed her on the mouth.

My whole body tingled, as if I'd been hit with a low charge of electricity. I shook my head. I certainly wasn't jealous of Julia. Kyran had to be at least ten years older than me.

The strange sensation ran through me again, causing the hair on my arms to stand up. Panic rose from my stomach. An overwhelming dread filled my mind. I turned to my uncle. "Something's wrong."

He broke away from his conversation with Andrew. "What?"

"Can't you feel it?" I rubbed my arms. "Something's coming."

Devnet went still. He breathed for a moment then his body went rigid. "We have to get out of here." He thrust himself up from the table, almost knocking Sidon and Andrew off the bench.

The healer stood. "What is it?"

Devnet made a frantic motion with his arms to get Vaschel and me up. "There's no time!" He ran toward the bar and yelled to Yaren, "Is there a back door out of here?"

The old man appeared stunned.

My uncle grabbed him by the shirt and pulled him across the bar. "Is there another way out?"

A hooded man entered the tavern. Unlike the Brethren, his robe was made of the fur of some animal, maybe otter. He held his arm straight out in front of him. In his hand he held an orb, similar to the one Quinn had carried in the woods, only smaller.

Devnet let go of Yaren. His shoulders slumped.

The noise in the tavern fell silent as the stranger took another step inside. The orb pulsated between blue and lilac.

He pushed back his hood with his free hand. He didn't seem much older than my uncle, but darker, both in skin and hair color. His brown eyes surveyed the tavern, stopping to rest on Julia. He walked toward her.

He paused several feet from her and stared at the orb. It didn't change color. His interest turned to Kyran. He tilted his head toward the younger man, as if in greeting. Kyran returned the gesture.

I tried to get Devnet's attention, but he still stood bowed toward the bar. I shifted so that I hid behind Vaschel. The robed man turned.

His brown eyes darkened and a cold smile crept across his lips as he caught sight of me in the corner. He took a step toward me and watched the orb. It pulsated, but stayed blue. He took another step and the crystal shifted to the lilac color I'd seen before. One more step and the orb blazed a deep purple.

The man lifted his gaze to me. "Your Majesty." His smile made me shiver. "Lord Braedon is anxious to meet you."

CHAPTER TWENTY-FOUR

Alone with the Stranger

"N o!" My uncle spun from the bar and rushed at the stranger.

The robed man swung the orb toward Devnet. "Stop."

A blue-white bolt shot from the crystal and hit my uncle, surrounding him in light. He froze in mid-stride, his face contorted in agony.

Recognition spread across the robed man's features. "Devnet?" He let out an arrogant snort of air. "Did you think you could keep Etain's child from Braedon a second time and live?" The orb pulsated again. My uncle screamed.

At least, I think he screamed. His mouth opened wide, but no sound escaped from the cocoon of light.

The robed man's hand flexed around the orb. It shot another bolt toward my uncle. "I thought you were smarter than that."

I tried to push past Vaschel. "Don't hurt him!"

Vaschel shoved me back to the corner as he pulled out his sword. Sidon unsheathed his weapon as well. The orb crackled and Devnet writhed within the energy that glowed around him. The robed man eyed Vaschel and Sidon with contempt as they stalked him.

"Fools! I have not come alone. Even now, Black Guards are coming to take Etain's child to my master. They will slaughter you where you stand."

Chaos erupted as the patrons rushed toward the only visible exit. Andrew turned to me. "Run!"

"Where?"

The strange voice I'd heard before screamed inside my head. *Up!*

The ladder to the second floor was blocked by the crowd trying to escape. Sidon made a swipe with his blade toward the robed man. He thwarted it with a wave of his hand. Sidon flew off his feet and hit the bar with a sickening thud.

Climb on the table, fool. Then pull yourself to the second floor.

I stood on the table and reached toward the balcony. From the corner of my eye, I saw Vaschel get thrown into the wall. The robed man grunted and pointed the orb toward me. My uncle crumpled to the floor as the light left him and electricity shot through my body.

The power that surrounded me also forced me to stay upright, even though I longed to collapse in pain. The robed man made a thrusting motion with the orb. A ribbon of white hot energy rocked through me. Every nerve shrieked as my blood seemed to boil within my veins.

"He said he wanted you alive." Another twist of the orb brought more anguish. "He didn't say unharmed."

Through the blazing light, I saw Andrew run at the robed man, but he too, was blasted across the room. I wanted to scream, but couldn't take a breath. My body jerked on its own accord. I cried out, at least in my mind, for the searing pain to stop.

And it did.

The bolt of light streaming from the orb to my body broke off. The robed man looked down in surprise. Then he caught sight of the sword protruding through his stomach. The crystal dropped from his hand, shattering on the tavern floor. I collapsed to my knees on the table, fighting to regain the use of my muscles.

The robed man fell face down. Kyran stood behind him, holding his bloodstained weapon.

Get to the second floor. The Black Guards are almost here.

I couldn't get my legs to cooperate. Each time I tried to put weight on them, they slid out from under me like a newborn colt's.

Devnet struggled to his feet. He eyed the door, but turned away when he saw the people still trying to push their way through. He stumbled toward me. Kyran yanked my uncle up by his arm and pushed him onto the table. He lifted Devnet toward the balcony. My uncle pulled himself up as the dark man turned to me.

"Move," he ordered. I grasped his arm and dragged myself to a standing position. Sidon and Vaschel stirred on the ground as a scream rose from the patrons near the door.

"Black Guards!"

The mass of people was blown from the exit as if a bomb exploded. Bits of the stone wall flew around the room like shrapnel. A smell like burning electrical wire filled the air. Kyran grabbed me by my waist and heaved me toward the balcony. My arms didn't have the strength to pull my body up. I fell back onto Kyran as two Black Guards strode in.

I'd never seen them up-close before, so I hadn't appreciated their size. They stood well over six feet. Everything about them screamed power; from their massive shoulders to their trunk-like arms and legs. Black leather covered their entire bodies, even their faces. Only their mouths and noses were exposed. Their teeth looked more like fangs and saliva dripped from their purple lips. Their pig-like snouts sniffed at the air as they swept into the room.

Kyran swore as he pushed me off and thrust me up to the balcony again. Devnet grabbed onto my hand. I managed to swing my legs up to the second floor. I lay sprawled on the balcony for a moment, trying to catch my breath.

Sidon and Vaschel pushed through the patrons that hadn't been injured in the blast. Once clear, they ran toward the Guards with their swords in front of them. The Black Guards lifted their hands and the brothers froze. Their swords clattered to the floor. The room filled with their high-pitched screams.

Devnet knelt beside me and grabbed my head, forcing me to turn away. "Do not look."

Kyran pulled me to my feet then kicked a door open. "Out the back window!"

I heard a sickening pop and turned back to the scene below. The brothers' bodies lay on the ground, a mass of blood and pulp where their heads used to be. The crowd shrieked in panic. Andrew flew at the guards, freezing the same way Vaschel and Sidon had.

Devnet pushed me through the door. Andrew's cries rose above the shouts of the patrons, followed by the same revolting popping noise. My knees buckled at the thought of Andrew's headless body falling to the ground. Kyran dragged me toward the window in the far wall.

My uncle squatted on the stone sill then thrust himself off. He let out a yelp as he hit the ground. Kyran lifted me onto the sill. Devnet lay in the dirt, his back arched with pain.

The dark man swore under his breath. "Bend your knees and roll when you get to the ground." He shoved me out of the window. I didn't have much choice as I landed. I had little coordination in my legs after the orb's electrocution. I hit the ground, collapsing in a heap. Devnet lay off to my right, writhing.

Kyran dropped down and rolled to his side. He jumped up, opened a gate next to us, and led out two horses.

I crawled to my knees. "He won't be able to ride with a broken leg."

Kyran glowered down at me. "Then he will die." He dragged

Devnet up and held him by the shoulders. "Is it your leg, man?"

"My ankle," Devnet gasped. "I can ride."

Kyran waved me over. "Let him lean on you while I boost him up."

Devnet wrapped an arm around my shoulders. He grunted when he had to put his weight on his injured leg so he could place his foot in the step Kyran made with his hands. The dark man hoisted my uncle up onto the horse. Devnet cried out but stayed on the beast. Kyran stroked the horse's nose and whispered something I didn't understand. Then he struck the horse on its hind quarters. It leapt through the gate, past the crowd streaming into the alley.

The tavern shook with another explosion. Kyran mounted the other horse, reached down, grabbed my hand and pulled me up behind him in one, fluid motion. His feet dug into our mount's sides and we galloped into the falling dusk.

A thunderous blast echoed behind us. The Black Guards stepped through the rubble of the tavern where we had just stood.

Devnet's mount galloped ahead of us, seeming to know the urgency of our plight. Devnet lay slumped over the horse's neck. I didn't know how long he'd be able to hold on. The horse turned another corner with Kyran and I close behind. People scattered out of our path as we pounded down the cobblestone alleys.

We came to a kind of open marketplace in the middle of town where merchants and peddlers packed in their wares as the sun set. They cursed at us as we crashed through several tables. Kyran let Devnet's horse speed down another street but pulled our horse up.

"People of Cyrene! Listen to me!"

Some merchants threw fruit at him. Others cursed as they tried to rescue their goods.

"Listen! This is your queen. If you want the heir of Etain to rule this land, you have to help us. Do what you can to block the Black Guards!"

A silence fell on the crowd for a moment until the drumming of the Guards' horses could be heard coming toward us. Kyran spurred our mount to follow Devnet's path. The peddlers pulled their wagons and tables in front of the alley we'd come through. Within moments, the Guards' way was clogged with rows and rows of obstacles.

We sped down several more streets before coming to the city wall. Uniformed guards lowered an iron gate as the city prepared for nightfall.

"Hold!" Kyran cried as we sped toward the barrier.

The guards didn't hear him or didn't care. The iron bars dropped further.

"Duck!"

Kyran folded himself against the horse's neck and it lowered its head as we charged forward. We skimmed under the falling gate to the cheers of rowdy townspeople unaware of the terror we were fleeing. I let out a shriek as one of the bars snagged my headdress, ripping it off.

As we galloped across the plains, I could see the outline of trees on the horizon. It had been a couple of months since I had been horseback riding, a year or two since I'd done it bareback. My legs could barely keep me on the horse.

Kyran reached behind him with one arm to pull me upright. "By Epona! Can you not stay on?"

"I'm trying!"

"Try harder!"

Did he think I wanted to fall off and into the hands of the Black Guards? Shooting pain stabbed through my thigh muscles as I forced them against the horse's side. Lifting my head, I tried to spy Devnet.

"Where's my uncle?"

"Seanna knows the way."

"Seanna?"

"The horse."

I tried not to let panic overtake me as we approached the forest. I glanced behind us, relieved I couldn't see any signs of the Black Guards. Yet.

Kyran looked back over his shoulder. His eyes appeared black in the dim twilight. They smoldered with rage. I turned away from him in fear. His anger pulsated from him. I could feel it all around me as we rode on. I had no choice but to tighten my arms around his waist and hope I could trust him.

We raced into the woods. Kyran seemed to have an idea of where he wanted the horse to go as we careened through the trees. We came to a stream. The cold water splashed up my legs. We followed it as night fell, sinking us into darkness. Kyran halted the horse.

He dismounted into the stream and lifted his arms up to me.

"What are we doing?" I asked as he helped me down.

"Hopefully, creating a diversion. Take off your dress."

I tried to step away from him, but his horse blocked my way. "What?"

"They cannot see as we do. They'll be following your scent and the sound of the horse. If Braga carries your dress in another direction, and we follow the river, we should be able to fool them."

This wasn't like stripping in front of Tegan. I'd had a blanket and Tegan hadn't hated me. And he'd been my size. This man had three inches and at least fifty pounds on me.

Kyran fisted the filmy cloth of the wedding dress before tearing it off me. I tried to take it back but he swore and pushed me into the water. He tied the ruined garment around the horse's neck.

I was left wearing only a long, linen slip. Kyran stroked the horse's nose, whispering in the same unintelligible language he'd spoken to Devnet's horse. I took the opportunity to get to my feet and run. The horse galloped out of the river to my left as I splashed awkwardly toward dry ground on my right. It took Kyran seconds to catch me. He seized my arm, yanking me to his chest.

"What are you doing, fool?"

I took the heel of my palm and pounded it into the bridge of his nose. His grip loosened enough that I could wrench myself free. I'd only taken two steps when he grabbed me again. He swore as he took hold of my wrists and pulled me against his body.

"Do you want to die?"

I didn't know what he planned to do with me. I could only shiver with cold and fear.

"Well?"

I shook my head.

I cried out when he tightened his grip on my wrists. "I'm trying to help you."

I growled under my breath, "By breaking my arms?"

He held me so close I could see his eyes burning, even in the dark night. "If I let you go, will you not run away?"

I scanned the black woods around me. What choice did I have? I nodded.

He let go of one arm. When I didn't try to escape, he loosened his grip on the other. Before I could pull free, his fist tightened again. I yelped.

He stood frozen for a moment, his head cocked to one side. His fingers dug between the thin bones in my wrist.

I tried to pry his hand from my arm. Kyran shook his head as if I'd woken him from sleep. He covered my mouth with his other hand.

"Do exactly as I say and you may yet get out of here alive."

He kept me muzzled as he forced me to kneel with him in the water, our eyes level with each other. He must have read the panic behind mine because the hardness had left his voice when he spoke again. "The Black Guards are close. I need you to lie down, putting as much of your body under the water as you can to keep them from catching your scent. Do you understand?"

His hand rose up and down with my nod.

The dark man let me go with a slight push and I flattened my back onto the silt. No more than a foot of water flowed along this part of the stream. I tried to dig my limbs into the mud so that my trembling wouldn't be seen. I lowered my head so that only my nose rose above the surface.

The horses' hooves echoed down the stream and thudded in my ears. When the pounding stopped, I held my breath and put my whole head under the water. My lungs burned sooner than I thought they would. I lifted my head up, so I could breathe. I spotted Kyran, two yards down the river. The Black Guards loomed over him. He patted the nose of one of their mounts then pointed in the direction his horse had galloped off with my dress.

One of the Guards raised his chin and sniffed. I slipped back under the water. It seemed like minutes, but it must have only been a few seconds, before the Black Guards thundered off after Kyran's horse. I poked my nose out again to breathe, but waited until I saw Kyran's shape standing over me before I sat up. I used my arms to cover my chest, knowing the thin slip would show everything when wet.

He lowered his hand toward me. "I think it may have worked."

I stayed in the water and washed as much silt off of me as I could. Kyran took off his shirt then held it out. I stood and put it on. It fell to the top of my thighs, the soft fabric offering warmth to my arms and chest.

He waited a moment. "Are you ready?"

"Now what?"

"Try to keep up."

He turned and ran in the river. I followed. The streambed was free of rocks and my feet didn't sink far into the soft bottom. Patches of moonlight danced atop the water, but for the most part, I ran with only the dark man's silhouette to guide me. It wasn't much to go on, but it's all I had.

CHAPTER TWENTY-FIVE

Into the Fey

We ran.

And ran.

And when I thought I couldn't go another step?

I ran some more.

I concentrated on Kyran's shadow ahead of me. Nothing else. If I let myself think about my uncle, my breath would catch and I'd stumble. Kyran never slowed when I fell so I'd have to fight my panic and fatigue and immediately get up and start running again.

If I thought about Andrew or Sidon or Vaschel, my stomach would knot and my throat would burn from the bile that rose from my gut at the memory of their headless bodies. I learned to swallow it back down. I'd stopped once to get sick and lost Kyran for several minutes before catching up with him.

My brain drifted to some new place. A place with only one thought. One goal.

Live.

And at this point, the only way to live was to follow Kyran.

I was so focused on this task that when he did stop, I plowed into his back. My legs gave out and I fell. In my exhaustion, I tried to breathe, but only succeeded in taking in a lungful of the stream.

Kyran yanked me out. I choked and belched at the same time. He pounded on my back until I coughed up the water. He tried to let me go, but I sank into the stream again.

He put his arms under my shoulders and dragged me to sit in a shallower area by the bank. "What is wrong with you?"

My body convulsed in a fit of laughter and tears. My voice came out in a shrill shriek, "Are you kidding me?"

He put his hand over my mouth. "Be quiet."

My exhaustion forgotten for the moment, I yanked his hand from my mouth and snarled, "Don't. Do that. Again."

His hand swung toward me as if he was going to slap me but he pulled it back at the last moment. He stared, saying nothing, until his breathing slowed to a normal rate. "Wait here."

I grabbed his wrist. "Where are you going?"

He pulled himself from my grasp. "Just wait here."

I tried to stand but could only get to my knees. "For how long?"

Kyran stepped past me onto dry ground. He delivered his orders in an angry whisper, "Remember. As soon as you leave the river, the Black Guards will be able to pick up your scent. Stay there and I'll be back."

I sat down in the water but found even that too tiring. The stream was only about six inches deep along the bank. I lay back and stared at the tiny piece of sky I could see through the trees. Gray clouds sped across the clearing above me, masking the silver moon. The cold water soon numbed my exhausted body.

I don't remember falling asleep but I must have because Kyran shook me awake some time later. He pressed his index finger to my lips to keep me from crying out.

"You must get up now. Only a little farther, then we'll take a raft across the river."

I let him pull me up. He waited before letting me go until I'd stood for a couple of seconds without falling. I forced my legs to take a step. He nodded and started down the stream. I dragged my feet forward, sloshing the water up around me. Unwanted tears poured down my face. I didn't have the energy to stop them.

I'd lost all sense of time. We may have travelled for minutes or it may have been hours before Kyran turned around and walked back to me. Without a word he picked me up, cradling me in his arms. I rested my head against his chest, still crying silent tears. He carried me out of the stream and through the forest, until we came to a river. The current ran fast enough that I could hear it splash against the shore. It was too wide to see the other side.

"Can you stand again?" He whispered as he walked into the water.

I nodded.

He grunted as he lowered me into the river. I gasped. This water was much colder than the stream we'd been in. The current tugged at my slip. Beside us lay a raft, the kind Huckleberry Finn rode down the Mississippi.

Kyran waved me forward. "Help me pull it out into the water, then jump on."

I stared at the twigs wrapped together by fraying rope, then at the river. It had to be at least a half mile wide.

Kyran pushed the back half of the raft. "Come on, pull!"

I grabbed the front corner and dragged it into the river. The water came up to my thighs before Kyran told me to climb on. I belly flopped on to the raft, fearing if I tried to sit on the edge, the thing would flip over. I squirmed across the branches until my whole body rested on it.

Kyran sat on the corner for a moment before swinging his legs over. He picked up a pole that lay next to me and stood. I let out a squeal as the raft rocked from side to side but I didn't move. Kyran shifted his weight until the raft balanced itself. He used the pole to push us across the river.

I lay with my cheek smooshed against the wood, too tired to lift my head. Water splashed up the sides and through the cracks between timbers but the raft stayed afloat. The moon hung low and the sky along the horizon showed the tell-tale signs of the coming dawn.

Kyran grunted as he pushed the pole through the river. I made out a dark mass on the other side. At first I thought it might be mountains, but as we got closer, I saw the ragged tops of trees. This forest was denser than any I'd been in so far, the trees so close together and so tall, I wondered if the coming sunlight would be able to get through. My heart sped up.

"That's the Fey, isn't it?"

"Aye."

I wished I had the energy to roll over to see his face, but I didn't. "I was told not go through the Fey."

He grunted again. "I wasn't."

I hated the taste of fear in my mouth. Dry like cotton, but hard as metal. I knew if Devnet or Andrew or even Tegan were with me, I wouldn't be this afraid. But I still knew next to nothing about the dark man behind me. The little I did know didn't make me feel better. Besides seeming arrogant and condescending, he knew my enemies. I had seen the Portal in the tavern nod at him. I'd also seen how Kyran communicated with the horses as well as the Black Guards. But if he was on the bad guys' side, why was he helping me escape?

I thought about what I'd overheard from Simon in the Sanctuary. Plenty of men in Ayden wanted me to help them achieve their own goals. Kyran must need something from me. It's the only reason he would fight his loathing to help me escape.

Trees stood like sentinels along the shore as far as I could see. The raft struck a rock, punching the air out of my lungs. Kyran dropped the pole and jumped into the water. He pushed until the raft came to rest in the mud.

I shoved myself into a sitting position. My head swam in exhaustion but I forced myself off the raft. I stood, shivering, ankle-deep in the water.

"Wait here." Kyran ordered. He picked up the front end and lugged it some distance into the trees.

He returned a minute later. He stared as I stood slumped-shouldered where he'd left me. "I should make you walk but I don't think you'd make it two feet."

Even my annoyance at his insult didn't give me the energy to straighten up.

He lifted his head and scanned the opposite bank. "Besides, I wouldn't put it past Braedon to find a way to allow his demons into the Fey." He looked back at me. "Do you think you could hold onto my back?"

"What?"

He turned around. "Put your hands around my neck and I'll carry you."

I shook my head. I hadn't had a piggy-back ride in years.

"Come now. The sun'll be up soon. We must get hidden."

His voice wasn't exactly friendly, but he didn't sound as angry as he'd been earlier. I stepped toward him, put my hands on his shoulders and pushed myself up, wrapping my legs around his waist.

He groaned and muttered something under his breath.

"What?"

He shifted my legs and arms to make himself more comfortable. "I said, you had to take after Geran in size."

"You knew my father?"

Kyran didn't answer as he set off into the Fey. I clung to his shoulders, careful not to wrap my arms around his neck and choke him. His smooth skin radiated heat, even in the cool air. He couldn't run with my extra weight but he moved quickly through the dense trees. I guessed the sun came up only because the forest came alive with bird songs, not because any light made it down to us. He carried me for a couple miles before setting me down in a circular clearing about ten feet in diameter.

He moved a boulder and brushed away dirt and leaves with his foot. Reaching down, he fit his fingers into a small hole in the ground and pulled. To my surprise, he lifted up a flat piece of earth. I realized after a moment that it was a wooden door disguised with sod and leaves to look just like the forest floor around us.

Kyran pointed down the hole. "Welcome to my home."

CHAPTER TWENTY-SIX

Down the Rabbit Hole

I took a step and stared down the black opening. "Are you some kind of rabbit or something?"

Kyran chuckled under his breath. "More of a fox. When you live in the Fey, you learn to be crafty. Now get down."

Every fiber of my rational mind told me to run away. Sixteen years of news and cop shows warned me not to let this stranger take me into his house, and yet, I didn't have any other choice.

His impatience sparked his anger. "I'm not carrying you any further. Go!"

I swallowed my fear and made my way down the hole. From above came a scraping noise and a soft thud as Kyran closed the "door" to his home. I stopped for a moment to try and bolster my courage as an oppressive darkness surrounded me. Kyran stepped on my hand.

"Ouch!"

He lifted his boot. "Why are you not moving?"

I resumed my descent. "Excuse me for being a little scared about climbing down a pitch black hole with a perfect stranger."

He snorted.

"It's not funny." I missed a rung and swore under my breath as I dropped to the next one. "I miss electricity."

A soft yellowish glow rose from below giving at least a little light to my way. I climbed down the last eight rungs and found myself in a large cave.

Kyran jumped down beside me then crossed the thirty feet to the other side of the room. I could barely make out his shape in the dim gray. As I took a step toward the center of the cave, the light pulsated. I looked around to find its source and saw another of the small orbs like the Portal had carried, sitting in an alcove to my right.

My muscles spasmed as they remembered the agony that thing caused. I looked to the shadows to see what Kyran was doing. He had his back to me. His arms jerked several times and I heard a faint scratching noise.

My gaze alternated between the ladder and orb. I considered my options. I could either try to escape back up the ladder, which was pretty unlikely, given Kyran's speed; or I could make a run for that evil crystal and smash it before he used it to shock my body.

A light sparked in front of Kyran and he lit a lantern. I figured I'd missed any chance to get a head start up the ladder so I opted to make a dash for the orb. It blazed purple as I raced toward it.

Kyran howled with rage, "Stupid girl! Don't touch it!"

My hand froze above it. "I won't let you hurt me."

He took a step toward me.

I lowered my hand so it stood only a half foot from the orb. "Don't come any closer."

He stopped. I could see the fear in his eyes.

The crystal gave me power over this dark man. I tried to sort out the myriad of questions spinning around my exhausted brain. My hand trembled.

Kyran swore. "Step away from it before you kill us both."

"Who are you?"

If I wasn't so terrified I would have laughed at the comic surprise that flashed across his face. "What?"

"Who are you? How do you know my father?" Every fear I'd lived with throughout the night came spilling out. "Why do you hate me? Where's my uncle? How did you know the Portal in the tavern? Why do you have one of these things?" My hand inched closer to the orb.

He reached toward me. "Pull your hand back." When I didn't move he grimaced as if he were in pain. "Please."

I lifted my hand away, but only a little.

Kyran's shoulders sagged. "Have you not seen an Elderstone before tonight?"

"The Portal in the forest, Quinn, had a bigger one. Treasa called it a Chrysaline."

Kyran looked like he wanted to ask me a question but he clenched his jaw and took a deep breath instead. "The Chrysaline is more powerful. There's only one Chrysaline, but many Elderstones."

"I've only seen men who work for Lord Braedon with them."

He lifted his arms to his sides. "They were originally a tool only of the Elders. When Braedon corrupted the Portals, he gained their power."

My heart skipped a beat. "Are you a Portal?"

He shook his head. "No."

"Then why do you have one?"

"It was given to me."

"By who?"

He licked his lips.

I raised an eyebrow. "Was it Braedon?"

"No." He kept silent, as if considering his answer. "One of the Elders."

"Why?" I studied him. He looked more like the Elders I'd seen in the Sanctuary than any of the Commoners. "Are you one of them?"

He let out a bitter laugh. "No."

My hand reached for the orb. "Look, you'd better start giving me some answers right now or I'm smashing this thing."

His voice echoed off the stone walls. "No!"

I could see him struggle with his desire to try and force me away from the Elderstone. I kept my hand poised above it.

Kyran closed his eyes. "If you touch it, all of Braedon's Portals will know exactly where you are. It wouldn't take long before the Fey, even this cave, would be filled with them."

"You might be telling me that just so I won't destroy it."

"It's the truth."

I stared at him, trying to read his face.

Nothing.

I thrust my chin in the direction of the back wall. "You step over there and I'll pull my hand away."

Kyran stepped backward until he stood by the lantern he'd lit.

I kept my end of the bargain and took my hand from the Elderstone. "Start talking."

"What do you want to know?"

"Who are you?"

"My name is Kyran."

I let out a growl. "I figured that out in the tavern. I know you're not one of the Commoners, they can't do the things you do. And if you're not an Elder, that only leaves one of the Mystics, and from what I've heard, they're not my friends."

Even with the glow from the lantern, his face darkened. Sadness and anger filled his voice. "I am nothing."

I trembled, both at his tone and the chill in the cave. My wet clothes clung to my skin. "What do you mean?"

He lifted his head. "My mother was one of the Elders. She was raped by a Mystic soldier during the last uprising. She died in childbirth. None of the Elders wanted to raise a bastard child conceived through violence. They brought me to the Mystics."

The coldness of my skin sank into my heart as I listened to his story. "What happened then?"

The dark man shrugged. "They raised me, but I was never accepted as one of them." He lifted his hand and stared at it. "My dark skin marked me as an Elder." He turned his arm, as if seeing it for the first time. "One of the enemy."

He dropped his arm to his side. "I had no standing in the community. When I turned fifteen, I ran away and sought out a home with the Brethren. I thought surely they would accept me."

"But they didn't?"

"The Brethren would have been happy to let me live among them." He glared at me. "But for your father."

My stomach rolled. "My father?"

Kyran nodded once. "The Keeper of the Keys, a man named Aren, sent word to King Aldred of my request. He left the decision to his most faithful counselor, your father. Geran met with me in the Sanctuary, then advised Aren not to take me in."

"Why?"

"He had his reasons."

I could tell Kyran hid something. "What were they?"

The dark man shook his head. "They're not important now. Suffice to say that I had nowhere to go. I'd abandoned the Mystics and been outcast by the Brethren. I took the only course left and joined the outsiders who live here in the Fey."

I stepped away from the Elderstone. Emotional and physical fatigue washed over me and I leaned against the wall. "Is that why you hate me? Because of my father?"

He frowned. "I don't hate you."

"Yes, you do. I can feel it."

Kyran's body tensed. "It's not you I hate."

"Then what?"

His hands clenched and unclenched at his side. "It's being forced to do something I don't want to do for people who discarded me."

"I don't understand."

"I inherited the gift of the unseen world from my mother. Even though the Elders didn't want to train me. I used my abilities to my advantage, predicting rain or droughts for profit. I got paid to lead travelers through the Fey because I could sense where trouble hid and steer clear of it."

Kyran lifted his head. The glow from the lantern reflected off his smoldering eyes. "And then, last year, I got my first glimpse of a Messenger. I tried to ignore him. I wanted nothing to do with any of them, Elders or Mystics." He shook his head. "But the Messenger was insistent. By the end, it was either do the will of Ruahk, or go insane."

I listened to Kyran's rapid breathing, waiting until it slowed before speaking. "What did the Messenger want you to do?"

A soft, sharp laugh escaped his throat. "Guide you to the Elders."

Kyran and I stared at each other in silence before the absurdity of our situations registered in my head. Both of us were stuck doing something we didn't want to be doing, with people we didn't want to be doing it with. Not only that, but other people wanted to kill us for doing the thing we didn't want to do.

I snickered under my breath.

Kyran's quizzical look made me laugh harder. I grabbed my stomach and slid down the wall until I sat on the ground.

The dark man raised an eyebrow. "Are you unwell?"

That started another fit. It was either that or cry. "I'm sorry . . . ." I managed to squeak out between giggles. "I'm sorry for everything."

He shrugged. "It's not your fault."

"I wasn't laughing at your story." I wiped my eyes. "I want you to know that."

He cocked his head. "Then what?"

I tried to slide myself back up the wall, but didn't have the energy. I collapsed to the floor. "Don't you find it funny that the two people who least want to be in this position, are in it?"

The corner of his mouth rose. He snorted softly. "I suppose you're right."

I rubbed my arms, trying to warm up a little.

Kyran walked over to a ledge in the cave wall. He pulled out a shirt and threw it over to me. "Put this on."

"Aren't you cold?"

He took out a pair of dry pants. "These'll do for now." He walked over to the back corner. I turned away from him so we could change clothes in relative privacy. I looked over when I heard his footsteps approaching.

He handed me a blanket. "Try and get some sleep." He stared at me a moment, as if weighing something in his mind.

"What is it?"

"I know you fear the Elderstone, but it's only a danger if you touch it. Or if someone desires to inflict pain."

I covered myself with the blanket, waiting for him to tell me whatever else he needed to.

"I must use it."

I shuddered. "What for?"

He squatted down in front of me. "The Elders gave it to me once they knew I would help you. I need to call to them. They can send us horses for the journey. Otherwise it will take us two or three days to get through the Fey."

I could see he understood how much I feared the orb. "Go ahead."

He stood up. I flinched as he took the Elderstone from the alcove. He carried it to the far corner of the cave then sat down, cross-legged, with the orb in his lap. The light turned to white. Kyran closed his eyes. His lips moved, but I didn't hear any words. I watched him for as long as I could before exhaustion overcame my will and I fell asleep.

CHAPTER TWENTY-SEVEN

Friends No More

I woke to the smell of ginger and garlic. My mouth watered. I opened my eyes, confused by the gray light that surrounded me. I rolled onto my back and looked up at a wet stone ceiling about fifteen feet above me.

"It's about time."

I sat up, struggling to remember who belonged to the familiar voice. Kyran squatted in the center of the cave near a circle of burning embers. He had a blanket almost the same brown hue as his skin draped over his shoulders. Wisps of steam rose from a pot that sat on top of the glowing timbers. He reached to his side and picked up half a loaf of bread.

"The Elders sent food as well as horses."

I caught the bread he tossed to me, eating several bites before speaking. "How long have I been asleep?"

"It's night again." He stirred the contents of the pot with a stick. "We'll leave before the dawn."

I finished the bread. "What are you cooking?"

"I caught a squirrel when I retrieved the horses. I've made a stew."

Squirrel stew. Wonderful. My stomach growled as I caught a whiff of it. "Smells like curry."

The dark man nodded and stood up. He walked over to the base of the ladder then opened up one side of a leather saddlebag. He drew out a dark bundle. "They sent this for you."

I tried to stand, but fell back to my knees with a groan. Sleeping in a cold cave after running through the night had caused my muscles to freeze up.

Kyran shook his head as he handed me the gift.

"What?" I asked.

He ignored me and returned to his pot.

I hated when people had things to say, but wouldn't say them. "What is it?"

He looked annoyed. "Will you put those on so I can have my shirt back?"

I guess whatever friendship, if you could call it that, we'd formed this morning had faded. Perhaps I'd only dreamed it. I undid the twine tied around the package and unfolded a hooded cape of deep green wool. The cape wrapped more clothes.

I pulled out a shirt made of golden thread. I had no idea how thread like that could be made in a place like this. It caught even the muted light in the cave and shimmered. A pair of cream pants, made of soft wool, came next. Under that, I found a long jacket, made of the same material as the pants. My hand traced the subtle design embroidered in cream and gold thread that decorated the front of the jacket.

I looked up at Kyran. "It's beautiful."

He kept his head lowered.

My stomach knotted. They hadn't sent him any new clothes. He still wore what he'd had on earlier. His other pants and the shirt he'd let me wear hung on a boulder drying.

I pushed the clothes off my lap. "This sucks."

He lifted his face to me, his eyes narrowed.

"It isn't fair. It wasn't your fault what happened. They should have sent you something to wear."

"I have dry clothes." He glowered at me. "If you'd give me my shirt."

I used the wall to help me stand up. Kyran muttered behind me.

"There you go again." I whirled around to face him. "What am I doing that's bothering you so much?"

He stared at me with a sullen expression. "You can barely stand. How're you going to ride a horse for a full day?"

"I just woke up. Once I stretch out the kinks, I'll be fine."

He kept silent, stirring his stew.

My muscles rebelled when I bent to pick up my new clothes, but I wouldn't give Kyran the satisfaction of groaning. I carried the Elders' gift to the back corner of the cave and turned away from him. I pulled the pants on under my slip, enjoying the instant warmth they gave me. I took off his shirt. Part of me wanted to toss it on the ground behind me, but I swallowed my annoyance and folded it then placed it at my feet. I hesitated to take off the slip, afraid Kyran might be watching me, but all he would see was my back. I pulled it over my head and put the gold shirt on. The fabric felt like silk against my skin.

Finally, I put on the jacket. For the first time in a while, I was warm. Slits had been cut up the sides and back of the jacket so even though it fell past my knees, it would be easy to ride a horse. The buttons started at the waist and continued up to a high collar that hid most of my neck. I wanted to ask Kyran's opinion on how I looked, but figured that wouldn't be a good idea. Instead, I picked up his shirt and brought it to him.

"Thanks again."

He shrugged the blanket off his shoulders and put on the shirt without looking at me.

My new jacket, though formal, wasn't constricting. I walked back to the corner and did a few stretches to loosen up. Despite some popping and pain, I enjoyed the exercise. My muscles reveled in the opportunity to stretch without adrenaline rushing through them.

After several minutes, I sat cross-legged and rested my hands on my knees. I closed my eyes, took a deep breath then exhaled slowly. I thought about Devnet. I wondered if my mind could reach out to him like I'd been able to with Kennis.

Don't.

I opened my eyes to find Kyran staring at me. "Why not?"

"If you haven't been properly trained in spirit travel, you could wind up anywhere. The first rule is, you have to know where you're going."

"Can you always hear my thoughts?"

"Only when I concentrate on them. I could tell you were being stupid."

I bit my lip to keep from saying something sarcastic. "I'm worried about my uncle. Where did you send him?"

"He's with the Elders." Kyran stood. "He's safe." He walked to the saddlebag and pulled out another loaf of bread. He ripped off two pieces. He held one out to me.

"Here."

I took the bread and started to eat it.

"Save some." He sat down by the pot then took it from the embers, placing it at his side. He dipped the bread into the stew and used it as a spoon. He didn't invite me to sit, but I did anyway.

We didn't talk as we ate. I tried to steer clear of the squirrel meat but the broth and carrots had a pleasing curry flavor. The thick sauce warmed my stomach and reminded me of a stew Kennis liked to make in the winter.

I missed her.

I wish she were here to help me get through all this. I wanted her to hold me, rub her hand on my back, and tell me everything would be all right. I forced myself to swallow. The stew turned to lead in my stomach as I fought off the wave of homesickness that threatened to overwhelm me.

I finished the bread, then turned to Kyran. "Thank you. It was very good." I stood up. "When do we leave?"

Kyran swiped the last piece bread several more times around the bowl before shoving it into his mouth. "Now."

He used a cloth to wipe the pot clean. Standing, he kicked dirt onto the embers he'd cooked on. He packed the pot into the saddle bags. While he prepared for the upcoming journey, I put on the green cloak the Elders had sent me. I guessed the heavy fabric would even keep me dry if it rained.

I wriggled my toes. "They didn't happen to send me shoes, did they?"

Kyran put out the lantern. "A man on your quest wouldn't wear them."

I couldn't make out his expression as the cave grew dark. "Excuse me?"

He strode past me and picked up the saddlebags. "You're wearing the outfit of a Bedouin pilgrim."

"But did you say a man?"

Kyran started up the ladder.

"Why a man again?"

"Because Braedon searches for a girl. By now the people of Cyrene will have told him of your outfit. He knows the Bedouins helped you, it makes sense that one of their princes would seek the Elders for aide."

So I'm supposed to be a prince now? I wondered if there were rules Bedouin royalty had to follow, but didn't have the courage to bother Kyran with more questions.

He pushed the earth door aside then climbed up into the Fey. I crawled out behind him. He closed the cover, replacing the boulder he'd removed in the morning. My head swam. Had we been here less than a day? The hazy darkness of the pre-dawn night stretched its fingers over the clearing, but because we'd spent the hours in the cave, my eyes had little trouble seeing.

"Put up your hood."

I scanned the clearing as I obeyed his command. "Where are the horses?"

He took a few steps into the wood. He bent his head down as if in prayer. A moment later he turned back to me. "All you need to do is stay on the horse. Do not try to steer her. I'll be telling her which way to go. Understand?"

"But what if—"

He held up his hand. "No matter what happens."

"Fine."

Two horses galloped into the clearing—one, a deep chestnut color with a black mane and tail. The other, a dappled gray with silver hair. Kyran's demeanor softened as the horses approached him. He spoke to each, rubbing their noses and kissing them between the eyes. I laughed to myself. If they had been dogs, I think they would have rolled on their backs so he could scratch their tummies. He mumbled something to the gray. They turned to look at me. I swear they both snickered.

"What are you saying about me?"

Kyran ignored my question. He led the gray over and gave me a boost up before mounting the chestnut horse. We headed into the trees. My mount followed without me signaling to it. We trotted at an easy pace for several miles. I got my balance, feeling how the horse moved underneath me and adjusting my weight accordingly. My legs, after resting all day then being stretched before the ride, had no trouble holding on.

Ready?

Yes.

Kyran kicked his mount in the flanks and galloped out of sight. The gray followed him. I resisted the urge to try and lead the horse as we sped through the Fey. Instead, I lowered my eyes, concentrating on the gray's neck, trying to lessen the sick churning in my stomach from fear and the jostling of the horse.

Random golden beams of sunlight broke through the dense branches, lighting up our way. We rode at a gallop through most of the morning. I wished I knew how to communicate with Kyran using just my mind, but so far I'd only been able to receive messages from people who knew the art. And my dark guide, just like every other man in Ayden except for Brice, wasn't much for conversation as he travelled. I smiled as I thought of Brice and Tegan. I'd felt safe with them, even after Tegan had pointed an arrow at me. The two of them were . . . normal, like me. They didn't talk with their minds or zap me with crystals. I missed them.

In the early afternoon, Kyran must have signaled the gray to slow its pace. We came to a pond. Kyran slipped down from his mount, then pulled something wrapped in cloth out of the saddlebag. I jumped down before he could make his way over to me. The horses meandered over to the water to drink.

Kyran grabbed a canteen. He passed it to me without saying a word.

I sipped as I walked to the pond. A dark blue sky reflected off the mirror-like surface. A few puffy clouds dotted the otherwise clear heavens. The sun stood past its high mark, so I guessed the time to be about one. I drank again then gave the canteen back to Kyran.

He'd taken out some leftover bread, unwrapped a hunk of cheese and placed them on a piece of woven cloth on the ground. I sat down next to the food then started to lower my hood.

Kyran put his hand out to stop me. "Leave it."

I scanned our surroundings. "Are we being watched?"

"Not that I can tell. But it's best to be safe."

A thin line of sweat trickled along my hair line and down the back of my neck, but I kept the hood up. Kyran took out a knife to cut a wedge from the cheese. I ripped off a piece of bread to make a kind of open faced sandwich.

We ate in silence, finishing the bread and cheese while the horses drank their fill of water. Kyran shook the crumbs off the small blanket before putting it back in the saddlebag. We remounted and, with another silent signal from Kyran, galloped around the pond back into the woods.

After about an hour, I let myself relax. My horse didn't need me to guide it and the scenery hadn't varied much in the miles of ground we'd covered throughout the day. I tried not to let my mind wonder about my future, as fear would start to reach its thorny tendrils from my stomach, up my spine and into my thoughts. Instead, I concentrated on the lyrics to a song we'd been singing in choir before . . . well, before everything had changed.

The gray lurched forward. I clutched its mane to keep my balance. My eyes shot open to see Kyran galloping ahead.

We're being followed.

I searched the surrounding trees, but couldn't make out anything but branches.

I cannot tell who, but it's not the Guards and they are not spirits. That is why I didn't sense them earlier.

I lowered myself closer to the gray's neck as we thundered through the forest. The horses zigzagged sharply. I pressed my thighs tight against my mount in an effort not to fall. The gray's breath came in hot, heaving gasps. We galloped hard for several more minutes before Kyran pulled his horse up to a stop. The gray slowed and trotted next to him.

"I cannot lose them," Kyran panted. "The horses are too spent from the morning's ride."

"What'll we do?"

"If I cannot talk our way out of this, I'll hold them off while you ride to the Elders."

"But—"

Kyran's hard countenance silenced my objections.

We trotted forward at an easy pace. Kyran stopped his mount as a horse whinnied off to our right. I turned to see a man about Kyran's age riding toward us. He appeared to be naked at first, but then I realized his pale skin was the same color as his filthy white shirt.

A branch cracked to our left. Another man meandered through the trees. This one older, maybe in his forties; stocky, bald, but with a thin black mustache and bearded chin.

Kyran patted the chestnut's neck as he watched the strangers approach. He nodded toward the younger man. "Samuel. What brings you this way?"

Samuel returned the nod. "I could ask ye the same thing." He lifted his chin toward his partner. "This is Kyran, Father. I've told ye about him."

Samuel's father squinted at me. "And who is this?"

I kept my neck bent to better hide my face. Kyran kept his eyes on the older man. "He is a pilgrim. I'm leading him to the Elders."

The two came closer.

"I have nothing, Samuel." Kyran raised his arms to his sides. "You know that."

"Aye, I know."

"And pilgrim's travel with none of their wealth. You know that as well."

Samuel nodded.

"Then what do you want?"

The older man circled behind me. "What's your name?"

"Vaschel," I answered, trying to make my voice lower.

"What's this about?" Kyran asked.

Samuel glanced at his father, then back at Kyran. "Have ye not heard the news?"

The dark man shrugged. "I hear a lot of news. What in particular?"

Samuel's father came along side me. "Lord Braedon's searchin' for a girl. A young woman."

Kyran acted the part of interested bystander well. "What is her crime?"

My mount sidestepped away from the stranger as he spoke. "He'll not say. But there's a hefty reward for the man who brings her in."

Samuel trotted up closer. Kyran did a good job of looking unconcerned, but I couldn't keep my muscles from going taut with tension. The gray sensed my nervousness, her hooves danced on the ground.

Kyran patted the gray's nose. "He thinks she's gone into the Fey?" He shook his head. "We've seen no one but you, and we've been riding since the early morning."

The older man reached over as if to grab my hood. Kyran's sword swung up so fast, I heard it whistle past my ear.

"You'll not touch him. He's on sacred business and my customer." The dark man's eyes flickered between Samuel and his father. "I'm being well compensated to see him to the Elders."

Samuel drew his own sword. He pointed it at me. "It seems we are at an impasse. You harm my father, I kill your Bedouin." His barely existent lips curled into a sinister smile. "I hope you've already been paid."

We stood as if frozen in time, Kyran with his sword to the old man's throat, Samuel with his sword at mine.

I'd had enough. Samuel was focused on Kyran, so I whacked the flat side of his blade with the back of my arm. "I'll thank you to take your sword from my throat." The move surprised his horse. Samuel bobbled for a moment to regain his balance.

My own horse skittered backward and, with a look from Kyran, bolted around Samuel into the forest. "No!" I cried and yanked the gray's mane in an effort to turn it around. The horse stopped short, nearly throwing me onto the ground. The sharp clang of swords echoed through the trees.

I turned around and caught sight of Kyran striking Samuel's sword away, as his father unsheathed a bow and nocked an arrow.

"Go!" The dark man swung his weapon in defense. His black eyes flashed with fury. "Go now!"

My horse sprinted forward. The gray's pounding hoof beats drowned out the sound of the fight. I gasped as intense pain shot through my shoulder. I wanted to cry out but couldn't take a breath. Sweat poured from my forehead. I tried to wipe it from my eyes, but when I moved my right arm, something stabbed me again.

The Fey darkened as if the sun had set at mid-day. My head grew heavy, too heavy for me to keep it up. I collapsed onto the horse's neck, groaning as each stride brought new agony searing through my body. Warm sweat covered my back. My hands went numb. I couldn't make them hold onto the gray's mane. The horse turned sharply. I knew I should squeeze my leg muscles into the beast, but I couldn't feel anything below my waist. I found myself weightless for a moment as the horse flew out from underneath me.

Then I hit the ground.

CHAPTER TWENTY-EIGHT

The Power of the Fallen

I lay on my side, my cheek pressed against the dirt. Sweat and tears pooled around my head, turning the ground into mud. I gasped for air like a fish out of water.

The gray trotted back to me. She let out a whinny and poked me with her nose. I couldn't make a noise even though my body screamed as if burning flames licked my back. The horse stood over me and whinnied again.

The realization broke through my half-conscious thoughts that I was dying. I would die in the mud in this stupid other world and no one would know. Not Kennis, not Josh or Renee. I doubted even Devnet would know where I ended up.

Hoof beats vibrated through the ground into my brain. I pretended to be dead already. Maybe Samuel and his father would leave me here. I don't think Braedon would give them the reward if they brought him my body. He'd wanted me alive, of that I was sure.

The rider stopped. The gray stepped away from me.

"Stupid girl. Why did you turn back?" Kyran knelt by my side.

"I thought . . ." It hurt to breathe. "I could . . ." I gasped again. "Distract them."

He growled, then rolled me onto my stomach. I shrieked at the excruciating pain.

"Hold still a moment."

I would have laughed if I wasn't dying. *Where would go?*

A sharp crack splintered the air. My mind went blank. When I came to, Kyran had me sitting up and was wrapping my torso with cloth. I looked closer, and realized it was a strip of my jacket he used as a bandage.

I tried to keep his face in focus as he leaned down to speak to me, but I couldn't. Sometimes he seemed to have four eyes and two noses, sometimes only one of each, but I heard his voice clear enough.

"I cannot take the arrow out. You'll bleed to death before I get you to the Elders." He slipped his arms under my shoulders. "This is going to hurt, but try and stay with me. You must get on the horse."

I screamed as he lifted me onto my feet.

"Stay with me, girl. Stay with me."

I panted hard, but forced myself to keep awake.

Kyran spoke to the chestnut horse. Lilting syllables of gibberish to me but the animal understood. The horse bent its front legs to kneel. Kyran sat me so I would ride backwards. He sat facing forward, shifting my body so I rested against him. His dark face appeared just inches from my own. "Now hold on while she stands. That's the last I'll ask of you. Can you do that?"

I nodded as my lungs heaved for breath. He called out to the horse and patted it on the rear. I started to slip as she pushed herself upright but Kyran's strong hands forced me back up. "Stupid girl." He wrapped his arms around my waist to grab the horse's black mane. "Why could you not do what I said?"

I drifted between dreams and reality, but had trouble distinguishing the two. Real life had become its own nightmare over the past week. When my eyes were open, I saw monstrous trees looming overhead. Their branches reached toward me as if they wanted to pluck me from the horse and swallow me inside their trunks. My body alternated between periods of numbness and moments of torture, depending on the movements of the horse.

Black Guards invaded my thoughts. Their snout-like noses sniffed the air. I could see them catch my scent then race towards us. I knew if they found us I wouldn't die quickly. Even in this half-conscious vision, I sensed them feeding off of my pain. It drew them toward me like sharks to fresh blood.

I relived the scene in the tavern and the blood soaked floorboards under the bodies of my friends. I heard Eben's cries as someone brought him the headless corpses of his eldest sons. The wails of his wives echoed in my mind as they clutched their ruined children.

Kyran's voice roused me. I don't know whether he spoke aloud or not, but he called me back from my visions. "Do not let your thoughts travel. Stay with me."

But I couldn't.

I dreamt of home. I cried out for Josh. Since second grade, he'd been my protector. He'd nursed every emotional wound. Could he help with this physical one? I heard his voice, as if he stood at the end of a long tunnel, but I couldn't see him. I pleaded with him to help me, but all he could do was call my name, as if searching for me.

I cried out to Kennis. I begged her to make Geran bring me home. They could heal me there. They'd give me drugs for the pain and surgeons would remove the arrow and sew up the wound.

A woman appeared. Tendrils of gray hair floated around her face, having escaped from the long braid that lay over her shoulder. Her blue eyes reminded me of Geran's—sparkling and intense. The lines around them indicated her worry and yet she smiled.

"Hold on, Alystrine. We can heal you. Hold on."

Andrew's screams interrupted her. I replayed the healer's death cries over and over in my head. I searched for his wife. His children. I wanted to tell them I was sorry.

Kyran shook me awake. "Stay with me!"

My hands clutched at Kyran's shirt. My body writhed as I tried to ease my pain.

"We'll be there soon."

My gaze drifted upwards. The sky shimmered pale blue. No clouds. "Where are the trees?"

"We're almost out of the Fey."

I closed my eyes.

A new voice beckoned to me, "Alystrine."

Its deep tone filled me with peace, "Alystrine. Do not fear me."

A sensation of warmth flooded me, as if I stepped into a bath. The pain ebbed away.

"Come to me. Let me tell you the truth. It is not what you have been told."

I let myself drift toward this new speaker. My body weightless, I took to the sky.

"Yes, Alystrine. You will know everything. Come to me."

Kyran called out, his voice filled with rage, "No! You will not have her. Not this way!"

My thoughts turned from my flight, to Kyran. I could see him stop, then shake my body. My consciousness was pulled in two directions; one side toward the beautiful voice that promised me knowledge, the other toward the dark man, desperate to see me to the Elders.

Kyran's fist pounded against my wound. The resulting agony reunited my body and my soul. I let out a wail as the punch reverberated through every nerve. An unholy roar resonated in my head as I opened my eyes.

Alystrine!

"Do not listen to him." Kyran's brown hand gripped my chin. He stared into my face. "You must stay awake." He let go, then kicked the horse into a gallop. I dug my fingers into his flesh as each step jolted through me like a knife. "We're almost there."

We broke through the last of the trees, the blue sky turning pale gray with the coming sunset. The visions no longer waited for me to close my eyes. I could see them, even as I looked at the sky. Hundreds of Black Guards thundered through the Fey, my pain a beacon for them as they crashed through the trees.

"Do you see them?" I asked Kyran.

"Who?"

"The Guards," I wheezed. "Can't you feel them?"

He kicked at the horse's flanks. "It is a dream."

"I don't think so." My vision of the Black Guards melted as I watched the pink rays of sunset streak across the clouds. My skin prickled with goose bumps, even as sweat continued to pour from my forehead. My stomach churned. I clutched Kyran's shirt, trying to shift my head so I could see his face. Whatever I sensed, I could tell he felt it too. His eyes scanned the horizon as if searching for something. He pulled me into his chest, then turned the horse sharply to the right.

I would have screamed if I had any strength left.

"Someone's coming," Kyran growled. "I cannot tell who or from where."

A strange sound of rushing wind filled my head, as if someone opened a door during a hurricane then slammed it shut. Kyran swore and stopped the horse. My head lolled to the side. I could make out the shapes of two men standing in front of us, both in dark robes. A light surrounded them.

"Quinn?" Kyran shouted. "How did you get through the barriers?"

The light around the men dimmed. I recognized Quinn from my first night in Ayden. The wizard who'd told me where to find help. He held the Chrysaline again in his hand. "An Elder can always come through."

Kyran's eyes narrowed. "He's an Elder?"

I struggled to see who stood next to Quinn.

"Faolan?" I croaked through my cracked lips.

The bald man smiled up at me. "Yes, Your Majesty." He looked up at Kyran. "Give her to us. We will see that she is safe."

The dark man pressed me close. I grunted in pain. My mind drifted into darkness. The three men spoke, their voices loud, but their words indistinguishable as I drifted in and out of consciousness. It wasn't until I heard a higher, female voice that I forced myself to wake up. But that meant I felt every fiber in my shoulder shriek in pain as the arrow tore at the muscle.

"Faolan?" A woman spat. "You would betray your people?"

Betray? How? Isn't he here to help?

"I'm doing what I think is best, Maris, for all the people of Ayden."

Maris? Where had I heard that name before?

I opened my eyes. Five horses stood near us, with a hundred more still a mile or so behind them. I recognized one of the riders as the older woman who'd spoken in my dream. The kind eyes I'd seen then now burned with venom. The gray-haired woman continued to glare at Faolan. "And what do you get for your help, Keeper? What has the Lord Regent promised you?"

Wait . . . isn't that Braedon?

The bald man smoldered, but didn't lose his temper. "The time of the Elders has passed. I look to guide our people into a new age."

Maris shook her head. "Do not lie to me. You seek the power of the Fallen. You have chosen evil over Ruahk."

"Enough!" Faolan roared. "I will take the queen to Lord Braedon. Whether you believe I act for our good or not, I will have her."

He was going to give me to Braedon? But I thought he was one of the good guys.

The gray-haired woman raised her arms. "Will you fight the power of the Elders? You cannot win!"

A sinister grin crept across Faolan's lips. "But we have the power of the Fallen." He turned to Quinn. "Call them."

The Portal seemed to sicken at the command, but he held the Chrysaline out and stared into it. A low buzz vibrated in the air as the army of Elders approached. From the trees behind us came a deep rumbling, as if the side of a mountain crumbled in an avalanche. I managed to turn my head in time to see hundreds of Black Guards pour from the Fey. The movement sent another bolt of pain through me and I blacked out.

I only stirred when Kyran shook me awake. He whispered into my ear, "No matter what he says, do not believe him." His brown eyes stared into mine. "Do you understand?"

"Who?" I croaked. "Faolan?"

He shook his head before Faolan's voice demanded, "Give her to me."

The dark man lowered me toward the Keeper, who grunted as I fell into his arms. He carried me toward the Black Guards. Panic consumed me. My panting grew faster as we drew nearer to the giant beasts.

I grabbed onto Faolan's robe. "You're not going to give me to them?" I could barely get the words out. "Please!"

His eyes held no compassion for my fear. "You are too weak to travel through a passage. They will get you to Lord Braedon safely."

I tried to push myself away. I tried to see Kyran's face or Maris's. "Please! Help me!"

Kyran galloped around the black horde into the Fey, abandoning me. Maris reached her hand out. "Do not fear, Alystrine. Be strong."

A massive leather-clad arm yanked me up. I shrieked in pain and terror as the Black Guard sat me astride the horse so I faced his massive body.

Faolan's voice rose up from below. "You may not harm her. She must arrive to Lord Braedon safe." He took a step closer and spoke in a low tone. "But when you reach the Fey . . . Break her."

The beast grunted, expelling breath that smelled of sulfur and decaying meat. I retched and threw up over the side of the horse.

The Black Guard let out what I could only assume was a laugh. Its voice scratched through my brain like nails on a chalkboard. It laughed again, leaning its snout down to my neck and inhaling deeply. My heart froze as it let out a contented purring sound. Somehow I knew what it was doing. It was drinking in my pain and my fear, reveling in whatever power it gave him. It breathed in again, letting out a victorious howl before turning its mount toward the Fey.

CHAPTER TWENTY-NINE

The Breaking

As soon as we entered the forest, I comprehended what Faolan had meant by "break her." It wasn't my body they sought to destroy, but my mind. My captors didn't have to slow down our flight to attack me, they did it with images thrust into my thoughts. Far worse than my own imaginings, the assault began the moment we crossed into the Fey.

I saw a cave filled with snakes. Hundreds dangled from the ceiling, thousands slithered across the floor. Then, I stood in the cave. Two giant serpents dropped from above me, each wrapping around one of my arms. The reptiles squeezed tightly, lifting my hands over my head. I struggled, but couldn't escape. Cold, dry scales writhed against my skin as smaller snakes climbed my body. More fell from the ceiling, coiling themselves around my shoulders, hissing into my ears. One wrapped around my neck. Its black and green scales crept past my eyes as it raised itself up in front of me.

The familiar man-faced serpent from my hallucinations in the Sanctuary stared into my eyes. "I told you, Etain's child, you are ours. There is no escape." I screamed in terror as the demon hissed out a laugh. It plunged into my mouth. I gagged as it thrust itself down my throat.

My body shuddered. I shook my head to clear out the sensations of the nightmare. I tried to focus on the Fey and the horses and the pain in my back, but another vision rammed its way into my thoughts.

Devnet's body lay on the ground, a Black Guard by his side. The beast knelt and took off its leather gloves. Thick brown fur covered its hands. Claws slid out from its fingertips.

My uncle moaned. His eyelids fluttered opened. He shrieked as the Black Guard stood over him, then reached down and ripped Devnet's chest open with its claws.

I couldn't look away.

I couldn't close my eyes.

These visions weren't anything I could control.

I was forced to watch as the monster stabbed his hand into Devnet's body. My uncle's screams ended as the creature pulled out his still beating heart.

My own voice took up his cries. "No! No! No!" I pleaded with my captor to stop the vision. The psychological torture kept coming. I watched the Black Guard take a bite of my uncle's heart, heard its blood curdling roar of victory as blood dripped from its mouth.

On the ground, the flesh rotted off Devnet's body. Maggots spewed out of his eyes and nose. I could hear myself begging the Black Guard to make it go away. I couldn't watch anymore and yet I had to. A giant spider crawled out of Devnet's mouth and my stomach retched again.

My muscles convulsed. For a moment, I felt myself falling, but then the brutal hands of the Black Guard pulled me back.

Back into the horror of another nightmare. Rusted chains bound Kennis' wrists to the ceiling of a stone cell. Blood ran down her arms in tiny rivers. Her blonde hair lay plastered against her head with sweat. Her tattered clothing revealed the bruises, welts, and open wounds of her torture.

A wooden door creaked open. My heart broke as my mother whimpered at the sight of the Black Guard. Kennis had never looked so frail and afraid.

"Not again!" She begged as the guard approached her. "Not again . . . not again . . . ."

The beast laughed, a cackling grunting sound, as it reached out to grope her body.

I couldn't watch as this demon raped my mother.

I wouldn't watch. My mind went numb with despair. I dug a hole deep within myself and tried to crawl inside. I prayed to die.

Around me, the shouts of the Black Guards rose in what sounded like a celebratory growl.

Listen.

A familiar voice whispered from somewhere inside me.

Girl, listen.

Was it Quinn? Kyran? Devnet? I couldn't tell, but I clung to the words like a piece of driftwood on an angry sea.

Do not let them break you. Focus inside. Turn your thoughts to your own heart.

I couldn't fathom how to stop the images being pushed into my brain. How? My mother's cries tore at my heart as the Black Guard forced himself on her.

Do not let yourself believe these things. Make your soul a fortress. Focus on all the good you know.

Once again my consciousness seemed to separate into two pieces. One watched in mute revulsion as the Black Guard repeatedly attacked my mother. But another concentrated on my life back home. I wrapped myself in sunsets down on Hammonasset Beach, warm spring rains, my mother's laugh.

Keep yourself locked there, no matter what else they show you. Do not turn to emptiness and despair or you will be lost. Do you understand?

I thought of Tegan's kiss, of Josh's hugs, and Renee's bright smile, even as another part of me watched the Black Guard slowly peel the skin off my mother's body.

I stayed in the cocoon of my memories until excruciating pain wrenched me back to reality. I opened my eyes to find myself laying on my stomach. I tried to flail, to jerk my body from whatever tried to rip it apart, but I couldn't move. My arms had been tied above my head to a hook in the wall. A leather strap had been stuck in my mouth. It may have been put there to keep me from biting my tongue, or maybe to stifle my screams.

Quinn's voice spoke from somewhere above me. "I told you she would need some kind of painkiller."

Something rooted inside me, pulling and yanking at my shoulder, telegraphing agony to every nerve in my body. My eyes searched for someone to help me. I hollered in protest.

"Stop this instant," Quinn ordered. "We cannot torture her like this."

For a moment my torment eased, then I heard Faolan's voice. "Her mind has been broken. Any physical pain she feels will soon fade to the memories of the Breaking. Continue."

I tried to tell them the Guards hadn't broken me. They ignored my sobbing pleas. Again something tore at my back. Adrenaline pumped through me and I kicked out as hard as I could.

Metal clattered to the floor. Someone swore. A new voice shouted, "I cannot work like this!"

I twisted my body as far as I could to the side. Quinn's pale face looked down at me. He took the strap from my mouth.

"Alystrine? Can you hear me?"

I was breathing too rapidly to answer him. Instead I nodded.

"Do you know . . ." He paused for a moment, glancing toward Faolan. "Do you know who you are?"

I nodded again.

Faolan glowered. "That is impossible."

"I'm . . ." I tried to catch my breath. "Ally Foster." I gasped for a few more seconds. "Daughter of Etain and Geran."

The Keeper's face hardened into a mask of anger. "No one can endure the Breaking of the Black Guards."

"I have," I said through clenched teeth. Someone tried to grab my legs. I thrashed on the bed, sending more pain through my body. "Don't touch me!"

A stranger knelt down by my side, an older man with pale skin and graying black hair. He held my shoulders. His strength surprised me. I couldn't budge him. He waited until I stopped trying to get away before he spoke.

"We have to remove what is left of the arrow." His breath popped and rattled as he spoke, like he'd smoked a pack of cigarettes a day. "The wound is beginning to fester. It cannot heal if we leave it in. Do you understand me?"

I nodded.

His soft hazel eyes stared into mine. "Malina can give you something to dull the pain. It won't take it away entirely, but it will help. Will you take it?"

I paused before nodding again. I had nothing to lose.

An old woman came behind him. Small and wrinkled, like an apple left too long on the window sill. She placed a hand on the old man's shoulder. "What has happened?"

"She needs something for the pain."

Her bright green eyes bore into mine. "You still have your mind, child?"

"Yes."

"Impressive." She walked away, returning a minute later. Her fingers played with something in her hand. She rolled whatever it was into a tiny ball before moving the old man out of the way. She knelt by my head. "Open your mouth."

Fear kept my jaws clamped tight.

The stranger's eyes filled with understanding. "I promise. It will dull the pain. Nothing more."

I opened my mouth and she placed the ball of leaves on my tongue. "Chew it."

As my teeth crushed the pill, my mouth filled with a bitter tang like aspirin, only with a citrusy after taste. I chewed and swallowed it as fast as I could.

The woman nodded. "I'll leave you in Greer's hands now to get the arrow out, but I'll be back to see how you are healing." She patted my cheek. "Be strong. It will be over soon."

Once she left the room, Faolan glared down at me. "How did you do it? How did you keep from going mad?"

"You gave me to those monsters." The leaf-pill burned my throat. "Why would I tell you anything?"

The Keeper reached out as if he was going to slap me, but the old man pulled him back. "Get out!" Faolan struggled against him but the old man held firm. "Guards!"

Several men in leather armor dragged Faolan from the room. Quinn knelt by my side as the old man swore several times and picked some metal objects off of the floor.

The Portal put a hand on my arm. I tried to pull away. His eyes saddened and he withdrew his touch. "I am sorry. For everything."

I wanted to be angry with him, but the medicine in the leaves fogged my brain. My body grew heavy.

"Turn her over," ordered the old man.

I grunted out a "no," even though my tongue felt twice its normal size.

"What's wrong? Is the drug not working?"

I licked my lips, trying to concentrate on forming my words properly. "Clean."

The old man's eyebrow's furrowed together. "Clean what? The wound has been cleaned."

"Clean the . . . the . . . ." I couldn't think of the word I wanted to say. "The stuff that fell on the floor. Clean it first."

A quizzical look crossed his face. He put a hand on my shoulder, but I scooted away.

"Clean it."

Quinn stepped forward. "What harm can it do, Greer? Give them to me."

Greer handed him the tools.

I fought to stay alert. "Alcohol."

Quinn stopped. "What?"

"Clean them with alcohol."

Greer frowned. "The alcohol won't help your pain."

"I know. Just do it."

The old man shrugged. "The captain probably has something. Douse the tools then bring them back." He turned to me. "Then can I do my work?"

I nodded.

Quinn left and Greer rolled me onto my stomach. My eyes struggled to stay open as he prepared to remove the arrow. He took a washcloth and wiped my back with cool water. He squeezed the blood-soaked cloth into a bowl then dipped it in fresh water to wipe my back again.

Quinn returned with the tools, putting them on the end of the bed. He picked up the leather bite strap. "You may need this again."

I opened my mouth and he slipped it in. He stepped away, out of my view. Greer leaned down. "Are you ready?"

I nodded.

I still felt Greer as he dug the arrow out of my back, but the drug deadened my reaction to the pain. I simply didn't care. That is, until the final tug before the muscle in my shoulder gave up its prize. Then a scorching fire ripped through the narcotic haze. My body twitched uncontrollably. My jaws snapped down in agony. My last thought before I passed out was that I was glad I had let Quinn put the leather strap back in my mouth, or I would have bitten my tongue in two.

CHAPTER THIRTY

Lord Braedon

A Black Guard held a wicked looking knife to my mother's throat while she sobbed. The knife sliced her neck. I screamed, jolting awake as the monster began to peel the skin from Kennis' face.

I lay on my stomach, my shoulder throbbing dully. My arms were at my side. The floor beneath me rocked. My stomach did a small flip.

The old woman hurried into the room. She placed a hand on my uninjured shoulder. "Do not try and move yet. Do you need something for the pain?"

"No." I thought maybe the drug caused my brain to remember the Black Guard's torture. I'd lived through it once, I had no desire to keep repeating it in my dreams. "Could I have some water?"

She filled a wooden cup then held it to my lips while drank. She wiped my chin with a towel she then tucked at her waist. The old woman sat down next to me and tugged gently on the bandages on my back. She made a hissing sound when she saw my wound.

"What's wrong?"

She rummaged through a saddlebag. "It's not healing as well as I'd hoped."

The bed rocked. I groaned as my stomach lurched into my throat. "What is that?"

Malina turned back to me while she mixed something in another cup. "What?

"Why is the bed moving?"

"We're on a boat." She came back and sat on the bed, placing the medicine next to her. She dug her fingers into the cup, lifting out a yellow paste. She rubbed the paste into my wound.

The medicine burned. I sucked a breath through clenched teeth to keep from crying out. The sensation dulled after a moment. Malina administered another glop before wiping her hands clean on the towel at her waist. She pulled a small roll of linen from her bag and covered my back with strips of the cloth.

The boat rocked again, waking me out of the stupor I'd let myself drift into while the old woman worked. "How long?"

"Hmm?" Malina tore off another strip. "Have you been asleep? Only a few hours."

"No. How long until we get to Lord Braedon?"

The old woman paused. She rolled the remaining linen back into a ball that she put into her bag. "We will be there before nightfall."

"When is that?"

"No more than three hours. The current is running swift today."

Oh, goody. I'll arrive early. I pretended to fall back to sleep.

The old woman shuffled around the cabin, muttering under her breath. I couldn't make out the words. A few minutes later someone else entered.

Malina grunted at the intruder. "What do you want?"

"How is she healing?" Quinn's voice inquired.

"The wound's infected."

One of them stepped closer to the bed. I kept my eyes shut.

"How is she?" Quinn asked.

The old woman let out a strangled laugh. "After all you've put her through, you have the gall to ask how she is?"

"I didn't–"

"Do not try and lessen your guilt. You transported Faolan to the Elder Lands. You helped Faolan give her to the Black Guards. I do not know how the girl survived the Breaking. I have seen it destroy the minds of far stronger men."

The two fell silent for a moment. I thought I'd fallen asleep, but then Quinn spoke again. "That is where Braedon has underestimated her. He thinks she's weak."

Malina sighed. "Do you know what he has planned for her?"

"A little," Quinn replied. "But the fact that she isn't broken will slow him down. I do not know what he'll do next."

"Can you sit up for me?"

I opened my eyes to see Malina's deeply lined face and green eyes. She placed her hands under my shoulders then lifted me into a sitting position. I marveled that I didn't shriek from the pain, but my mind was consumed by the sensation that my body was on fire.

The woman's bony fingers worked deftly to wrap my shoulder and torso in fresh bandages. She tied my right arm down against my side so

I couldn't move it. Through the haze of fever, I could see blood and pus stained bandages on the floor.

"I told Faolan it would be no bother to see you properly wrapped."

My head lolled to my shoulder, my neck too weak to hold it up. The woman looked into my eyes. "The fever is bad, is it?"

I panted through my nose and nodded.

"We'll find you something, don't you worry. Once you're settled in the palace, we will make you well."

She draped a cloak around my shoulders and fastened the clasp. "There now. You look . . ." She lifted her eyebrows. "You look awful, but at least you're covered. We cannot have the future queen making her first appearance with her bosom hanging out for all to see. I told them it wasn't right."

I smiled weakly as the woman continued to babble. She fluffed up several pillows then propped me up against them so she could brush my hair.

"And who did this to you, poor child?" She smoothed the short locks away from my face. "I can tell you have beautiful hair, but mercy to Epona, they've cut it all off." She continued the soothing brush strokes. "It'll be no matter. It'll grow back sooner than you know. Then they'll see how beautiful you are."

Greer entered the room. He frowned. "Aye, Malina! What are you doing?"

She didn't look at him. "I'm making her Majesty a little more presentable."

He pulled the brush away. "She needs to be resting. The infection's raging through her. She does not need her hair fixed."

Malina stood. Even though she only came up to Greer's chest, I could tell she made a formidable opponent.

"Listen, old man. You're the surgeon. I'm the healer. The girl's been through plenty, so I've been told. She'll not want her people to see her for the first time with her hair awhirl and half naked."

Greer glared at her for a minute before his face broke into a wide grin. He leaned down and kissed her forehead. "I love you."

She lifted herself onto her toes so she could kiss his lips. "And I you." She glanced back at me. "Let me wash her face before they take her."

"Quinn has sent for a coach."

Malina soaked a cloth then sat on the bed and wiped my brow. I shivered. The cool water shocked my hot skin.

"It won't be long now," she cooed as she put the cloth against my neck. "Don't you worry. You will pull through this. I can tell. You're a strong one."

My breath sounded labored in my ears. My eyelids shut as Malina kept chattering.

"Can she walk?" Faolan's voice woke me out of my daze.

Malina mumbled something under her breath. It didn't sound good.

"No," Greer answered loudly. He stepped between me and the Keeper. "She'll need a litter."

"We don't have one. The carriage is at the end of the wharf. She'll have to walk that far."

Malina swore under her breath. "Are you deaf, man?" She stood. "Her fever's such she'd as likely fall into the river and drown as make it to the carriage."

"And I'm telling you Lord Braedon will not want to wait for a litter to be brought."

The tiny woman's face turned pink, then red. "You tell Lord Braedon—"

A commotion in the doorway cut her off. Several uniformed men crowded into the cabin. My irrational brain started to wonder how many people could fit before the bottom fell out of the boat.

And then I saw him.

He stood several inches taller than the soldiers, a good head taller than Greer. The sun streamed in through a porthole, illuminating his face.

Lord Braedon.

The Lord Regent stared at me from the doorway. His pale skin stood out in stark contrast to his thick black hair. A well-trimmed mustache grew into a charcoal colored beard. He reached out a gloved hand and rested it along the threshold.

"What happened to her?"

Except for my heavy breathing, no one made a sound.

His black eyes flashed in anger. "Who did this?"

Faolan swallowed hard. "My Lord, she was set upon by brigands in the Fey. She was shot with an arrow when she tried to escape them. We brought her to the healer as soon as we could."

Braedon nodded and took a step into the room. I held his gaze, trying to read what lay behind those dark eyes, but I couldn't.

Malina coughed. "Infection has set in, My Lord."

Braedon appeared not to hear her, but then he pulled his eyes away from mine. "How bad is it?"

She lowered her head. "It is bad, My Lord."

"What can be done? What medicines does she need?"

"I sent for my best herbs as soon as we made shore. They should arrive by the morning." Malina glanced in my direction. "If she can make it through the night, she'll have a good chance of surviving."

I trembled at her honesty.

The Lord Regent nodded. "As I came in you were saying they needed to tell me something. What was that?'

Malina took a moment to swallow. "The Keeper here was refusing to bring a litter for the quee— for the girl. Said you wouldn't wait for it to come." Malina threw back her shoulders. "My Lord, she cannot walk to the carriage."

Braedon stared at the woman for a moment, then looked toward me. "We cannot wait."

I could sense the anger boiling under Malina's skin. "My Lord, she cannot walk!"

"Of course she can't." He seemed surprised at her outburst. "I will carry her."

My muscles tensed. For over a week, I'd been told to fear this man. My fever-wracked brain couldn't comprehend the compassionate person in front of me. He sat by the side of my bed and took my hand. His brown eyes glistened with tears.

"Alystrine, I have longed for your return. I will do everything in my power to get you well. I am anticipating with joy the day you will sit on the throne of Ayden, as its rightful queen."

I tried to shake the confusion from my head, but the infection kept me unfocused and perplexed. This wasn't at all how I'd expected to be greeted. I didn't know how to react, what to say, so I didn't say anything.

He reached out, sliding one arm under my back and another under my knees. "I apologize if this hurts you. I will try and be as gentle as possible." He lifted me up with little effort. I let out a moan as my back throbbed. He shifted my body so that my head rested against his chest. "Are you ready?"

I gave him a slight nod and the Lord Regent carried me out of the cabin. He had to turn sideways to make his way out of the narrow corridor that led out onto the ship's deck. The cool air hit my face. My teeth chattered.

Braedon looked down at me. "Only a few more steps, then we'll be to the carriage." He pulled me closer to his body then stepped up onto a ramp. He smelled of well-oiled leather and some kind of spice. The breeze chilled the sweat on my forehead. I shivered.

From somewhere ahead of us, a horse neighed. The wind carried another sound I had trouble deciphering at first—the low rumbling of a thousand voices all talking at once. Braedon stopped halfway down the ramp and lifted his head.

"I hold in my arms the child of Queen Etain and the Elder, Geran!"

The steady murmuring swiftly rose to a cacophony of cheers. The shouting continued for what seemed like minutes before Braedon spoke again. "I call on you now, all of you; Mystic and Elder and Commoner alike, to pray for her. Pray for her health and recovery. Will you do that for her?"

The crowd I couldn't see roared their consent.

Braedon kissed the top of my head then lifted my body away from him. "People of Ayden, your queen has returned!"

The hem of my cloak fluttered in the breeze as the people welcomed me home. I groaned when the Lord Regent pulled me back against his chest to walk down the ramp. The cheering followed us even as Braedon stepped up into a gilded carriage and lowered me onto a cushioned bench. He tucked the edges of my cloak up around me before sitting on the opposite seat. He rapped the ceiling with his fist.

"As fast as you can to the palace. But mind you take the smoothest road as well." He ran a gloved finger across my cheek. "We don't want anything more to harm the queen."

CHAPTER THIRTY-ONE

Dying

I drifted in and out of bizarre dreams. Sometimes they were of home, but most were of what the Black Guards had shown me. Fortunately, the fever seared any lingering effects of the nightmares from my brain. The heat melted its terror and the images floated harmlessly in the nothingness of my mind.

What I saw when awake scared me more than the dreams. The fear behind Malina's eyes as she tried to get me to swallow the medicine she brewed. The way her fingers trembled as she cleaned my infected wound. She muttered under her breath as she worked. I think she was praying.

I didn't have the energy to take in a deep breath. I panted instead, as if I'd run a marathon. Every joint in my body ached. My skin hurt. I remembered enough from living with Kennis, a nurse, to know I was dying.

I'd just woken up from another nightmare, the one with the snakes, when Lord Braedon entered the room. I had no idea how many days I'd been sick. The light from the torches in the room burned too bright. I barely opened my eyes. I made out the Lord Regent's shape by the doorway.

"She isn't better," he said.

Malina bowed slightly from the waist. "No, sir."

"And why is that?"

The old woman shook her head. "I don't know."

"You don't know?"

"I've used my best medicines but . . . ." Malina's voice drifted off.

"But what?"

The healer took a step toward me. "I don't know what else to do."

An angry silence filled the room before Braedon finally spoke again. "You had better think of something. If she dies, I promise you, I will see you hanged in the market square, but not before you watch your husband and your children slaughtered before you. She must live! Do you understand?" Braedon stalked out the door.

Malina grabbed the bedpost.

"I'm sorry," I panted.

The old woman gasped in surprise. "You're awake."

I blinked as my eyes struggled to adjust to the light. "Unless you're a dream."

The corner of her mouth rose in a smile. She pulled a pot from the fireplace in the corner and poured steaming liquid into a cup. "Stay awake now for me. You need more medicine."

I studied the woman's hunched shoulders; the deep circles under her eyes and the lines in her face as she blew on the cup to cool it off. "He wouldn't do it, would he?"

"What?"

"Braedon," I tried to swallow. "He wouldn't really kill you, would he?"

Malina stopped blowing. A wisp of steam swirled up around her face, but it didn't hide the flash of dread in her eyes. She gave me another weak smile. "There'll be no need, will there? You're going to get better."

A wave of fatigue crashed over me. "I don't think I am."

The old woman slammed the cup down on the table by the bed. The scalding liquid sloshed over the rim onto her hand. She let out a shout and stormed out of the room.

My body wanted nothing more than to go back to sleep, but I felt bad about upsetting Malina. I edged myself to the side of the bed and was trying to sit up so I could reach the medicine with my good arm when Malina came back in the room.

She let out a shriek. "What do you think you're doing, child?"

I collapsed back onto the pillows, exhausted from my efforts.

"Are you trying to kill yourself?" She pulled the covers over me then held the medicine to my lips.

I closed my eyes as I sipped the tea. It smelled of lavender but tasted like eating a radish that hadn't been washed, all earthy and pungent. "I don't want to die."

Malina's voice quaked. "Hush, now. No talk like that. You have enough to fight without the spirits hearing you say that."

"I wish." The old woman made me take another drink before I could go on. "I wish I could tell my mom I loved her."

"A mother knows."

I took one more sip then fell back to sleep.

A Black Guard laughed as blood dripped from his purple lips. He held my uncle's half-eaten heart out toward me, as if offering me a taste. I screamed and tried to break out of the hellish vision. I thrashed at the beasts that kept me captive—kicking, hitting, punching at the claws that sought to hold me down.

And then I woke up. At least I think I did. Faces of men I didn't know stood over me. And there were hands. Lots of hands. They pulled me out of the bed and carried me down long marble hallways.

And then I was cold.

And wet.

I remember sitting in water up to my chest. Malina sat behind me. My body trembled violently. A strange sound came out of me—part moan, part scream.

The old woman grabbed hold of my shoulders, either she forgot about my wound or she didn't care anymore. She shook me hard. My head rocked back, pounding against her chest. She did it again. And again.

"You will not die! Do you understand me? I will not have it!"

I remember looking up into the night sky and thinking the stars were falling. Tiny white specks floated and danced around my vision. Malina wrapped her arms around me and sobbed onto my shoulder as my body shivered uncontrollably in the freezing water.

My pillow was wet.

And the sheets.

Everything felt clammy and cold against my skin. I wrinkled up my nose and groaned.

"Greer?" Malina's voice shouted. "Greer! She's waking!"

I turned my head, again surprised at the dampness of my pillow. "Why am I wet?"

"Why are you?" Malina laughed and clapped her hands. "Praise the gods!"

Greer stood by her side, looking down at me. "The fever's finally broke."

"Aye! Look at her eyes. Clear." His wife beamed. "Go tell Lord Braedon."

Greer hurried out of the room. Malina didn't move. She didn't even blink as she stared at me.

"I don't like being wet," I said.

That seemed to push some kind of button. She sprang into action. "Of course not. Let's see what we can do for you." She ran to the doorway. "Rhoswen? Fetch some new sheets and bring 'em to me. And fetch us a strong back along the way."

She ran over to the bed. "Not long now and we'll have you freshened up." She removed the covers, throwing them into a pile on the floor. She'd put on a pot of water to boil then washed my face with a cool cloth before the other servants arrived.

A red-haired girl about my age ran in, carrying an armful of linen; followed by a tall young man with a wild mane of yellow hair. They stood at the foot of the bed, waiting for Malina's orders.

"Colm, good lad! Come here." She waved the blond man over. "Pick her up."

His round cheeks flushed as he looked down at me. Bandages covered my chest but a linen half-slip was the only clothing I wore. Malina swatted his arm. "Do what I tell you, boy. We need to change out the sheets!"

His rather large Adam's apple bobbed as he leaned over and scooped me up. His eyes widened as I moaned in discomfort. He chanted under his breath, "I'm sorry, I'm sorry Your Majesty, I'm sorry." He lowered me back.

Malina swatted him again. "Don't you dare, you big lug. She'll be fine. Take her by the window so she can breathe some fresh air while I fix up the bed."

Colm crept toward the window with tiny steps, careful not to jar me. The young man's face paled as I grimaced.

"Don't worry," I whispered. "I'm fine."

He nodded, but his eyes revealed his concern.

I could just make out a faint yellow sun in an overcast sky and another wall of the castle outside the window. I shifted my gaze to the room. It was bigger than my bedroom at home, but not by much. A full-sized bed sat along one wall. Curtains hung from four tall posts at the corners, but weren't drawn closed. A fire burned low in the fireplace in the adjacent wall. On the other side was a large wooden table with two rung backed chairs.

Malina and the red-headed girl removed the sheet that had lay under me. They grunted in unison as they flipped the straw mattress over. Rhoswen fluffed it up. Malina put on new pillows while the girl put fresh sheets on the bed. Once that was done, the old woman waved Colm over.

"Now you can put her back."

Colm gently placed me on the bed so I sat up, resting against the pillows. Malina shooed the boy out of the room, then helped me put on a new slip. "Rhoswen, fetch the blankets like a good lass and bring them to me."

The red-haired girl rushed to do the old woman's bidding. The two of them stretched the heavy woolen spread over my legs.

"There now," Malina clapped her hands together. "How's that?"

"Much better."

Rhoswen bowed before leaving the room. From the hallway came the sounds of a near collision. A low voice barked, "Get out of my way!" while another apologized.

Lord Braedon entered. He stood flushed, as though he'd run the entire way. He grinned when he saw me sitting up in the bed. "Alystrine!" He bowed his head. "Your Majesty." He took several hurried steps to my side. "You can't know how relieved I am that you've recovered."

I still had no idea what to say to this man.

He was far less intimidating than the first times I'd seen him. Instead of the black leather armor, he wore only a white shirt, opened at the collar. His brown pants were tucked at his knees into leather boots. He reached for my unbound arm and lifted my hand to his lips. Then he sat down on the edge of my bed, still holding my hand.

He stared at me. "Can you speak?" His eyes darted to find Malina. "She can still talk, can't she?"

The old woman bobbed a curtsy. "Yes, My Lord."

He kept hold of my hand in one of his, while his other hand reached up to cup my face. "What is wrong? Will you not speak to your uncle?"

My heart raced and I tried to swallow. Too many thoughts crowded around my head. I couldn't seem to pick one out so I could verbalize it.

Braedon's dark brown eyes searched mine. The bright excitement I'd seen when he first sat down mellowed. "You are afraid of me, aren't you?"

I swallowed. "A little."

He lowered his head. "It is what I feared. Why I tried so hard to find you first."

"You? Afraid?"

"Aye." He lifted his chin.

He was a very handsome man; movie star handsome with well-proportioned features. He had eyelashes a girl would kill for, long and dark. A tear hung on one of them. He didn't wipe it away, even as it dropped onto his cheek.

"What were you afraid of?" I asked, feeling a little uncomfortable under his scrutiny.

"That they would turn you against me. You have to believe me, Alystrine." His fingers squeezed my hand. "I have only ever wanted you to sit on the throne of Ayden. It is my dearest hope."

Kyran's warnings came back to haunt me, believe nothing he says. I remembered the fear in Treasa's eyes as she spoke of the man sitting in front of me.

The tear that tracked down his cheek came to his chin. It dripped onto our hands. He lifted my fingers to his lips again and kissed them again. "You rest now. Perhaps, when you are better, you'll give me the opportunity to defend myself."

He rose from the bed, his broad shoulders slightly stooped. He nodded toward Malina in the corner. "Thank you. For all you have done. You shall be greatly rewarded." He walked over and placed his hand on Malina's shoulder. "Money? Land? Whatever you desire, it shall be yours." He patted the old woman's arm before walking to the door. He stopped in the threshold, turned back to me and bowed. "Your Majesty, I would come and speak with you again tomorrow, if you allow it." He seemed to be waiting for some kind of answer.

"Sure."

His lips rose into a smile before he bowed again and left the room.

CHAPTER THIRTY-TWO

Believe It or Not?

True to his word, Lord Braedon visited me after lunch the following day. Greer and Malina insisted I stay in bed, so the Lord Regent pulled a wooden chair over from the desk along the wall and sat it next to me.

His face glowed. "I cannot tell you how much the sight of you eases my heart. I have waited so long."

I smiled in spite of my reservations. "I don't understand."

"What?" He leaned forward. "What can I explain?"

I lowered my eyes. "Why the others were so afraid of what you'd do to me, if you really do want me on the throne?"

He placed his fingers under my chin to lift my head up. His brown eyes bore into mine. "I know this will be difficult, Alystrine, but you must try." His fingers left my face and found my hand instead. He circled the back of my wrist with his thumb. "The Elders wanted you to serve them. Be the ruler who would reinstate their authority and subjugate the others who live in this land. To do that, they had to convince you I was evil."

I thought about what Simon had said back at the Sanctuary. Everyone wanted to use me for their own advantage. "And what kind of ruler do you want me to be?"

When he chuckled, a spark lit in his eyes. "Whatever ruler you desire. But I hope a fair and just one. A queen for all of Ayden, not just the Elders."

That's what I wanted, wasn't it? And I thought that's what the Elders had wanted too. I stared at his thumb, still rubbing the back of my hand. "That's not what they said you wanted."

He snorted softly. "Let me guess, they told you I killed your mother. That I want nothing but my own power?"

I shrugged my one good shoulder. "Basically, yeah."

He dipped his head so he could see my eyes. "Alystrine, I swear to you, I did not kill Etain."

My stomach churned. My head hurt. What was real and what wasn't? "Then who did?"

"The Elders. They knew if the people believed I killed the royal family, they would fear me. They would refuse to accept my rule over Ayden and the Elders could keep their ideas of segregation and hatred alive for another generation."

He continued to stare into my eyes, so I shut them. I couldn't think straight anymore. "Go away."

Braedon let go of my hand. The chair scraped against the stone floor. He kissed the top of my head. "I know it is difficult when those you trust lie to you, but you must believe me. It is the Elders you need to fear, not me."

I kept my eyes closed as his footsteps walked away. They stopped for a moment. "May I come back again tomorrow, Your Majesty?"

I nodded.

He sighed. "I will continue to pray for your recovery. Good day."

Braedon came after breakfast the following day. He stood in the doorway and cheered me on as Greer and Malina helped me to my feet for the first time in I didn't know how long.

"I can stand on my own," I insisted, but the older couple wouldn't hear of it.

"And what if you fell?" Malina asked. "Can you imagine the damage you'd do yourself?"

"I feel fine."

The two led me around the room, one on either side of me. I gave Braedon a pleading look as we walked past him for the second time.

He grinned at me. "How do you feel now, Your Majesty?"

"I'm fine!"

Braedon took a step in front of us. "Why don't I take her for a walk down the hallway and back?" He chuckled at my healers' worried looks. "I promise, any sign of weakness and I'll carry her back immediately."

I could tell Malina and Greer didn't like the idea, but as I was the queen and Lord Braedon was the Regent, they had little choice. My uncle gripped my elbow. Together we stepped out into the hallway.

"Free at last! Free at last!" I muttered under my breath.

"What?"

I shook my head. "Nothing."

We walked in silence about fifty feet down the length of the hall.

When we got to a marble staircase leading to the floor below, we turned around. A thin opening in the stone wall let in light from the outside. I paused to look out.

A dusting of snow lay on the ground. The trees stood barren and brown.

My uncle tightened his grip on my elbow. "Are you well?"

"I haven't seen anything but that room in a while. How long was I sick?"

Braedon shifted so he too could see out the window. His chest pressed lightly against my back. "It's been eight days since you arrived here."

"Eight days?" I never assumed I'd lost that much time.

He placed a comforting hand on my shoulder. "I can't tell you again how grateful I am that you are well."

The snow outside reminded me of the night my fever had spiked. A small pond lay in the middle of the rectangular courtyard. I smiled to myself.

"What are you thinking?" My uncle asked.

"I think Malina put me in that pond when my fever got too high." I chuckled at the memory. "I remember I thought the stars were falling. I guess it was just the snow."

Braedon laughed. "The stars falling . . . that's very poetic."

I took a step back toward my room. Braedon shadowed my every move. I grew out of breath by the time we reached the doorway. My uncle swept me up into his arms and carried me to the bed.

"She did just fine," he answered Malina's worried looks. "But I didn't think she should overdo it on her first walk."

I groaned in mock exasperation, but the truth was I was glad he'd carried me the rest of the way. My legs trembled after just that small amount of exercise.

Braedon stepped away as Malina tucked me back into the bed. Greer gave me a cup of water. When they finished hovering, Braedon asked, "Do you mind if we talk more today, Your Majesty?"

I shook my head, glad to have something to do besides stare at the four stone walls of my room.

He pulled up the wooden chair again and sat by my bed. "Is there some question I could answer for you? Something that might help ease your mind about my intentions?"

I asked the question that had plagued me the most since I woke up.

"Why did you send the Black Guards to find me?"

"I can see how they would frighten you. They're intimidating are they not?"

"That's an understatement."

My uncle smiled. "You have to try and understand. The Elders hold all the power here in Ayden. We Mystics have some magic, some ties to the unseen world, but it is the Elders who control it." He rested his hand on top of mine. "I was desperate to find you first. The Black Guards were the only supernatural power I could call upon to aid me."

I thought about this for a moment. "What about Quinn and the other Portals?"

His gaze dropped from my face. "Without having met you, they wouldn't be able to find you."

"That's not true." I pulled my hand out from under his. "One of your Portals found me in Cyrene."

"Pure luck. I'd sent some of them to the river cities in case you traveled through. It was all I could think of."

"Then how did Quinn find me?"

"Through Faolan. Since the Keeper had met you before, could picture you in his mind, he was able to use Quinn and the Chrysaline's power to transport to you."

I turned my head away from him, afraid to ask my next question.

"What is it?"

I concentrated on the wall and tried to shut out the pictures flickering through my mind. All the scenes the Black Guards had forced me to watch. A lump lodged in my throat. I couldn't swallow.

Braedon put his fingers to my chin and gently turned my head to face him. "Alystrine, please. Whatever you need to ask so that I can prove I intend you no harm, you must ask."

I closed my eyes but the images of torture came in clearer. I sought relief in my uncle's concerned gaze. "How could you order them to show me those things?"

Confusion spread across the Lord Regent's face. "What things?"

I couldn't talk through my sobs as I struggled to regain my composure. Greer stepped forward.

"My Lord?"

Braedon jerked toward him. "What is it?"

The old man bowed at the waist. "My Lord, Faolan instructed the Black Guards to Break her."

Braedon's face paled. He turned back to me. "Tell me it isn't true."

The anger I saw in his eyes frightened me. It reminded me of the Braedon I dreamt of in the forest. My throat froze.

He grabbed hold of my hand. "I swear to you, Alystrine. Faolan ordered it without my approval. I would never do that to you." He put my hand on his heart. "I swear on my very life. I will not harm you."

I still didn't know whether to believe him or not, but he looked so sincere I nodded as if I forgave him. He kissed my hand and placed it down on my lap.

"Faolan will pay for his transgression. Believe me." His brown eyes burned. "He will not hurt you again."

With that, he stormed out of the room. Malina sat down on the bed. She lifted her arms to me. Sobbing, I fell into her embrace. Who told the truth? Who could I believe?

CHAPTER THIRTY-THREE

A Secret Lesson

The next afternoon, I insisted on bathing, as best I could, with only a small tub of water and my arm still bound. Braedon had provided me with a new gown of green velvet which Rhoswen and Malina helped me put on. It had been made for a larger woman, but the extra fabric allowed me to wear it over my bandaged arm and still button up the back.

"I look like a beached whale," I moaned as I flapped the empty right sleeve.

Rhoswen frowned. "And what is that?"

"It's a very large sea creature full of blubber."

Her eyebrows furrowed. "It doesn't show off your figure. That's for certain."

Malina shushed her. "Now don't be makin' the girl feel bad. She looks beautiful."

Rhoswen's cheeks turned almost the same color as her hair. She curtsied toward me. "Sorry, My Lady. I meant no disrespect."

I chuckled. "I'm glad to know you'll tell me the truth. It means we can be friends."

The red head's cheeks grew even pinker.

Malina clucked her tongue and fixed me with a stern stare. "I know you're feeling a bit lonely right now, Your Majesty, but you mustn't say things like that. Rhoswen and myself, we're but your servants. It wouldn't be right to be treated better than what we are."

"Where I come from, there aren't distinctions like that." I straightened my shoulders. "Anyone can be anything they choose and friends with whoever they want."

The old woman tilted her head. "But we're not in your world. You must live by the rules of Ayden."

A spark of defiance lit in my stomach. "Unless I change the rules, when I'm queen."

Rhoswen gasped. Malina's eyebrows rose in surprise.

I looked over at the younger girl. "What do you think we could do to make a dress fit better, while my dear nurse forces me to keep my arm wrapped?"

Rhoswen circled me, her face a mask of concentration. She circled me again then grinned. "I have it! Give me a day or two to work on it and I'll have a dress that'll fit you like a glove!"

"Wonderful! Go to it!"

The girl curtsied then ran to the door, pulling herself up short before colliding with Quinn.

Rhoswen curtsied again. "I'm sorry, sir."

"It's my fault. I should have announced myself first." He watched her leave then turned to me. "Your Majesty." He bowed. "It's good to see you looking so well. How do you feel?"

I shrugged my good shoulder, not sure what to tell him. Quinn was right up there with the people I wasn't sure I could trust. "I'm okay."

He shifted his weight from side to side, like a nervous high school actor. "I would like to discuss something with you. If you'd allow?"

I watched him for a moment, trying to get a read on him, but got no divine revelation as to whose side he was really on. With a nod of my head, I directed him over to the cushioned bench under the window. We sat and I waited for him to speak again.

He glanced at Malina. They shared an unspoken message. She nodded and went to the fireplace, her back turned to us. Quinn bent his head toward me.

"Your Majesty . . . I suspect . . . that is to say . . . the little I've heard about you revealed . . . ."

"Just say it!"

He lowered his voice. "Faolan suspected that you were gifted with at least some power of the Elders. Your ability to defy the Breaking may be an example of that." He studied my face. "Is it true?"

I hesitated. I still hadn't made up my mind about who I could believe. Quinn had brought me here, but he'd seemed sorry about it. He'd also given me advice my first night in Ayden, directing me toward Tegan's farm. "Why should I trust you?"

He started to answer, then seemed to think the better of it. "I cannot give you a reason."

I snorted. "Then I don't think I'll be telling you anything."

"I am not the bravest of men, Your Majesty, or the most gifted, but I am loyal to those I give my friendship. No matter what Maris and the Elders believe, I keep my word. I have a debt that needs to be repaid, and it is through you I believe I can repay it." His voice never wavered, even though his inner pain was evident. He rested his elbow on the window sill and leaned toward me. His voice was low. "What gifts do you have?"

Maybe I would have put my trust in anybody by this point, but I didn't think it would be misplaced in Quinn. "My Uncle Devnet wasn't sure. I've seen some of the unseen world. And I kind of travelled back to my world. At least, my mind did."

The portal's eyes sparkled. "Excellent."

"Why?"

He pulled back his enthusiasm. "Is there anything else?"

I shook my head. "Not that I know of, but Devnet said the Elders would test me and then train me."

"Aye. They would have." He leaned toward me again and whispered, "I would like to do the same, if you would be willing to let me."

"You could train me?"

"It would have to be done in secret. I might not have the power of some of the Elders, but I know a lot."

I smiled. "When do we start?"

"What about now?"

For the first time in weeks, my body had energy. It tingled up from my toes in my excitement to be doing something besides staring at the walls.

Quinn called to Malina. "Would you mind closing the door, my good lady?"

She glanced between the Portal and me, but did as she was asked before returning to the fireplace.

He grinned at me. "You say your spirit travelled to the other world, while you were here?"

I nodded.

"Then let us see if you might be a Portal as well. We'll start slow." He put his hand on my shoulder and turned me so I sat facing forward on the bench. "Relax your muscles." He watched me as I wiggled a little, trying to ease the tension out of my body. "Now, close your eyes."

I closed them.

"Paint a picture of this room in your mind. Try and draw every stone in the walls, every piece of furniture. Do you have a vivid memory of it?"

I concentrated for a moment, but the task was an easy one since I'd spent so long staring at the same four walls. "I see it."

"See yourself sitting by the window, like you are. Can you do that?"

I got a clear image of me in the hideously big dress and nodded.

"Now, breathe deep. Feel the air flowing through you. Imagine it flooding you from the inside out."

I filled my lungs, ignoring the throb in my shoulder. I let the air out slowly. I did it again.

"Think of the air as water in a stream and you in the middle of it. Let the air carry you from here to there on a current. I want you to picture yourself in the bed. You've spent a lot of time in it these past few days. Think of how it feels. And remember where it is in the room. Can you see it clearly?"

The weird separation of my mind and body happened again.

Quinn's voice rose. "Try not to let just your soul go! Let the air pick your body up as well, and take you with it."

My muscles tensed.

"Do not try so hard, Your Majesty. Relax."

I took another deep breath and exhaled it through my nose. I thought of the bed. I thought of how warm the blanket would feel around me. I pictured tiny oxygen molecules pushing themselves into my tissues and my blood and lifting me up like a giant balloon.

"Now, picture yourself in the bed and push yourself through the air. Push hard!"

The sensation was like when you dream you're falling and before you hit the ground, you wake up. My body dropped. When I jerked awake I found myself in the bed.

"By the gods!" gasped Malina.

Quinn stood. "Extraordinary!"

The door swung open. Lord Braedon entered the room. My companions looked panicked. I just smiled.

Braedon surveyed us. "And what is so fascinating?"

I thought of a quick lie. "I'm trying to convince them about cell phones."

The Lord Regent frowned. "What?"

"They're machines . . . tools . . . and with them, you can talk to anyone in the world. Instantly. Like if I wanted to talk to my Uncle Devnet, I could pick up my phone, dial his number and he would answer his cell and we could talk to each other just like you and I are now."

Braedon laughed. "That is extraordinary. To have such magic at your command.'

"It isn't magic." I hugged my knees to my chest and tried to hide my grin while I thought about what I'd just done. "Not like what you have here."

I could see Quinn duck his head to suppress a smile. He bowed toward me. "I have taken enough of your time, Your Majesty. I'm sure your uncle has things he wishes to discuss."

I thought I glimpsed a flash of anger in Lord Braedon's eyes, but it melted as he turned to acknowledge the Portal's departure. "Come see me this evening, Quinn."

"Of course, My Lord." He left the room without glancing my way again.

Braedon took in my new clothes. "Green becomes you, Your Majesty." He took a step toward me. "It brings out the color of your eyes."

I stood up. "Thank you. Shall we go for a walk?"

A deep crease formed along his forehead. "If you're not too tired. I thought perhaps you were getting ready to rest."

"No. I came over weak for a moment while Quinn visited. But I'm better now."

Lord Braedon studied my face. "And what did you two talk about?"

I let him take my elbow. We walked toward the hallway. "Nothing in particular. He asked about my health. How much exercise I was getting. Boring stuff, really." I glanced up at Braedon. "I'm sorry if he's a friend of yours, but he's really kind of dull."

"I've often thought that as well."

We strolled to the stairwell and stopped at the top.

I lowered my head then lifted my gaze up at him, giving him my best "sad puppy eyes" look. "Can we go down today?"

Braedon seemed surprised. A roguish smile crept across his face. "If you'd like."

"Yes, please!"

The steps were wide, but the rise fairly deep, maybe six inches or so per stair. My knees ached by the time we made it to the bottom.

Braedon paused. "Too much, Your Majesty?"

I shook my head. "Not if we can sit somewhere for a moment."

He guided me along a marble corridor. A wide archway opened up to the courtyard I could see from my window. I missed the fresh air.

Braedon noticed my longing gaze. "There's a room around the corner that looks out into the garden. We can sit there."

Roaring flames burned in the fire pit which dominated the center of the room. Several stone benches formed a semi-circle around it. We sat facing the courtyard with the fire at our backs.

The stone bench held some of the fire's heat and the warmth spread through my body. I looked outside and wished it were spring, instead of autumn. It would have been nice to sit out in the sunlight. I could feel Braedon's eyes on me. I gave him a sideways glance. His face held an odd expression.

"What's wrong?" I asked.

He gave his head a slight shake as if waking from a dream. "Nothing."

"What are you thinking?"

I couldn't believe my eyes when he blushed. He looked away, but I had seen his cheeks flush.

"You look very much like the queen. She was a beautiful woman."

"So I've heard."

Braedon turned back and studied at me. "You are more so."

I had the strange thought that he was flirting with me. But he was my uncle, if only by marriage; and he had to be at least ten years older than me. I shuffled over to archway, confused by Braedon's actions. A little bird flitted along the edge of the pond, dipping his head into the water and shaking his wings out.

Braedon leaned against the opposite side of the arch. I knew he watched me, but I wouldn't look at him. Instead I kept my focus on the bird. It flew up onto the barren limb of a small tree.

"You shouldn't let a man's compliments unnerve you. Modesty is a virtue a queen cannot afford. You must know your strengths, as well as your weaknesses. Come." He took my elbow. "We should get you back before Malina worries too much."

My legs weakened half-way up the stairs. I gasped as Braedon swept me up into his arms as if I weighed nothing.

He carried me to my rooms where he placed me on the bed. "Perhaps now you need to rest?"

I nodded but didn't speak.

Lord Braedon left the room. Malina approached but I rolled onto my side and closed my eyes. I couldn't decide whether I had imagined Braedon's flirtations or not, but I did know the whole thing had left me missing my mother. I wanted to talk with her over dinner. Laugh with her at a TV show. Argue with her about whether or not I could stay over Renee's house on the weekend. I missed my bed and being able to sleep through the night without being scared. I wanted to be home.

CHAPTER THIRTY-FOUR

Betrayed

Rhoswen returned the following morning with a new dress for me to try on. She showed it to Malina for her approval.

"I thought at first I should cut off the sleeve." The red-headed servant laid the deep russet-colored gown on my bed. "But then, I thought to make that the sling." She demonstrated how the sleeve could be tied down to the dress to keep my arm from moving. "Will it work?"

The old woman examined Rhoswen's handiwork closely before she nodded. "I think it might."

They helped me remove my nightgown. Malina cut off the bandages that still covered my wound and held my arm in place. I tried to stretch out the muscles, knowing the less I moved them now, the harder it would be to regain mobility later. In the end, Rhoswen had to help keep my arm raised as Malina wrapped new linen around my shoulder.

While the women worked, I decided to ask the question that had kept me awake for most of the night. "Can I trust Lord Braedon?"

Malina pulled a little too tightly on the bandage and I gasped. Rhoswen nearly dropped my arm. The young girl's eyes were round with fear. "Sorry, My Lady."

I tried to see Malina's face, but she stepped behind me. "Please. I don't know what the truth is. Devnet told me one thing, the Brethren something else, and now Braedon has his own story. I don't know who to believe."

Malina stopped working for a moment. She lifted her face to mine. "Believe them all, for they all tell a version of the truth."

I frowned. "That doesn't help."

Her eyebrows rose. "No?"

"No."

The old woman went back to wrapping the bandages. "Braedon is a hard man, Your Majesty. But he sees himself as right in his quest to bring equality to our people."

I jerked away from her in surprise but she pulled me back with the linen leash that bound us together. "You're a Mystic?"

"Aye."

I considered this for a moment. Simon had made the Mystics sound evil and deceitful. Malina and Greer had done nothing but serve and comfort me. Her tender hands wrapped another layer of bandages around my wound. "What do you mean 'equality'?"

"Our ancestors were promised things before they took the passage from the Other World. King Gedeon said we'd be free to worship our gods, as we'd done for centuries. But the Elders lied."

"How?"

Malina made one final circle with the linen, then tucked the end deftly into the other folds of cloth. "They came to fear our religion because it differed from theirs. They called it evil and insisted we abandon our beliefs. But by then, our numbers had grown too strong for the Elders to defeat us in battle without destroying themselves."

"So all this hatred . . . it's because of your faith?"

"Basically." The old woman nodded. "Of course, over the centuries it's grown deeper than that."

"So Braedon wants someone on the throne who will allow your people to have religious freedom?"

Malina lowered her head. "For the most part."

I glanced at Rhoswen. Her eyes darted away from mine. She appeared to study a thread on her dress. "What's wrong?" The two women remained silent. "Please. I need someone to tell me the truth."

Malina turned away and picked up the new dress from the bed. As she and Rhoswen helped me step into it she whispered in my ear, "He's a hard man. His passion and quest for power have become his gods. It is best to be . . . cautious."

I nodded. "I will." I could read the apprehension in their eyes, so I didn't press either woman any further. Instead we set about getting me into my new clothes.

The sleeves to the velvet dress were fairly wide, so it wasn't too difficult for me to slip my arms through, even the injured one. Rhoswen again supported it while the older woman laced up the back. Then the girl bound my arm to my waist with a series of ties she'd sewn into the dress. She'd expertly hidden them so they wove into a belt that circled the gown.

When they were finished with all the laces and ties, they took a step back to admire their work. Malina nodded with approval. "Aye, that looks fine, it does."

Rhoswen smiled.

I smoothed the fabric where it had puckered at my stomach. I could tell the dress accentuated my few curves. "I wish I had a mirror."

The three of us looked up when someone coughed softly by the door. Lord Braedon's gaze roamed up from my toes, stopped for a moment at the low cut bodice, and then came to rest on my face. I blushed at his frank stare.

Rhoswen and Malina curtsied and hurried to the corner of the room.

Braedon's eyes held mine. "You won't need a mirror, Your Majesty. Your beauty will be reflected in the face of everyone who sees you. You are a vision."

I struggled to find my voice. "Thank you."

Braedon held out his arm. "Shall we walk again today?"

I glanced at Malina and Rhoswen but they had their backs to me. I stepped over and rested my arm in his.

"I'd like to show you more of the palace, if you're feeling well enough?"

I nodded as we made our way down the stairs. When we got to the bottom we turned to the right, down a long marble hallway.

"You're quiet today," Braedon observed. "Is anything wrong?"

I shook my head.

We stopped in a doorway. "This is the library, Your Majesty. I've heard that you are able to read. Now that you're feeling better, you could find your way here and study in the afternoon."

Shelves of books lined the walls from the floor to the eight foot ceilings. Candles burned behind glass sconces and oil lamps provided more light on the tables. It wasn't as big as the library at the Sanctuary, but it was still impressive.

"I can summon one of the bards to assist you in your learning, if you'd like."

I walked down the first aisle and touched the leather bindings. The books here appeared to be written in Latin as well. "Bards?"

My uncle leaned against one of the tables as he watched me. "They are Mystics who study words—written and spoken. They can help you improve your knowledge."

"That would be great."

Braedon smiled when I looked at him. The same strange smile he'd given me the day before. I looked away.

"Come." The Lord Regent held out his hand. "There's much more to see."

He led me out of the library. Several servants stepped aside and bowed as we passed them in the hallway. Shafts of sunlight illuminated the gray stones and a cold breeze chilled my shoulders whenever I walked past the openings in the walls. Soldiers with long pikes stood guard near an arched wooden door at the end of the hall. My uncle stopped at another room. He motioned for me to look inside.

A tapestry hung on the far wall, its threads depicting a hunting scene somewhere among forested hills. A mosaic covered the wall to my right. I walked over to it, entranced by the beautiful tiles of blue, green, red and yellow that made up the picture. It was of a lush garden with a stream running through it. Birds flew in an azure sky and a lion stalked among the bushes. I reached out and touched one of the tiles. It was cool on my fingertips.

"It's Ayden the way it was meant to be." My uncle came up behind me. "At least, that's what I was told."

My heartbeat sped up as he put his hand on my good shoulder. His fingers brushed against the skin of my back. It gave me goose bumps, not good ones, but like I'd walked through a spider's web. I moved away, walking along the length of the mosaic, pretending to study the different scenes.

Braedon didn't move, but I felt his eyes on me the entire time. When I got to the end of the wall, I walked back to the door.

My uncle joined me and took my arm again. He led me toward the doorway that the soldiers guarded. They tapped their pikes on the ground as we approached, the sound reverberating down the hallway. Braedon nodded. One man opened up the tall door.

My uncle let go of my arm and placed his hand on the small of my back. "You enter first, Your Majesty."

I walked into a huge open room of polished marble floors and massive stone walls. Colorful satin banners hung from wooden rafters in the ceiling. Another mosaic, this one depicting the crowning of a king, dominated one of the walls. Angels hovered all around the figure. A beam of sunlight seemed to be coming straight from heaven to shine on the man. At the far end of the room, some one-hundred yards away, sat an ornate wooden chair on a dais.

"The throne room." Braedon again put his hand on my lower back.

"It is here that you will be crowned queen."

I shivered at his touch. "And when will that be?"

"When you are fully recovered and the leaders of our country can come together to celebrate."

He took my hand to pull me toward the throne. "You should sit, My Lady." He gave me a wink. "You must grow accustomed to the view from here." He swung me in a wide arc, letting go of my hand as I stepped up onto the dais.

I walked behind the huge chair, running my fingers over the dark wood. I turned slowly to face the massive room. I refused to look at my uncle. Instead, I imagined what the room would look like filled with people. Performing in concert choir at school was the only time I stood in front of a crowd. I avoided them at all costs, so the thought of standing on the dais alone made my palms sweat.

Braedon chuckled. "You'll need to work on that."

"What?"

"Getting rid of the look of terror in your eyes. You must be confident in your position." His own dark eyes twinkled with humor. "Try sitting down. Perhaps that would help."

I made my way to the other side of the throne and sat down, resting my free hand on the arm of the chair.

"Try smiling."

I couldn't help but laugh at his at his gentle teasing.

"That's it!" He clapped his hands together. "Much better."

It was easy to forget all the negative things I'd heard about my uncle when he acted like this. Now he wasn't the evil Lord Regent, he was a goofy young man. His face glowed with amusement as he kept up his instructions.

"Now, straighten your shoulders, if you can, and sit up."

I shifted my position. He studied me, as if looking at a piece of art then shook his head. "It's not quite right. How about something a little more relaxed? Turn a bit so your back is in the corner."

I did as he asked.

"Now slouch down."

I laughed out loud and gave him my best impression of a bored teenager. I let my hips slide forward on the thick cushion, until I almost fell out of the chair.

"Very imperious. You look like you don't have a care in the world."

I put on a mock English accent. "I say, be a good lad and fetch me my slippers."

Braedon stepped up onto the dais and reached out his hand toward me. I let him pull me off the throne. He brushed his fingers along the side of my face then down my neck. I tried to step away but he drew me closer. His eyes sought mine.

"Alystrine—"

The door swung open behind him. Before I could get away, Braedon bent his head down and kissed me. My muscles froze in disbelief as his lips pressed against mine. A wave of panic swept through me as I tried to process what he was doing. I yanked my hand from his and pushed him away. I stumbled back into the throne, wincing when I grazed my injured shoulder against it.

Braedon turned to face whoever had come in.

One of the guards walked into the center of the room. He pounded his pike on the floor. "A contingent from the Elders here to see you, My Lord."

My thoughts swirled in my brain like a kaleidoscope. I concentrated on jamming Braedon's kiss to the back of my mind to focus on the five people following the soldier. I remembered the older woman, Maris, from my brief encounter with the Elders before the Black Guards took me. I'd never seen the three men behind her. A fourth limped up from the back of the group.

My heart soared when I recognized him. "Devnet!" I ran past the others to get to my uncle. I'd expected him to greet me with a hug or at least a smile. Instead, he stood glowering.

I stopped in front of him. "What's wrong?" His cheeks grew pale. I thought he might get ill. "Are you sick?"

His gaze flickered between me and Braedon. "How could you?"

"How could I . . ." I realized he must have seen Braedon kiss me. "I didn't ask him—"

My head rocked back when Devnet slapped me—its sharp sting like ice against my cheek. Two of the Elders rushed over to restrain him from hitting me again. Braedon strode up and rested his hand on my shoulder. I jerked away from him, taking a step toward Devnet.

My uncle trembled with fury. I could read the loathing in his eyes. "After I told you what he did? He slaughtered your mother and my brother. He's killed anyone who stood in his way to find you. And you would allow him to kiss you?"

"No! I didn't!"

"I saw it, Alystrine."

"But I didn't ask him to."

"You didn't stop him."

"I didn't know what he was going to do."

Devnet shook off the men who held him. "You should never have allowed him to get close enough to try." He gave me a final look of reproach before stalking toward the door.

"Wait!" I ran after him, but he refused to stop. When I caught him, he tore my hand from his robe. "Please. Let me explain."

He wouldn't look at me and instead walked out the door. Braedon approached me, but I turned on him. "You planned this, didn't you? You knew he was coming and you manipulated me."

He didn't deny my accusations. "It's as I told you, My Lady, the Elders see only what they want. They refuse to listen to reason."

"How could you?" I looked down the empty hallway where Devnet had disappeared. Despair weighed on my heart.

Maris spoke from somewhere behind me. "Leave us."

The three Elders exited without glancing my way.

"I would like to speak to my granddaughter alone, Lord Braedon. It is a reasonable request."

I stared at her. Of course, that's where I'd heard the name. Devnet had said my father had taken the name "Maris's son," in honor of his mother.

Braedon's dark eyes simmered with malice. "So you can spread your lies about me? I think not."

My grandmother opened her arms. "Come to me, Alystrine. Let me hold you."

I hesitated only a moment before running to her. She folded me inside her embrace and rubbed my back as I cried. "I'm sorry. I'm so sorry. Please don't hate me."

My head bobbed as she let out a hearty chuckle. "Hate you? I could never hate you, Child." She ran her hand over my hair. "You look so much like your mother, and yet I see my son in you also." She kissed my cheek.

Lord Braedon's voice echoed in the great hall. "This is all very touching, but what is the point of your visit, Maris. What did you hope to obtain by coming here?"

"I wanted to meet my granddaughter. Your horde of demons took her before I had the opportunity to see her face up close."

"Again, touching, but I don't believe for a moment that was your only goal."

I wouldn't leave my grandmother's embrace, even as she argued with Braedon. "And if it was, would you leave us alone?"

He barked out a laugh. "Of course not. I trust you even less than you trust me." He took a step closer. "What do you want?"

Maris pushed me so I stood behind her. She drew herself up to face Braedon. "I want permission to take her back to the Elder Lands. I want to train her."

"Never."

"We don't even know if she has gifts. Let us test her."

The Lord Regent raised an eyebrow in my direction. "Do you see now, Alystrine, how the Elders lie? Devnet would have told the Elder Council about whatever powers you possess, and yet your grandmother tries to deceive me to my face and tell me she is ignorant of them." His attention turned to Maris. "My spies may not have discovered what her gifts are, but know this, you will never get the chance to manipulate them."

"How will you stop her once she is queen? She will not be under your guard forever."

He appeared to think twice about the first retort that came to his mind. "I think we will come to a mutually acceptable agreement." He turned to the doorway. "Guards!"

The four soldiers who'd been posted outside the door rushed into the hall. Braedon gave me an apologetic smile.

"I'm sorry, Alystrine, but your grandmother needs to leave."

I clung to her. "No! You can't do this."

She kissed my forehead as the guards tore her away from me. "Be strong. Pray for discernment."

I trailed behind as she was dragged toward the door. "Please, talk to Devnet. Tell him I'm sorry." With a violent yank, the soldiers pulled her across the threshold while the guards slammed the door before I could follow her into the hall.

The noise reverberated through my body. My grandmother was gone. I willed myself not to cry. Instead, I focused my anger on Lord Braedon. I whirled around to face him. "There is nothing, nothing you could ever say to me that would make me trust you again."

He grinned at me. "Alystrine–"

"That's 'Your Majesty,' to you."

He bowed. "Your Majesty, I'm sorry if you feel betrayed, but my actions were not for the Elder's amusement. My motives were purely selfish. I wanted to know what it would be like to kiss you, and so I did."

"You're my uncle!"

"Only by marriage and, as I'm no longer married to Kennis, I'm not even that anymore."

"You divorced her?"

He shook his head. "Kennis divorced me. Under Ayden law, if a spouse deserts their mate for longer than five years, the marriage is considered void."

Before I knew what was happening, he grabbed my hand and pulled me close to him again. "Tell me you didn't like it."

"I didn't."

His dark eyes sparkled. "You don't lie well, Alystrine. Your cheeks have turned pink. But since you insist you didn't enjoy it, I will have to try again."

I turned my face away as he bent to kiss me. "Why are you doing this?"

Braedon's fingers tightened around mine. Since he couldn't kiss my mouth he settled on my neck instead. His hot breath whispered in my ear. "You are alone, Alystrine. Devnet has abandoned you, your grandmother wouldn't fight for you and your friends are dead. I am all you have left. Think on that, Your Majesty." He kissed my neck again then let me go. "Shall I take you back to your room?"

I shook my head. "I can find the way myself. Leave."

"Very well." He took a step toward the door. "You should know there's only one way out of this room and the guards will be instructed to make sure you get back safely. There is no escape from this palace."

The metal hinges on the door squealed behind him. I shut my eyes and let the noise echo through me.

I was a prisoner.

I was angry.

But someday soon, I would be queen.

I let my emotions boil within me until I couldn't stand it anymore, then I made my way up to the dais, sat on the throne, and plotted my revenge. Somehow, I would find a way to destroy Braedon, but it would have to wait until the palace and its servants were under my control. Right now, the guards and their weapons were loyal to the

Lord Regent, but it wouldn't be long until I ruled.

CHAPTER THIRTY-FIVE

To Save a Life

I played the part of petulant teenager well over the next week, refusing to speak to or even look Lord Braedon in the eye. I barred the door to my room and refused every dinner invitation he sent. The only reason I didn't hide from him completely was because of all the officials I had to meet and history I had to learn before my coronation could be announced. Every morning a guard would escort me down to the library or council room, where my uncle would be sitting with some new dignitary or Druid bard I had to listen to. I would love to have taken notes, but Malina insisted my arm remain tied down so the shoulder muscle could heal properly. It was hard enough to understand all the newcomers' accents, and without notes to look back on, I found it impossible to understand all the ins and outs of Ayden politics or the Mystic faith. And while I met consistently with individual Lords of the Mystics and the Commoners, no one from the Elders came to visit me.

I returned to my room after a particularly boring conversation about ancestral land rights with several members of the Commoners Council. "What does he expect me to do with all these?" I tossed another decree onto the already teetering pile on my desk.

"Do with what, My Lady?" Rhoswen poured steaming liquid from the pot over the fireplace into a mug.

I plopped down on the edge of the bed. "I can't read enough of what any of these parchments say to understand them." I kicked my slippers off and sent them flying across the room. They hit the wall with a satisfying thud. "Braedon's doing this to drive me crazy. I know it."

"Why don't you appoint a secretary?" Rhoswen asked as she handed me a cup of hot tea.

"What?"

"You can appoint anyone as a secretary. I'm surprised Lord Braedon hasn't given you one already."

I blew into my mug, trying to cool down the brew so it wouldn't burn me. "He's probably hoping I'll fall on my face the first chance I get. Or better yet, he'll offer to do the job for me so he can still run the country."

Rhoswen crossed her arms over her chest. "Is there anyone you trust? Anyone you know who can read who will help you?"

"My Uncle Devnet, but I don't know that he's forgiven me yet." I took a sip. "And Quinn of course." He'd been coming up to see me whenever he could, to help me practice with my new powers. I'd gotten fairly adept at the Mind Speak, the ability to cast my thoughts into another's head. I'd discovered that it only worked with other Elders. Rhoswen and Malina hadn't heard anything when I tried it with them since they were Mystics.

Rhoswen frowned. "Quinn's position as a Portal means he couldn't be your secretary. He has too many other duties."

I wondered what Portals did besides train other Portals, but I didn't ask. "I'd trust Simon from the Sanctuary."

"What you do now is, open that door and tell the guards outside you want to post a message. They'll bring a scribe."

"It's that easy?"

Rhoswen's crooked teeth flashed as she smiled. "Aye, it's that easy, now that you're going to be queen."

Within the hour I'd sent out my requests. Now all I had to do was wait to see if Devnet or Simon would respond. I finished another cup of tea then dismissed Rhoswen for the afternoon. It would be the first time in weeks that I'd had the opportunity to be alone. I couldn't wait to stretch out on my bed and think. I stared at the ceiling, enjoying the silence, letting my mind wander over everything that had happened over the past month.

A wave of homesickness washed over me like the waves of ocean I missed so much. It would be summer in Connecticut by now. I tried to remember the feel of the sticky June air clinging to my skin. Instead of gowns made of heavy brocade fabric, I'd be in shorts and t-shirts. Mom and I would jump in the car and drive to Hammonasset Beach to watch the sunsets, stopping for a cherry-dipped, chocolate soft-serve cone on the way home. My chest ached when I tried to picture Kennis' face, my mind struggling to remember the exact shade blue of her eyes and the shape of her mouth.

Reality hit me again. I didn't want to be queen. I wanted to go home.

Quinn had been training me to Spirit Travel, but I wasn't very good.

I couldn't get past the idea that I might get stuck in a wall if I tried to go through it. Once, when Braedon had been out riding his horse, Quinn had sent the guard posted outside my room on an errand, then left the door open. That time I'd been able to let my conscience roam the hallway and even went down the stairs.

I thought again about Kennis and decided to try to reach her as I had on the Plains of Sharne. I relaxed my breathing, letting the tension leave my muscles. Inside, I felt the strange tug and snap as my spirit separated from body. I floated up to the ceiling and looked down, barely recognizing the form on the bed. The butchered hair from Devnet's attempt to disguise me as a boy, the formal gown of green wool. Never in my wildest dreams had I imagined I'd look like this. I forced myself to turn away. I set the picture of my home firmly within my mind and tried to travel there as I'd done before. Instead, it felt as if someone pressed down on my head, pushing me back to the bed. My spirit re-connected with my body. I sat up with a frustrated groan.

What was the problem? I'd done this before without any training. Why couldn't I do it now? Maybe it was the walls. After all, the last time I'd done it I'd been outside. I walked over to the window, drew back the tapestry and opened the wooden shutters that kept out the frigid autumn air. Settling myself back on the bed, I relaxed again and focused on the shaft of blue sky I could see. With a mental push I thrust myself outside.

As I didn't have a body, I didn't get the sensation of flying. This spirit form of mine didn't have hair that the wind could blow through or skin to chill. I tried to push myself up toward the sky and was hit again by invisible hands that thrust me instantly back to my body. I sat up, cursing, trying to rid myself of the sensation that I'd just bungee jumped off a cliff. A cold wind blew in from the open window and helped to revive me. I stood to close it when a guard knocked then opened the door.

"My Lady?"

I took a deep breath of fresh air before I fastened the shutters. "Yes?"

"There's someone here who wishes to see you."

I pulled the tapestry free and turned to meet my visitor. A Portal, hooded in deep blue wool, stood beside the young guard. I hadn't seen any Portals in the castle besides Quinn. I wondered how many more Braedon had turned to his side after he killed my mother.

The robed figure took a step toward me and bowed. "If you please, My Lady," the voice was higher than I expected. "I've been sent to honor your request for a secretary." The Portal drew back his hood to reveal not a man at all, but a stunningly beautiful woman. The woman's violet eyes sparkled with amusement. "My name is Sigal."

I blinked in surprise. "You're portal?"

"Yes." A smile mirrored the humor in her gaze. "You seem astonished."

"All the others I've seen so far have been men."

"Women of the Elder race are also gifted."

My arms broke out in goose bumps. I turned to make sure the window hadn't come open again. It hadn't. I looked back and shivered as I caught Sigal's intense stare.

"Are you well, My Lady?" she asked.

I nodded, then glanced at the guard. "You can go."

He shut the door as he left. I sat down on the bench along the wall and studied my visitor. Her skin was lighter than many of the Elders I'd seen so far, the color of tea with cream. She'd pulled a few strands of her straight, black hair off her face and fastened them behind her head with a simple silver clip. The rest spilled out of her hood, down her back. "Who sent you?"

Sigal looked confused. "I beg your pardon, My Lady?"

"How did you know I wanted a secretary?"

She clasped her slender fingers together in front of her. "Please, don't be angry." When she'd first removed the hood I'd guessed her to be in her early thirties, but her face seemed to grow younger as she dipped her head in apology. "I've so wanted to meet you, but Lord Braedon has put a tight rein on those he'll let serve you." She wrung her hands. "I bribed one of the guards to let me know if there was ever any service he thought I could perform for you. When he'd heard you'd sent for a secretary, he told me."

Her story sounded plausible, but my arms still tingled with electricity. It reminded me of when the Portal had found me in the tavern. Maybe it wasn't her at all though, maybe I was still recovering from my attempt to Spirit Travel. I chewed a hangnail on the side of my thumb. Whatever she was, if she could read Latin, she could help me with some of the paper work overtaking my desk. I gestured to it with my head. "Can you read those and translate them for me so I know what they say?"

Sigal smiled. "Of course." Her long robe hid her feet and she moved with such grace she seemed to glide rather than walk to the desk. "Do you mind if I sit down?"

"Go right ahead."

We worked for about an hour, until a servant arrived to deliver my uncle's request that I join him for dinner.

"Just bring me something from the kitchen. Anything will do." I glanced at Sigal. "Do you have somewhere to go, or would you mind eating here and working some more?"

"I would be honored to eat with you."

"Bring two trays please."

Sigal kept silent, but her violet eyes flickered repeatedly over to me while we worked. When she'd stopped herself from speaking for the third time, I'd finally had enough. "What is it?

"My Lady?"

"You obviously want to ask me something. What do you want to know?"

"Why won't you eat with Lord Braedon?"

"Because he's a liar and a pervert."

Sigal made a choking sound. "What?" She coughed a couple of times, until she could breathe normally again.

"I don't trust him. He drove away my only blood relatives and he's creepy." I shivered. The Portal continued to watch me with curiosity. "Why do you work for him?"

She lowered her eyes for a moment, in shame or anger, I couldn't tell. When she looked up again, her face was neutral. "Those of us who would not voluntarily turn to the Mystics, like Quinn, were forced to endure the torture of the Black Guards."

Before I could process what she'd said about Quinn she asked, "I believe you are familiar with the Breaking, are you not?"

I pushed back the images that ran like an unwanted movie through my mind. "Yes."

"I could not fight them like we've heard you did. They showed me my child—my daughter, and the things they would to do to her if I didn't use my gift for the Mystics."

I felt as I'd been punched in the stomach "I'm sorry." Sigal remained silent, her body rigid. "That must have been horrible."

She let out a shuddering breath. "Yes. But I don't know if this life is worse."

"What do you mean?"

"My child lives, but the Elders refuse to let me see her. I am banished from the Elder Lands and she has been told that I am dead."

"What?"

"All of the Portals who gave into the Mystics were exiled. Did you not know that?"

I shook my head.

"I saved my sanity, but at the cost of everything else I held dear. My family. My faith. My identity."

"That's awful."

She shrugged. "Ruahk may have abandoned me, but I still hold on to the old religion, even though I serve at the palace now."

"Braedon doesn't make you worship his gods or anything?"

"No." She traced a grain of wood in the desk with one of her delicate fingers. "The Elders won't let me pray with them, but your uncle has never made any of us practice the Mystic ways."

Once again the familiar doubt crept into my head. Maybe my uncle wasn't such a bad guy after all. Maybe I was misinterpreting his advances? Then I thought of him kissing me and the threats he'd made in the throne room. No, the dude was seriously disturbed. Maybe schizophrenic, a multiple personality or something, for him to be so rational one minute and so twisted the next. But what about the Elders? Was it right to punish people who were forced to become traitors? I hated to think that there were no clear "good guys" in this equation.

"May I ask another question?"

"Sure."

"Your ability to survive the Breaking has been told throughout the land. It would seem you were blessed with much power from Ruahk." She stared up at me. "Did you inherit any of your father Geran's gifts?"

"I can Mind Speak," I answered before the hairs on my arms stood on end.

Her porcelain face beamed with excitement. "Really? Who taught you?"

"At the Sanctuary." I thought quickly, not wanting to divulge my work with Quinn. "A man named Goram. I didn't get much time to practice, though."

"Is there anything else?"

I got up and poured a goblet of cider from a pitcher Rhoswen had left by the fire. "Not that I know of." I took a sip before turning back to her. "Braedon wouldn't let my grandmother take me to the Elders to train me."

A strange spark lit up Sigal's eyes. "I could train you." The spark went out and she lowered her head as if embarrassed. "That is, if you would trust me with such an honor."

I didn't, but had nothing to base my fears on except some goose pimples and a feeling in the pit of my stomach. I took a long gulp of cider then gave her what I hoped was a convincing smile. "First, I need to get through all this paperwork and be crowned." I plopped myself back down at the desk. "Then I can think about training."

I jumped as the door behind me swung open and struck the wall. Lord Braedon strode in. His voice was measured but still echoed against the stones. "Enough of this, Alystrine. You will eat with me in the dining hall this evening."

"I'm not hungry." I turned back to the parchment in front of me.

"Portal," his voice was filled with contempt. "Who gave you permission to be here?"

Sigal stood. "I'm sorry, My Lord. The Lady Alystrine sent a request for a secretary."

Braedon came to my side, the heels of his black leather boots clicking against the floor like a drum beat. "Did she?"

I ignored him.

"You should have come to me first." He put his hand on my shoulder, but I pushed my chair away. "I would have found someone worthy of the station."

I sensed Sigal prickle, but commented before she could get herself in trouble. "I wouldn't trust anyone you brought to help me."

Braedon glared between the two of us before speaking again. "I have a matter of state I need to discuss with you. It involves a friend of yours as well."

"What friend?"

His smile made me shiver as if someone had poured ice water down my back. "Come to dinner and you will see." He spoke over his shoulder as he walked out. "I'll be sending up a new dress for you to wear. I expect you to be ready within the hour."

I stuck my tongue out at him as he left. Childish, but satisfying. I stood up, almost running into Rhoswen, as she entered carrying a gown of dove grey velvet.

The red-haired maid stepped back. "Sorry, My Lady." She glanced over to Sigal. "We've not much time to get you dressed for dinner."

The Portal bowed. "I can return tomorrow if you'd like to continue with our work here."

I didn't answer, too distracted by Braedon's threat. What friend could he be talking about?

Sigal stopped in front of me on her way out. "Shall I come in the morning?"

"What?" I asked as Rhoswen began to unlace the back of my gown.

"Tomorrow?" She raised her hood to cover her face. "Shall I come in the morning?"

"Sure."

The Portal left. Malina entered moments later to help Rhoswen get me ready. I subjected myself to the women's pampering as they bathed and dressed me. The gown Braedon had sent fit perfectly. The women laced up the snug bodice, which in turn pushed my breasts up. Paired with the low cut of the dress, I actually had the appearance of cleavage. Embroidered flowers of navy thread and pearls bordered the neckline, sleeves and hem of the dress.

I groaned as Rhoswen secured my right arm to the waist of the gown with a series of ties. "How much longer do I need to do this?"

"Another week at least." Malina gave me a steely look. "The wound may be almost healed, but it's the muscles I be worried about. They need time to mend properly."

Rhoswen finished by sticking tiny silver pins adorned with pearls into my hair. Malina stepped back to take in my appearance.

"You look lovely, My Lady. A vision."

"Thanks." I stared down at the silver satin shoes Braedon had sent as well. "What do you think he has planned?"

Neither woman answered. I couldn't tell if it were out of ignorance or fear. Before I could ask, someone knocked on the door. A guard entered.

"Your presence is requested in the dining hall."

Rhoswen stuck my hair with one more pin before she deemed me fit for the evening. I followed the guard until we met up with Braedon. He waited for me along a corridor I presumed led to the dining hall.

We wouldn't be eating alone. I could hear boisterous laughter and loud conversation coming from behind closed oak doors. "Who else is here?"

"The members of the Mystic Council wish to welcome you. I hope you will be gracious to my friends and advisors. Much about your future depends on making them your allies as well."

I glared at him, but didn't say a word.

"As you have not yet been officially crowned, we will enter together." He stepped around to my left side so he could take my unbound arm. He gave it a painful squeeze as he accompanied me into the hall.

Rows of tables and benches lined two of the walls; along a third stood one table with two ornate chairs. Several gray haired men in monk-like robes of silver sat along benches on either side of the thrones. Banners hung behind the head table with what looked like coats of arms emblazoned with brightly colored satin. At least forty men sat around the hall dressed in the manner of medieval lords—heavy woolen tunics and high leather boots. They went silent as the guard at the door announced our entrance.

"Lord Braedon, Regent of Ayden and Lady Alystrine, daughter of Queen Etain."

They stared at me, taking in every detail of my appearance. I kept my head high and focused on one of the banners behind the head table.

I didn't smile.

Braedon led me to my chair and pushed it into the table. He leaned down to whisper, "I hope you enjoy your meal. I'm sure you'll find the evening . . . most interesting."

My stomach churned, not only because I wondered what friend of mine he could have business with, but because of the men who watched my every move. I glanced around the room for a friendly face and found none, except for a young blond man sitting at one of the nearby tables. I felt my cheeks flush when he caught my stare. His lips rose in a gentle smile. He lifted his goblet out in front of him as if offering me a toast, then tilted his head back to pour the wine down his throat.

I chuckled at whatever tribute the young man was trying to give me. A voice croaked to my left.

"What do you find so amusing, young lady?"

I turned to the white haired man next to me. His milky eyes seemed to be focused on something over my shoulder. "I'm surprised at how much some of your nobles like to drink."

The wrinkles on his face deepened as he frowned. "You should not find amusement in the weaknesses of others."

I sat up straighter. "I don't think he has a weakness, he's just enjoying himself."

"Nevertheless."

The old man left the word hanging over the dinner table. I turned back to my meal and forced down a roll and a slice of meat.

"Don't you like the food, Alystrine?" Braedon asked.

I cringed at his slimy tone. "It's the company I can't stand. Why did you bring me here?"

He gave me a look of innocence. "I need you to help me judge a case."

"What kind of case?"

"One of treason. I think your perspective will be most helpful."

I gritted my teeth in an effort not to scream. "Can we get on with it? Or do you like to torture me? Is that really how you get your kicks?"

His eyes flashed for a moment before he smiled. "If you insist." He stood and clapped his hands to get the attention of the room. "Dear friends and nobles all, I hope you enjoyed the meal."

Shouts of, "here, here," and scattered applause filled the room.

"I'm afraid although you all knew you'd be meeting Etain's heir tonight, she did not know she'd be meeting you. It's left her quite speechless."

Chuckles and murmurs drifted around the tables.

"As she hopes to one day sit on the throne of Ayden, I thought she would benefit by seeing how the rule of law operates in our land." He clapped his hands once. "Guards! Bring in the prisoner."

I kept my face impassive as I waited to see what Braedon had up his sleeve. My heart beat like a scared rabbit's. I tried to swallow, but found my mouth too dry. I took a sip from my goblet of wine as two guards dragged a man into the hall. The man attempted to walk, but he'd obviously been beaten. Only the guards' arms were keeping him upright.

My heart froze when one of the guards lifted the man's head so he could face his judge.

Tegan.

He had a cut on his cheek and another along his forehead.

I stood up. I wanted to leap across the table and run to him, but I didn't know what the crowd of Mystics would do.

Every one of them watched me, judging my reaction. Somehow they all knew what he meant to me. I spoke low enough so only Braedon could hear me. "I swear to you, if you hurt him again, I will kill you."

He sneered at me. "Tsk-tsk, Your Majesty. The boy is a criminal."

I tried not to scream, but my voice rose in pitch and volume. "What has he done?"

"The prisoner has been found guilty of treason. Treason against the Regent of Ayden."

Tegan's eyes sought mine. We held each other's gaze. I wanted to comfort him, but I didn't know how.

Braedon continued, "As punishment, he will be hanged in the city center a week from today."

My voice rang out through the hall. "No!"

"He has confessed to disobeying an official edict. For that he must die."

"What edict?"

"That anyone finding a traveler must bring them directly to the palace at Uz, where they will be questioned by the Regent of Ayden."

I wanted to tear Braedon's eyes out. If I'd had the use of my right arm, I may have tried. Instead, I forced myself to ask, "What do you want?"

He didn't answer, but a smile slowly spread across his lips.

"You brought me here for a reason. If you had wanted to hurt me by killing him, you would have done it already." My chest tightened. I couldn't take a breath. I reached out to stable myself on the back of the chair, hoping it would stop the room from spinning. "What do want me to do?"

He leaned down so we stood face to face. "Marry me."

A sharp laugh escaped my throat. "What?"

He gave his head a slight nod. "Marry me."

I took a step away. "You can't be serious?"

"Deadly serious, Alystrine. The only way the boy will live is if you, as the queen, pardon him. The only way for you to become queen in time to save him, is by agreeing to make me your consort."

I grabbed my stomach in an attempt to ease its nauseous churning. I glanced at Tegan, my heart breaking at the sight of his bruises and cuts. Yet another person hurt because of me. He must have seen something in my eyes because he shook his head.

"Whatever he's asked of ye," Tegan called. "Do not do it."

Braedon waved his arm and the guards dragged the dark haired boy between the tables toward the door.

"Do ye hear me, Ally?" Tegan yelled. "Do not do it!"

They pulled him out the doorway. The dining hall remained silent as the Mystic Council stared at me. Tegan's pleas were cut off sharply. My legs turned to jelly. My hand groped to find the chair and I sank into it. Four men rose from the table to my right. Two carried a piece of parchment, one a quill pen and the last, a jar of ink.

The oldest looking of the group placed the parchment on the table. It was written in Latin.

I spit out the words, "I can't read it."

"No?" Braedon asked. "It is a parchment in which you agree to marry me once you become queen. It is a binding document, unable to be broken by any other royal edict, even after you are crowned."

"I want to know what it says."

The Lord Regent pushed the parchment toward me. "I've just told you." He nodded toward the other men. They put the quill and ink in front of me.

I stared at the paper with revulsion. I couldn't sign it. I couldn't bind myself to this monster. But, I couldn't let him kill Tegan.

I closed my eyes. "You said I had a week."

Now it was Braedon's turn to be confused. "What?"

"You said the sentence wouldn't be carried out for a week. I want someone I trust to read this document."

Braedon thrust the quill into my hand. "I've told you what it says."

I threw the quill onto the floor. "I. Don't. Trust you." I stood up and faced him. "Bring my Uncle Devnet back here. Or my grandmother. Bring me someone I can trust to read what that stupid paper says, and then maybe I'll sign it. Not until then!"

I stared at him a moment longer before I stormed out of the hall. I refused to make eye contact with any of the men who sat among the tables. I walked with my shoulders back and with what I hoped was a look of determination on my face.

Until I got outside the hall.

Then I grabbed the wall for support. My chest heaved. I stuffed my fist in my mouth to keep myself from screaming. I had bought myself a few days at the most. But I knew in my heart I would sign the paper. I'd marry the devil himself if I thought it would save Tegan's life.

CHAPTER THIRTY-SIX

I See You

M alina and Rhoswen jumped up from the corner by the fireplace when I slammed the door open.

"My lady?" Rhoswen hurried to my side, her face pale. "Are you well?"

I waved her away as I paced around the room, calling Lord Braedon every foul name I could think of. I grabbed the pillow off the bed and screamed into it until my throat was raw. Then I whacked the thing against the wall, until feathers surrounded me like snow.

I whirled around to faced Malina and Rhoswen. They stood with their backs against the wall. Rhoswen held her hand over her mouth as if trying not to scream. Malina showed less fear, but her eyes were bright and round. I dropped the shredded tatters of the pillow. "I swear to you, I make a solemn promise to you now, I will kill that man. No, he's not even a man. I swear I will kill that monster if it's the last thing I do!"

Malina tip-toed through the remaining feathers still floating to the ground. "What has he done?"

I pictured Tegan's battered face and my knees buckled. I knelt on the floor. "I love him."

Rhoswen gasped. "You love Lord Braedon?"

"No," I fought back sobs. I couldn't give into despair, I had to keep my anger and let it help me defeat my uncle. I told the women all that had transpired in the dining hall. Their faces whitened as I told them about Braedon's proposal.

Rhoswen sat down by my side. "But how did the Lord Regent know of your feelings for this boy? Did you tell him on one of your walks?"

"No." The answer came to my mind in a flash. "Faolan."

"Who?"

"That bastard." I stood up and paced the room again. "The Keeper of the Keys, he told Braedon, I know he did." I picked the cushion off the bench and threw it across the room. It didn't give me the satisfaction of breaking anything as it landed. I strode over to the wooden chair by the desk and smashed it against the wall.

That felt better.

The wood splintered around me, letting out a gratifying crack. I heaved the remaining leg I held into the fireplace.

The guard from outside opened the door. "Your Majesty? Is everything–?"

I hurled a book from the desk at his head. "Get out!"

His eyes widened as he dodged the missile. "My Lady?"

I searched for something else to heave at him. "Get out!"

He scrambled to catch his balance.

I couldn't find anything to throw that would leave a sizeable mark so I stalked up to him. "And I'll tell you another thing. If you let Lord Braedon into my room, so help me, my very first order as queen will be to cut off your head and stick it on pike. Do you understand me?"

The poor man backed out of the room. "Yes, Your Majesty."

I slammed the door again before he had a chance to shut it. I rested my back against it, sliding down until I sat on the floor. "What am I going to do?" I looked between Rhoswen and Malina. "I can't marry Braedon." The thought of him touching me, kissing me. I wished I could take a long shower to wash the slimy feeling off my skin.

Malina's hushed voice broke into my thoughts. "You could go to him."

"Braedon?"

She knelt by my side. "The boy. I've been listening to Quinn. If the boy's in the prison here in the palace, you should be able to...to do whatever that thing is that you do."

"A passage?" I grabbed her arm. "I could make a passage to Tegan!"

"I think you could, as long as he's here. If he's left the grounds, you cannot get out."

Rhoswen stared at us. "Do you have the Elder blood then? Can you use the passages?"

I struggled to my feet. "I've been learning how." I had no doubt I could do it, however, to reach Tegan. My connection to him was strong. I made my way over to the bed and got comfortable. "Keep talking to each other, so the guard doesn't suspect I've gone." I'd only tried to create a passage from one place to another. This time, I thought only of Tegan. I imagined the stream of air that separated us. There may be walls between us, but he was somewhere nearby and I would find him.

I opened my mind up to the air around me and let it flow through my body. I concentrated on Tegan. How he looked, his smell, the touch of his lips on mine. I imagined myself wrapped in his arms and allowed the current of air to carry me to him. A strange whooshing sound filled my head. When I opened my eyes, I was blind.

I had transported out of my room, but to where? I couldn't see a thing. I moved my arm and legs to convince myself I wasn't stuck in a wall. I gagged when I took a breath. The air here, wherever here was, smelled of urine and feces. Underneath those powerful scents was the faint copper odor of blood. Something crawled across my hand.

I swore under my breath and stood up.

A sound from the corner, almost a laugh, got my attention.

I didn't move.

An odd droning noise started. I kept still, even as something scurried near my foot.

The murmuring continued.

"Whatever it is . . . ." The words trailed off.

I took a step toward the voice.

"Whatever it is, don't do it. Whatever . . . don't do it."

I inched myself through the inky blackness, until my foot hit something soft.

The droning stopped. Somebody moaned.

I knelt on the floor. "Tegan?"

His voice got louder. "Whatever it is, Ally, don't do it."

I placed my hand as gently as I could on him. "It's all right, Tegan. I'm here."

A soft chuckle interrupted his chanting. "I'm hearin' things."

I pressed my hand a little harder against him, unsure of what part of him I actually touched. "Tegan, I'm really here."

He choked out a sob. "Ally?"

"It's me."

His hand flopped against my wounded shoulder and I pushed down a groan. "Ally?"

I'd figured out he was lying on the floor. I crawled down in front of him, my hand seeking out his face. I knew I'd found it when I felt him kiss my fingers. "I'm so sorry."

"How'd did ye—" He sucked in a ragged breath. "How'd did ye get in here?"

"I can use the passages," I told him. "I've learned how."

His hand reached out and stroked my head. "Where's your hair?"

"Devnet cut it." I twirled one of my fingers in his shaggy locks. "You have more than enough for both of us."

He groaned as he laughed, but then his hand tightened against me. "Ye have to go."

"No, I won't leave you in here. Not like this."

He tried to push me away. "What'll happen if they find ye?"

I grabbed his hand, holding it to my chest. "Braedon doesn't know I'm gone. I'll go back before anyone notices."

His fingers were warm against my skin. "It feels so good to touch ye."

"Can you move at all?" I asked.

"A little."

"Then come rest your head on me." I lay flat and stretched my arm out on the filthy straw. "I promise," I repeated the words he'd told me in the cave, "I'll not take advantage of the situation."

Tegan shifted his body to do as I'd asked. I stroked his hair for several minutes before he rolled into a fetal position, one arm lying on my chest and one leg over mine. His body trembled as he told me how the Black Guards had come for him and his family. How he'd confessed to anything they'd asked in order to stop Treasa's and Galvyn's screams of pain. I comforted him the best I could, with gentle touches and words. Once he'd poured out his story, he answered with touches of his own. But his were more urgent. His kisses more forceful.

His voice sounded low and breathless. "I wish I could see your face."

"You've already seen it." I pulled him back to me.

His tongue pushed my lips apart and found mine. Electricity prickled across my skin as he pressed me even closer. Unlike Braedon's kiss, which turned my stomach, Tegan's filled me with hunger.

His hand raked through my short hair. He groaned and rolled away. "When I saw ye up there, lookin' like ye did in that dress, I thought ye were one of the Messengers, a vision from Ruahk." He couldn't seem to stop touching me, as if to prove I was real. His hand ran down my neck, to my shoulders to the skin on my chest. This seemed to fascinate him most of all. His fingertips danced along the edge of my bodice, sending shivers throughout my body.

He moaned. "You're still wearin' it? Are ye mad, girl? Lying on this floor in a dress like that?" He kissed my neck. "But I'm glad ye did. I'll hold the vision of ye, and this touch of ye," his lips brushed against mine, "when they lead me to the gallows."

I pushed him away. "Stop it. You're not going to die."

His mouth pressed against my neck again. "Don't ye see? It doesn't matter now that I had this time with ye."

"I won't let him kill you!"

Tegan stopped. "What are ye goin' to do?"

I didn't answer him.

"Ally? What does he want from ye?"

"It doesn't matter." I tried to kiss him but he turned his head.

He let out a sharp gasp as he sat up. "I told ye not to agree to anythin'."

"I haven't." I didn't say *yet*.

"But yer thinkin' about it. What does he want?"

I knelt in front of him and reached for his face. When I found it, I cupped it in my hand. "It doesn't matter." I kissed him. "I won't let him hang you."

He pulled my hand away but held it. He tried to find my other hand but discovered my right arm fastened to my waist by Rhoswen's ties. "What happened?"

"I got shot with an arrow. In the Fey."

He cursed. "What were ye doin' in the Fey?"

"Trying to get to the Elders. I didn't make it."

"And what does Braedon want in exchange for my life?"

I laughed. "You can't trick me like that."

His hand caressed my bandaged arm. "Please Ally, whatever it is, I'm not worth it."

"Yes, you are." I gave him one more kiss, then stood up. "I have to go."

"Ally, wait!"

"I can't. I have to find a way to get you out of here." I put my good hand out in front of me and walked until I found the cell bars. I pictured the bed in my room, I imagined the air flowing through me and taking me back, but when I opened my eyes, I was still in Tegan's cell.

"I can hear ye breathin'," Tegan's brogue called from the other side of the room. "Why are ye not leavin'?"

"I was drawn to you. It's harder when I'm only thinking about returning to a room."

"You said ye could get back!"

"I know! Give me a minute. I'm new at this." I tried again to find the passage back to my room, with no success. I sat down on the straw and held my head in my hand. I thought about Quinn, about what he would tell me to do. *Quinn! I need you!*

I felt as though an arrow had been shot from within me. I sent out the message again. *I'm in the prison, I need you!*

"Ally!" Tegan called. "Ya have to go!"

"You're not helping!" I grabbed onto one of the cell bars to pull myself up. A breeze whipped through the corridor outside of the cell and someone stood on the other side of the bars.

Quinn's voice whispered from the darkness, "Alystrine?"

"In here."

His hand fumbled against the bars before he found mine. "How did you get in there?"

"I found a passage, but I can't find my way back!"

"And why would you want to put yourself in prison?"

"I'll tell you when you get me back. Please!"

He took hold of my hand. "Think with me about your room. Concentrate."

I focused on the picture in my head and the currents of air. Quinn's hands gripped mine even tighter then he pulled me up and out of the jail. I kept my room in my mind until I heard Quinn's voice again.

"By Ruahk, you smell horrible!"

Rhoswen and Malina both stirred from their pallets on the floor. Malina sighed. "You had us worried half to death and now look at ye, you've ruined that dress."

Rhoswen's eyes searched mine. She grinned. "You found him, didn't you?"

I nodded. We giggled like a couple of normal teenagers. For a moment I could almost believe I was home talking with Renee, until Malina yanked on the ribbons that secured the back of the gown.

"We need to get this off of you, look at it, covered in filth and hay and the gods know what else."

"What were you doing rolling around on the prison floor?" Quinn asked. Rhoswen and I started laughing again. The Portal looked so confused, it sparked a whole other fit.

"I told you to find the boy," growled Malina. "Not make love to him." Her hands froze and she spun me around to face her. "You didn't, did you?"

"No!"

She twirled me back to finish undoing the laces. "That's all we would have needed."

Quinn's cheeks turned a deep crimson. "What did you do?"

"Nothing!" I explained to him about Lord Braedon's twisted plot to make me marry him. By this time, Malina had gotten my gown unfastened. She shooed Quinn to the corner while I stepped out of the ruined dress. "Malina suggested I try and make a passage to Tegan, and I did." Rhoswen helped me slip on my nightgown. "You can turn around now."

The anger in the portal's voice surprised me. "And what did you do in the prison with this boy you just met,?"

"Why are you mad? I'm the one who's being blackmailed."

"Selfish, stupid, arrogant—" He strode up to me. "You would risk everything your parents' sacrificed for you, everything Kennis, Devnet and I have done, and for what?" He grabbed the gray dress from Malina's hands. "For this? To let some peasant grope you on the floor of a prison?"

"Quiet," the old woman hissed. "The guard will hear you."

My left arm swung in an arc toward Quinn's face, but the move was awkward and he caught my wrist. He dug his fingers into mine to keep me from finishing the blow. Our eyes locked.

"That peasant saved my life. He brought me to the Brethren. He's been beaten and now they want to kill him because of me." I yanked my arm from the Portal. "I went to give him some comfort. Just to hold him for a moment and let him know everything would be all right. I owed him that much."

Quinn's eyes held mine. "Promise me you won't go there again."

I couldn't look away, but I couldn't answer him either.

"You don't know all that is at stake. It is imperative you not see him again."

I lifted my chin. "I won't let Braedon kill him."

The Portal's face paled. "You cannot marry Braedon."

I saw Vaschel, Sidon and Andrew's faces in my mind. "No one else dies because of me."

Quinn's gaze softened. "If you take Braedon as your husband, more people will die than you can possibly imagine."

"Isn't there anything we can do?"

He exhaled slowly. "I will do everything I can. But in the end, I need you to promise you'll do what I ask. Anything I tell you, without question."

I hesitated.

"Alystrine, you must trust me."

Sigal's words danced inside my head. Quinn joined the Mystics willingly. Was it true?

The portal's face showed his concentration. He focused on my eyes for a moment, then tilted his head. "Sigal has been here."

He'd read my thoughts. I hated that he could do it without me sensing him in my mind. "She asked if she could be my secretary." I pointed to the parchments on my desk. "She helped me translate this sh—stuff."

His gaze turned hard. "Is that all?"

I squared my shoulders. "Why do you care?"

"Have you told her about your gifts?"

"That I can Mind Speak. Nothing else."

His body relaxed. "Good."

Malina and Rhoswen stood awkwardly by my side. I stepped away from them and toward the bench under the window, but I didn't sit down. "You don't like her, do you?"

"It's not a question of like, it's one of trust. She is Braedon's servant."

"Funny," I played with the gold tassel hanging from the corner of the tapestry on the wall. "She said the same thing about you."

He tapped his thigh with his fist. "What, exactly, did she tell you?"

"Only that you willingly joined Braedon when he asked."

He took several deep breaths before he spoke again. "You have no reason to believe me. After all, I helped to bring you here."

Malina turned away to pour water into a pot. She set it over the flames burning low in the fireplace. Rhoswen thrust the gray gown into the corner of the room. I tried to cast my thoughts out to Quinn's but I couldn't.

It takes time to read another's thoughts, Alystrine. For now, you will have to trust me.

I didn't trust anyone in this place. "I'm tired now Please go away."

Malina damped down the fire, throwing Quinn's face into shadow.

He bowed before he turned to exit. Stopping at the door, he stared at me over his shoulder. *Someday, I will be free to tell you my story. Then you will be certain of my loyalty to you. You are my Queen, Alystrine. I will do all I can to protect you and your throne.*

I sat down on the edge of my bed with an exaggerated groan. Malina presented me with a mug of tea. The teas Rhoswen brewed always tasted fruity and sweet. Malina's smelled of lavender, but left a bitter aftertaste in my mouth.

"Drink it all." The old nurse ordered before she left. "It will help you rest through the night."

I sipped on it as Rhoswen turned down the covers of my bed. "I wish you'd left your hair long," the younger woman sighed. "I'd love to brush thick hair like yours."

I pulled at the short tuffs. "It's already grown some. It'll be long before you know it."

The maid removed the hairpins she'd so carefully decorated me with just a few hours ago. She put the baubles into a wooden box and set it on a shelf by the fireplace. She stirred the fire so only embers glowed. I finished my tea then slipped under the covers. The red-haired maid pulled the blanket up and closed the curtains around the bed to keep out the chill.

Was there any way I could know who to trust? If I could read their minds, like Quinn could read mine, it would be so much easier. Then I'd know for certain which of the Portals I could trust, Quinn or Sigal. They obviously didn't like each other, which meant that one of them was on Braedon's side, and one on mine.

Malina must have put something in my tea because I felt warm and relaxed even though my thoughts continued to spin. I struggled to stay awake as my body grew heavier and heavier, as if it were sinking into the feather mattress. Afraid I'd be forced to go to sleep, I focused my mind on separating from my physical self. The woozy feeling disappeared as I left my unconscious form on the bed. Empowered by my ability to transport myself to Tegan, I knew I should be able to Spirit Travel throughout the castle. Malina had said I couldn't leave the grounds, which explained why I couldn't find Kennis earlier, but I figured I should be able to find Quinn and Sigal. Maybe discover who told the truth.

I hesitated at the door. If I'd had a body, I would have taken a deep breath. As I didn't, I counted to three then stepped into it, surprised that I felt nothing as the door went through me.

Two guards leaned against the stone wall opposite my room, their eyes open, but unfocused. They didn't see me as I drifted past them and down the marble staircase. I concentrated on Quinn first, trying to open my thoughts to where he might be. As his picture became clearer in my mind, I found myself drawn down certain hallways and passages, until I stood outside another door.

I passed through the barrier. This room had no fireplace; several melting candles provided its only light. A simple cot lay to the right of me. A table with books and papers strewn about sat to the left. A portal's robe hung next to it. Quinn knelt on the stone floor, wearing black linen pants but no shirt or shoes. His pale skin seemed to glow in the candlelight. Unlike my Uncle Devnet's, his back was unmarked. However he had come to serve Lord Braedon, it didn't appear to be through physical torture. He rested his elbows on the wooden stool in front of him, his hands folded as if in prayer. As I came closer, I could see puffs of condensation rising as he muttered to himself. It must be freezing in his room.

I couldn't make out the words, but whatever they were, he said them in earnest. Sweat beaded along his forehead even with the cold air. He rocked on his knees, the top of his head occasionally hitting against his hands.

Looking around the room I could find nothing but the sparsest furnishings. Not even a window broke up the gray stone walls. If Quinn willingly worked for Braedon, he wasn't being rewarded for it.

"Give her wisdom . . ." Quinn lifted his face toward the ceiling. "Give her discernment . . ." The words faded to an indistinguishable mumble, but I'd heard enough. He was praying for me. That was a point in his favor.

I slipped out of Quinn's room and wandered the palace halls. Occasionally a thin strip of light slipped out from under a door, but for the most part I drifted in darkness. When I finally found my way back to the more public areas, torches flickered along the walls. I recognized the hallway outside the library, following it down toward the dining hall. The sounds of musicians and laughter grew louder the closer I drew to the guarded entry. I paused in front of the soldiers, so used to them opening the doors and announcing me wherever I went that I forgot for a moment that they couldn't see me.

I stepped into the grand hall. The earlier formality of the evening had degraded into a frat party. Several men lay sprawled across tables, pools of vomit at their feet or heads. At least a dozen women now occupied the room. Some sat on men's laps, others coupled against the wall or under tables, oblivious to the crowd around them. I turned to leave, but spied Braedon at the head table, talking with several men. I focused on them and not the stuff going on around me.

"Here's to my betrothal!" The Lord Regent lifted a goblet.

"Here, here!" cried the men around him.

The young blond man I'd seen earlier drained his cup again then poured another. "She seems–" he belched loudly. "She seems a stubborn one."

Braedon sat back in his chair. "Stubborn, but stupid."

"She can't be that dim-witted." The blond wiped his mouth with the back of his hand. "She wouldn't sign it."

Braedon's eyes narrowed over the rim of his goblet. "I expected as much. Tomorrow, Sigal will translate it and then–"

"I see you!"

The old man I'd sat next to earlier stood up. The others around him talked over his exclamation, but his words echoed in my mind. His milky eyes stared at me. "My Lords," his ancient voice rose, growing in strength as he straightened his back to stand taller.

Even without a physical body, his stare froze me. It's as if he'd trapped my spirit inside a jar.

"My Lords."

The others around him quieted down. They turned to give the old man their attention. He pointed his bony finger directly at me. "She is here."

Braedon looked where my betrayer pointed, but remained oblivious to my presence. "What are you talking about, Malcolm?"

"She is here, My Lord."

The men by the Lord Regent chuckled and mimed pouring drinks down their throats.

The old man shrieked as if his clouded eyes had seen their actions. "I am not drunk like those around me." He thrust his finger again in my direction. "Her spirit is here."

Braedon slammed his goblet onto the table. The sound jarred me out of the trance the old man had put me under. I fled down the aisle between the tables as the old man shouted, "I have seen you, daughter of Geran. I have seen you."

His cries woke the Mystics around me out of their lethargy. They lifted their heads. Others ran as if they were going to block me from leaving. A pair of men stood in front of the door. I paused for a moment, stepped to the side, and pushed myself through the wall. The door opened behind me and Mystics poured into the hall. I had no idea what would happen if they got to my room first and found my unresponsive body, but I hoped I wouldn't find out.

It wasn't as if I had legs that I could force to run faster. Instead I concentrated on my room and imagined being reunited with my physical self. I got the sensation of a rope being tied around my stomach with someone pulling very hard at the other end. In moments, I floated above the bed then felt as if I were being poured through a funnel. I gasped for air as I reconnected with my body.

Footsteps thundered outside my door before it was thrown open. I instinctively wanted to sit up at the noise, but I couldn't make my body move. It was as if my brain hadn't fully reconnected with my muscles yet.

Braedon yanked open the curtains surrounding my bed. I managed to throw a hand over my eyes to block out the sudden intrusion of torchlight now illuminating my room. I let out a screech as if I'd been surprised at his arrival.

He watched me for a moment, not saying a word. His eyes narrowed. "Is it true?"

I felt a tingling through my fingertips and toes as the nerves finally sparked to life again. I rolled away from the light just like I used to when Kennis would wake me up for school. "Go away."

He pulled off my covers.

I yelped and hid my face in a pillow.

He climbed onto the bed, grabbed me by the shoulders. He panted from his run, the smell of wine beating across my cheek with each breath. "Is it true?"

My shoulder throbbed. "Is what true?" I swear he was trying to read my mind.

"Did you Spirit Travel?"

I shook my head like I'd never heard the term before. "What?"

His face grew red with anger. "Did. You. Spirit Travel?"

I pushed him away and flopped back onto the bed. "I don't know what that is." I rolled my face into my pillow. "Leave me alone."

He loomed over me but I did the best imitation of a person trying to go back to sleep that I could.

"I saw her." The old man's voice crackled from somewhere near the doorway. "My sight in this world may be dim, My Lord, but in the spirit realm, I see as one in their youth. She was with us."

Everything went quiet. Braedon leaned over and whispered into my ear. "It doesn't matter what gifts you possess, Alystrine. They will be mine once we are married."

CHAPTER THIRTY-SEVEN

Signing

R hoswen frowned when she found me sitting at my desk the following morning. "You're up early, My Lady."

A yawn escaped my lips. "I didn't sleep."

The young woman tsked under her breath. "That won't do you any good. You must rest and keep your health. The coronation's not far off." She put a log onto the fire then stoked the embers. "You don't want to fall ill again."

She took the blanket off the bed and started to drape it over my shoulders. "You must be–" She stopped and inhaled deeply. "I can still smell the prison on you." Throwing the blanket back on the bed, she then hurried to open the door. "My lady wishes to bathe this morning. Please inform the kitchen maids and have several buckets of hot water brought up immediately." She slammed the door on the guards outside before they had a chance to answer her.

I lifted my arm and sniffed. "Is it really that bad?"

"Others would not notice at first, but I've gotten used to your lack of scent." She scurried over to the corner of the room. "Where's the dress?"

"I burned it."

Her mouth dropped open. "What?"

I wrapped my arms around my chest as if giving myself a hug. "I threw it in the fireplace last night." Most girls wanted to keep every memento from the night they were proposed to. Me? I wanted to forget it ever happened.

After a quick rap on the door, Malina entered. "How are you feeling this morning, My Lady?"

I growled under my breath. "Apparently I stink and I didn't sleep a wink last night, so I'm not doing very well, thank you."

I spent the next hour being poked, prodded, bathed and re-bandaged as Rhoswen and Malina washed the stench of Tegan's cell off my skin and out of my hair. Nothing could take away the sliminess of Braedon's offer. I remembered the prostitute I'd seen in the tavern. I'd be no better than her, selling myself to my uncle, but at least my price was a man's life and not a pint of beer.

As Rhoswen secured me into yet another new gown, this one made of dark green silk, someone knocked on the door.

"Come in," I called, ready to have something else to occupy my mind rather than my creepy uncle.

Quinn entered, appearing out of breath. "There's a rumor going about the castle this morning." His brown eyes surveyed my face. "That you Spirit Traveled into the dining hall last night." He paused to catch his breath. "Is it true?"

Rhoswen stopped lacing. I focused on the floor.

The Portal's voice sounded strained. "Why, in the name of Ruahk, would you go there?"

I shrugged. "I couldn't sleep. I wandered all through the halls. You never told me people could see me."

"People, no," Quinn grunted. "A Druid Ovate, yes."

I lifted my head. "A what?"

"Malcolm is an Ovate. They communicate with the unseen world."

"Like the Messengers?"

"No," Quinn snapped. "The Messengers speak only to the Elders. It is the Fallen the Ovates seek."

"I still don't understand how he could see me."

The portal sighed and sat on the bench by the window. "It only matters that he did and now Braedon knows of your gift."

"I'm sorry." When Rhoswen finished tying my gown, I sat next to Quinn. "I won't do it again."

"It's too late now, but we must keep him from learning anymore." He folded his hands in his lap. I was reminded of his prayers for me the night before. "I've been thinking about what you told me last night. About Sigal helping you with your work." He gestured with his head toward my desk. "Did you request a secretary from Braedon?"

I shook my head. "Rhoswen said I could send a request out by myself."

He looked back in surprise. "Whom did you ask for?"

"I told her I wanted to ask you but she said Portals had too many responsibilities." Which made me wonder, how did Sigal have the time? "So I asked that a message be sent to Devnet and another of the Brethren, a man named Simon."

Quinn's gaze grew distant, as if he focused on something from his memory. "This Simon, to which of the divisions did he belong?"

"He studied the law." I shuddered, thinking of Javan and Zaccur. "But he was nice to me. And honest. I trust him."

"And how long after you sent the requests did Sigal arrive?"

I puckered my lips as I thought. "I don't know. An hour or so. She said she'd bribed a guard to tell her if there was some service she could do for me."

As if on cue the door opened and a guard announced Sigal's arrival. She gave Quinn a hesitant smile. "Good morning, Portal."

Rising from the bench, he smiled at her. "Good morning." He bowed toward me. "I'm glad you are well, Your Majesty. If you'll excuse me." He didn't wait for me to actually give him permission to leave before he stepped around Sigal and left.

Her body shook slightly. "Why was he here?"

I shrugged. "He likes to check up on me. I think he feels responsible for bringing me here."

"Any one of us could have used Faolan to find you." Her violet eyes held mine. "It's odd that he takes such an interest in you."

I pretended to fiddle with a non-existent loose thread on the cuff of my gown to get away from her scrutiny. "Perhaps he's like you."

Her voice was cold and sharp like a knife. "He is nothing like me."

"I meant only that, like you, he might want to know me better."

She stared at me a moment longer. "There's a rumor running through the castle this morning."

Before I could comment, a guard entered to escort me down for the day's meetings. I groaned as I stood up. "You don't have to stay."

Sigal picked up a parchment. "I could read through these so that we could work this afternoon."

"That isn't necessary. I'll call for you if I have time later."

She pursed her lips. "As you wish, My Lady."

Sigal and I walked out together through the hall and down the stairs, but at the bottom she turned left, while the guard and I turned right. As soon as the Portal was out of sight, I stopped.

"Tell Lord Braedon that I'm not feeling well. I'm going back to my room." The truth was, the thought of being anywhere near my uncle made my stomach turn.

"But, My Lady—"

I ignored him and made my way back up the stairs. I had a week before I was crowned queen. That gave me seven days to try and save

Tegan. I wanted to spend them trying to figure out a plan.

That evening, Braedon again ordered me to have dinner with him. This time he promised me a solution to our standoff.

Three men, including Braedon, already sat at a long wooden table by the time the ever present guards led me to a private dining room. Two candelabras cast the room in golden light. Richly embroidered tapestries hung on the walls.

Braedon met me at the doorway. "Alystrine, I'm so glad you could join us today."

I bristled at his use of my name, but didn't have the courage to start a scene in front of strangers. The others stood to greet me. I recognized one as the drunk man from last night. He seemed to be my uncle's age, maybe a year or two younger, clean shaven with blond hair. He wore a gold-threaded tunic and dark blue pants tucked into brown leather boots. His blue eyes sought mine as I approached, but I wouldn't hold his gaze.

At the head of the table stood an imposing figure, dressed in black. He had hair like Braedon's, thick and dark. Silver whiskers ran throughout his full beard. A gold design, similar to a Celtic knot, decorated the center of his tunic.

My uncle presented me to this man first. "Alystrine, I would like to introduce you to my father, Lord Donagh of the Mystic Council."

He had the same serpentine smile I'd seen on his son's mouth. Lord Donagh took my hand in his and bowed to kiss it. "I'm pleased to finally meet you." His eyes betrayed the lie. This man found no pleasure in me at all. He surveyed my face. I knew he looked for resemblances to my parents.

The blond man gave a quiet cough. Braedon led me over to him. "This is Caradoc, one of my younger brothers."

He too, bowed and kissed my hand. "I never had the opportunity to meet your mother, but I know no one exaggerated the tales of her beauty, if she was even half as lovely as you are."

I bit the inside of my lower lip to keep from saying anything snarky. Braedon guided me to my chair. "My brother has paid you a compliment, Alystrine, don't you have something to say?"

I lowered myself into the seat, giving Caradoc only a cursory glance. "You'll have to excuse me for being rude. Your brother's proposal, and the ransom involved in it, has put me in a bad mood." I took hold of the goblet in front of me. "We have something in common, you and I."

Caradoc's smile was softer than his brother's. "And what would that be?"

I took a sip of wine. "We neither of us met my mother, before your brother had her murdered."

Caradoc surprised me with deep belly laugh.

Braedon shut him up with a black look. He stood between his brother and his father. "I've told you what happened."

"Yes, you did. But in light of the current situation, I think I'm leaning toward believing Devnet's version of events, rather than yours."

Lord Donagh slammed his fists on the table. The candelabras shuddered, but remained upright. "Enough of this!"

My heart pounded. Braedon always appeared in control. His father, however, had already showed his temper. Could he be even crueler than his son? I clasped my hands together under the table to try to still their shaking.

The moment the men sat down, servants hurried in like ants, carrying tray upon tray of food. Lamb and goose, carrots and bread, dates and pomegranates made their way around the table. I took a little of everything even though I didn't think I would be able to eat much.

Caradoc noticed me picking at my bread as the men ate. "Don't you like our food, Your Majesty?"

I glared at his brother. "I seem to have lost my appetite."

Lord Donagh dropped his knife against his plate. I jumped at the sharp clang of metal which caused everyone to look his way. "This is what we have to deal with? This is the queen?"

Braedon shrugged. "I'm afraid so, Father."

From somewhere deep inside, I dragged up the courage to confront him. "If you're not happy, you can leave." I took another sip of wine to calm my nerves. "No one is forcing you to stay."

"How dare you." Braedon rose slowly from his chair.

"I spoke the truth!" I stood to meet him. "I'm the only one being held against my will." I turned my head at Lord Donagh's sinister chuckle.

He sipped from his goblet. "That's not entirely true now, is it?" He leered at me from over the cup. "What is the boy's name? In the dungeon? Thomas? Terrance?"

My breath left me like I'd been punched in the stomach. I reached out for the table and lowered myself into my chair.

Braedon hovered over me. "That's right, Father. I'd almost forgotten about him." He placed his hand on the arm of my chair and leaned down. "Alystrine, what is his name?"

I stared at my knife, wishing it was sharper.

"Well?"

"Tegan," I whispered.

He spoke the name into my ear. Soft and low, like a lover's kiss. "Tegan."

I tried to swat him away like an annoying fly, but he caught my hand, pressing it to his lips. "And what have you decided about Tegan's fate?"

I refused to let my voice tremble, even though my body did. "I told you what I wanted."

He strode back to his chair. "I'm afraid I cannot let the Elders know of my proposal." He poured himself more wine. "If I did, they wouldn't agree to crown you queen."

"Then I'm afraid I won't be signing your parchment."

Lord Donagh leaned back into his chair. His fingers toyed with the stem of his goblet. "Then your friend will die."

I dug my fingernails into the fleshy part of my palms. "You told me you had come up with a solution to this problem. That's why I came here tonight."

Braedon adopted the same casual pose as his father. "I saw the Portal, Sigal, with you yesterday. Would you consent to having her translate the decree?"

I caught my breath, my brain trying to make sense of his offer. "Sigal?"

My uncle nodded. "I'll send for her immediately." He lifted his arm to signal to one of the servants that stood along the wall.

"No." The word came out without me thinking about it. The men looked at me with surprise.

Braedon lowered his hand. "What?"

My mind whirred. I felt like I was in the scene from *Princess Bride* where two characters have a battle of wits, one trying to deduce which cup of wine the other has poisoned. There was no poison, as far as I knew, but I had to decide which Portal I trusted. Did Braedon suggest

Sigal because she was working for him, or because he knew I wouldn't trust him and so pick Quinn instead?

Braedon broke the silence that had settled around the table. "I thought you and she had an agreement?"

"Not really." I wished I could read my uncle's mind, but I got nothing when I tried. My only clue was the sick feeling I got whenever I thought of trusting Sigal. I lifted my chin. "Quinn."

"What?"

"I'd trust Quinn to translate it."

Lord Donagh looked at Braedon. "Who's Quinn?"

The Lord Regent stroked his beard. "Another of my Portals."

Donagh shook his head. "An Elder."

I stood up. "Like Sigal, a traitor. But he's the only one who's shown me even a little kindness in this place. That's my last offer. It's either Quinn or you kill Tegan and lose your chance of ever marrying me."

Caradoc surveyed the tense faces around the table. "Come, Brother." He slapped Braedon's shoulder. "The invitations to the coronation have already been sent out. The Councils and dignitaries will be arriving day after tomorrow. You have her counteroffer. Take it."

Lord Braedon clapped his hands a servant ran into the room. "Find Quinn, the Portal. Bring him here."

I sat back down and ate a cube of lamb. The meat was well seasoned with rosemary and melted against my tongue. It fell to my stomach like lead.

The servants cleared the table of food but brought a new pitcher of wine while we waited. Quinn entered. He bowed toward us. "I am at your service."

Braedon stood. "Alystrine wants you to translate something for her."

The Portal's eyes glimpsed mine as he approached the table. "Of course, My Lord." He didn't ask why Braedon or any of the other men present didn't read the parchment to me. He simply sat down in Braedon's empty seat and lifted the pronouncement so he could hold it up to the candlelight.

"I, Alystrine, daughter of Queen Etain and Geran the Elder, do hereby pledge, on this the fourth day of the tenth moon, to wed Lord Braedon, son of Lord Donagh, by the end of the first year of my reign as Queen of Ayden. Any children the gods or Ruahk bless us with will be given all rights of

inheritance. If no children are given to us, upon my death, my husband shall be my heir."

If I'd had food in my mouth I would have choked. "Are you insane?"

Braedon's cheeks reddened. "It is a standard betrothal contract."

I leapt from my seat. "It's a death warrant. You'd have me killed within a week of the wedding. Maybe two if you decided to torture me first with a honeymoon."

I guess the term "honeymoon" confused them. They muttered to each other about what it meant.

"Forget it." I pointed my finger at the parchment. "I'm not signing that."

Braedon flew across the room. A shriek of pain left my lips when he dug his fingers into my shoulders. It didn't faze the Lord Regent. "You will sign it, or so help me, you will watch your lover tortured for the next six days before the coronation."

"He's not my lover."

"Whatever he is, are you willing to watch him suffer unimaginable pain for your stubbornness?"

"I hate you."

Spittle hit my face as he ordered, "Sign it!"

"No!"

Quinn's voice rose above the din. "Wait!"

Braedon still held me. My wounded shoulder burned. I bit the inside of my cheek to keep from crying.

Quinn's eyes locked onto mine. "Would you consent to marry him, if the final clause were stricken?"

What had happened to *you cannot marry Lord Braedon?* I tried to decipher what he was thinking.

Lord Donagh pounded the table. "I will not have my grandchildren disinherited if that . . . girl," he made "girl" sound like a filthy word, "outlives my son and takes another husband."

Quinn shook his head. "No, My Lord, I'll rewrite the document in such a way that it assures your son's children, and only his children, will inherit the kingdom."

Lord Donagh nodded. "Do it."

Braedon pushed me away. "What?"

His father fixed him with the kind of look only a parent can give their child. "The Portal will write the new document and you will sign it."

My eyes couldn't leave Quinn's face. *What are you doing?*

You promised you would do anything I asked. Without question.

I bowed my head toward him and was rewarded with a quick smile before he lowered his.

A servant brought in new parchment and Quinn bent over the document as he wrote. Braedon and his family stood in the corner, drinking wine and arguing amongst themselves. I walked to the opposite end of the room and stared at a tapestry on the wall. Hunters carried in the carcass of a deer to roast for a feast. I felt like the animal—hunted, gutted and ready to be eaten, only no one had actually killed me. Yet.

It took Quinn an extraordinarily short amount of time to complete the betrothal contract. He put powder on the ink to fix it then stood and read it quickly to his captive audience until he got to the sentences he'd changed.

"In the event my husband precedes me in death, only the children of our union will have legal right to the throne. If we should not have children, and I, Alystrine, precede my husband in death, then the Joint Assembly of Ayden shall elect a Regent from among their ranks, by a three-quarter majority vote, to rule the land."

Lord Donagh and his sons strode over to the table. Quinn placed the parchment down, dipped the quill into the ink and handed it to Braedon. The Lord Regent shot me a glance of pure hatred before scratching his signature onto the contract. He pushed himself up then held the quill out to me.

"Your turn, wife."

I shook my head.

Quinn's eyes widened. Braedon looked practically apoplectic.

I stood my ground. "Release Tegan first."

Lord Donagh marched toward me. "Damn it, you wench! You will sign that agreement and you will do it now!"

"And your lying bastard of a son will have Tegan killed tonight in his cell." I darted away from Braedon's father before he could grab me. "Let him go!"

We seemed to be at another stand still, but this time I had thought things through. "Another compromise. Bring Tegan here. Bring Malina to treat his wounds. I'll sign the paper and seal it so it can't be altered. As soon as the seal is on, Quinn transports him out of the palace."

Braedon shook his head. "It cannot be done. There's a protection around the palace that thwarts passages in or out."

I looked to Quinn. He nodded. "It's true. But there is a way."

Braedon's face registered his surprise and then anger. "Do tell us, Portal. How you think you can get out of the palace?"

He swallowed. "I could transport him to the one open passage." His eyes flickered to me and I knew it had been built to bring me here. "I could then send the boy . . . anywhere."

Lord Donagh crossed his arms over his chest. "Let's get this over with."

Malina hurried into the dining room with Greer in tow. She took one look at me and let out an exaggerated sigh. "Thank the gods! I thought you'd gone and torn your wound open. Or worse."

I didn't have the heart to tell her that Braedon had done just that. I could feel the blood seeping through the bandages and spreading across my back.

Malina bowed. "I am at your service, My Lords and Lady."

Lord Braedon paced about the room. "Your patient is not here yet."

I made my way over to Malina and whispered my plan to her. She, in turn, filled in her husband. I stayed close to them as we waited. Braedon continued to pace, his father to stand, and Caradoc drank.

The guards dragged Tegan into the room. His eye had been blackened since I'd seen his face in the dining hall last night. The other searched frantically around the room until he spied me.

"Ally?" His voice was panicked. Strained. "Why am I here?" Greer pressed Tegan's shoulders until he sank to the floor. "What have ye done?"

I shook my head, but wouldn't answer him. I couldn't. If I spoke the deal aloud again, I'd lose my courage.

Greer took off Tegan's torn shirt while Malina prepared bandages. Her hands trembled as she cleansed his wounds with a washcloth and water. Greer mixed ointments and medicine. I sat in front of Tegan while the two of them worked, my eyes never leaving his.

I thought about our night together. I tried to help him remember it too. His eyes questioned mine. *Was it real?*

I gave him the slightest of smiles. Yes, it was real. I knew, no matter what lay ahead in this sham of a marriage with Braedon, no matter what he would do to me, I would hold on to my two nights with Tegan, the starry night in the forest and last night in the prison. Passionate touches and gentle kisses. I would remember what real love felt like.

Greer and Malina finished their work. I bent forward and kissed Tegan's lips one last time. I saw the fear in his eyes as I stood up.

His voice cracked. "What have ye done?"

"Bring him to Quinn," I ordered.

His face paled as they lifted him up, but I think it was from the fear of what I'd agreed to rather than any pain. "Ally? What have ye done?"

I wiped away my tears so they wouldn't smudge the contract. I took the quill in my hand and dipped it in the ink. Quinn nodded when he had a firm grasp on Tegan's arms.

The boy's brown hair covered his eyes. "What is that?"

Braedon put a hand on my shoulder and kissed my cheek before he turned to Tegan. "She's agreed to make me her husband."

Quinn stumbled as Tegan's legs weakened. "God, no, Ally!"

The Lord Regent's breath danced across the back of my neck. "Sign it. Or I will kill him here before your eyes."

I scribbled my name as best I could with my left hand and poured the powder on to make it final. An animal growl rose up from Tegan's chest as I rolled the parchment and melted wax to seal it. Braedon took off his signet ring and stamped the puddle of blue wax. Tegan lunged for him, but Quinn's eyes closed and yanked him away. The air rushed in to fill the space where they had been.

Braedon held the parchment in his hand. "It is done, Alystrine." He turned me to face him. "No one must know about our agreement until after your coronation, do you understand?"

I nodded.

"Not Devnet. Not your grandmother. Not any of the Brethren who are on their way to witness your crowning."

"Believe me, I don't want anyone to know about this."

"If you betray me, those you care about will pay dearly. Now, come. Let us seal our contract." He pressed his mouth on mine. It wasn't a kiss, it was an assault. His lips pushed and bruised and bit. When he finally stopped, I slapped him. It wasn't as hard as I would have liked because I had to use my left hand, but it made a satisfying cracking noise against his cheek.

From the end of the table, Caradoc rose unsteadily to his feet. He grasped the stem of his goblet and lifted it up in the air, causing wine to slosh over the rim and onto his tunic. He didn't seem to care. "Here! Here!" he crowed. "May you have a long and happy life together!"

Here Ends Book One of the Portals of Ayden

ABOUT THE AUTHOR

Kim Stokely lives in Nebraska with her husband and three crazy dogs. Her son-in-law wants you to know she makes awesome "spaghetti cake" (aka lasagna,) and has great taste in ice cream.

Visit Kim's website www.kimstokely.com
LIKE her on Facebook
www.facebook.com/kimstokelyauthor
Follow her on Twitter
@KStokelyWrites

ACKNOWLEDGMENTS
Thanks to my First Draft Readers, especially: Sherry Harris, Shannon Smiley, Vicky Grous and Rebecca Holt. And to my Beta Readers, Gina Barlean and Bryan Hankins, thanks for your eagle eyes in spotting those missing words! My awesome editor, Annie Weir—you totally rock! I couldn't have done it without you. This is the first time I've included a map in one of my books. Shout out to Michael Weir for his awesome artwork— Woot Woot!

To my husband, John—thank you for letting me ignore you and write the stories in my head. I can write novels about imaginary people, but I can never seem to find the words to express how much I love you.

63163171R00172

Made in the USA
Middletown, DE
29 January 2018